The Short Stories of John Joseph Mathews, an Osage Writer

The Short Stories of John Joseph Mathews, an Osage Writer

John Joseph Mathews

Edited and with an introduction by Susan Kalter

UNIVERSITY OF NEBRASKA PRESS | LINCOLN

The University of Nebraska Press is part of a land-grant institution with campuses and programs on the past, present, and future homelands of the Pawnee, Ponca, Otoe-Missouria, Omaha, Dakota, Lakota, Kaw, Cheyenne, and Arapaho Peoples, as well as those of the relocated Ho-Chunk, Sac and Fox, and Iowa Peoples.

◎

Publication of this work was assisted by Illinois State University's Department of English, College of Arts and Sciences, and Office of Research and Sponsored Programs.

Library of Congress Cataloging-in-Publication Data
Names: Mathews, John Joseph, 1895–1979, author. | Kalter, Susan, 1969– editor, writer of introduction.
Title: The short stories of John Joseph Mathews, an Osage writer / John Joseph Mathews ; edited and with an introduction by Susan Kalter.
Description: Lincoln : University of Nebraska Press, [2022] | Includes bibliographical references.
Identifiers: LCCN 2021046864
ISBN 9781496230911 (hardback)
ISBN 9781496230980 (paperback)
ISBN 9781496232083 (epub)
ISBN 9781496232090 (pdf)
Subjects: LCSH: Short stories, American—20th century. | BISAC: FICTION / Indigenous | FICTION / Short Stories (single author) | LCGFT: Short stories.
Classification: LCC PS3525.A8477 S56 2022 |
DDC 813/.52—dc23/eng/20220207
LC record available at
https://lccn.loc.gov/2021046864

Set in ITC New Baskerville by Mikala Kolander.

Contents

Introduction

John Joseph Mathews's writing career was effectively launched in 1932 when he became a Book-of-the-Month Club author through his first book-length study: *Wah'Kon-Tah: The Osage and the White Man's Road*. That 359-page volume narrated the reservation experiences of members of the Osage tribal nation following their 1872 removal from a reservation in Kansas to their last reservation in Indian Territory (later to become Oklahoma), located just northwest of Tulsa. It traced the period from 1878 through 1931 and also included a 15-page "Notes on the Osages" afterword that scanned Osage history from 1673 to 1878. Mathews's enduring legacy was secured shortly thereafter, in 1934, when *Sundown* was published. The novel forged—among a few compatriots, such as Mourning Dove's *Cogewea* and D'Arcy McNickle's *The Surrounded*—the genre of the "mixed-blood" narrative. These novels explored the crises of identity and belonging faced by American Indians with partial European American heritage or—closer—parentage. Three more decades saw three additional Mathews works. All were nonfictions: on living with the earth and within the multispecies earth struggle, on an Oklahoma oil magnate, and on long Osage history in comprehensive perspective. Thus Mathews was known until the second decade of the twenty-first century entirely through his longer works.[1]

To discover in him a prolific short story writer is therefore something of a surprise. Yet he was the author of at least thirty pieces never published prior to his death in 1979 as well as several other works of fiction and creative nonfiction for which publication venues have remained hidden from the view of his contemporary audience.

His short stories for children were published in 2015 as *Old Three Toes and Other Tales of Survival and Extinction*. Our edition presents for the very first time seventeen additional stories, all of which were written for adult audiences. The majority were written in the half-decade following the dropping of the first two atomic bombs, and so might be considered stories for a nuclear age. Their topics range from adulterous murder to Cherokee removal, from the thrill of the hunt to the cultural impasses between U.S. citizens in Mexico and their hosts, from the modern Middle East to the fantastical future. They bear the consciousness of a postwar world: its confusions and regrets, its orthodoxies and hypocrisies. They also bear the mark of a practiced and prolific writer.[2]

We now know Mathews's first publication to have been in high school. As he later wrote, it was an "over-dramatized story about . . . three brave, plucky high school boys in a devastating tornado . . . illustrated with snapshots taken by" his older sister. We also now understand that he began writing as early as 1904, at about the age of nine or ten, through daily diary entries containing scrupulously detailed observations of the lives around him, human and nonhuman. By 1929, three years before his first book was published, Mathews was submitting work to his alumni magazine, the *Sooner*, beginning to reach a wide audience of Oklahomans and setting the foundation for his long career in the blackjack prairies of Osage country.[3]

Wah'Kon-Tah and *Sundown* would come next. *Wah'Kon-Tah* was based on the diary of a former Osage reservation agent, a white Quaker from the upper Midwest, born in Ohio, as well as on Mathews's conversations with Osage elders. *Sundown* has been thought to be based upon Mathews's own childhood, college, and military years, and certainly was in part, though the contrasts with his actual life and thoughts are striking when compared to his autobiography. Within two years of *Sundown*, Mathews was beginning to conceive of the book that would become his quiet masterwork—*The Osages*—published in 1961. But his studies and extensive travel for that work led him to Mexico on a Guggenheim fellowship, and the decade leading up to and during World War II saw instead the drafting and publication of *Talking to the Moon.* It was a nonfiction work about his own decision to withdraw from urban life—and the competitive self-centeredness of the human struggle with other humans—to try to live again in harmony with the natural flow of life and within the earth struggle amidst all living beings, eschewing what he called earth-detachment. It was following the publication of this third major work that he seems to have first turned back to shorter genres and more toward the taste for fiction and fictionalization. These stories appear to have emerged during this period. By the early 1960s Mathews had completed two distinct runs of short story writing: the first his production of the 1940s and possibly the early 1950s, collected here; the second his nine-story "boy book," *Old Three Toes and Other Tales of Survival and Extinction.* But he was also still at work. At his death, he was still trying to craft his autobiography (posthumously published as *Twenty Thousand Mornings*), possibly combing through old diaries to reconstruct events.[4]

Although there is no way definitively to date eight of the seventeen stories collected here, all seventeen appear to have been produced between 1930 and 1951, most after 1945. Those uncertain eight were likely—and in some cases definitely—the work of August 1945 or later. Mathews appears to have recorded every one of his writing endeavors in his diary on the days on which he was writing it, editing it, or otherwise working with it. We know from these records that in August 1946 he wrote "The Apache Woman" and "Yellow Hair," in November 1948 "The Talk of the Face," and by the end of December 1949, eleven more. Of those fourteen, only eight appear here. One was published with his children's stories. The story "Laughter" we leave to other editors, as its plot duplicates in most essentials a different story, "Alfredo and the Jaguar," also already published with his children's stories. Four others could not be located ("Dance at Dawn," "Imported Cheese," "Echoes among the Junipers," and "Joy Finds the Old Trail").[5]

Mathews was motivated in the late 1940s by far different motives from those which animated him in 1963 to produce his children's book in a few short months. By that stage he wrote for love of his grandchildren or step-grandchildren; in 1946 his impetus was economic. Within days of penning those first two stories, they had been mailed off in the hope of publication. A little over two weeks later, he was deciding to cut the second to fit a popular magazine. He had accomplished that task within the next fortnight. The extant diary for the following year is quite incomplete, but there is no mention that either was ever published. However, it would become clear that he was writing for money and not just love. On New Year's Eve 1946 he would write about the dull, disjointed year he had had: "I am ready to live as a gentleman lives once more." We must remember that Mathews and his four sisters had lived more than comfortably during the 1920s, the peak of oil production in the Osage, when Osage tribal members were some of the highest per capita earners in the world. It was a unique history among federally recognized tribes at the time and still is today. Despite his nostalgic statement, Mathews did not fail in his works to examine the dark side of this unique history—the anti-Osage and anti-Indian side. Many Osages were murdered or placed under guardianship (whether minors or not) in order for whites to obtain control over their oil revenues. The father of the central character in *Sundown* dies in a gun battle related to these intrigues and the general influx of money and technology into the Osages' territory.[6]

Each Mathews sibling appears to have had not only his or her own headright in the tribe's collective ownership of the oil beneath the reservation, but a fifth of a share in their deceased father's headright. Still, by early 1948, he felt comparatively poor. While he continued to receive oil royalties and an income from the leasing of his allotment (what he called his "natural income"), he was also still in debt and still putting one of his stepchildren through boarding school and college. In April 1948 he remarked that he was unable to pay his taxes and insurance, and he was still borrowing from friends and patrons to fund the travel he needed to perform research to write *Life and Death of an Oilman*. By September he wrote: "I shall be compelled to write [short stories] while writing the Marland book. A matter of being obvious and rather stupid. One ought to be able to do what others do. I *must* write for money." That day and the next he spent a total of ten hours researching short stories. Later that month he remarked that he wondered how he was going to make it, since *Life and Death* could not come out until at least spring 1949, "and there is some doubt that the public will want to read my short stories. My agents, Brandt and Brandt have sent back 2 of the 3 I sent them last month. Terrific food prices and Ann's college and interest keep me broke, so that I have nothing for myself."[7]

November 1948 sees him composing "The Talk of the Face," originally "The Talk of Your Robe." Yet in December of the following year he notes that no short story had sold yet. The country during that time had been in a recession. By the end of 1949, he took inventory. He had written eleven more short stories that year and sent a total of thirteen (two written in 1948) to his agent as part of his story-a-month plan. They were arrayed as follows:

January—"What Thing Is Fairest"
February—"The White Sack"
March—"Only a Blonde"
April—"Dance at Dawn" as well as "The Apache Woman"
May—"Imported Cheese"
June—"The Liberal View"
July—"Lady of the Inn"
August—"Echoes Among the Junipers"
September—"The Flower of Cadron Creek"
October—"Joy Finds the Old Trail"
November—"Laughter"
December—"The Talk of the Face"

"I saw my short stories as liberators, but they didn't sell though the agent still has four of thirteen. This failure dimmed my confidence quite a bit." Mathews felt himself to be "a prisoner on the ridge" and blamed himself for having "played the fool the few preceding years."[8]

After this we cannot trace his thoughts or productivity until January 1952. Given that the diaries are relatively complete from then until his death, and that he never mentions short story writing again until the spurt in 1963, where he names every story he wrote, it is fair to assume that the eight undated stories here ("The Thinkin' Man," "Too Small for a Horse," "Allah's Guest," "Moccasin Prints," "Bad Medicine," "No Time," "Natural Science," and "The Meek Shall Inherit?") were written between 1946 and 1951. Not one of them resembles in its first pages the later nine, the children's stories. Nor do their themes—especially the themes of the latter three—seem to conform to his later production. The typeface used and the faded paper resemble the others here. Possibly they were written earlier, between 1925 and early 1939, another gap in the diary record. But that seems unlikely. For the latter three, it is impossible. He sent one more to the *Wild Catter* magazine in March 1952. "That Day" was pulled from his missing novel *Within Your Dream*, completed in early December 1949. Whether it was published, or where the manuscript resides, we do not yet know. At the time the magazine itself had not yet gone into production. Regardless, these efforts and continuing efforts to date Mathews's literary endeavors will help us to understand better his development as a writer among writers and the roadblocks he faced in different eras, whether linked or disparate.[9]

Each of these stories is a surprise and a delight for anyone who is already a Mathews aficionado or simply interested in mid-twentieth-century Native American writing. They reveal a dimension of his writing and thinking as yet unrecognized. For those new to Mathews, they give a new angle of insight into what I have elsewhere called his reverse ethnography: his turning of the anthropological lens upon its wielders in the United States who had become complacent consumers of Indian images. In other words, Mathews made great study of non-Indian and particularly white America. Had these stories been published—and perhaps this is one reason why they were not—several would have revealed to that America sides of itself that exposed its foibles and hypocrisies from the subtle standpoint of a French-Welsh-English-Osage American, of predominantly Osage and French cultural heritage and Osage reservation upbringing in a multiracial family. There are aspects that might have made Americans uncomfortable, even those used to reading or eager to read "insider" critiques.[10]

So, until quite recently, Mathews has instead been known as the author of those five important books already mentioned: *Wah'Kon-Tah, Sundown, Talking to the Moon, Life and Death of an Oilman,* and *The Osages.* Most were groundbreaking, unique in their day, in some cases still unique in ours. In the stories being published here we see an extension and development of his thought as well as greater diversity in his interests. By 1945 he had traveled extensively, including beyond the United States, a fact not at all pronounced, not at all obvious in those five major works. As with many Native American authors of his day, his published—his public—persona remained largely circumscribed by the popular and editorial imaginary of American Indians as localized, parochial, and stationary rather than worldly and far-ranging. In addition to displaying the subtlety of his social critiques and political observations, these shorter narratives help to show the shaping of a Native American intellectual through his thirst for travel and cultural comparison, one who has heretofore been confined in large part to his hometown, reservation identity.[11]

The arrangement of the stories in this volume roughly traces how his experiences shaped his life and writing. Readers may appreciate cues here reminding them of the basic outlines of Mathews's experiences, which are much more fully fleshed out in his partial autobiography *Twenty Thousand Mornings* and in other sources. After growing up in Pawhuska and enrolling at the University of Oklahoma, Mathews soon joined the war effort and became a pilot and flying instructor during World War I. Despite his yearning for overseas combat, his world travels began only after the war when he enrolled at Oxford University. Spending a brief time in the Rockies in 1920 just prior to this transient four-year expatriation, he was able to launch from Oxford trips to Scotland, several European countries, and Algeria. After living briefly in Switzerland and marrying there, he and his American wife returned to the States, residing first in her home state of New Jersey and then in California.[12]

The onset of the Great Depression saw Mathews leaving his wife and children to return to the Osage. During the first half-dozen years of this traumatic time for the country was when Mathews established himself as one of the handful of pioneering Native American writers who brought to the attention of U.S. citizens the conflicts and contradictions of the centuries of pressure that had culminated in the Reservation Era, the policies of assimilation and allotment, and the affinities and tensions among Natives of mixed and unmixed heritage. Others who took up these subjects or ranged beyond them included Mourning Dove and D'Arcy McNickle, as already mentioned, as well as Zitkala-Ša (e.g., *American Indian Stories*), John Milton Oskison (e.g., *Black Jack Davy*), Ella Cara Deloria (whose ethnographic fiction *Waterlily* would not be published until the 1980s), and Luther Standing Bear (e.g., *My People the Sioux*). They were succeeding several earlier Native writers such as Francis La Flesche (*The Middle Five*), E. Pauline Johnson (*The White Wampum, Flint and Feather*, and others), Charles Alexander Eastman (*Indian Boyhood, Old Indian Days, The Soul of an Indian*, and others), Alexander Posey (poems, stories, and the Fus Fixico letters), and Arthur C. Parker (e.g., *Seneca Myths and Folk Tales*), who themselves had taken up the mantle from earlier writers.[13] Perhaps Mathews's most famous work today, *Talking to the Moon* (1945), was partly made possible by his Guggenheim fellowship in Mexico in 1939–40, after which he returned to live outside Pawhuska for the remainder of his life, touring many parts of the United States and Canada both with his second wife and on solo excursions or with parties of fellow hunters. The writing published during his lifetime was bookended by works on his tribe, the Osages, with his vastly underappreciated history of the tribe published in 1961.[14]

Mathews's self-confidence came in part because the Osages were a tribe that—like the Caddos, the Haudenosaunee, the Cherokee, and a number of others—had been able during the colonial period to position themselves advantageously with respect to European colonizers and surrounding tribes. At the height of their postcontact power, they controlled most of the territory now represented by the states of Missouri, Arkansas, Oklahoma, and Kansas. In Willard H. Rollings's ethnohistorical terms, they formed a political, economic, and social hegemony on the prairie-plains. Other researchers have suggested the strong possibility that they had been instrumental in the building and political prominence of Cahokia, a mound-culture settlement of the eleventh through fourteenth centuries near present-day St. Louis. The urban space of Cahokia centers on the largest mound known to have been built north of the Rio Grande. Its multifarious actors shaped exchanges of ideas, ceremonial goods and artwork, foods, minerals, hides, and other wares and raw materials across the continent through trade routes stretching toward Echota in the Appalachian Mountains, toward Florida, toward Mexico, toward the north and northwest, toward the Caddo confederacies of present-day Oklahoma, and toward the Pueblo and Apache regions even before those names became attached to them. Dhegiha Siouan entities such as ancestors of the Osages, Omahas, Poncas, Kansas, and Quapaw are thought likely contributors to Cahokia's development, along with other ancestors to tribal groups among the Algonquian Illinois, the Muskogean Choctaw, Chickasaw, and Creek, the Caddoans, and the Chiwere Siouan societies.[15]

After writing the "Stories from Indian Country" included here, and perhaps as unconscious historical contextualization for them, Mathews would take this history even further back. He relied upon keepers of Osage tradition like Chief Fred Lookout rather than solely upon written western scholarship to do so. *The Osages* begins with the land itself, the Ice Age, and the people from the stars who descend to earth from the Sky Lodge, search for and join with an earth people indigenous to the sacred planet, and become the Children of the Middle Waters, Ni-U-Ko'n-Ska (rather than "Osage"), "long before the Europeans found them." Robert L. Hall writes that one "Dhegiha tradition describes the lower Ohio valley as the starting point for Dhegiha migrations" and says "Osage-Kansa and Omaha-Ponca traditions move the balance of the Dhegihas through the greater Cahokia area at one time in their histories." While Mathews's story "Moccasin Prints" in this collection suggests there may be something to the Ohio valley connection, he writes later, in this 1961 work:

And no matter where they lived in the beginning of dawn-thought, and no matter what dim tribal memory indicates about their coming from the southeast, their religion reflecting the earth indicates a region of river-abandoned water in general, exactly like the region at the forks of the river now called Osage in modern Bates and Vernon counties, Missouri. If they had lived in the vague prehistoric times at the head of the Mississippi River, where there are lakes—glacial, not river-abandoned—and lazy meandering rivers and marshes and lenses of water, one might expect to find the moose and the loon among their life symbols, and if they had lived in the vague Southeast, they ought to have a word for sea.[16]

Perhaps what Mathews is responding to here is the tendency for the intermingling and intermarriage of peoples—across a continent characterized more by sedentary agriculture and widespread trade than the imagined nomadism of savagist theories—and the infusion of stories from beyond a particular group into that group's consciousness through that trade and intermarriage to be confused for the basis of their self-identity. After all, the western imaginary of precontact North American life is nearly always mixed with an unconscious theory of the migration of static self-isolating groups. In any event, Mathews's increasing grounding in a long-historical sense of his Osage heritage as distinct from his thorough consciousness of the recent history of the Osage reservation life of his father and grandmother and their Amer-European spouses likely developed more during his U.S. travels in the 1950s, after writing these stories, than beforehand.[17]

During the late 1940s and early 1950s period of writing, however, Mathews focused in any event more on stories reflecting his European heritage and specifically reflecting upon and critiquing the bourgeois aspects of what he called Amer-European life (because it transplanted European culture onto the Americas more than adapting and assimilating into the cultures already here). The fact that he did so from an anticommunist perspective as an American Indian writer may have seemed incongruous or unappealing or unexpected to literary agents or magazine editors unfamiliar with political landscapes in Indian country; we do not know. One might think instead—given Mathews's established political connections through his engagement in tribal politics in Washington and his family connections (one sister, Florence, being married to Michael Feighan, a longtime Democratic member of the House of Representatives from Ohio)—that they might have been delighted to tout him and his anticommunism as exemplary of the solidarity of Indians with the cause, however distorting. Yet his very presence in the discourse could have been seen as thrusting the warts of U.S. imperialist sins on its own continent into the prominence of global scrutiny. In any event, these critiques of the middle class are perhaps a unifying trend across these multitextured contributions. Arranged here thematically, the stories include "Westerns," which display Mathews's embeddedness in rural working-class vernaculars, and "Travel Stories," for which he drew upon his tours in Scotland, North Africa, and Mexico. Only one of the seven stories in these first two sections ("Allah's Guest") seems obliquely to suggest a mixture of reflection upon his Osage experiences and his colonialist heritage, though "Yellow Hair" and "Only a Blonde" get at familiar themes through explorations of mestizo consciousness. The third section, "Stories from Indian Country," exhibits a sweep outward toward the Osages' tribal neighbors as well as a look within at their private challenges. Meanwhile, "Stories of World War II and the Cold War" expose a little known, poorly understood side of Mathews's personal, political, and ideological formations while offering perhaps the least hint of his Osage identity.[18]

This aspect of the stories may offer insight into why they saw no success in the New York literary magazine market Mathews was aiming for (aiming for perhaps because he both saw it as the most promising of cash returns and associated it with prestige). In the aftermath of World War II, U.S. publishers and intellectuals on the East Coast and in Europe were beginning to engage in a cultural Cold War against forces of totalitarianism. These intellectuals later included Mathews's own stepson, John Hunt. One might think therefore that Mathews's sympathies with that Cold War effort and the preceding war effort would have gained him a way in. Who he had already (and recently) established himself to be, however, may have worked against him. And the onset of the Termination and Relocation Era, which was assailing the very concept of a sovereign Osage nation and a multiplicity of American Indian polities distinct from yet within the larger nation, may also have continued to shape Mathews's successes and failures. These were successes and failures in a publishing industry sensitive to various fluctuations in its public's receptivity, along with the economic and social forces during the late 1940s recession that were his very impetus to write.[19]

Mathews had in many ways come to the public's attention due to interest during the 1930s in folk, vernacular, and regionalist literature. Both *Wah'Kon-Tah* and *Talking to the Moon* defy those strictures while also fitting into them. *Sundown* had broken molds, but Mathews complained that his publisher had not marketed it widely. So the literary modernism that characterizes the work, according to Christopher Schedler, may not have had wide recognition among the public or publishers in its day. At the same time, these works would not have had the widespread popularity of a John Steinbeck or an Ernest Hemingway because most white working- and middle-class readers had no experiences comparable to those in the 1930s works; they also had no ability to withdraw into the rural earth-struggle of *Talking* if they were not already in it, and perhaps feeling trapped there, because of the intensifying economic pull toward the cities. And as Mathews later observes, readers in this nation tend to read not for the beauty of the writing but for the pleasures of the reader in vicarious self-identification with the characters.[20]

So, by the time Mathews directed his stories as entries into the fray of a literary publishing industry in New York, then burgeoning since its slump during the war, not only would he have had greater competition in terms of numbers of authors submitting, but his recent publications may have fixed a particular image of him in the minds of agents and editors. The three Indian- and mestizo-themed stories that he sent first may have reinforced that image at the very time when tastes and moods were taking a turn away from regionalism and ethnic affiliation and toward a sense of unified, global, cosmopolitan identity to face down the threat of a communism perceived as divisive. By the time he sent those entries more in solidarity with the Cold War effort, perhaps his chances had been sealed or his entries scrutinized on a different level than those of others, and certainly they would not have been seen as "inside" the East Coast version of the national conversation, even if submitted first. Entries from Middle America in general may have had less of a chance regardless of the writer's ethnicity. John Tebbel notes that "best sellers," humor, short stories, westerns, and mysteries were in demand by 1945. As the war ended and the decade progressed, literary magazines and book publishers began also to focus on the global implications of the war's end, the reconstruction of Europe, rivalries with the Soviet Union and China, and an anticommunist, prodemocratic, pro-U.S., antitotalitarian discourse being covertly driven by the CIA. Ideological debate was beginning to dominate American letters, a terrain in which Mathews was certainly familiar and which he had engaged within *Talking to the Moon.* Yet his ideological angles in four of the five "Stories of World War II and the Cold War" poke at the emerging American hegemony and readers' wishful view of themselves and their leaders even while abetting their racializing views of others and band-wagoning onto the cause.[21]

Shaped by these forces still, readers today may focus on what they perceive as regional, parochial, or workmanlike aspects of Mathews's short story production. They may tisk-task him for experimenting, on the one hand, or, on the other, for being insufficiently experimental, writing too much in a tradition or traditional style. Yet what writer does not do both at some point in a career? Those judgments are part of the interest of this collection, as we see him fully with the flow of anticommunist, antisocialist, and antitotalitarian sentiment, while at the same time refusing to give up his grounded folk, vernacular, regional identity—his injunction to the reader to know-my-history, know-thy-history, know-the-basic-conditions-of-your-consciousness. His irritation at the privileged pretentiousness of the very eastern literati who might determine the trajectory of his career must have been palpable to them when reading "The Liberal View," even if its targets were disguised as their ideological enemies. If satirical critiques of the bourgeoisie were now being typecast as communistic, Mathews refused to be typecast. He refused to soothe. If reminding Americans of the contingency, privilege, danger, and ludicrous chance of their power were grounded in certainty that ethnicity would always play a role, Mathews refused to play the un-self-critical cosmopolitan. He refused to pretend.[22]

Like many writers writing for money, Mathews was well aware of what he was doing, and the audiences to whom he was catering, but also of the limits of his willingness to compromise. The very basis of his artistic skill was grounded in his life experiences and unique epistemological standpoint. It was also grounded in his concept of what a writer was and did, what a writer's function in a society ought to be. To abandon any of those would have run into the ground the very writing career he was trying to fund through the stories. It seems likely that both editors and readers during this time would have typecast even mixed-race American Indians as nonideological; that is, as not having an intellectual or political stake in the global debate despite their massive contribution to the war effort. Ethnicity did not sell anymore, but it still defined and confined. Mathews wrote snidely in his diaries during the 1960s about the New York publishing industry, and one must imagine that the irritation had been building since his disappointing experience with Longmans, Green in the mid-1930s and the failure to place his postwar short stories.[23]

In his 1962 contribution to the *Sooner Magazine* entitled "Author Joseph Mathews Discusses the Limited Impact, Influence and Dollar-Importance in Books of the Indian and the Southwest," he seems to be silently interpreting his failure to place these short fictions as an issue not so much of ideologically minded editors among the East Coast establishment but of the readership to which they catered. He saw U.S. readers as unable, through their Cold War fears and self-centered comforts, to appreciate writers from complex Middle America who were "writing as naturally as the meadowlark sings."

The future of Southwest literature probably depends upon the cold war jitters now, as it was affected for some time in the past by the extremely clever, insinuating termite action of Communist propaganda . . . to support [the intellectual] in his rebellion against the atmosphere created by the dollar powerful. . . . One expects little . . . because of the jitters over international relations, and any literature which fails to give the reader some comfort for his fears, his obesity, his heart's defects will not produce dollars for the publisher or the author. . . . Even with the jet boost of publicity to get him off the ground, he can't remain airborn [*sic*] long if the jittery reader, the salacious reader, the nascent hypocondriac [*sic*] cannot identify himself with the characters or the themes.

In his argument, the previous era's Communist propaganda had expressed and provoked in the U.S. public "dramatic . . . concern for the . . . underdog," a stance hard not to see as being in contrast to Mathews's depictions of the common man in "A Thinkin' Man" and "Too Small for a Horse." His authoritative, masculinist tone and his self-knowing irony throughout this *Sooner* piece deftly put on display the "mixed-blood" complexity of his and his father's heritage while also pointing to his rejections by and rejections of the dollar consciousness within which he had been forced to write in the decade previous: "Now—what will happen to the very heart of Southwest culture, the literature of the Indian, is impossible to say. One might assume that by the time he becomes, after hundreds of years with European contact, a human being finally, with warm blood and philosophy, and a soul and a pre-God concept which came out of his own earth, the Southwest, it will be too late." Had Mathews become a human being in the eyes of his audience? Probably so. Had his fellow Osages without mixed-race heritage?

Since 2016 Americans of all political persuasions have become quite familiar with why a person might retreat from an elitist culture, even one that believes itself to be upholding democratic virtues. Why might Mathews have retreated? It is clear in these lines that the very structural economic conditions that made his writerly consciousness possible also made him dollar-dependent upon the very site of economic power along the coasts that that consciousness had arisen to critique.[24]

Mathews does not ever appear to have been dismissed, mocked, shunned, or openly made unwelcome by the eastern intelligentsia, and he seems to have networked with relative ease among them. Yet he was always aware of more than they were, always saw more than they saw. Often he conveyed this consciousness to his readers, as in *Wah'Kon-Tah*, *Sundown*, "Only a Blonde," "Yellow Hair," "The Liberal View," "What Thing Is Fairest," "Natural Science," and "The Meek Shall Inherit?" But he did not always do so in a national aesthetic atmosphere welcoming of it. The Cold War period and the aesthetic sensibilities it solidified on the East Coast (distinctive, although allied with those in Middle America, and perhaps still adherent to the previous regionalist and ethnicity-based aesthetics that it was supplanting) proved a cold reception for Mathews's reverse ethnographic observations. These aesthetic sensibilities may still reign today.[25]

For those interested in the fullest landscape of American writing in the late 1940s and early 1950s, published contemporaneously or not, the stories are invaluable. Short story writers like Mathews hoped to compete for the attention of the American public with authors like Jessamyn West, Vladimir Nabokov, John Cheever, Shirley Jackson, Kurt Vonnegut, Ray Bradbury, J. D. Salinger, Eudora Welty, Flannery O'Conner, Robert A. Heinlein, William Faulkner, Arthur C. Clarke, Isaac Asimov, and even Jorge Luis Borges and other international figures. Mere talent or skill was far from the determining factor in success or lasting renown. Science fiction and fantasy were on the rise. Thriller, horror, mystery, political, and philosophical genres also had traction. Where regionalism persisted as a national obsession seems to have been in regard to the South, as opposed to Middle America and the Southwest, with continuing attempts to reconcile the former Confederacy with the rest of the country through examinations of southern mentality, culture, and race relations. Younger writers like Salinger, Bradbury, and Vonnegut may have had some advantage among editors due to their recent status as WWII soldiers, a saleable profile. Writers who lived on one of the coasts or in a larger city and could mingle among agents, publishers, and other social influencers probably also fared somewhat better in the competition for columns. African American, Native American, and other U.S. writers of color, even well-established ones, seem to have received fewer opportunities for publication.[26]

Mathews had been called by Joseph A. Brandt, the first director of the University of Oklahoma Press, "one of the best stylists in America," yet the immediate postwar years saw him largely forgotten except for *Talking to the Moon*. Ironically, both his attempts to range beyond Osage themes and his attempts to write Native stories may have had something to do with that neglect. Ironically, the writer who had helped to put the "mixed-blood" subject before the attention of the mainstream public was never truly accepted as a mixed-blood writer. His Osage heritage was what was valued, except when it was not. He was only once successful in publishing a major work without a major Osage aspect to it: the biography of oil magnate E. W. Marland, wherein the Osage perspectives allow their Amer-European subject to take the lead and become a vehicle for subtle critique of him. Of his five postwar stories in the present volume that take place in "Indian Country," only one—"The Talk of the Face"—would likely have appealed to a late forties audience, though the others match or exceed it in quality. As already observed, many of his other stories seem designed to provoke discomfort in their readers' bourgeois habits and complacencies, something his first three books had never done so directly. Perhaps in hindsight we can appreciate these stories for their nuance, their care, their complexity, and their range. And we may wonder what the world and the field of literary study would have been had Mathews's luck been better, his agent more persistent, his regional identity more "marketable," or his talent for seeing through that other Middle America (and letting them know it) more veiled.[27]

The John Joseph Mathews we are coming to know in the beginning of the twenty-first century is a vastly different Mathews from the writer that the twentieth century knew. From novelist and nature writer, historian and biographer, aviator and tribal council member, museum founder and Guggenheim fellow, he has become all these plus a short story writer, a children's author, an autobiographer, a diarist, a correspondent, and the author of lost novels, essays, and works of creative nonfiction that we are still trying to track down. And while sometimes flawed by Mathews's lack of access to a caring and careful editor, and by the financial pressures under which he wrote, the stories published here for the first time give us important new insight into his ideologies, his travels, his composing processes, and many other aspects of his life and career.[28]

The Short Stories of
John Joseph Mathews,
an Osage Writer

Westerns

Readers who wish to avoid plot spoilers will
prefer to skip to the stories and then return.

John Joseph Mathews's unpublished westerns derive from two sources: his sojourns in the Rockies starting during his young adulthood prior to embarking for Europe, and the peripatetic impulses of his adolescence, delimited for the most part by the outskirts and borderlands of the Osage Nation, later Osage County, Oklahoma.

After he had ended his service in the WWI forerunner to the U.S. Air Force, he returned to the University of Oklahoma to finish his bachelor's degree. However, he felt the university had been forced to rush the veterans through. There were many flooding back all at once, while the school was also trying to maintain its service to students newly graduated from Oklahoma's high schools. So Mathews decided to apply to Merton College in Oxford for a second bachelor's degree, encouraged by his mentor Walter S. Campbell (whose pen name was Stanley Vestal). After being admitted, though, he caught big game hunting fever. He and his mother and three of his four sisters had gone on a road trip through Oklahoma, Kansas, Colorado, Wyoming, Montana, the Dakotas, and Minnesota, and down the Mississippi River through Samuel Clemens's stomping grounds of Keokuk, Iowa, and Hannibal, Missouri. It was a four-thousand-mile "grand tour of the Rockies and the Plains": they called it "le Grande 'Tower.'"

"The Thinkin' Man"

Having tented with his family for some time in Yellowstone, Mathews decided to fill the time between his return to Pawhuska and the start of Michaelmas term at Oxford (in October 1920) by returning west. The "bull wapiti would be challenging" and the black and grizzly

3

bears would not yet be in hibernation. "My big game hunting fever had attacked on Mt. Washburn in the Yellowstone when I had ridden into a band of Rocky Mountain bighorn. I remember distinctly when it struck, and I had descended the peak in a sort of trance." He had spoken with several hunting guides, including one Bill Barron, before leaving, and telegraphed Barron to make arrangements. He and his sister's husband Henry Caudill and their three companions started their pack-in along the Shoshone River east of the park. With them were Barron, the cook Jim Milstead, the wrangler Wuff, five saddle horses, and fourteen to fifteen pack horses.

Whether one of these men told Mathews the story that takes shape here as "The Thinkin' Man," we will probably never know. The location made an impression on him: he wrote about it not only in this unpublished story but also in his children's story "Ole Three Toes of Buffalo Fork"; at length in his autobiography; and in a story for the *Sooner Magazine* in 1929. Readers will notice that it forms a nice mirror to the upcoming "The Lady of the Inn" in the next section, "Travel Stories": the paranoid, or narcissistic, or highly perceptive young narrator there is removed here in favor of a man who has had a lot of time to think things over from the point of view of others.

"Too Small for a Horse"

"Too Small for a Horse" seems to emerge from this same period of life and location. After lighting out for Yellowstone in his "big game hunting fever," Mathews did not want to return in October 1920 to catch his berth on the *Aquitania* for the start of Michaelmas term at Oxford. So he telegraphed from Cody to the Cunard Lines to cancel his passage. He had "decided to try for bighorn in the Sunlight country" of Yellowstone. One day he caught sight of a cougar playing in the snow, and after literally exhausting his sixty-year-old guide, he went hunting with the Cougar Hunter of Holmes Lodge on the Shoshone River (shooting only a mule deer buck and a late season black bear). The Hunter was really a Trapper, catching the cats for the most part, rather than shooting them. When they got back, the guide, Bill Barron from Cody, Wyoming, introduced him to novelist

Caroline Lockhart, perhaps the model for the "dainty little novel-ist . . . from New York," Violet Smythe, in "Too Small for a Horse." A midwesterner, Lockhart had worked in Boston and Philadelphia before moving to Cody in 1904 on an assignment about the Black-foot Indians. She never left, and she made a name writing westerns that fed the motion picture industry while managing her ranch and a newspaper she owned.

Perhaps Mathews heard the story of Buff Calvert at the dance Barron threw in his honor, where guests brought their own moon-shine because Prohibition was in full swing, and he danced with every woman and spoke with every man and saw his host only once. Perhaps, though—given the setting in the "San Martinez Moun-tains," Guerrero, hombres, and the coast cattle wintering in the canyons—"Too Small for a Horse" came instead from his time in Southern California before the Depression or his hunting trips to New Mexico. There are Wild Cat Canyons or Wild Cat Mesas in Cal-ifornia and in Utah, but not obviously in Wyoming or New Mexico, nor can White Skull or Balsam Tank be located readily on any map. The story's beginning must have amused him, as Mathews was quite a tall man, so he was perhaps making fun of himself. And why not make fun too of his reputation from *Talking to the Moon* for shooting innocent, unarmed poultry? A white Plymouth Rock chicken is the model of the domesticated breeds, the picture in every schoolboy's and schoolgirl's mind of what a chicken should be. With perfectly white body, and perfectly red face and comb, and perfectly plump and perky struttitude in perfect front-to-back and side-to-side symmetry, they make the perfect enemy and epitomize the perfectly invasive species with the perfectly symbolic name. If you aren't guffawing by the time the shooting ends, Mathews *would'uv had to give up on yu.*

"Old Bob"

Despite some impulses to do so, however, Mathews rarely gave up on himself and his own writing. We conclude this section with two never-published versions of the same story, "Old Bob," that in revised form appeared in print during the Depression: one an unedited and apparently first draft, the other a typescript antecedent to the published version.

Mathews published ten short fictions and nonfictions in his alumni magazine, the *Sooner Magazine*, between April 1929 and April 1933. Their topics ranged from hunting red deer in Scotland to hunting in the Rockies to stories about Osage elders. He did not use that venue again until 1962, and then only once: for a well-received and important tract on the fate and future of southwestern literature, entitled "Author Joseph Mathews Discusses the Limited Impact, Influence, and Dollar-Importance in Books of the Indian and the Southwest." The earlier pieces were written around the time Mathews moved back to the Osage, leaving his young family during the break-up of his first marriage. The earliest has him still in Los Angeles: "Mr. Mathews is a graduate of the Universities of Oklahoma and of Oxford England. He read natural science at Merton college, Oxford, and then enrolled at the University of Geneva, where he met his bride-to-be. Mr. and Mrs. Mathews reside in Los Angeles, California, where Mr. Mathews is a realtor. He devotes a part of every year to hunting, either on his ranch in the Osage hills of Oklahoma, in New Mexico, or in the Rockies."

Given the online accessibility of these short works at the University of Oklahoma's Digital Collections, we republish here only these draft versions of "Old Bob," for the benefit of those interested in how Mathews's first drafts sometimes changed drastically prior to publication. A version of "The Passing of Red Eagle" that was published in the *Sooner* and the "Old Bob" drafts, both of which he kept for some reason of his own, offer insight into Mathews's writing and revision processes and into the kinds of shaping his writing faced from editors and the expectations of the reading public.

Distinct from all the other short stories, the earlier version of "Old Bob" placed here first was completely handwritten on five-by-eight-inch lined notepaper, each page but the first numbered at the top, 2 through 12. The voice is Mathews's, though in character, with the barely perceptible overtone of a narrator's double-voicing. The handwriting appears to be Mathews's, exhibiting his characteristic penchant for placing the apostrophes of contractions before the last two letters, as in "was'nt" and "could'nt." However, compared to the handwriting from his 1920s diaries and his 1930s letters (largely typed), it is a great deal larger and more sprawling, almost unrecognizable, perhaps most resembling the 1922 diary though certainly written with a different instrument than the calligraphic pen used there. We must leave for our own curiosity and imagination whether he pulled out a notebook to record a story as it was being told to him, or a short time afterward, to capture it before it fled his recollection. Or perhaps he invented or recalled the incident in midride as he ranged the Osage hills on horseback while writing *Wah'Kon-Tah* (1932) or *Sundown* (1934).

The story was eventually transformed into the draft reprinted second in this volume, which appears to be the rough for the one that the *Sooner Magazine* featured in April 1933. Though perhaps only a very rough sketch always intended as fodder for that later version in the third person, the original entices. Did Mathews at some point toy with the use of first-person stream-of-consciousness as an eligible technique for his craft? If so, what made him abandon it? Considering how raw the power of the handwritten story is compared to the more mundane version that follows it, was it a mistake to reject it, and was that mistake his or an editor's? The direct address, the breakneck speed of the narration, even the unorthodox spellings, are far superior to the distanced pacing of the public version. Though the lack of punctuation, especially in the printed copy, slows the reader through backtracking and interruption, it fits old Bob to a tee to have almost no periods and certainly none at the end—even at the end—of his life.

Perhaps the most evident revision from the handwritten version of "Old Bob" to the penultimate version is the addition of the Osage character Che Sabe (a character readers would assume to be fullblood given Mathews's patterns of naming and broader conventions), excising the characters Frank Simpkins and Ralph Johnson. The change begs the question: Whose idea was it? Mathews had been published in the *Sooner Magazine* before and would be published there afterward without needing explicit association with Osage or Indian themes to gain audience. So the substitution may have been his own fancy rather than the pigeon-holing of an editor. Che Sabe does not appear elsewhere in Mathews's work, so it is unclear whether he, Ed, Ben/Jim, or the others are men he knew or invented. *Sabe*—though sounding Spanish—means "black" in the Osage language; the meaning of *che* is less apparent, unless he really did intend a Spanish "who knows?" (¿quién sabe?) or "what do you know?" (¿qué sabes?). Mathews had changed his Osage orthography by the time he wrote *The Osages,* and so it is not clear from his text or index what *che* or its likely alternative *tzi* means literally; possibly "sky" or something to do with peace.

Our typographical editing of the second version has been minimal—mainly correcting transposed letters such as *acorss* for *across*—in order to retain Mathews's raw spirit. Unambiguous misspellings (those spelled correctly in the same word in close proximity) have been corrected, but ambiguous ones such as *doges, puled,* and *afterwords* have been retained. Mathews's geography deserves mention as well. Pearsonia is directly in a line northwest of Pawhuska toward Grainola, with Foraker being several miles farther northwest and closer to Grainola. In the original version, he erroneously locates them sixteen miles apart: Foraker eight miles west of the Blackland hills and Pearsonia eight miles east of them. In the presumably later version, the towns are more appropriately eight miles apart and the topographically more intricate Blackland is no longer mentioned in relation to them.

The Thinkin' Man

Yu kin hole up here as long as yu want, rekon, if you wanta take the top bunk, but 'fore yu throw in with me—me livin' out here in the mountains like a wolf—maybe I'd better tell yu a little sometin' 'bout myself.

Well, I'm an ex-con. That don't mean I done anything, 'cause the Man up above knows damn well I didn't. But rekon yu oughta know 'fore yu throw in with me. This storm's liable to last fer maybe a day er two, but the pass'll clear 'fore the heavy stuff comes on; they might be fine weather fer a month er two yet. These first snows that come down lazy and heavy flakes 'fore the aspen leaves fall, never last long. So rekon since yu cain't git out nohow, even if yu aimed to, looks like me and you's gonna be partners fer a few days, and a man oughta know who he's-a holin' up with. Rekon I oughta tell yu how things is.

A ole boy might call it hard luck. That's the way I look at it, and it sure cain't hurt me none now, sence I got my papers and I'm clean as a hound's tooth, and sence I ain't got no guilt on my conscience in no way, shape er form. The Man up above knows all about it.

Maybe there ain't no call to say much about it, but I figgered you bein in Packsaddle fer several days, Bill Maze a-guidin' yu, they might a-bin talk.[1] If yu did hear talk 'round Packsaddle, and ole Bill blowed off any, yu might lay awake nights a-wonderin' about me. I'm a stray, yu might say, and yu know, they's kinda open season on a man that's bin in the pen, sence I never had no call to go 'round tellin' people the straight of it. But sence ole Bill left yu to go after grub, and cain't git back through this snow, and you-a dude, and your outfit blowed down, I sure oughta give yu the straight of it.

Yu know, I never done nothin' worse'n git drunk, and ride my ole pony down the middle-a Dusty with the other ole boys of the Crosshatch outfit, after we'd loaded. The boss paid our fines if we'd happen to shoot out a winda light. That's all I ever done that was on'ry; that and a little tom-cattin' round.

Whin I quit the Crosshatch outfit, I got me a guide licence from the state, and tuk hunters up on Buffalo Fork fer elk, and maybe bear if they was still out and a-berryin'.[2] I hadn't chounced steers outa the mountains all my life th'out knowin' somethin' 'bout bull elk. I almost could tell a man what they's thinkin'. I've seen 'em fightin' and a-raisin' hell 'long 'bout the first moon in September. They's many the nights I couldn't sleep fer them a-buglin' and coughin' all over the mountains. Yu kin see I wasn't no green hand whin I tuk to guidin'.

They was good money in it; sure good money. Rich dudes'ud come out in fancy outfits and special made rifles with their names on 'em. They'd bring radios and sich stuff, and sometimes they'd bring their ewes with 'em. When I seen them women along, I knew I hafta git their bulls fer 'em but they's some of 'em that wouldn't have it that way. They'd ride and shoot like a man; hell of a lot better'n some. It's many a bull I've shot fer some dude, never lettin' on, 'course. Maybe yu think I didn't git some fancy honorums, like one ole wind-broke dude used to call the extrys. Hell, a hundred dollars wasn't nothin fer killin' a man a good head. They's one ole boy shuk hands with me five times and put a roll of bills in my hand that'ud choke a mule.

Like I say, they sure was good money in it, and hell, lotsa fun. It's a sight the stories some of them fellas could tell, after they'd had 'em a few 'round the camp fa'r. I had one law fer myself though; I never tuk a drop when I's out guidin'. Hell, I wasn't 'fraid of it, it was the way they kep forcin' it on yu. If yu lied a little and said yu never touched it, then they'd never force yu.

Well, one day I got me a letter from New York. From an ole boy who was big boss of some company up there; cain't 'member the name, but it musta bin some outfit. His name was Fortune, James A. Fortune.[3] I met him and his outfit at the train in Packsaddle, 'en we got ole Jake to bring us as fur as Dusty where we outfitted. Hell, they's three pick-ups a-followin' Jake's station wagon, loaded with their soogins and stuff.

They's three of 'em. They's this James A. Fortune and his wife Grace, they called 'er, and then they was this other fella Jack. I never did ketch his last name. Figgered he was a kinda friend at first, but it kinda turned out different, rekon yu might say.

Tell yu what they looked like: This James A. Fortune was a soft kinda fella; kinda grass-bellied. Look like he'd never done a lick in his whole life, but I guess he sure had the headpiece. He was a thinkin' man. He give orders like he aimed to have 'em 'tended to, but it wasn't long 'fore he was a-lookin' at me ever time he give one, and sayin' "what d'yu say Jim, Grace wants to wear them hobnail boots, wouldn't her composition soles be better on this granite," and things like that, and I'd give 'im the straight of it.

That Grace sure was some good lookin' woman. She didn't say much but kinda smiled all the time, just like she knew a lot she wasn't tellin'. She could turn them black eyes on yu, and make yu feel she knew what you's a-thinkin, and laff about it 'stead-a turnin' her head like a schoolmarm and actin' uppish. Tell yu the god's truth she had me lookin' at the ground 'bout half the time. Sometimes whin we's throwin' the hitch ona packhorse, I could feel her eyes on my back.

This fella Jack was jist a damn good ole boy. He smiled too, a lot, and he'd do whatever I said jist like a kid. If I tole 'im he'd better not try to pass the pack string on the trail whin we's rimmin' out, and it narrow, he'd stay right where he was, smilin'. First thing he done when he forked ole Brownie, was to put 'im into a lope 'crost the flat, then set waitin' fer us with ole Brownie a-blowin'. Whin I tole 'im ole Brownie sure would have enough work 'fore we reached the Meadows after that two thousand foot climb, he said, "I'm turble sorry, Jim, I won't do it no more."

I had me a purty good string. 'Course they wasn't no show horses. Ole Brownie'd bin jist a sure good ropin' horse, was gittin' agey. The roan Grace was ridin' was a jug-headed ole horse, sure-footed but lazy as a terrapin. I had my dun; a Waggoner, that could git outa the chute and on a fast calf right now. He was sure a good horse. Kep lookin' whin we's huntin' and never missed a chipmunk. Hell, all yu had to do was watch his ears whenever you's huntin'. The horse Mr. Fortune was ridin' sure wasn't much fer looks but he's hell fer strong. I jist called 'im Ole Hammer. He reely had 'im a hammer head.

Whin I's tryin' to kinda put things together a-settin' in that cell, seems like I thought mostly 'bout Ole Hammer and the thing that happened the morning we hit the trail. Commonly, it was that Jack sayin' short things and laffin' and lookin' crosst at Grace, and her a-comin' back with one of them smiles without sayin' nothin'. The kinda smile that might give a man a notion that she savvied some-thin' extry behind what yu was sayin'. Her and Jack was allus sayin' short things and lookin' at each other, like they's the only ones that savvied. Well, this time it was her that made the say, and she looked at Jack in that way they had, and he smiled. I heard it but I cain't say it now. Mr. Fortune didn't hear it 'cause he was climbin' on Ole Hammer, and gruntin'. I looked for the saddle to slip plumb under Old Hammer's belly.

Anyways, it was more than one word that Grace said—seem like about Mr. Fortune and Ole Hammer. Part of it sounded like "'rozy-nanty.'" After a while they gotta callin' Ole Hammer, Rozy. Even Mr. Fortune laffed and called 'im Rozy, but when they first said it, seem like they didn't care 'bout 'im hearin' it.

They was a lotta that kind-a lookin' at each other 'en short-talkin' whin Mr. Fortune wasn't lookin' er listenin', and I never tried to savvy it 'til I gotta thinkin' back over the trail a-settin' in that cell. I never had no head fer nothin' that-a-way. I quit school whin I's no bigger'n-a picket pin gopher, and never even found out what hap-pened to Little Red Ridin' Hood. It was them savvy looks Grace and Jack made at each other whin I's back-trailin' there in the pen, that come to my mind. Maybe if I coulda savvied them words that went with them looks, I mighta had it straight.

Whin we come to the Meadows, I seen smoke, and I couldn't fig-ger it. We's aimin' to hunt on the other side of Two Ocean Pass, and they was an understandin' with the other boys that they'ud take their dudes some'urs else.[4] Whin we come close I seen it wasn't no dude outfit, only Henry Wolf. He come up to us with his teeth shinin' 'en tuk off his hat, and helt Grace's stirrup. I seen right then I had me a bunk-mate, and Mr. Fortune had har'd 'im two guides 'stead-a jist me.

I tell yu 'bout Henry. I rekon whin I tell yu 'bout how he come up that-a-way, and tuk off that big hat-a his'n, and showed them tomb-stone teeth, yu can see why I didn't like 'im none too well. I figgered up to that time that I was doin' good, but whin he come a-struttin' out it seemed like ever'thin' I done was wrong, 'en I felt like a bear cub at a tea party. That's the way that bastard made yu feel.

He was so busy a-showin' them teeth and a-talkin' to them dudes, like he savvied dude talk, that he didn't as much as say "what'du'ya say" to me or the cook or the wrangler. I sure didn't like the way things turned out, but yu know, I's a har'd hand and I aimed to do what'us right.

I could-a tole how it was gonna turn out whin we got to camp on the Buffalo Fork. Henry'ud take Grace and Jack out and I'd take Mr. Fortune. 'Course I knew what Henry aimed to do; he aimed to cross over into the Park, yu know, the Yellowstone, git 'im a coupla bulls 'en high-tail it outta there 'fore the rangers smelled 'im. Ever body 'round Dusty and Packsaddle knew he done that kinda business, but us ole boys guidin' kep our mouths shut. They suspicioned 'im alright, but yu know that hombre was slick, and it'ud-a tuk several rangers along the boundary to ketch 'im 'en him a-knowin' whur they was most of the time. 'Nother thing; that was why he didn't come up the Stinking Fork trail with us, but come 'round by the Hole a-purpose so's the rangers wouldn't know he's out.[5]

Well, me and Mr. Fortune seen enough cows and short yearlin's and some spikes, and we seen plenty bulls too, but they didn't have the heads. Ole Rozy was stayin' under Mr. Fortune good, but he was sure gettin' enough of the saddle.

Like I thought, Henry slipped over the boundary of the Park and got Jack a sure 'nough good head, but I couldn't savvy why he didn't git Grace one too while they's at it. Hell, some of them Park bulls had got plumb tame, a-watching tourists from them lodge-pole pines all summer and nothin' happenin' to 'em. I thought funny at the time but I never said nothin'. But ever' mornin' out they go with Henry, actin' like they's huntin' like hell fer Grace's bull.

Ole Henry sure wasn't a-showin his teeth one mornin' whin they pulled out. The night before I had to carry 'im to our tent with his feet a-draggin'. I never said nothin' to 'em 'bout how he couldn't drink fer sour apples. Wasn't none'uh my business then; later I figgered it sure as hell was, if a man'ud only knowed it.

But anyways this mornin' damned if ole Henry didn't look green 'round the gills, and that Crow blood of his'n was jist nacherly dreened outa his face 'till it was plumb white. I knew they's gonna hafta carry a bottle along with 'em, if they aimed to do any good gettin' Grace's elk.

Me and Mr. Fortune went up Pilgrim Creek agin' and hunted the rim rock. I figgered them big ole boys hadn't come down yet sence we hadn't seen any reely big'uns. I kinda felt sorry fer Mr. Fortune. He sure was saddle sore, but he stuck to 'er. I'd look back as we clumb a steep trail and he'd be a-pullin' leather and a-jerkin' like a sack-a flour, 'en a-frownin' at the mountains like they wasn't a-doin' 'im right.

Finely we stopped on a saddle to eat lunch. Commonly, he never said nothin' 'bout stoppin', but I kep watchin' 'im and made out like I wanted to stop to have a look-see through his glasses. But this stop on the saddle was his'n.

It was on a saddle whur yu could look down on Pilgrim Creek and Buffalo Fork at the same time, and he was hell-bent to stop on this particular saddle seem like. Both branches looked from there, like little ole strips-a tishy paper somebody'ud throwed away monxt the pines.

Mr. Fortune tuk the glasses out and looked fer a long time down into the canyons. He'd look at Pilgrim and then at Buffalo. While he's lookin' I walked along the saddle lookin' fer sign. Elk pass over saddles passin' from one canyon to another. They's some sign but mostly cow. I come back en Mr. Fortune said, "Henry tuk the others up Buffalo Fork didn't he?" "That's the way they left out," I tole 'im. "Did yu see any sign," I asked 'im, and rech fer the glasses. He held 'em back. "Wait a second" he said, "the eye piece is loose agin."

He fumbled at it, 'en purty soon he asked me would I could git his cam'ry. I went over to ole Rozy and it wa'nt there. "A four hundred dollar cam'ry" he said, "musta lost it on the trail." "We ain't bin off-a the trail hardly" I said, "I kin go down a piece and look fer it" "Oh, never mind," he said, "we can find it tomorrow."

"Maybe I'd better go now, while yu ketch a little sleep," I said, "it could snow tonight, 'cordin to sign," I said. He looked at the sky and got reel interested; "think it WILL snow," he said. "Well," I said, "if it don't it'll sure miss a good chance."

Maybe yu wonder why I'm giving this stuff in dee-tail, but it's what come to me whin I's back-trailin' a-settin' there in the pen. I never would'a remembered it so good, if they hadn't corralled me, and I hadn't tried to kinda put things together.

I rekon I's down three-fourths of the way—yeah, a good three-fourths, 'cause I could hear Pilgrim Creek, where it fell, maybe a hundred feet right off-a ledge. Yu know a man cain't hardly hear himself think the water pourin' over a ledge like that. I's jist figgerin' on goin' back up trail, knowin' that Mr. Fortune sure musta fergot that cam'ry of his'n at camp, whin the dun come up with them ears of his'n; lookin' off 'crosst the canyon.

'Course, first thing I felt fer was the rifle, figgerin' if it was a big'un, one of them ole cap rock bulls, Mr. Fortune wouldn't give a damn now if I killed it fer 'im and him tar'd.

But hell, there wasn't no rifle. I'd bin carryin' Mr. Fortune's Newton. Yu know a small grain bullet that'll carry to hell and back, but no shockin' power, but like I say, all yu needed was a man's address to git 'im with that outfit. Mr. Fortune had 'im-a telescope sight outfit too, but I wasn't carryin' that; he had it on his saddle.

Like I tole 'im, a hell of a velocity, but noways near enough shockin' power fer them ole bulls. Go clean through 'im and him a-thinkin a hornet had stung 'im. Even if it nicked a bull's heart, I tole Mr. Fortune, he'd run to hell and gone and we'd never find 'im.

"Take my ole 45-90," I tole 'im. I knew he'd probley hafta take a close shot in that thick timber under the cap rock, and that ole 45-90 had the shockin' power. He could hit a bull in the horns with it 'en knock 'im flatter than a flapjack; give 'im a chance fer another shot, I figgered.

Well, he carried my old 45-90 and I carried his Newton. I rekoned that's why I didn't have no Newton when I rech fer it; it was jist too small fer my scabbard, and had fell out. That's what I figgered then, but yu know that's bin botherin' me ever' sence; how I didn't know whin she fell outa my scabbard. Mr. Fortune kep a-tellin' me I'd lose it, the scabbard too big, but I've come off-a many a mountain with a rifle in the boot, but damn if I ever lost one th'out me a-knowin' it.

Well, I didn't have no rifle, and I figgered on seein' the biggest bull in the country, standin' a-lookin' at me, the way the dun's ears was stickin' up. That's the way things go. But hell, it wasn't no bull, but Henry's ar'n grey a-standin' while Henry was bellied down gettin' 'im a drenk outa Pilgrim Creek.

I set my dun and waited fer 'im to come toward me, but they wasn't no body with 'im. He tried to flash them teeth of his'n, but he couldn't cut 'er much. Looked like he'd bin a-sleepin' one off. They's pine needles still a-stickin' to 'im.

"What the hell yu a-doin' on this side," I ast 'im.

"I chounched a big bull 'en some cows outa the canyon," he says. "Looked like they mighta went over the saddle; rekon they didn't, 'er they'ud run clean over yu," he says. "Guess they musta went 'round under the rim rock. Didn't yu hear my outfit a-shootin' at 'em whin they started down Buffalo?" he says.

He looked me in the eye like an ole boy will, whin he wants to see how yu figger his lie. Right then I knowed fer sure they's something fishy 'bout the whole deal. Him layin' out drunk on the Pilgrim side and his dudes on the Buffalo side, and him a-makin' out like he's-a bird-doggin' fer 'em, I didn't aim to let 'im see nothin' goin' on behind my foretop, so I says, "HELL, no, I never heerd no shootin"

"Grace musta got 'er bull," he says as he steps on his ar'n grey, and led off back up the trail.

Funny how clear things come to me whin I's a-settin' there in the pen, a-puttin' things together. I 'membered how the first thing Henry looked at whin he come up to me there on the trail was that empty boot on my saddle. It wasn't 'till we stopped to blow the ponies up the trail a piece, that he says, like he'd jist then seen it gone, "whur's your gun?"

"Rekon she slipped outa the boot on the way down" I says.

"Hell," he says, "that's a thousand dollar gun—yu better find it."

Yu'll probley laff, but it's the god's truth, things come so clear to me whin I'se a-back-trailin' there in that cell, that I 'membered ever little thing; the way Henry's hands laid on his saddle horn, and the goddam yellowjacket that kep-a buzzin' 'round his hat, and him only 'bout half there with a hang-over. En a-'course, him-a lookin' at that empty boot the first thing, 'en-a actin' like he didn't see it 'till we's up the trail a piece.

'Course ever'body in camp knowed I's a-carryin' Mr. Fortune's rifle. Mr. Fortune himself sure thought it was funny—me a-carryin' the pea shooter as I called it, and him-a carryin' my ole 45-90. Ever' day he'd say somethin' 'bout it. He'd pick up one of my shells and put it agin' one-a them pointed Newton shells, and laff at the difference in the size of the bullet. He'ud say the 45-90 bullet was'us big as this thumbnail 'en as slow as the seven-year-itch, 'en yu'd hafta shoot in a high loop to hit anythin' a hundred yards off. He laffed a lot 'bout it, but sure rekoned it'ud bring a big bull to his knees, pronto. He wasn't wuffin' 'bout that.

Me an Henry was almost to the saddle, jist under the ledge of rock, whin Henry seen the butt of the rifle a-stickin' up outa the rocks. He got off 'en kinda rubbed it off, 'en handed it up to me.

"Sure lucky we found it," he says.

Whin we got up to Mr. Fortune, he says to Henry, "Grace and Jack musta had some shootin'," 'en Henry says, "I chounced a bunch-a cows and a big bull right over 'em from the Pilgrim side." Then Mr. Fortune says, "yu better git down there and hep 'em gut it," 'en Henry turned his ole ar'n grey down the Buffalo canyon.

It sure was a hell of a night. Snow comin' down slow and heavy and kinda hissin', Mr. Fortune a-settin' on a log by the fa'r with his head in his hands, 'en Grace a-layin' in their tent a-sobbin', while me and Henry was a-wrappin' Jack in a tarp. The cook and the wrangler was a-packin'. We figgered we'd better git outa there that night, it a-snowin' and us with a dead man.

That shootin' that Henry and Mr. Fortune said they heered wasn't Jack and Grace a-tall—that shootin' that I couldn't hear fer them falls on Pilgrim. 'Course now, lookin' down the back-trail——.

But anyways right there's whur I got my dirty deal. It come-a hell of-a early fall storm 'en it whiped out ever track and sign in the whole country, 'en they wasn't nobody could git up there to read any sign, if that storm had-a left any to read. Whin they did git up there, hell, 'course, they wasn't nothin'.

I don't know how they figgered it, but they sure as hell figgered me into the pen. The bullet in Jack was a Newton, 'en I had the Newton. His pocketbook was missin' and whin I come clean, they made out like I'd hid it. That there missin' pocketbook was what the lawyers called the motive. They said the way the Newton was layin' in the rocks, 'cordin' to what Henry tole 'em, it looked like an ole boy might-a had it in his mind to hide it. They cleared Henry on what I tole 'em 'bout what I seen and knowed 'bout him-a bein' asleep in the pine needles, and how no man could-a made it 'round on the other side less'n two hours. They can figger time purty good whur a man's shot that-a-way, rekon. Grace had her 30-06, and Jack had 'im one jist like it. Henry carried a 30-30, and I had the only Newton in camp, which I said was Mr. Fortune's I's carryin'. 'En the bullet in Jack was sure'n hell outa that Newton, 'cause I seen it.

They wasn't much they could do, rekon. Snow whipin' out all the sign, and them not able to git up to the headwaters of either one of them forks fer a week. They jist put me in the corral fer a few years, 'til finely Mr. Fortune got me out.

'Course I don't know, but like I's tellin' yu, a man a-settin' in them cells a-back-trailin' can savvy a lotta things. Things sure come clear. I 'membered them smiles and them little looks 'tween Jack and Grace 'en them a-callin' Ole Hammer rozy-nanty, secret-like 'tween themselves.[6] 'Membered 'bout them a-takin a bottle along ever' mornin'—the wrangler tole 'bout this later—'en ole Henry comin' in ever' evenin' 'bout half cocked. 'En him an Mr. Fortune sayin' they was shootin' and me not-a hearin' a goddam thing. 'Course, if that snow hadn't a-come.

Yu know a lotta little things come clear to me a-settin' there. Mr. Fortune a fumblin' with that eyepiece to his glasses, and me a-lookin' through 'em not ten minutes 'fore that. Us a-findin' that cam'ry in his beddin' when we got back to camp. But, yu know what reely got me to thinkin', was that Newton a-slippin' outa that boot th'out me a-seein' it. Hell, I've knowed dudes to lose their rifles a-comin' off the rim rock, 'en ever' damn one of 'em seen it fall.

Then one night I couldn't eat a goddam bite, and I walked up and down, up and down that cell, like a wolf. It was the time whin the bulls-ud be a-buglin' and it a-echoin' down them canyons. Purty soon I knowed that Newton couldn't-a bin in that boot whin I went back on that trail to find Mr. Fortune's cam'ry. I wasn't a-studyin' 'bout it no more, I KNOWED it. Then I reely got down to thinkin'. They was only one way a man could-a picked Jack off down there in that canyon from that saddle. The Newton'ud carry. Hell, it's a sheep gun. Yu can pick them ole bighorn rams off clean crosst a canyon so big it'ud take yu so long to head that canyon he'd be spoiled time yu go to 'im. But yu hafta have a 'scope-sight.

Well, whin I got out, I come back, packed me-a horse and went up to that saddle 'tween Pilgrim en Buffalo, and got to scratchin' 'round there jist under that saddle. They's a deep, narrer little feeder canyon that heads right up agin' the saddle, 'en maybe it's a five hundred foot drop down to its head from whur me and Mr. Fortune et lunch that day. Hell, yu know, it's one of them wild, deep and crooked little feeders, that a blue grouse couldn't fly down th'out gittin' dizzy. Well, after scratchin' 'round down there at the head of that little canyon, fer maybe a week, I found a 'scope-sight.

Jist thought I'd better tell yu, so yu won't be a-losin' no sleep. The way she'd comin' down now, me 'en you's gonna hafta be partners fer maybe a week.

Too Small for a Horse

I guess you have noticed how cocky a little man can be; how touchy about his size, and how he'll often choose a big stridin' woman for a wife, like he might be tryin' to satisfy a desire as best he can. We've had 'em out here that were actually overbearin' cause they were small, and would fight you if you called 'em Shorty.

Big men are different. Looks like the real big ones go around sorta apologizin' 'cause they're so damned big. But did you ever see one of these big boys in love?

Buff Calvert didn't really develop, you might say, until he fell all over his six feet eight and two hundred and fifty, sixty pounds, for the dainty little novelist that came out from New York. Buff wasn't his real name. I don't think I ever knew his real name. He just went by the name of Buff which is short for buffalo.

Like most big men, he was kindly and peaceful as a lamb, and was afraid of hurtin' things. He wouldn't fight you at all. He'd rather hold you away with his big hand clutchin' your shoulder, while he talked the fight out of you. He could do this 'cause he never got mad. I've seen him leave Guerrero's place by the back door when someone with fight in his eye came in the front. There were lots of fights in the San Martinez mountain country too. Over water rights and line fences and 'tween sheep men and cattle men. Some of the boys of the cattle outfits carried guns like in the old days, but the law was too careful now-a-days for much of that. Oh, you could carry a gun alright without runnin' into the law, and we all carried rifles on our saddles for eagles and maybe bear and wolves, but you couldn't carry a gun and a reputation at the same time; a reputation for braggin' and quarrelin'—you know. So when Buff started carryin' a gun, nobody said anything 'cause he was so peaceful and apologetic about his size. But we boys didn't look at it the same way the law did, 'cause we were on the inside, you might say. It was on account of love.

Old Buff never had a girl in his life. He's always shied like a bronc when women tried to talk to 'im. He acted like he wanted to get away 'fore he hurt 'em someway with his big hands or step on 'em with his big feet. Round the campfires at round-up time though, when the boys talked about women, you could see he was interested. He would sit there on his haunches and look at the speaker soft-eyed, with his mouth open and a light in his face that didn't come from the light of the fire but from the inside. He kinda leaned forward as if he aimed to catch every word as soon as ever it came from the speaker's mouth, so's not to miss it.

But I don't believe anybody cared much about what went on in Buff's heart. Come to think of it, if anybody had ever mentioned anything about Buff's heart, ever'body would have stopped to think about whether ole Buff had any of the inside gadgets of the ordinary man. He was a tough hombre; as hard and as strong as a line-back dun. Jim Frazier said one time that he'd bet if you'd cut old Buff, it wouldn't be blood at all but some kind of sap; pine rozin maybe, and that's what we all figgered about 'im. When we got it into our heads that old Cupid had shot an arrow right through that thick hide of Buff's, we had to stop and scratch our heads and do a lot of studyin'.

But it was a fact. Some of the boys had seen 'im drivin' past Violet Smythe's house out on Wild Cat Canyon trail, in that old T-Model of his, two, three time a day, when he was in town. I'll never tell you how he got his long horse legs into that little rattletrap, or how he ever got out without tipping it over. I've stood around waitin' to see one or the other, but I never had any luck. I've seen 'im goin' hell-bent down the road in it, though. He had to bend over that wheel so's his head wouldn't scrape the top, and he'd look down on that wheel somewhere down 'tween his legs and fight hell out of it. I'll swear he never looked at the road. That wheel was all he could manage at one time.

'Course the roads were only a coupla sandy trails with grass growin' in 'tween the sandy, crooked ruts. Ever'body in the country learned to turn out of those ruts and let old Buff pass, I can tell you, when they saw or heard 'im comin'. You could hear that old wreck for a mile; two, if you met 'im in the mountains on account of the echoes. At night, you got clean off the road when you saw a lone headlight, flickerin' as if it was just about to die. The only trouble was that old Buff's headlights spelled each other. One night the right would be on and the next time it'ud be the left, and you'd never know how far to pull out.

Well, as I say ole Buff was just a big old good-natured bear without much to say, as if like his feet and his hands, he was afraid to hurt things with his words too. But suddenly he started swearin' and throwin' his weight around and that got us to studyin', till we found that arrow of Cupid's stickin' in his breast. The first thing I noticed was one day at Guerrero's when there were some dudes in town from the Lazy-T. They began lookin' at 'im, like anybody 'ud be bound to do. But there had been many a dude look at old Buff before; this time I could see by his face that he was madder'n a wet hen. He kept movin' the fingers of his big hand on the bar, and cuttin' his glances their way. Mikel, the bartender kept sayin' funny things to make Buff laff, 'cause he saw some thing happenin' in Buff's face too. But old Buff didn't rekon anything funny this day.

Suddenly he threw his head back and downed his drink, then walked out. I stayed for a while and watched the dudes by the mirror back of the bar, pretendin' not to, of course. One of them had on a leather jacket—doeskin—with a thunderbird painted on its back, and he had a rattlesnake skin band around his ten-gallon hat. He kept lookin' at himself in the mirror. All of 'em, were actin' free and out-goin', like they fancied themselves in all this space. I was glad old Buff had quit us, and him in a sour mood.

I had no more than thought this till I heard the floor give a little and the boards creak, and there was old Buff again. The first thing I noticed was the holster and the butt of his gun stickin' out. He walked up to the bar and called for a drink, but paid no 'tention to the dudes. They stood and gawked at 'im again, like men lookin' at the lion in the zoo. I saw Buff's fingers twitch again, and there was that look on his face that no one had ever seen before. Something came over me, and when I caught the eye of the dude with the grey hair and the melon belly, I jerked my thumb at the door, and then looked up at Buff. They paid up and left pronto.

That was the first hint we had that old Buff had been hit, and that he was a changed man, but soon we didn't laff anymore and got to worryin' a little. 'Course we never laffed where he could hear us, you might know. We'd get together and now we'd talk mostly about old Buff and Violet Smythe, and each one of us would have some new thing to tell about 'im. He didn't want people lookin' at 'im even.

'Course Violet Smythe didn't know anything about Buff's romance, and it looked a lot like he didn't aim for 'er to. He'd run from 'er. He wouldn't even look at 'er. He'd just drive by her little house several times a day, when the work wasn't heavy.

When we shipped in September, Violet Smythe asked old man Cason, if she could ship some of her calves along with ours; she didn't have enough to make a car to Denver. She just dabbled in cattle; just a plaything, I guess, so's she could wear those fancy duds of hers. She had goats too, and a few head of woolies, some chickens and a Russian wolf hound that looked like he might break his leg if he ever took it into his head to run right fast.

She was a novelist and she had come out to the San Martinez country to get away from it all, as they say. Or maybe for material for one of 'er books. She was a dainty little thing, and they said the Lazura family did ever'thing for 'er but bathe 'er. Some said she was a widow, and some said she had run away from her last lover who was a drinker and saw snakes. It didn't matter much; only the women of White Skull cared anyway. That was our post office: White Skull.

You see Buff worked for old man Cason at special times, at round-up time and when they worked calves, but he had a little place among the brown foothills, that he had filed on as a homestead someway, and you'd a-thought he had a bluegrass farm in Kentucky to hear 'im tell it. He took good care of it alright, and was always talkin' about "my place."

He liked to call himself a rider too, but you know a man that big just can't do any good unless he has a horse big enough to pack 'im, and when he gets one that big he is just not fast enough; can't handle himself to do any good with those wild mountain steers. So you see Buff wasn't really a rider, but he was a good hand. He could handle the most stubborn cowhorse. He was a kind of a handy man; a filler-in, I guess you'd say. Old man Cason said, he was too big for a man and too small for a horse. Said when he first hit 'im for a job, he didn't know whether to throw a saddle on 'im or give 'im string of ponies. The calves we's workin' used to look up at old Buff scared to death when he flopped 'em for the iron. And as for horses, they really respected 'im. Guess they thought he was one of 'em, only brighter and could walk on his hind legs. Old T-N-T used to stand on his hind legs and paw at you when you went into the corral to bridle 'im, or maybe he'd run in circles for ten minutes every morning, but when old Buff appeared, he'd look open-nosed and whistle, two, three times like he'd smelled a grizzly, then come to old Buff bobbin' his head, and almost put his own head in the bridle.

Well, anyway? I'm tryin' to tell you about love, which I don't know much about, and gettin' off on horses which I generally do, cause I know horses.

We gathered out of the mountains, and were holdin' at the old corral by Balsam Tank, up on the rim of Wild Cat. We had a fire there 'cause we had to put the iron on some of the cut backs that we'd missed the spring before when we worked the calves. Well, we were standin' around waiting for some of the boys to bring in the rest of the steers; you know just talkin' like cowpokes will, about this and that. There was always somebody each year who had seen grizzly sign, and this was always good for talk.

While we were talkin' a reflection like the reflection from a shavin' mirror hit me in the eye, and I looked down the canyon trail, and there was Violet Smythe drivin' up in that fancy station wagon of hers. The other boys stood and gawked like a bunch of does, but soon's I saw who it was, I looked at Buff's face. He just stood there and wouldn't look, puttin' his hands forward toward the fire as if he needed to warm 'em on this September day with the sun ridin' our backs.

When Violet stopped, old man Cason went over to 'er and swung that big black hat off, and started tellin' 'er about 'er cattle—I guess. She cut 'er eyes over the outfit just once, then smiled back into old man Cason's face as they talked. She could have nose-ringed any one of us if she a-tried. That's the way she was; all neat and good-smellin' and smilin' and twinklin'.

You've seen women dudes in levis and boots, and you've seen 'em in slacks and high-heel shoes? You've seen dude women pour themselves into levis and slacks, strainin' the container, and becomin' real coltish, but this Violet Smythe was as cute as bug's ear in her outfit. She left a curl just outside of 'er big hat just right. Nothing butt-sprung or knee-sprung about her britches.

The boys got ashamed of themselves gawkin' at 'er and old man Cason, so they started on the grizzly sign again, but old Buff just stood there pretendin' to warm his hands when they didn't need warmin' and lookin' at nothin' just the other side of the fire. I bet he was thinkin' the same thing; nothin'. His thoughts bunchin' up like sheep in a storm, not knowin' which way to go.

I watched 'im. You know his face has a pink color, like some kinds of granite all summer and winter, but now there was a little different red creepin' up from his collar. I watched it climb. It was like if you dropped a redhot into a glass of water. But never once did he cut his eyes to the station wagon; not even when Violet got out, and it looked like she might be goin' to have chuck with us.

There was no need for her to come to the fire, 'cause like I said, it sure wasn't cold. She just stood there in her silk shirt splashed with all the brands in the country, and her Pendletons, that cut just right on the instep of her alligator boots. When she looked up into old man Cason's eyes, smilin', you could see the light glint on her teeth.

They took a step or two toward the fire, then stopped, while old man Cason pointed out something to 'er. You could see 'im steppin' proud. Then just at this time, there was the damnest wild cat squall you ever heard, and we all jumped. That white-eyed sorrel of Cliff's set back and broke the reins, and took off through the junipers.

Old Buff had raised his face to the sky and let out a "EE-ee-ee-ee-yowh-yowh-yowh-yowh, oo-oo-oo-oo-ah," then took off his big black hat, threw it on the ground and tromped on it. Then, he pulled his gun and shot that old hat full of holes. When he had emptied his gun on it, he kicked it into the fire, and then went over to his shiverin' wide-eyed, snorty horse, forked it and took off in the direction the sorrel had taken.

The next think I knew Violet was backin' her station wagon and turnin' it among the pine saplins'. She waved her hand and started back down the trail.

But there was never a word about old Buff among us boys. When old Dogmeat Henry banged the dishpan we went to eatin', and never a word. Of course later, each one of us tried to tell the other the way of it, but there wasn't a man could figger it any other way than love.

The winter dudes started comin' in—dudes that had never got their lookin' out at old Buff, like the summer ones. The San Martinez country is all winter for dudes. Down in the deep canyons, it stays mild most of the winter, and that's where the ranches are. So here came some new dudes and we knowin' now that old Buff just couldn't stand anybody gawkin' at 'im. Some of us figgered on trouble. You could never tell. Love had just plumb queered old Buff.

You know the son-of-a-gun was as straight as a lodgepole pine, and now seems like when he talked with us boys, he'd stoop, so's to be closer to our size. He'd hunch over like he never did before when we were sittin' whittlin', so's he wouldn't stick up.

Listen, you know a mountain lion has tawny-grey-blue hair, and you can't see 'im in the mountains where he stays, because of the natural kind of hair he carries. It suits 'im like a skunk's black and white suits him, 'cause it's natural, and nobody would want to dress a roadrunner in red or purple, so you might know what I mean when I talk about the suit old Buff bought in town, just to come back to White Skull to loaf in. The son-of-a-gun put a tie on too. You know, you take a cowwooly in his faded jeans and shirt, with his get-along like a winged eagle when he's off his old pony, and you got you a hombre you're goin' to look twice at. The look in his eye which never misses much but you can't tell it; the thin, hard face, the narrow hips and no butt to speak of. Even with his bow legs, he'll make you want to be a real man yourself, if you've spent a lot of time in a swivel chair.

But you take an old cowwooly at a funeral at Packsaddle, dressed up in his town suit; the green shined off his boots, and his face shinin' with soap, and shaving lather still in his left ear, and his big hands hangin' like they wanted something to do quick, you got you a lion with pink hair, a skunk striped like a barber pole, and that roadrunner, I was talkin' about in purple or red.

Now, do you see old Buff in his town clothes? You guessed right; we sure didn't laff. We didn't say, "Hey, Buff, where you goin' to preach?" or sad-like say, "Whose dead, Buff?" We only winked at each other when he spooned himself into that old Model-T and drove out Wild Cat Canyon trail, speedin' up as he passed Violet's house, and never lookin' her way.

It was Thanksgivin' Day. Old man Cason usually had two, three turkeys and all the fixins' out at the ranch, but that day I got back from Packsaddle too late to make the ranch for dinner, and started toward the Little Dandy Café. I saw old Buff comin' and I waited for 'im. He was all duded up in that town suit. He come up watchin' my face, like he might be half-expectin' me to draw, but I wouldn't even look like I was lookin' at his suit.

We sat up at the counter. We didn't say much. I believe old Buff did say: "Looks like that cake oughta be a-comin'. Ordered a car more'n a month ago."[1]

And I said, "Yeah, looks like it."

Clara put water down and started layin' the forks and knives, then we heard someone come in. You know how a café is on Thanksgiving and Christmas? Empty as the railroad depot 'tween trains, and the people in it feelin' sorry for themselves.

So both Clara and I looked around and there was Violet Smythe comin' in, and Clara went to see what she wanted. I told you about that smile of hers. Well, she turned it on women and men alike. She wanted some kinda seasonin' for her turkey, I guess, and Clara started back to get it. Just as she was passin' us, old Buff pulled out his gun and hammered the counter with the butt.

"I wanta steak as big as John Mason's apron," he roared, "and want 'er pronto."

Clara stopped, surprised. This just wasn't old Buff at all. He was usually bashful, and was the only one of the outfit that never tried to pinch 'er leg. She looked puzzled, then smiled, figgerin' he'd had a little Thanksgivin' cheer.

"Want it as black as John's apron?" she asked. John Mason was our blacksmith.

Old Buff pulled his big hat down over one eye and kinda looked up from under it.

"I want 'er bloody and still a-quiverin', and I want 'er fast. Pass it over the fa'r two, three times, and slide 'er down the counter, and bygod, I'll stab 'er when she comes by."

Of course, he never let on that he knew Violet was within fifty miles of the Little Dandy. When Clara came out with the little can of seasonin', I could see through the winda, the dust boilin' from her station wagon. After this old Buff was as quiet and as dumb as a plow horse.

I guess it wasn't long after this when some of the boys were talkin' at Guerrero's. It seemed that a wild cat had come down outa the mountains and had taken ever last one of Violet's chickens. We talked about what ought to be done, but mostly what she should-a done in the first place. But old Buff just stood there with his mouth open, turnin' his face to each speaker in turn. Finally, he set his glass down on the bar, wiped his mouth with his sleeve.

"Hell," he said, "if a man could ketch that'ar trail soon enough to put the dogs on it."

"Hell, it's fresh," said Cliff, "fresher'n dew on a rose. Git that pack-a biskit eaters of your'n Buff and les have us some fun."

"Hell fa'r," said Buff, "time a man'ud git out to the ranch fer horses, the trail'ud be as cold as a Eskeemo's butt."

He walked out and got into his old rattletrap, and lit out. We heard later what he'd done. He went to his shack and picked up his hounds. Just damn good lion hounds they were too. He set 'em in right in front of Violet's house, and let his pack spill out. He had 'im a rope 'tached to the back door handle which he worked from the front seat. It was a good thing that spindle-legged Russian hound was in the house at the time, we 'lowed, 'cause those floppys of old Buffs are fast and not particular at all. Anything out a mile from the post office, or something they had never seen one like before, was just plain meat to them.

Accordin' to the way Violet told it later, old Buff set his hat down over his eyes and looked from under it at her a-standin' at the door.

"Whur WAS your goddam chickens when that cat come fer 'em?" She showed him the place, and she said those hounds didn't even circle. She said they picked up that scent and were off up the mountain and old Buff with 'em. He didn't follow 'em, accordin' to her, but he was WITH 'em. She said old Buff let out a squall that echoed along the canyons for a minute.

Sometime later that afternoon, he came down with the cat. His hounds had their mouths wide open and their tongues were touchin' the ground when they lay down to rest, but he wasn't even sweatin'. She said he flung that dead cat down on the kitchen step without even lookin' at 'er, walked out to his car and held the door open for his hounds, then he crammed himself in and after back-firin' two, three times got off in a cloud of dust.

Two days later, he drove up to her house fast with the dust boilin', set 'em right in front of her house and pulled that rope from the front seat. When the back door opened this time, out fluttered six of the prettiest white Plymouth Rock hens you ever saw. By the time she could savvy what was goin' on, he was gone.

I was in the post office when he got the letter from 'er. It was a sight to see those big old steady fingers, that could choke a wolf, tremblin' as he opened that letter. He said he didn't have his glasses with 'im, and would I read it for 'im. Nobody ever saw 'im with a pair of glasses, and he was always talkin' 'bout what he had "read" in the papers.

When I started to read that letter, a cheque fell out, and that's just about what the letter was about. She was payin' 'im a dollar and fifty each for those pullets. Hell, I couldn't look at his face. He took that cheque and rolled it into a thin tube like a spill, then shoved it into his gun barrel, raised his gun and fired through the ceiling, and walked out just as old man Bird stuck his head out the Gener'l Delivery winda, and hollered, "Hey, go easy there, this here's Federal."

Well, it finally came. Some of the boys had noticed a dude sittin' on Violet's front porch, but you know, never a word to old Buff. You know, there's a time when hoorawin' is just not in place. You don't hooraw an old boy 'bout his mother dyin' or his wife leavin' 'im. See what I mean?

But we watched 'im to see what he'd do. We'd see this dude come into Guerrero's and take a seat at a table. We didn't figger that because he didn't belly up to the bar with us, he was insultin' us as we might have done about somebody else. This dude was like us in a way. He just didn't see us, and he musta figgered that lookin' at us just wasn't the thing to do, since he was 'tendin' to his business and we's 'tendin' to ours. You know how dudes try to sidle up to you for a talk, or slap a ten-dollar bill down on the bar and holler for drinks? Well, he just came in not noticin' anybody, went to his table, and thanked Mikel when he brought his whiskey, then sat there turnin' his glass 'round and 'round and thinkin'. You could watch 'im through the mirror without him knowin'. He musta got pretty soggy sittin' there, 'cause he'd be there a long time. But he'd get up, and walk out steady and straight as a magpie, just as if there wasn't anybody else there.

It sure goes without sayin' that Buff had seen 'im there on Violet's porch and knew about his visits to Guerrero's; figgered out someway that he and Violet didn't have the same last name. He knew from the familiar way they talked there on that porch, and him a sitting there in his pajamas sometimes on a hot afternoon, that he wasn't sellin' sewin' machines. You know the sun hangs right on your back out here some days even in the fall, and a man hunts the shade like a trail hound.

Well, one day Buff came in to Guerrero's when the dude was at his table turnin' his glass in his long, white fingers. Ever' eye went to

Buff's holster and sure enough he had his gun. He carried it most of the time now. Buff a-course pretended he didn't see the dude, and came up and bellied up at the bar. I watched 'im, and I think Cliff and Gary watched 'im too. I could see 'im watchin' the dude through the big mirror back of the bar, and we all could see that he was drinkin' more than usual. 'Course that didn't mean much, 'cause that hombre could walk and work when the rest of us were layin' round in windrows. It'ud take a lot of whiskey to spread through his carcass, just like the rattlesnake poison one time when he was bit up on Wild Cat mesa. It just got so thin tryin' to cover his big body, that all he did was throw up, and went right on workin'.

Even if old Buff wouldn't really get plastered, we all knew that he could get enough to change his ideas mighty quick. We all knew if that dude hombre got outa place in any way, shape or form, or even looked at old Buff, there might be hell to pay.

But you see we's countin' on that dude. He had that way of not seein' you, and that alone might have made old Buff mad, and him drinkin', but there's a difference. You see, a man can see you and pretend that he don't, pretendin' that you are below his notice, and that'll make a drunk man madder'n a wet hen. But when he ignores you like an Indian, there just isn't anything to make out of it. It might even be a courtesy, guess you'd call it. Then you know, public opinion is just against you if you walk over and pick a fight.

Anyway, that's the way it was that day, and we sure felt good to get outa there. I guess maybe it was a week later when the real showdown came. It happened that there was quite a bunch of us there at Guerrero's. Old man Cason had bought a lotta Coast cattle to winter in the canyons, and we were waitin' for the train.

We were talkin' 'bout whether there might be a better price the next fall, when we heard shootin'. It was a good ways off, but you know how canyon walls bounce it around. There were maybe ten shots; two, three at a time, then a few seconds another, and after a few seconds another, or two bunched. We didn't stop to count 'em. I jumped into the bed of a pick-up as it started off, and we went like a bat outa hell toward Violet's place, 'cause that's where the shots came from.

There wasn't a soul in sight. Not a Lazura in sight, and I bet they had a dozen kids. That spindle-legged hound was in the house, I guess. Finally we saw a buck goat looking at us through a sage bush with his yellow eyes; that's all. You know it looked like we were face to face with tragedy like in the papers, and you know how a man feels in a situation like that. There wasn't a gun among us, and the five or six of us just waited for something to happen, but we didn't know exactly what we wanted to happen.

I'm tellin' you I like to jumped outa my skin when I heard a flappin' noise in the grass. I looked and there was something white. It was a white hen in her last kick. She had been shot right through the head. We looked and found the rest of 'em, all shot in the head.

Just then the curtain parted a little and there was a white face at the winda. It was Violet Smythe. When she saw us, she screwed up her pretty face like she's 'bout to cry, and motioned for us not to go away. We could hear 'er run to the front door and heard the lock click, then she came out on the porch. She looked each one of us in the face, then she told us what had happened.

Ever' day 'bout four o'clock, the hens would forage in front of the house. You know how chickens have habits about eatin' and restin'? Well, old Buff knew their habits. This afternoon he had rattled by in his old Model-T, then when he was in front of the house he had set 'em in, raised his gun and cracked a hen, then drove off up the road. Soon's he got turned around, he came back and cracked another. Sometimes he'd get it with one shot and sometimes he took as many as three on one hen, driving at full speed back and forth six times, until he had 'em all. He'd slow up to shoot; not bad for a handgun. She said he left out when the last one was floppin'.

Well sir, we didn't see old Buff for maybe a month. Some said he took his beddin' and his hounds and went off up the mountains. But the next time I saw 'im, he was out to the ranch loadin' cake to take to the steers in the canyon. He was his old self again. A big, kindly hombre, a-walkin' over the earth with the careful step of an elephant; afraid to hurt it.

Old Bob

Unpublished and unedited version

It was early in the fall of 1926 and about the second or third Coyote hunt we had been on we already had one Coyote on our saddle they are quite easy to catch early in the fall. that is the young ones.

We had the best bunch of dogs that year we had ever had we were just coming to the big hills west of Blackland when suddenly on the side of the hill a coyote got up and run a few yards up the hill then turned broad sides to us, he was an unusually large Coyote and had a mane like a lion.

The dogs all saw him and the race was on, he would only run a few yards then turn and look back again he run to the top of the hill and just before he went out of sight on top of the hill he stopped and looked back again when he turned to go on the dogs were not more than 25 feet from him.

We spurred our horses to the top of the hill expecting to find him there but imagine our surprise when on topping the hill we saw him and the dogs going north across the perfectly flat country the prettiest country for a race you ever saw, we rode off the hill expecting them to catch him at any minute and we kept on expecting that for three and a half miles when we saw him go up a short raise too far ahead of the dogs to even hope to catch him.

We sat on our horses and waited for the dogs to come back which was'nt long for they realized about the same time we did that he had outrun them while we were waiting Ben said was that Coyote bob tailed I said I dont know I said maby he was bob tailed and his ears

33

cropped too, we both agreed that he looked as much like a lion as he did like a Coyote certainly I never saw such a mane on a wolf and Ben had'nt either.

In the next two weeks we had chased him three more times and other folks had reported seeing him he had been saw in the hart of town in the little town of Pearsonia then a booming little oil town of about one thousand population he had shown up there a couple of times at 11 or 12 oclock at night and run the dogs of town off the streets and they seemed willing to let him have the streets. then he would disappear as quick as he came, we also had saw him in Foraker at the same game Foraker was about 8 miles west and Pearsonia was about 8 miles east of the Blackland hills

From that time on we heard of him often from the ranchers between Foraker and Pearsonia he would come into a yard and take a chicken in broad day light with apparently no fear and leave before anyone could get a gun and get back to shoot him.

Frank Simpkins had a pack of wolf dogs in Pawhuska heard of old bob and brought up his dogs and ask us to show him old bob we got our horses and rode over to the Blackland hills we took Franks dog and also our own as usual we had no trouble in getting up old bob as usual he ran up the hill turning every few yards to look back at the dogs and when he topped the hill the dogs were only a few feet from him Frank was certain he was on top of the hill as his dog Dalis could'nt miss him, Dalis was a track Greyhound and I'll admit a good one we loped our horses to the top of hill and to Franks surprise not ours old bob was going across the flat country as usual Frank was sure he would'nt get clear across them three miles of pretty country but we finally persuaded him to stay there where we could see the race when we finally saw old Bob drop off the flat country into Bird creek he was several hundred yards of the pack

We visited Ralph Johnson Ben's Brother in Tulsa and while there we got two track dogs a black and a buckskin that sure looked good, we could hardly wate to try them on old Bob, well our second day out with them we got him up and as usual he did'nt run till the dogs were in a few feet of him and as usual he outrun them and across good country

Well to make a long story short old Bob stayed there till 1931 every fall we would catch 6 or 8 young Coyotes in the Blackland hills and they would have the big manes but though every winter we would run old Bob from one to three times a week we never caught him we always got a good run at him there were other packs of dogs in the country that run him too, with the same luck we had

Then early in the fall of 1931 old Bobs unlucky race was lost and you know though he had won several hundred races one lose and he could never try again, it was a beautiful morning and just after sun up we had only rode a mile from home we saw a Coyote standing on the point of a hill we looked at him for a minute then Ben announced Old Bob we sat still on our horses and watched him for five minutes and wondered was he bob tailed or just a short tail was his ears cropped or just short no one was ever quite sure and all the time he stood there between a quarter and a half mile away and watched us.

Then the subject was how can we get a better run at him, so we decided to ride on so the shoulder of the hill would hide him from view then the wind would be blowing from him to us too that would be in the dogs favor too, so we rode around and turned back towards him, when we came in view of the hill point Old Bob had left and before we got within fifty yards of where he had stood the dogs winded him he had went in to a corn field at the foot of the hill the field was probably a quarter of a mile across and on the other side of it there was a ditch or small creek about 5 ft deep and 10 feet wide we stopped at the point of the hill and wated to see the dogs bring him out when we saw him come out of the ditch and stand on the opposite bank there he stopped and watched us we were wondering where the dogs were at when suddenly we saw old snow a pure white scotch Deere hound come out of the ditch nearly on top of old bob and nearly caught him before he ever moved, then the race was on Snow wasnt over two feet behind him and the rest of the pack right at his heels they run in a half circle to us with no [chance] in the race for a mile and a half the snow made a super effort and caught old bob, we rode over to them about a half mile distant and when we got there old Bob was up on his feet with light dogs doing their best to put him down we helped the dogs as he was cutting them up bad when we had put him on the saddle we found he had cut every dog in the pack and some of them bad when we got home with him we found three of his feet had been in traps his tail was short but not bobbed, his head was battle scarred his ears were scarred was the reason they were short when we skinned him there was four sized shot in him, his mane masured seven inches and he weighed fifty one pounds we were proud we had caught him but sorry he was gone he looked as though he had had a double breakfast or probably we never would have caught him

Ben and I have probably caught more than a thousand Coyotes but never anything like old bob's equal

Old Bob

Manuscript antecedent to the published version

One saturday afternoon I saw Ed standing in front of the Smoke House, looking out over the street where the saturday afternoon traffic was moving slowly. The winter sun was warm where he stood with one high boot heel caught up behind him on the sill of the window. He was smoking his saturday afternoon cigar with a sensual contentment, and the toothpick in the corner of his mouth indicated that he had just enjoyed a little town chow, and had found it good.

When he saw me he raised his hand and shouted, "howdy," then clanked up to meet me, his girl-leg spurs rattling as the high heels of his boots hit the pavement. "Well," he said, amiably, "whur yu bin grazin—haint seen yu, I guess since me and Jim and you was out after old shep."

"I've been stayin out at the place. Had any good huntin this winter?"

"Purty fair, I guess—got my best hound all tore up—shore hated it."

"Which one, the little black bitch."

"Yeah—yu know how she fights. Jist can't learn her to take care of them legs of hern. Me and Jim was out last sunday and ole shep dang near et her up."

"Too bad. Think she get over it."

"Yeah, guess so. Taint very bad—kinda lames her up, so she can't do nothin'"

"Wasn't Old Bob by any chance was it? That old coyote eats hounds like Belle for breakfast every morning."

His face brightened and he smiled broadly. "Hell, me and Jim done ketched Old Bob."

"When?"

"Musta bin a month er so ago, rekon. Yeah we shore ketched that old shep."

"Whats the matter, was he sick?"

"Yeah, sick like a quarter hoss. No sir, by golly that old Snow dog of Jims brothers jist reached out and gathered him in"

"Was it a good race?"

"One hell of a race and some of the purtiest fightin yu purt'near ever saw. It was apurty mornin and we had only rode a mile from the ranch. The sun was just comin up. We seen a coyote standin on the point of the hill. We looked at him for a minute and Jim said "Old Bob." We sat still there for five minutes and watched him and was wonderin whether that short tail of his'n had been cut off or whether it was jist nacherly short; his ears too we wondered if they had been cropped. You could see that long mane of his'n like a lions mane. You've seen it? Well, he looked like a purty good wolf standin there broadsidin', astandin' there awatchin' us as much as to say, like he always did, 'come git me if yu can git her done'

"You know how bad ever body in the country tried to catch him, and how ever come to know about him. I know me and Jim had ben achasin' him for five years—sometimes as high as three times a week from the first time we seen him astandin' there on the Blackland hills. The first time we seen him was in 1926, in the fall. We had a young shep on our saddles, and we had the best bunch of dogs that year that we ever had, I guess. We was jist comin' to the big hills west of Blackland when suddenly on the side of the hill we seen ole shep. He had bin layin' down, and when he heard us he got up and trotted up the side of the hill, then turned broadside to us. We jist stopped and set on our horses and looked at him. He was the biggest coyote we had ever seen. His mane looked like a lion's mane. Yu could see the prairie breeze a blowin' his mane.

Purty the dogs seen him, and they was off, but the coyote would run a few yards then stop and look back. When he reached the top of the hill he stopped and looked back again, and the last time he stopped the dogs was not more'n twenty five feet from him. We poured on the steel to the top of the hill, and by golly if that coyote wasn't racin' across the flat prairie—the purtiest country for a race yu ever seen. We rode off the hill expectin' the dogs to catch him at any minute, and we jist kept on expectin' this for three and a half miles, but finely we seen him go up a short raise so fur ahead of the pack that we knowed that they wasn't any hope and jist set there on our blowin' horses and waited for the dogs to come in. It wasn't long as they realized that they couldn't catch him about the same time that we did, and here they come pantin' and fox-trottin' back to us. Jim said 'was that shep bob-tailed?' and I said I don't know: maybe he had his tail bobbed and his ears cropped too, but we both agreed that he was the biggest shep that we had ever seen, and me and Jim's seen aplenty. We thought he looked like a lion with that mane the way it was.

In the next two weeks we had three more runs at him and all with the same luck. Then seems like we begin hearin' about him more and more. Other fellas tried to catch him but with the same luck as me and Jim. They was stories about him acomin into the heart of Pearsonia and running the dogs off the street, and the people in that little village said that the dogs seemed willin to let him have the dark streets. He disappeared as quick as he come they said. He also was saw in Foraker about eight miles from Pearsonia. Yu heard about him from all the ranches within ten and fifteen miles around. He would come up and take a chicken in broad day light.

Well one day Che Sabe come to the ranch with his pack. He pulled off his saddle and forked that pinto bare-backed, and away went me and him and Jim for the Blackland hills. It wasn't to git a run at Old Bob. We seen him in the usual place, and purty soon we was off; Old Bob runnin' and stoppin' ever few yards to look back. Che Sabe fed that pinto the leather, but me and Jim jist loped along behind; we knowed that Injuns dogs couldn't do nothin' with Old Bob, though

I'll admit that he had one of the best packs in the Osage, and that dog Shonkah of his'n was one of the best. We had a hard time persuadin' that Injun that he might as well stay with us and watch the race from the hill, but he was sure that Shonkah would catch Old Bob. Well, it turned out jist as we thought. After the three mile run across the flat prairie, we seen Old Bob drop down into the breaks of Bird Creek. That Injun come a-lopin' back like a pichur across that flat prairie, but he didn't say nothin'. Well, we had a nice race out of another shep afore we went back to the ranch.

Yu know, a funny thing, most of them Blackland hills coyotes has got long manes jist like Old Bob, only not so long of course, but seems like they all got 'em, unless me and Jim is seein' things.

Most ever man that had a pack took a run at Old Bob and me and Jim run him, I rekon a hundred times du-in' the next four or five years, till as I was a tellin' yu we finely ketched him about a month ago. Old Bob's unlucky race come: he lost though yu know he had won several hundred races agin' the best packs in the Osage, besides some track dogs from Telsa—one lose and he could never try agin'. Wasn't no special dog that first laid holt of him neither—jist one of them things that yu read about in books—the Fate of the wild I guess yu'd say maybe.

The Old Man had me and Jim purty busy this fall, and we didn't git shipped out till along in October, then one beautiful mornin' Jim looked at me in a certain way, and went out and got to foolin' with the dogs. I seen ole Star, Jim's ropin' hoss a-standin' saddled, and I knowed what was up. Jim never used old Star except for somethin' special, and I'll admit that he was one of the best hosses a man ever forked. I went down and got my ole Jazzbo, which was so bad himself fer a quarter. When I come up Jim was a-waitin' with the pack at his heels.

When we got to the hills the sun was jist comin' up and what should we see a-standin' there on the hill but Old Bob. We stopped and Jim said kinda like he was a-seein' him for the first time: "Old Bob." We set there on our hosses and watched the old fella for some minutes while the doges was a-payin' their respects to the carcass of a old dead steer. He stood there and looked at us in the same old way of his'n. We was both a-wonderin' the same old thing; whether them ears was cropped and whether that tail was bobbed. I guess he was thunkin'; well there's them fool men agin' that thinks they got some runnin' dogs—I was jist needin' a little exercise for my digestion anyway.

Jim looked over at me and said: "No use a gettin' the dogs tar'd on that sun-of-a————." I said "No I rekon not," when ole Spot scented him—the wind was favorin' us. It was the same story. He jist waited till the dogs got mighty nigh on him then he turned and run off, the dogs a-snappin at his rear, it seemed like. Jist as we had done a hundred times we loped to the top of the hill and aimed to set and wait for the dogs to come a-pantin' back. But when we got there we didn't see him. We looked around. There was a old corn field at the foot of the hill, which had belonged to a farm that had been "throwed out," and there was the pack runnin' down the middle of it, and Old Bob about forty yards ahead of 'em.

The field was about a quarter of a mile across, and at the other side was a ditch about five feet deep and about ten wide. We stopped, cause we knowed he aimed to pull a fast one. He would make the ditch and then run along it and come out way down at the end, and the dogs goin as fast as they was and running by sight would pile up in the ditch and when they got untangled would run straight ahead, while Old Bob would climb out way down the ditch and trot off about his business. He aimed to pull a shananigan—didn't feel like playin' this mornin'.

But right here's where that Fate yu read about comes in. The little trick worked. Purty soon we seen Old Bob climb out of the ditch way down the ravine, and stand there, with his tongue out and lookin' back. With his tongue out that a way he looked like he was a-laffin'. We wondered where the dogs was—we guessed they was kinda gettin untangled in the bottom of the ditch, when that Fate come in. She musta bin a-straddle of the oneriest dog in the outfit; a big Scotch Deer hound, ole Snow, which was pure white, and had never ketched nothin' more than beef scraps at butcherin' time. He was fast as hell, and would run a jackrabbit clean out of the country, but he always laid back when the pack run ole shep, but savage as hell at the kill, and growled like he was mean.

Imagine our surprise when somethin' white come out of that ditch right on top of Old Bob. We figured afterwords that ole Snow was on him before he knowed it and bein' scairt to death jist set in fightin' like a 'possum that is cornered. Well, him and Old Bob mixed it. Ole Snow was big and strong, and he could fairly fight when he had to, er when he was scairt like he was now.

We poured in the steel and got to the fight about the same time as the rest of the pack. Now, I've seen some fights in my time, but I never seen one like that Old Bob put up. Yu know when a pack hits a coyote, he goes down and up again two or three time before he is finely kilt. But not Old Bob; he wasn't down once but ever dog in the pack was down more than once. Well we had to help the dogs kill him. I believe he would have whupped that whole pack, and Jim thinks so too. Finely he was stretched out there in the long grass, and the dogs was a-layin' around lickin' their wounds, and me and Jim was blowin' too. My pants was ripped down the leg, and Jim's hand was cut.

We throwed him on the saddle and started home—no more runs that day, and as it turned out no more runs for several months cause ever dog in the pack was cut up purty severe, and we had to go back after ole Dan and Socks in the wagon—they jist couldn't make it.

As we rode along slow so the limpin' dogs could keep up we wondered why ole Snow had run down the ditch, and we come to the conclusion that they musta bin a rabbit got up jist as the dogs puled in, and ole Snow perferred rabbit to coyote so he got unscrambled and took down the ditch after the rabbit right onto Old Bob, and both of them was surprised. But if Old Bob had played as he usually did he would be singin' to the moon yet, I guess. I don't know what was the matter with him that morning, unless as Jim said, he musta had a double brakfast.

We stood there in the sun for a short time in silence. Ed was studying the end of his saturday afternoon cigar, which had gone out during the recital, then he pushed his hat back on the back of his head, took out his knife, squatted on his high heels and picked up a piece of pine box which had fallen into the cutter. He said as if reminiscing, "I was ridin that country the other day lookin' about some strays. Yu know its kinda funny not seeing that great big wolf standing on the point of the hill, a-looking as if he owned the Osage. He weighed over fifty pound—haint never seen his match—don't guess they make a common coyote any bigger. Seemed like I could hear them teeth of his'n comin' together when he missed a foreleg du'in the fight, and them yellow eyes of his'n that made you feel kinda funny after he was stretched out there in the grass—seemed like them eyes was a-sayin' that he hadn't quit yet, even he was a, they wasn't much left of him but some yellow hair matted with blood."

During the short silence that followed he had shaped the piece of pine box into a smooth peg. He arose, put his knife back in his pocket, pushed his big hat forward and looked up the street, squinting as though the sun was in his eyes as he would squint riding across the prairie. Then with a touch of embarrassedment; "Yu know I wish he was still kinda a-kingin' it over them hills—shore wush we hadn't ketched him." Then after a brief pause: "Shore'n hell do."

Travel Stories

Readers who wish to avoid plot spoilers will
prefer to skip to the stories and then return.

One could argue that most of the stories in this volume are travel stories. Many were made possible by Mathews's travel beyond his home or travel by the original source of the story: two from the "Westerns" section, all but one of the "Stories from Indian Country," and all but one of the stories about World War II and the Cold War. But the four gathered together here are more specifically stories of the adventures and misadventures of travelers, to Scotland, the Middle East, and Mexico. That point of view of the stranger in a strange but familiar land forms the basis for his excursions here.

"Lady of the Inn"

Unlike for the final story in this section, "Only a Blonde," the diary that might be associated with "Lady of the Inn" is no longer extant. We are left to conjecture whether the incident is based upon an actual experience Mathews had in Scotland or merely fed by his familiarity with the setting. "Lady of the Inn" is a bit more anonymous than his other Scottish stories, taking place in a generalized Argyllshire. While on vacation in Scotland in July 1921, Mathews had made arrangements with a Mr. Tedcastle for a hunting expedition in October. He enjoyed traveling alone, finding himself of a solitary nature and liking to do things others might not enjoy. It is quite possible that the now missing October 1921 diary or a later installment contains an earlier version of this short story. By then Mathews was already nearly twenty-seven years old. He was still an undergraduate, having piloted and air instructed in World War I and dissatisfied with having been rushed through his first bachelor's degree, he'd gone to England for a second. Likely not lost upon him at forty-five, if the story is little embellished from reality, is the irony of his probable persona believing at twenty-seven that Mrs. Atherton at thirty-five is aged rather than still ripening. But of course the ever careful writer keeps such details to himself to enhance the youthful narcissism and immaturity of the narrator. His potential exaggerations are pronounced; he behaves throughout as if his arrival were of importance, as if people and things were happy to make him the center of their attention. He even falls into a deep slumber desiring to polish up the little story! That detail fits nicely with the risible orientalist touches Mathews provides: the sinister, scheming Milford reading a magazine called the *Arab*; an au revoir revealed to be insincere at the Turks Head Hotel. Even Mrs. Atherton, conveniently for the young writer, is a cougar.

"Allah's Guest"

Meanwhile, "Allah's Guest" might fit into another category of orientalism, but one complicated by Mathews's complex mixed heritage. This narrative takes us back to the beginnings of intensive oil production in the Arab countries, which has led to a great diminishment of the stateless, nomadic lifestyle of the Bedouins and an increase in the power of the nation-state. Mathews could hardly have been unaware of the parallels between the Little Old Men of the Osage tribe in one hemisphere and these sheikhs and their tribes in another: both sets of leaders thrown from positions of independence and hegemony into a forced though fortune-bringing bargaining with the powers of Big Oil. More generally, the geographical range of the Bedouins can be compared to the territorial expansiveness of the Plains tribes. He subtly links these oil discoveries in the Osage nation to the colonial development of oil reserves in Saudi Arabia, by surfacing their accompanying tribal-colonial politics. The oil context of the story is never more than a whisper. Yet it hovers incessantly over the action in a way seldom found in the romances of British and American adventurers to the deserts, which often leave unspoken their hero's reasons for being present. The presence of the adventurer here is accommodated, not welcomed. John Hamilton is a heathen, not just an infidel, in this narrative. At one critical point he intentionally associates himself with child marriage such that he becomes a momentary object of his host's derision. Previous readers of Mathews can hardly help recalling his lengthy chapters on child marriage and polygamy in *Wah'Kon-Tah*. In "Allah's Guest," the Aniza remain safely out of the judgmental reach of the American civilizationist with respect to polygamy, and show themselves contemptuous of child marriage. Indeed, Mathews showcases customs that protect Bedouin and Muslim women rather than participating in the clichéd myths of their ever and ever being at the mercy of men. Though several of his sentences are stilted—perhaps intentionally—his outlook ultimately reflects an admiration for the ability of Hamilton's hosts to exert their power in situations that nominally give multinational corporations or the strongest man the upper hand.

Mathews's diaries for the 1920s are sparse. Most are either no longer extant or else not publicly accessible. Hence it is difficult to know for certain that he never traveled to this area of the world, but that seems likely. In his autobiography he writes of his yearning during World War I to join the British commander Edmund H. H. Allenby in his push toward Damascus in 1917–18. The dream was never to be. Later, while at Oxford, Mathews traveled to Algeria. Some of the features of "Allah's Guest" can be discerned in his diary of that 1922 sojourn, transplanted onto Saudi soil. Travels beyond Europe after January 1922 cannot be ruled out, but Mathews was married by April 1924. If he had not been in Damascus or Saudi Arabia by then, his only chance would likely have been a job with Standard Oil Company of New Jersey (the founder of the Anglo-American Oil Company in the story), either in his first wife's home state of New Jersey or in Southern California, where they apparently relocated in order to follow a prospect with the company. That prospect may never have panned out, given his 1929 byline in the *Sooner Magazine* as a realtor. There is no indication between 1929 and 1979 that he ever journeyed to the Middle East after relocating to Pawhuska, particularly prior to the probable writing of this story between 1946 and 1951. However, Mathews gobbled up Charles Montagu Doughty's *Travels in Arabia*

Deserta. Much of the terminology of "Allah's Guest" seems to follow Doughty's language, which Mathews "grazed" for style and pleasure on and off through the end of his life.

"Yellow Hair"

The final two stories in this section are both set in Mexico. Written in August 1946 shortly after "The Apache Woman" of the next section, the complex associations of "Yellow Hair" take some time to penetrate its deceptively simple exterior. It is one of four stories, including "Only a Blonde" (1949), "Laughter" (1949), and "Alfredo and the Jaguar" (1963), made possible by Mathews's 1939–40 residence in Mexico while a Guggenheim fellow. All these reference jaguars or pumas or leopards, leading us to draw tentative conclusions regarding Mathews's familiarity with the canonical indigenous works of Mesoamerica such as the *Popul Vuh* and the *Chilam Balam.* In "Yellow Hair" he explicitly pictures the "black leopard" swallowing Mayan civilization: one of the multifarious ways in which Mayans treat feline and feline-adorned relationships to and between human societies.

In his diaries Mathews remarks on the towns converted to tourist danger zones by the increased traffic from the States, and the opportunistic manners of the mestizo men in those gassing-up places that he avoided. On October 13, 1939, on his way into the country, he noted his disappointment in Monterrey as less Mexican than San Antonio, and remarked his location at the end of the day driven part way by a White Cap boy: "This the Hotel Valles, in the village of Valles, in the jungle, in the State of San Luis Potosi, in the Republic of Mexico." In January 1940, on a trip to Acapulco, he said,

> Tierra Colorada is a native town which is being changed very rapidly by the tourists who whizz by on the way to Acapulco, yet it is not quite spoiled. It is in the transition stage, and it is for this reason alone that it is interesting. It was a distinctly unfriendly village before the highway came, I am told, and now the wits and shrewdness which animated the people, are adjusting themselves to fawning and pleading with tourists to buy. . . . Thus far, I have

found that where the tourists and civilization (if one wants to use that word) have touched, petty thefts occur, along with insolence and brazen determination. Where the people are still untouched, they are charming, reserved and dignified.

A few days later, in Mexcala, the children had

the boldness of half-witted pirates, and the elders are no better. Those who have ambition enough to turn in their hammocks, show faces in which light is rather dim. Having had to, to stop here several times on my trip along the Highway, I have noted the difference here from other points along the Highway, where the people are often spoiled by the tourist—that is they become very, very unattractive in their urging the sale of their wares.

This tourist-consciousness, depicted best in "Yellow Hair" by the description of Miguel's favored roles as "a poor, struggling Indian genius, a gay, lovable mestizo, yearning for higher education, or a drifting Don of good family destroyed by the revolution," Mathews links without hesitation to the unequal economic relationship between Mexicans and Americans. Born to a family that apparently migrated northwest to find work, rather than being caught across the moving border of the nineteenth century, Miguel recognizes Helga for the chance that she is to change his condition either momentarily or more permanently. She is a rung on the social ladder and he a clever though trite innovator with cinematic know-how and latent undervalued prowess. Mathews ironically has "the girls" dreaming romantically of pith helmets and slinky half-castes, so Helga gets not only the thrill that she seeks but the fright that she deserves. And yet, ever empathic (and still slightly cynical, gender-role-bound), he paints her too as a woman betrayed by the nonconformity of her own body to the dreams cinematically implanted in her mind. Also ironically, Mathews described himself in his diaries as wearing a helmet throughout his time outdoors in Mexico, pith or otherwise we cannot tell! He himself frequented hotels run by the "efficient"

Swiss, in part so that he could use his better polished French rather than his so-so Spanish.

"Only a Blonde"

Like the Orientalized relationship between the fabricated East and the fantastical West, the experience of the U.S. tourist encountering the Mexican police is the stuff of legend and repetition, and therefore should also be fodder for skepticism. However, whatever assessment we throw over the fiction of the second Mexico story in this collection, "Only a Blonde," with its hardened anticapitalist Radcliffe girl and its petty-power-glorying "park where you like" officials, its origins must be a part of that assessment. It may well be the only story Mathews ever wrote in which he transformed himself into a woman. The encounter with Mexican police in the "wild mountains of the Mexican State of Guerrero" was in fact his own experience. It occurred in Chilapa on his way back to Cuernavaca from a short vacation in Acapulco in early January 1940. Even in those diary entries from January 7 and 8 where he recorded it, Mathews writes self-aware, as an author, saying that the encounter was one of the handful of events that had given him "a greater insight into Mexico and the Mexican character than any thing I could have experienced. The carbons on these two days may seem long and filled with rather unessential details, but to the heart of a writer . . . are the individual stones necessary to the structure—a literary structure, which become an unconscious short story, through the simple scribbling of impressions. . . . If I ever write successful Short stories, they will never follow a conscious form laid down by magazines."

In writing this short story installment for March 1949, presumably from the nearly identical incident that spans sixteen pages in his 1940 diary, he changed significant details beyond the gender of the lead character. For example, when first approached about his car, Mathews deems himself to have been consciously malicious and intentionally condescending, insulting the men for being uncultured and not knowing any English. He also eliminated the genuine but ultimately ineffectual efforts of the hotel's owner to put him in touch with a translator—his daughter-in-law—for his morning in court. The note from the professor is almost the same, but the nonfictional one baldly acknowledges the bribe being sought. Clearly Mathews is amusing himself too by changing the doctor from the Department of Health who assisted him into "a poor engineer of Sanitation from the Department of Mexico." Perhaps most important, Mathews saw Mexico and his role in Mexico very differently than did Shelly Peters and does not appear to have looked with hard eyes or vindictiveness on the Indian women kneeling in the earthquake-stricken church:

And because these children of the sun have the dignity of the saints whom they worship, the spasmodic ferocity of the big cats that pad over their mountains, the humanity of their own burros, and the souls of Oriental poets, I am fascinated by them when they come into the caressing coolness of their churches. When they come in silently on bare feet, and in weathered huaraches, to talk to God, the dignity of the Saints, the ferocity of the lion, the struggle-hardness of the burro, and the heart of the poet, are fused by the fire of faith into poignant Beauty.

Lady of the Inn

As I look back now I suppose it was because I was so filled with enthusiasm over my first red deer shooting, that I seemed to be little impressed by the lady of the inn during the first two days of my stay on the moors. I say this because she was a rather strange, startling person one would naturally remember. I had made arrangements to shoot the deer forest the summer before and since that time nearly all my thoughts were colored by my plans, and she became simply an element. The lady of the inn was in fact just a woman, a person aiding me in my all-important plans by owning the lonesome little inn far out on the moors of Argyllshire. And in those days I had some idea that people and things were happy to make my plans effective, and it seemed only natural to me that she should come along at the proper time with her inn and her staff for my convenience.

But even though absorbed by my plans for shooting as I was, the lady of the inn was notable. When she watched me, especially from the dark corner of the dining room, I thought of her as being a charged person, with a species of primitive urge which generated a spirit of discontent; her charged silence as being inspired by a suppressed force within her. She was, it seemed to me, like the brooding moor, and I romantically thought of her as being the embodiment of a force under the heavy silence and the mists, which if not actually menacing then certainly mystical. Her placidity was that of black water which is very deep and flows so silently that you get the impression that danger lurks there. As I say, she might have attracted my full attention if I had not been absorbed by the prospects for my first red deer shoot in the romantic land of Sir Walter Scott and the clans.

The train that had twisted and labored through the highlands, and had finally stopped at the little station among the conifers, seemed impatient to get on; get away from the forlorn little station, and was actually moving again before the guard could hand down my rifle to me, and I had to walk along with the moving van to take it from him.

I was the only passenger to descend there at the dismal little station. There was no sign of life, and the rain whispered as though it didn't care to be too obvious and cause comment. Yet it fell gently with assurance, as if it realized that resistance to it had been found to be quite useless centuries ago; from the time the Pictish gods had accepted it.[1]

There was no one to meet me with my duffel, and the inn was not visible. I threw my duffel bag over my shoulder picked up my rifle and shotgun and set off down a needle-covered path that wound its way down among the boles of the firs. The smoke from my pipe floated over my shoulder and remained on a level with it, and my hat brim dripped water into the bowl, causing it to sputter.

Suddenly the inn loomed as if it had decided to come to meet me. One moment I was unable to see it through the mist and the next moment it was there in front of me with its sheds and outhouses. It was like coming face to face suddenly with a family of hikers on a mountain trail. In the shut-in loneliness of the moor, the sheds and outhouses seemed to be crowding close to the inn for protection.

I opened the door with one hand and threw my duffel into the room with the other, so that I could get out of the rain as quickly as possible. Boots and a maid came to my aid from somewhere out of the shadows as if they had been disturbed in whispered conversation. While I was wondering what effect my dripping hat and coat would have on the neat floor, I looked up to a small desk with a light over it, and saw the lady of the inn watching me. Her eyes were the eyes of the Mona Lisa but there was no inscrutable smile. She did answer my "Good afternoon—I'm Mr. Girard," with her mouth, but made no response.[2] She twitched the corner of her mouth as if the muscles there were attempting to pull the rest of her face into a conventional expression of welcome, but that movement of the corner of her mouth was the only sign of recognition. Her eyes were intent and amused, apparently because I had thought that my arrival was of importance.

She had apparently been watching me from the moment I opened the door, and the faint movement at the corner of her mouth and her inscrutably amused eyes that were also strangely hungry-appearing, seemed to say, "you're just another male, so don't give yourself the trouble of strutting, and don't say things to impress me; I know the stupid, vain lot of you."

I felt her watching me from a shadowy corner of the dining room as I ate, and it was then I felt the suppressed force of her. The feeling that there was something pent up in her, was the same feeling the moors gave me, and that is the reason I thought of her as being the embodiment of the heavy silence and the whispering rain and the mystery of the mists.

I never knew when she moved from the desk to the dining room shadows, but since she said nothing but sat silently watching me, I felt instinctively that she had come to watch me from her corner on the pretext of dining room supervision. I was the only guest in the room.

The silence was so complete within that I could hear the water in the roof gutters and the dripping from the eaves like the voices of a contented flock of migrating warblers. Boots had disappeared and the waitress moved about without even the slightest creak of a board. She was so silent that I was startled to find her at my side.

While eating the sweet, I ventured to look at the lady of the inn in her shadowy corner, so charged with a mysterious, primitive force which disturbed me. She didn't lower her eyes as I had expected her to do, and I guessed that she believed herself invisible.

I was startled again by the waitress as I started up the stairs to my room. Suddenly she was standing in front of me, and was asking when I should like my tea brought up in the morning, before I was completely conscious of the situation. I suppose I was still absorbed by my own awkwardness when I had left the dining room and had said good night to the shadowy corner, and had heard no response.

I say these things must have impressed me at the time, even though by the time I was in my room and laying out my clothes for the morrow, I seemed to have been lost in my plans for shooting. I might have forgotten them entirely, if I had not had occasion to recall them within a few days. The incidents of the lady of the inn's eyes and the silence which was like expectant brooding of the moor were noted by me as one notes objects in the outer edges of one's headlights while looking straight down the highway to some very pleasant objective, only to be recalled and remembered vividly when one drives back to search with the spotlight of knowledge and high interest, throwing the light beams upon the vague forms one has passed in one's absorption with an objective.

As often happens in Scotland the morning after the night of heavy silence and mystery, the sun shone down on an extremely happy and beautiful world, and I met Mr. Milford as he drove up to the inn with a quivering enthusiasm.

The lady of the inn was not present when he arrived to pick me up, and it wasn't until afterward that I realized he had seemed to hesitate as though waiting for her to appear. This would have meant nothing at all under ordinary circumstances. He could have been waiting for a message, or to give one.

He was a very pleasant sort of person, and was dressed very neatly in plus fours and wore the latest shoes with the tongues flapping on the outside.[3] His stockings were gay. As a matter of fact I noticed immediately how neatly he was dressed, a thing I seldom notice in men. It occurred to me that he must have taken very great pains to appear well. He had the fastidiousness of a successful boxer rather than the carelessness of a country gentleman whose life revolved about horses and who had leased a large deer forest. Of course, this impression of his perfect plus fours and his perfectly combed hair came back to me later, and there seemed to be reason for such careful dressing, but at the time I wondered why he should care to impress a shooting guest, who in his turn was dressed for the purpose of stalking stags.

This first day out was not too successful. McCarriker, the ghillie, wanted to show me the big stag which he said was a "royal," and we spent so much time listening for his bass roar, that we ignored the roaring of lesser stags.[4] It was only after we had despaired of hearing the royal that I shot a very ordinary stag.

As we sat by the kill eating lunch about 3 p.m., the warm air from the Gulf Stream began to condense the moisture over the highlands, and a fog rolled in, and we could see only the vague outlines of the hills. On our way back to the lodge, the furry outline of a hind, enlarged by the fog became to me, at least, the royal which we hunted. She watched us, then with a whistle of alarum, she wheeled, and it was disappointing to see on the skyline only a hind's bare head, and not the pulse-quickening truly majestic antlers of the royal. If the term majestic means anything in reference to man or animal, it must apply to the uplifted, antlered head of a stag on the skyline.

The great granite boulders carelessly left by the receding ice of the Ice Age became, in the mist, a herd of grazing elephants, and the roar of the stags became completely disembodied, and the querulous voice of the blackface sheep became the very voice of the half-lighted world.

Soon the rain began to fall through the fog, and the fertile earth odor of moss came up to us as we tread on it, and the bracken swished against our legs to wet us to the knees. The stags now began to roar on every side, as though expressing their discontent that the half-light should come to their world to disturb their wooing, to which nature had allotted such a short time each year.

As we walked along, McCarriker kept listening for the bass voice of his royal. Then suddenly he stopped and remained motionless as if to give accuracy to his hearing.

"In yon vale," he said, and pointed to the opaque west.

"The royal?" I asked.

"Aye."

But I could see by his shoulders as he strode on, that the day was finished.

Again I sat at table in the silent dining room at the inn. It seemed utterly silent and lonely after the tea with Mr. Milford in front of the great fireplace of the lodge. We had talked of horses and stags, then he had driven me back to the forlorn little inn in the rain. The shut-in loneliness was not so much a romantic and comfortable refuge from the whispering mysteriousness of the moors, as it had been the evening before, but I could appreciate the rhythmical tinkling of the water from the eaves.

I knew that the lady of the inn had taken her place in the shadows of the corner again to look at me with her hungry eyes, and perhaps turn the corner of her mouth down in her Mona Lisa smile, as she watched. I was not so aware of her this evening; I was tired, and my bath had left me sleepy after the day in the fog and rain. Also I was recapitulating the incidents of my first day stalking the classical highland stag, and anticipating the morrow when we should again attempt to locate the royal.

My bed looked like an éclair with pink frosting, extravagantly applied. I was happy to be shut in by the charged solitude of the moors, and there was delicious comfort in the whisper of the rain and the tinkling of the water, and here in my room I could hear the sluicing in the gutters.

As I came out the next morning to meet Mr. Milford in his shiny Vauxhall, I saw him standing in his meticulous plus fours, and she, the lady of the inn, stood with him.[5] He had been talking rather seriously, I thought, as people of some intimacy might talk with each other. Her whole attitude was defensive, as though he had been disapproving of some thing she might have done. She was looking at the ground as a child might do who had been scolded, and who though recognizing the justice in the reprimand might still persist in stubborn resentment. When Milford saw me approaching, he said something flippant about her terrier and his ill luck in catching moles.

"Good morning," he said to me. "I was just telling Mrs. Atherton that she ought to stop the little beggar's digging; awful mess, really."

The lady of the inn walked out among the shrubs without greeting me. It was plain that she was upset, and his flippant talk was a cover up for a rather intense conversation.

On the way to the lodge, Milford, while never loquacious except when talking about horses during tea by the cavernous fireplace, was now perfectly silent. When we arrived, he said, "well, here we are," as if he had been totally absorbed by other thoughts all the way from the inn.

That morning on the moors, McCarriker sighted a large band of hinds immediately, and we searched the hills for the stags we could hear roaring, but we saw only indifferently antlered ones. It was then that we heard the bass roar of the royal, and McCarriker put up his finger.

The challenge of this classic animal has little beauty, but has the flatness of the bawl of a discontented steer on the ranges of the United States. The roar was deep, and I noted McCarriker's excitement. He wet his thumb and held it up to the air.

"We'll go 'round," he said, "yon hind'll no ken if we keep it close."

We immediately fell to our hands and knees and began to crawl through the whin and bracken. I saw the soles of McCarriker's big brogans in front of me, and wondered why that clumsily articulated body was not more graceful, nurtured as it was here on the moors and constantly serving him in his profession as ghillie.[6] One expected the litheness and beauty of a dude ranch cowboy; the type with whom American heiresses fall in love. I found that I was unhappy that this stalker of the majestic stag should be more the work-distorted clod than the beautiful son of nature. I always lighten thoughts that inspire high excitement by concentrating on something near and of little importance. Thus in my tingly excitement about the royal, I must study the gnarled man crawling in front of me during this high moment.

We would stop crawling to listen, then the bass roar would come to us, and I could see McCarriker's stub-fingered hand shaking with nervousness. It seemed ridiculous in a way; this hard, gnarled, earthy man so under the influence of tingly nerves. It was like an English oak bowing to a zephyr.

We crawled to the crest of a hill and looked over, and there stood the royal in the valley. We crawled back carefully, and McCarriker whispered: "It's nae guid." His face was troubled, and his hands shook more, "yon hinds'll——"

"Shall I try?" I whispered.

"Aye, try."

I moved up to the edge of the hill's crest, but just as I did so, one of the hinds whistled, and the band bolted. I got to my feet and sent three flying shots after the great stag, then he showed himself momentarily against the skyline, and his majestic antlers caused me to choke with emotion.

McCarriker let his hands fall to his side, and I felt sorry for him. He wanted me to kill a royal and he knew that this would be the only chance I should have. He sat on a small boulder and took off his cap, "yon hinds," he said and shook his head.

We walked down into the valley, and he pointed to the royal's tracks, and shook his head in defeat again.

We ate our lunch. He pointed to a spot not far away and said as if musing, "yon lassie lost mate there."

I thought of the lady of the inn, Mrs. Atherton, the only "lassie" we knew in common—or would a Scot ghillie refer to the lady of the inn as "lassie." Yet it must be.

He continued as if he might be talking to himself: "T'was accident—that was what t'was said." He peeled his orange. "Yon laird found body—yon laird'ud ken well where to sairch that nicht. Too mony guns that day, yon." He paused for some time and ate several segments of his orange before he continued, "T'was said t'was accident."

I wanted very much to ask questions but there was something about McCarriker that stopped me. Anyway he rose rather abruptly and pointed to a long band of fog lying in the valley, picked up his things and started off over the hill.

Soon the mist enveloped us and the rain whispered about us, and soon we were walking again on the spongy earth. The stags began to roar again like disembodied creations; like discontented spirit stags. But my thoughts were now with the lady of the inn. Who could imagine that she and Milford could plan such a fiendish way of removing poor old Atherton. It had been called an accident; just another accident of the field, but old McCarriker knew the facts. I dare not ask him to reveal his secret, but really it was not necessary.

Milford had shot him during a time when the moors were full of guns, and it had appeared to be an accident.

The day closed in fast and soon it was twilight in the fog and mist. As we moved over a hill we could see the early lamplight from the fog-fuzzy lodge. Suddenly McCarriker stopped and pointing a very crooked finger toward the lodge said, "yon laird'ud ken well where to make sairch, I obsairved," then we moved on toward the light. I felt that he might answer my questions now since he seemed to be moved. Perhaps he had liked Atherton very much. I decided however, not to attempt to urge the exposure of his secret. He would become wary if asked one question and immediately wonder how much he had revealed in his reminiscent musing.

The fire in the fireplace blazed as usual and the tea things were on the little table reflecting the flame dance. Mr. Milford put down a magazine called THE ARAB, and smiled at me.

"I'm afraid you're wet again," he said, "hope you've got fresh linen."

"Oh, no," I said, "I'll just change socks, if you don't mind."

"Oh, by the way, you can have a complete change here if you wish. Daresay, I've done a rather abrupt thing."—He seemed confused and colored a little as an Englishman who had intruded upon your privacy would do. "I've, as a matter of fact, had your duffel brought here; I hope you won't mind."

"Not at all, if you find it more convenient that way."

"Well, as a matter of fact t'will be. You see I've gone a little lame and my old business—I believe I've told you about the horse falling back on me——has come back as it usually does in cold weather; before a weather change. That leaves no one to drive you to the inn or fetch you in the morning. I was sure you wouldn't mind."

"Quite alright; I hope the proprietress won't think——." I checked myself just in time to keep from saying, "'that I've been murdered or something'"——"that I've been lost on the moors or something when I don't turn up for dinner."

"It's all arranged; look here, I even have your statement——what did I do with the ruddy thing?" He looked on the table under the horse magazines and the breeder's manual. "Oh, yes, here it is; all paid y'see, and you can give it me when you pay my statement."

"That's perfect," I said.

But it wasn't perfect at all. I was indefinitely upset. I was suddenly aware of that curse of youth which comes of the fact that your mind is, or seems to be, in a glass bowl for older people to read. My thoughts were certainly not crystallized, and even if they weren't, I didn't want this impeccable and apparently sinister and scheming older man even guessing that my thoughts might be disturbed since McCarriker had pointed out the scene of the murder. He knew where we had been stalking, and he might suspect that McCarriker knew more than had come out at the autopsy, therefore he would catch at the merest hint from my manner.

I knew that I must put him off the trail by talking enthusiastically about the royal we almost had, but the point was not to be too obviously eager to tell him about it. I had a thought. As I left to change my socks, I stopped at the door and then said casually, "why don't I change for dinner now? Will that make tea late?"

"Oh no, not at all; just as you wish, no hurry. I'll just show you your quarters."

As he came toward me smiling, I noted that his limp seemed a bit exaggerated. I didn't notice his limp at all when I first came in from the moors.

As I bathed, I thought I could understand the whole story. When I remembered the eyes of the lady of the inn, I felt a little shock and my stomach tingled. That's what it was behind those eyes; a pent up primitive force that was relentless like death, only it was not sure like death. It was more like an uncomfortable possibility; an explosion at the least expected moment. It would be like the combustion in a hay barn where the flood waters from some creek raced through the stored hay to create friction and possibly combustion. There would be no fire near; only the harmless hay and the silently, relentlessly flowing flood waters.

It had happened to them alright, I felt sure, but I also felt sure that would not be the end. Atherton had been in the way and they in their primitive intensity had removed him as an obstacle; as perhaps only an inconvenience, but Milford was not the complete answer to the insatiable, exigent force of the lady with the hungry eyes. I guessed that he had been certainly overwhelmed by her primitive force, but he also knew that he was ineffective in the absorption of it, and he could not stand in the path of her inevitable self-assertion, if she were pleased to look at another with her hungry eyes.

My thoughts produced a sudden rather hot fear. I knew suddenly that his complete and submissive infatuation would make him almost clairvoyant, and he had noted her manner since I had come to the inn. I supposed that there was a manner visible to a love-tortured man; certainly I hadn't seen it—I was putting two and two together now. We had scarcely spoken to each other and to me she seemed aged anyway. She was all of thirty-five, I guessed.

As I came from my bath however, I was sure that I had unraveled the story and Milford's having my things brought to the lodge was of the greatest importance to me.

I never drink Scotch, my favorite drink, raw, but I did that evening. I was still dripping when I poured the top from my vacuum bottle half full, and I watched the water from my arm drip into it.

When I was dressed and was ready in spirit to join Milford, I believed I was ready for the evening.

I'm sure he saw nothing in my face or in my manner which would indicate my thoughts that evening, either when I told him of the royal during tea or at dinner when I told him about the cow horses of the American Southwest. However, I "felt" the thoughts back of my conversation about the royal, like ordinary people crowding up to get into the focus of a newsman's camera. As I talked, I kept seeing the pallid form of poor Atherton lying there on the moor, with his hair plastered down by the rain and laying against the earth like fine rootlets. I saw this impeccable man sitting there by the fireplace with the flame dance on him, sneaking through the whin with an intense expression on his face. I even wondered how he was dressed for this primordial business. Strange how I could talk of the days stalking and the royal fleeing from my rifle, and yet have in my mind the image of a Mr. Milford crawling, disheveled through the whin with an intense animal look on his face. You see, I had taken for granted that he had done the job himself; not daring to leave it to possibly incompetent hands. The impeccable Mr. Milford just wouldn't do that.

But I kept talking of the royal, and really had no fear that the thoughts and images in the background might be indicated in my manner. At dinner I talked of cow horses and held my host completely, so that I could allow my background thoughts and images to come even closer to the surface; or better to say, come closer into focus.

After dinner, I was tired and there was a silence as we sat over our brandy by the fireplace. I was now so stupefied by Scotch, a heavy dinner and the brandy, that I was confident that my face or manner could reveal nothing.

When Mr. Milford rose and walked to the fireplace to knock the dottle from his pipe, I knew he would then mention the blackcock shooting planned for the morrow.[7] My mind became alert again. A beater, I thought, could "accidently" shoot me. But, no beater would be carrying a gun. Then I thought, but he might. Falcons were sometimes seen, and beaters might be instructed to shoot them on sight. If not that, then an erratic blackcock might fly toward me and Milford might—yet would his lameness improve sufficiently? If not, how would he arrange an "accident."

Then I realized that I was being very stupid. He'd got me away from the hungry eyes at the inn, and tomorrow would be the last day of shooting, and it would be devoted to blackcock and grouse, then he would be rid of me. I didn't consider the feeling of relief that came to me suddenly one bit ridiculous at that time.

"I daresay," said Milford as he came back from the fireplace, "you'd like to turn in. I do hope I shall be able to shoot with you tomorrow."

A thought came to me. "Look," I said, "you know I believe I've been rather stupid—I'm sure I've been, if this is the 12th." He looked at me. I knew quite well it was the 12th, and I hadn't planned to leave before the morning of the 14th, but I continued, "I've only got until the 13th and——"

He smiled one of his very charming smiles, and I was sure that I could see relief in it, "my dear fellow, unfortunately, this is the 12th."

"That's it, then," I said with histrionic disgust, "I must be off tomorrow morning."

"How disappointing for you."

"Yes—damn it."

"You can't possibly stretch it?"

"Looks impossible."

I rose and said, "I think I must turn in—goodnight."

"Goodnight—jolly good idea, I shall do the same."

I suppose it was due to the fact that I had made my intentions clear to him, and to the final certainty that he would have no cause to sneak up the stairs with a knife and do a little bloodletting during the dead of the night, that I could fall immediately into deep slumber. I was worn out by the day on the spongy moors, and the drink and the food had made thinking impossible, however much I desired to polish up the little story which I seemed to have stumbled upon. Fear, personal fear, had been only momentary, and I was relieved of that.

The next morning Mr. Milford had finished breakfast when I came down.

"I don't know about the train," I said, "it seems to me it leaves here at nine."

"I'm having the motor brought out," he said, "I've decided to take this ruddy leg into Glasgow for an opinion. Your duffel will go into the boot, and if you don't mind, you can drive."

The old boy really intended to get rid of me. Ride me out on a silver rail, so to speak. I felt that I should like to go by the inn to say goodbye and leave tips, but I noted that they had been included in the statement. I knew that it would not be the thing to ask to stop there, but I must confess that in the light of my new knowledge, I rather wanted another look at the hungry eyes of the lady of the inn.

As we approached the inn, Milford pretended that he didn't see her standing there waving us down. I looked at his face turned to the other side of the road as if he saw something very interesting there.

"There's Mrs. Atherton," I said.

He pretended to see her for the first time: "Oh, I say, she'll be wanting letters posted—yes." The letters in her hand gleamed in the mists of the morning.

As I stopped the car alongside of her, I seemed to be seeing her for the first time. My knowledge had made of her not only a definite personality but a dangerous and tragic one in the old Greek drama sense. She ought to have been wearing a Grecian mantle and sandals with a bloody dagger in her hand. These thoughts had time to come to me with their attendant images even before she spoke; even before the car had come to a complete stop.

"I'm OH'fully sorry," she said smiling, "but would you mind taking these along. There're quite important, so mind, don't let them get rained on."

As she handed the letters to Milford, I noted for the first time the womanly fullness of her figure; her square shoulders and her bosom that strained under her sweater. Her grey skirt seemed to have been the mould into which the perfectly measured liquid for her hips had been poured. My nervousness was like a narcotic since it sharpened my senses, even though it seemed to concentrate in the pit of my stomach and quiver there.

She paid no attention to me, but was in conversation with Milford so that I had a chance to study her, if I had been able to do so. I found that in the few moments I had that I couldn't reason about her at all; I could only feel the power and the fascination of some thing smouldering within her.

Then she turned her hungry eyes on me, and I choked slightly.

"I shall save a room for you for fishing, Mr. Girard. You ARE coming up during your Easter vac, of course?" I had a feeling that as she looked at me she must know all secrets of man, and she must then have seen my hesitation, because she continued: "The salmon are really tremendous in The Kidney—even big enough for an American." Her very mobile lips were pulled away from her teeth as she smiled as if they were too willful for the muscles to handle, and her eyes had a queer look which was half challenge and half surrender, and I had to avert my own and concentrate on the man driving a flock of sheep along the road.

I don't know why I said I'd be up for fishing during the Easter vacation from the University. It might have been because I felt I could escape those eyes and that power of the something suppressed within her, and which sent out impulses under its pressure that enveloped me, by saying that I would come. I wanted to fish for salmon and trout in the Scottish streams, but under the circumstances I felt that I was slapping Mr. Milford in the face with the glove of a duelist.

So great was the primordial hunger of the woman that I wanted to look back, but I dared not. I knew, however, that she would be standing, looking at the vanishing car, as a cougar might look at a bounding deer he had just missed.[8]

The mountains gave way to rolling hills, then the smoke of Glasgow smeared the sky that had been the color of soiled pearls all the way, but at least unpolluted until we neared Glasgow. And all this time Mr. Milford had not spoken. I felt that he had dropped all pretense now. His face was set and he looked straight along the road. I had often said with the smart-aleck histrionics of an undergraduate that civilization is only a veneer, easily scratched or easily rubbed off to reveal the natural wood of cave mores under the influence of primitive urges. Now I knew that truth had come out of at least one conference of the renovators of the world, held in my rooms at the University.

I was afraid of the man beside me. His face seemed bigger and his neck seemed to be too big for his collar. There was the impression of swelling through his body. For the first time, I was happy to enter Glasgow.

When we were stopped at the Turks Head Hotel, he extended his hand and said: "Goodbye. We shall be seeing you then, for fishing?"

I wanted to say as fast and as definitely as I could: "No, I don't have the least intention of coming up."

"Really? What a pity. Well, then it is goodbye." There was no change in the expression of his face, even with the smile of courtesy which he forced.

I went immediately to cancel my room reservations, then asked for the train schedule for London. It would be a long, tiresome trip in the night, but I was fleeing now; actually fleeing from fear. I had read about that too and hadn't believed it. It had been only the language of novels until now.

Allah's Guest

The sand wilderness was dazzling, stricken by the pitiless sun. Men talked little or not at all; not wishing to open their mouths to say things which all must have in their minds. Their speech-opened mouths would have let into their lungs the fire of the desert in mid-summer.

At this time of the year other Beduin tribes were camped by the wells, by the water stations, somewhere under the volcanic cap rock. But here the Annezy were strung out over the burning sands, and the people must jolt on their rocking camels, with the tails of their headdresses drawn over their mouths and noses.[1]

The odorous water was low in their water-skins. The women swayed in their creaking basket frames atop their camels, with their babes in the depressions between their crossed legs. The little boys trotted along on bare feet; some bare-headed and naked with their little water-skins flapping at their sides. The hounds, starved and lean, trotted in the shade of the baggage camels.

John Hamilton, the "Nasarene," as the people of the Annezy called him, was unhappy with fear.[2] He had lost his fear of the water he must drink, heavy and infested with visible forms. He had become accustomed to that. He was not especially afraid of the purposeful heat over the shimmering land, where images were created to dance over the sand. He had long since become accustomed to the black bandit's eyes boring into him from over the tails of the headdresses which covered the men's mouths and noses. The blinding brightness where hot puffs from the heated sands came whimsically to his face and inspired thirst that could not be assuaged by the fetid water, frightened him no more. He knew he could make it if the women could make it. For courage, he had only to look at the naked boys, grim dwarf men, marching along with the sun drawing from them all the gay juices of youth. When he looked at them he felt ashamed of his fears.

It was Haafa of whom he was afraid; the dark eyes of Haafa, the sheykha of sheykh Abeyd's harem.[3] She had been born in the tent of a sheykh, and her bold eyes proclaimed this fact to the world. It was when these bold eyes began to talk to him, that fear came to him.

Only that morning as the sheykh's harem were striking camp, and he and Abeyd were having coffee, he had heard her scolding and shaking audibly in the cold thin air of the plateau, as she helped pack the kneeling camels. But in her histrionic misery she had looked at him, and had smiled boldly, and he saw that there were the arts of Damascus on her face. Her lips were made red and her cheeks glowed, and her ear lobes were as rubies.

The Annezy believed that the faces of women should be seen, so that men might more easily read their souls. Thus did they wear no veils. John could see that Haafa had abandoned all thought of duty that morning, and thought only of his attention. He had looked quickly to see if Abeyd had also read the face of Haafa.

When John Hamilton had come to sheykh Abeyd, there had been an arrangement between King Abdullah and the Anglo-American Oil Company, that he should be the guest of the sheykh of the Annezy, since there were geological structures on this lord's domain, or dira.[4] There had been paid to sheykh Abeyd a certain amount of gold, the other half of which would be paid later when he should arrive back in Damascus safely. Thus was he a guest in the camp of Abeyd.

As he rocked along wearily on his camel, John had become acutely aware of his obligations to his host, the sheykh, and he was also aware of his host's obligations to him. Abeyd, following the old law, would know himself to be responsible for the safety of the heathen as long as he was his guest, and could never raise his proud head again, if aught of harm came to him. He would have this obligation even if there had been no gold passed.

John Hamilton knew this, but there was no refuge from this new fear, which the eyes of Haafa had brought. He had seen hate in the eyes of some of the tribesmen for the Nasarene, the unbeliever, as they came to Abeyd's coffee fire. The very narrowness of their understanding of the world was frightening. They knew the world to be totally of sand and volcanics and scattered oases, where each Beduin tribe had its dira, its range. Somewhere beyond the range of the Annezy lay, they assumed, the dira, the range of the Engleys they knew as "Hamulum," and it was the land of the heathen. If they were to cut his throat as he slept, the act would be looked upon with favor by Allah. But this Engleys, this heathen was under the protection of their sheykh. For this Nasarene, the sheykh had drawn his sword and given his word. In the understanding of the Annezy, he was Allah's guest now.

With deep appreciation of his host's obligations, John had ridden no more away from the sight of the Annezy; not even over the curvature of the sand ridges. He had learned his lesson, the day when the Shammar came riding toward them firing joy-shots.[5] When the Shammar raiders had found themselves outnumbered, they had said to Abeyd: "This Nasarene, let us kill him." And Abeyd had answered: "Allah forbids it; he is my fellow."

Later Abeyd had said, as he made marks in the sand with his camel stick, "Now Hamulum, hast thou seen? Is this that I told thee the peril of lonely riding in the country? Have thee not tasted now of their hospitality?" And like a man in any clime, Abeyd had felt his own importance in the eyes of his guest, and John Hamilton had experienced a great surge of gratitude.

But now what of his gratitude and his obligations against the bold looks of Haafa. What could he say and how could he act? Would the law of Allah protect a guest who had breached the crystalline traditions of his host's beyt?[6]

He looked back over the rahla; over the philosophical camels with their loads. He knew that Haafa would be lost somewhere in the dazzling brightness, riding with the harem among the baggage camels. Ahead was Abeyd with his men, riding silently on his mare, who of all things in the world was of the most value to him. His beard with its grey strands would hang down below his mouth covering like the tail of a skunk. He would probably be thinking of the coffee he would make as the harem put up the tents, or perhaps he might be thinking of Haafa and her youth and boldness, which was the boldness of a sheykh's daughter. Or, he might be thinking of the gold which King Abdullah held for him; the other half. John believed that it would be better if he thought much of the gold.

He knew he should be riding with the sheykh and his men, as the sheykh's guest, but they had sold him a slow camel, since such a camel was thought worthy of a Nasarene, and thus did he ride in the middle, not being able to make his camel keep up. He couldn't torment his weary camel into a faster gait.

He had some comfort when he thought of Abeyd's lack of formality. He thought back to the time when he had arrived at the semi-permanent camp, where the camels were fattening on the lush rabia and were calving.[7] He had not thought much of that first meeting with Haafa, but his mind was occupied with the thoughts of how well he managed the Arabic of the Annezy. He talked to anyone about anything just to feel the new words on his tongue. Not much else had occupied his mind. He remembered how astonished he was when Abeyd had led him into the women's apartment and presented him to Haafa. "Hamulum," he had said, "here is thy new aunt, and Haafa, this is Hamulum, see that thou take good care of him."

It was after the rabia was dry in the spring sun, and the water heavy with camel trampings, that the tribe began their wanderings. It was after the long rahlas, the rides across the sands, when the tents were being set up by the harem, on the sandstone or among the volcanic blocks, that his eyes would leave the coffee fire where he sat with Abeyd, to follow the movements of Haafa. It was as if the movements of Haafa were purposeful, not in duty, but in attracting his attention. She laughed and her white teeth shown in her olive-brown face, and her eyes would seek his, as though she would challenge him. At such times he would turn back to Abeyd's talk, as though listening intently.

And even now he could think of the black eyes of Haafa, even when he was sore and weary and blinded by the reflected light; when his throat was parched and he could not drink the fetid water in his water-skin. Even in this world of lifeless, black volcanic crust, which was the set frown of nature who had forgotten how to smile, he could think only of the eyes of this Annezy girl. The sun singled him out no more as the invading heathen as it had seemed to do on his first few rahlas, and he felt no more as if he were a gnat in all this nightmare land; an accident of matter and spirit of no importance. The dark eyes of Haafa were giving him some strange, inscrutable importance, even as they brought primitive fear.

With his uncomfortable thoughts, he prodded his camel into a trot so that he could be near Abeyd, in his traditional place as a guest. This conventional place near his host would, in some vague way, balance his tingling feeling of fear.

Soon the sun fell behind the black, twisted land, just as it had been noted by many poets who had traveled in the land of the Beduin; sliding quickly into the riven land. Soon, as on the moon, the air would grow cold in the sun's absence, and the surprised bodies of the people would begin to shiver.

Abeyd kicked his mare into the lead, and entered a crack in the lava cap, leading the tribe down from the volcanic plateau into the sand waste. The way led through large blocks of lava broken away from the mother crust, and in the twilight were like great beasts of the older world, grazing, even where there was no blade of grass or bush.

Then the stars came, and shone down upon people humped on their camels shivering. There had been some walking on the hot sands when the sun blazed upon them on the plateau, but now all rode. Here among the great lava blocks lived the horned adder.

The sheykh had the camels stopped, and soon they were kneeling to be unpacked. Ungraciously they knelt, the cows complaining and the few bulls snarling like fiends.

The people lay on the sand where they had stopped. There was no coffee fire this night; no gathering of sticks for the fire when the fallen limbs of the acacia looked much like the adder in the starlight.

Sometimes in the cold of the sun-deserted sands these serpents came to the warmth of the sleeping bodies.

John Hamilton had been taught how to sleep in the sands under the lava caps where lived the horned adder. You did not move once you had hollowed out the sand for your body. You chose immediately the side on which you would sleep, using your arm for a pillow.

But he slept little. He woke suddenly with a cramp in his leg but was afraid to move. All night, the hounds barked back at the howling of the wolves and at the maniacal laughter of the hyenas. Thus did he judge the coming of the dawn by the hoarseness and huskiness of the hounds' voices.

As the hot light came, he turned his eyes down his body without moving a limb. Carefully he surveyed his body from his arm. Seeing nothing, he rolled quickly forward and jumped to his feet, but he found that no adder had sought the warmth of his body during the chill of the night. That, he realized, would be a perfect way for Abeyd to eliminate him, and there could be little question. But, he thought with some comfort that there was still the other half of the gold held by King Abdullah, and the terms of the agreement could not be carried out if he were killed by an adder.

The smoke of the coffee fires climbed out of the sand as the hot light spread. He sat with Abeyd at his coffee fire, but there was little conversation. Abeyd was in deep thought. John was nervous. Now he thought, he will talk of what he must read in Haafa's eyes, and fear came to him again and he found himself hating the mannerisms of Abeyd, which he had scarcely noted before. He hated him as he stroked his beard as if milking the thoughts from his dark mind.

He looked about the place where they had stopped last night in the starlight, and the people were doing nothing. They seemed to be waiting for something and they looked at the spot where he and Abeyd sat. Nowhere is thought and the expression of it transferred faster than among the Annezy. They seemed to act upon instinct like flocks of birds. Rumor which is as thin as vapor creeps into every beyt, with the freedom and silence of the heat-dazed hounds, and with the assurance of the riding mares to sniff at those about the coffee fires.

Idleness is the feeding ground of rumor, and the Annezy were idle. He imagined that the scandal of Haafa's bold looks was in every mind and on every tongue. Why were the people watching for movement about the coffee fire where he and Abeyd sat?

But soon, Abeyd turned to his harem who had been waiting in the background and said, "Make the beyt," and immediately they became busy with the tents. Then the people who had been watching in idleness became busy putting up the tents of their own beyts. John had forgotten that the tribesmen watched the sheykh's harem, to note if the tents went up and they would spend the day, or travel. When they struck the tents in the mornings that meant the rahla, when the tents remained up long after sunrise, that meant that they would stop for a day, two days, or perhaps a week if there was good grazing and the water plentiful.

Fear crept back again to the dark corners of John's mind when he saw the people busy. He heard Haafa ask in that bold daughter-of-sheykh's manner of hers, which had in it a shout to John's attention, and which made him wince, which way must the tents face.

"Dress the face to this part," said Abeyd, as he waved his hand to the north.

This meant that they would be here for several days. This meant that the hellish sun would not shine into the space where was built the coffee fire, and visitors with the usual freedom of the nomad could come to the coffee and talk throughout the day without discomfort. If Abeyd had directed that the tents should face to the south, this would mean that he wanted no visitors; that the sun would persecute those who did come during the hours of the sun's rule, and they would not stay long and Abeyd could thereby save precious coffee, and he could sleep out the hours in the apartment of the women.

John was glad that there would be no rahla this day, and now he waited a chance to talk with Abeyd, or awaited nervously for Abeyd to talk. He was nervous and John knew that he would talk of intimate matters. He must have seen what lay in the eyes of Haafa. As John waited he felt the tingling at the very ends of his fingers.

"Hast thou not a harem to weep for thee in thy land?" asked Abeyd. "We will give thee a maiden to wed, and dwell among us."

John answered nervously: "What would she do in my country? Can she forget her language and her people in this wilderness?"

Abeyd was proud and very jealous of his station as sheykh when he felt that such an attitude might be profitable, or where there was neither profit nor loss. Where there was definite profit, he hinted that the Annezy had been ill-colored by Allah and their bodies wracked by disease and weakness and hunger, and their minds as the minds of children.

"Here is but famine and thirst and nakedness," he said, "and thine is a good life, I have heard many times. A wife would follow thee and serve thee by the way—this were better for thee. The lonely man without his woman is low in mind and looks much toward the harem curtain of his brethren. The woman would learn thy tongue as thou hast learned Araby."

John had to think quickly and find the Arabic grooves for his thoughts before he turned them into words: "Some say," he answered, "and I have heard them around the coffee fires that it would be malice in a Nasarene to take a daughter of Araby—a malice to Christians, since the religion of Islam should grow thereby."

Abeyd turned to him and smiled: "Dost thou listen to the words of bandits or to the words of your host who is a sheykh, Oh Hamulum. It were meritorious to give thee a wife to this end: that true worshipers might rise among us, of him who knew not Allah. Wed thou and leave us a white daughter that she may wed some great sheykh."

John saw the point now. The old fox would marry him off, and keep his honor as a host in the eyes of Allah. He would not be compelled to send Allah's guest away to be lost in the sand ridges that looked exactly like each other to the end of the world. There would be no need of secret poisoning or an "accident," or an adder in his bed. He had to think fast again. Abeyd was certainly giving him a chance to live, and himself a chance at the other half of the gold.

There was a silence and Abeyd, believing that John was considering his offer seriously, spoke again and thereby giving John the escape his thoughts sought.

"Wellah, Hamulum, I and thou art brethren. In proof of this, I ask thee, hast thou a mind to be wedded among us? See, I have four wives, and billah, I'll give thee one of them; give thee to choose among three. Say which of these thee choose, and I will leave her and she shall become thy wife. Haafa I shall keep, the next in beauty and youth is Salema, which means peace, great-eyed and a holder of her tongue. Billah, they who look at Salema from the coffee fire, are not less than they who look at Haafa."[8]

John had his escape now: "Would they needs marry me, then be it not with other men's wives, which is contrary to our belief, but give that pretty one, Atheba, that child of your sister who comes daily here to play with other infants near our beyt."

Abeyd's face lightened with great pleasure: "Hearest thou, Oh Haafa? Women? Hamulum prefers a child before thee all."

There had been no movement behind the harem curtain for some time; now came movements of impatience, and then the voice of the bold, assured Haafa.

"Well, be it so, and I make no account of Hamulum's opinions."

Abeyd laughed. His humor was running high and warm now. He called for dates and the milk of the camel.

Through the noise of his eating, he said: "Ho, Hamulum, thy camel has little mind for travel. Her knees respond not well to thy mind. I will fetch a young one for thee; she that swims over the sand."

But John knew that there must be a greater price for the swift she-camel than simply Abeyd's peace of mind. With this fast camel, he could make el Wejh with small escort, and Abeyd would have some excuse to send him away.[9] Abeyd might tell him he would be going on a ghrazzu, a raid on another tribe or on the caravans from Damascus, and therefore the guest must not invite death. John knew now he must ask to be sent to el Wejh. No one, no talk, no pretext could control the eyes of Haafa, that was plain. Should he ask Abeyd now? He could say that he must look for signs of the oil mystery elsewhere; in some other dira, some other sheykh's range.

But Haafa was listening. She would fit her wild, bold strategy to the new circumstances. Then the whole matter would stand before their eyes, and man's pretexts would be as the fog over the irrigation ditches of Hayil, making the facts bolder to the eye, as figures in a thin morning fog.[10]

Abeyd spoke again: "Ho, Hamulum, I have often seen thee reading in thy books. Canst thou discern there the mind and intents of man?"

"No," answered John, "I find there only the things that men have found and tasted and smelled and taken apart; men's thoughts sewed together, nothing more."

"But mayst thou not see in thy books where are the enemy, and how many, and what is in their minds, or whether one absent be in life or dead?"

"No, only things are here that run through men's minds; where thee findest the water stations and the wells, and where the rabia grows, and when and where the rain falleth in good measure, so that thee mayst take thy camels there for the calving, and the people for well-being. They tell of what other men know of the face of the earth and where may be found the oil mystery. Here things are set down, and are there even when men sleep; even when men die; unlike the mind of man in this wise."

"But surely," insisted Abeyd, "thou seest thy own household, so far away and how they fare?"

"No, there is no revelation there. There are only man's words to himself."

There was silence. Abeyd spoke again, and there was an interest in his voice, as if that which he now asked were the very core of his thoughts.

"Then, mayst thee not see from thy books into a woman's heart, and mayst thee not turn that heart to her husband. Couldst thee not make signs with thy reed upon a leaf and sell to him who needeth its magic? Would such magic equal the value of a she camel?"

"There is no magic," said John again, "it is only man's talk to himself; the talk of many men sewed together, which is there when man sleeps and which remains after men die, as in the "writing stones," in that valley where thou hast knelt thy camels many times."

"Eigh, be it so."

As he said this, Abeyd rose and walked toward the tent of the mejlis, the tribal council. Here the tribesmen talked of many things: the direction of the rahla on the morrow, where rain had fallen to leave water in the rock depressions, or whether their enemies had been seen lurking, or they discuss what might be in their enemies' minds.

As John watched Abeyd walk through the sand, he noted that he carried his sword. This meant that he would not return from the mejlis, the council, until after darkness had fallen. If he had intended to come back during the daylight hours he would have carried only his gaily-colored camel stick. No one went abroad at night without his sword.

When Abeyd was gone, John heard the jangle of ornaments from behind the harem curtain, and fear came back to him like an electric shock. He knew he must get away from Abeyd's beyt. He should have spoken to Abeyd about leaving despite the ears of the harem. Probably he ought to overtake Abeyd and tell him of his intentions; tell him that he must go to el Wejh, and ask for escort there.

But he was too late. Haafa had seen Abeyd leave, and she too had noted that he was wearing his sword. She came out from behind the harem barrier as though she would perform routine wifely duties. But she wore the golden circlet of her ancestors about her gazelle-like ankle. Her lips were as red as sand berries, and bracelets jangled on her arms, and vitreous beads glistened on her neck. The red tassels of her bodice danced with the lazy movements of her breasts, and lacked much of touching the waist of her pantaloons from Damascus, leaving her olive-brown middle bare.

The sidewalls were tucked up for the free passage of air, furnace-hot though it was. Thus anyone who wished could see into that part of the beyt not curtained off for the harem.

Haafa picked up a goat-skin of sour milk, sat cross-legged opposite John and began to shake the skin with the movements of her legs; from side to side and up and down on her knees. Thus would she be seen in housewifely duty, and people might think naught of her raiment.

"I have sent the others away," she said. She was obviously nervous now, and had lost her boldness. "One called Salema has gone to cut food for the mare, and another, Gorma, she who has borne our lord a son, to the rocks that are like grazing sheep on the hillside, for herbs."

"There are many horned adders there," said John. "This I have heard."

"That is true," said Haafa, "the sun has stricken her eyes, and she does not see well."

A coldness ran through John's blood, and his throat seemed to close against words he might have spoken. But he couldn't keep his eyes from Haafa. He knew he must leave but he couldn't. He watched the rise and fall of her bare middle as she breathed, but she kept her eyes modestly downcast at the rocking goat-skin.

"Oh Hamulum," she said suddenly, "I have heard that thee hast none to weep for thee if thou are wounded. If I come to thee, wouldst thou receive me?"

He choked, then he spoke, and his voice was strange in his own ears.

"There is much to think about."

She laughed. "He hath a beard with the white of years in it. When he rises from the sand the years pull him back again, and he needs must bow to the camel dung before he can stand erect like a man. Even after a long rahla when there is nothing in it, his belly is like the watermelon from the oases of Hayil. Allah has taken from him his juices; he can get no son. He can get no daughter even. In his arms there is no forgetfulness, and he breathes a foulness that makes the hyena laugh with hope. Wouldst thee think him "much," Oh Hamulum?"

She laughed. It was a throaty laugh, like a laugh that comes from a scolding throat, but John deemed it beautiful, because she and her laughter were beautiful in the wilderness of sand and sterile lava rock.

She looked at him now: "Oh Hamulum, is it that a woman of Araby tells a man of many books that which he knows not? I can be held and I can be put away. Knowst thou that I have borne no son to one from whom Allah has taken the son-power. When I am old, he can say, 'here, camel driver, is thy woman.' The camel driver will show a great hole where there are no teeth, and cast his eyes over me as one at the market for camels. I was an orphan and many camels were left to me by my father, sheykh Zeyd. When the cow camels had calved fifteen times, I had lived only that long. He married my camels, seest thou, Oh Hamulum?"

"Hearest thee not what I said at the coffee fire?" asked John.

"Didst thou not hear what I said?" she replied. "Didst thou not hear me say that I made no account of Hamulum's opinions? Seest thou ever, Oh Hamulum, a believer put forth his hand in greeting, as one puts forth words, holding the other hand behind his back as one with words unspoken? Dost thee find in thy writings that women of Araby are free only in the wilderness? Dost thy books tell that they mayst leave their lord's beyt and there will be none to look for their prints in the sand? Thinkest thou a sheykh will ride after a fleeing woman? Canst thou see in thy writings that which lies in a woman's heart? If so, thou knowest much."

The sun had begun sliding into the sand waste, and the shadows of the tents and the volcanic blocks were like fingers on the sand. Life stirred. A hound left the shade and trotted off on some personal business. There was the sound of women chattering, growing. Haafa rose quickly and clanked into the women's apartment.

John had no fear of adders that night, as he had when sleeping on the naked sand, but he heard the wolves, and the hounds challenge them all night. He heard every movement and every surly groan of the camels by the beyt to which the camel-boys had driven them at nightfall. He heard every movement of Abeyd's mare as she wandered about restlessly, stirred by the cold of the sun-deserted world. His fear was more real than it had ever been before. It tingled in his stomach, and made him whisper to himself in the darkness about what he must do on the morrow. Tomorrow he would talk with Abeyd about going to el Wejh, and all his fear would be over. This thought stopped his wild images.

The morning was the same as the others. The sun splashed the land with blinding fire, and life became a murmur in the beyts of the Annezy. John decided to ask Abeyd to give him an escort to el Wejh the first thing that morning, but Abeyd was gone quickly from the coffee fire, and none knew where he had gone. John sat in Abeyd's beyt and waited. There were only stirrings from behind the harem barrier but no heads popped above the breast-high curtain.

Then came some tribesmen who were relatives of Abeyd. They arranged themselves about the dead coffee fire, and one called to one of the women to bring coffee, then he said: "Well met, Hamulum, where is thy uncle Abeyd today. Does he lie in his mood slumbering under the acacia?"

One said, smiling, "But tell us? Know you Haafa was beat? What news then, Hamulum? Do you love your uncle?"

One who had been once exiled by Abeyd said: "Abeyd is not a man. It is a woman that will strike a woman. Do your people do so, Hamulum?"

"No, surely, unless it be some outrageous wretch," stammered John. He felt sick at his stomach.

"It is thus among us Beduin, a shame, wellah," said the one who had been exiled, as he stirred his coffee with his finger and drank.

The dirty womanish gossips, thought John; the devilish mischief makers.

When the relatives had left, a man came whom he had never seen before. He gave greeting and then sat down beside John with evident weariness. His face was drawn and he seemed very tired. He turned to John: "Has your uncle Abeyd come?"

"I know not where he has hidden himself," said John.

Just then the light was shut off from the entrance of the tent, and John was startled to see Abeyd standing there. His heart came into his throat, but when he saw the sheykh's face, he saw misery there and no menace, and he regained his composure. But Abeyd greeted him not. He had greeting only for his visitor, his relative, and as he greeted him, he asked a question with his eyes, and the relative answered.

"She is fleet, that filly. I followed her print in the sand for a league. Then I saw her, but she ran like an ostrich, and with this Shammar's bullet in my leg, I was no match for the gazelle."

Abeyd seated himself heavily. The relative rose and left the unhappy atmosphere of the beyt. John knew he would now speak to Abeyd about the escort to el Wejh, but before he could speak, Abeyd turned to him and said:

"Seest thou how it goes with one in this famished land of the devil? Is there no magic in your books to aid one who is naught to his wife?"

John was relieved. Abeyd seemed defeated and humble. He said: "No, there is no magic; there are only words of men. The bones of wolves who once spoke to the beyts from the darkness. One fingers the bones and sees in his mind the wolf again in all his manners."

He was about to speak about the escort, when a messenger came for him, and as John rose, he looked at Abeyd for understanding.

"Go," said Abeyd, "the mejlis honors thee."

John followed the messenger to the mejlis. The sheykh's relatives were there in council, but there were smiles behind the solemnity.

"Eigh," they said. "Here comes Hamulum. Welcome, Oh Hamulum. Make place for Hamulum. Is your uncle lying in the sun in melancholy? Can the sun touch brains that are not there? Can the sun dim eyes that are dim?"

The laughter was general, and cold sweat came to John's forehead.

An old man looked at him and saw his fear, and he said softly: "It is this way with the Beduin, Oh Hamulum. It is your honorable office to go for Haafa."

John's fear became deeper. So this was it. This was the trick; they would take him with Haafa. But as he looked about him, he saw only half-hidden humor and no menace. Anyway, there was nothing he could do but accept the office of tradition. He would have to think later.

Abeyd lent him his mare, and seemed pleased that his guest would ride after Haafa.

John rode out into the blinding sun. He saw at once that the wind had not come to sweep away the tracks of Haafa in the sand. He could see them far ahead, as the sun darkened them with shadow. All knew where Haafa had fled. There was a small encampment of her relatives some two leagues away, and in that direction the dark spots on the sand led.[11]

There were women in the tent to comfort Haafa and she sat among them with another's baby in her lap, laughing with him merrily. She was not surprised when she saw John standing tall and brick-red in the entrance.

She smiled up at him roguishly: "I will not hear thy words, Hamulum, unless they are other than those thy bearest from Abeyd."

John was embarrassed. He knew that the smiles of the women, who were making little attempts to hide them with their hands, were from amusement over his awkwardness.

An old aunt said: "She is ours now, Hamulum, and we will not let her go. Abeyd cannot claim her."

He held out his hands in a gesture of futility. "What am I to do?" he asked. "I have my honor."

"That is well spoken, Hamulum," said the old aunt, "and you have your life. Which will you choose? Will the hyena stop at your body by the acacia, saying, 'Here is honor. We shall circle and walk softly past in the presence of honor.' Did you ever hear of how fared honor in the belly of the hyena?" Here she changed to the familiar. "Didst they tell thee, Oh Hamulum, in Damascus of one who ever found honor in the belly of a hyena when they let in the sunlight with a knife?"

A young cousin came into the tent and said to no one in particular: "I am her father and her mother, and I will not give her more to Abeyd."

The sweat became cold under John's clothes. He looked down at Haafa and her eyes were soft and full and starry, and then he noted that softness had come to all the faces in the tent.

The young relatives spoke again: "We will untie the mare, and she will find her way to Abeyd, since she knows little of good men. The camels are ready and there are baggage camels and a camel driver, and I shall be head of the guards, and there will be only the people of Haafa."

John looked at Haafa and his voice trembled a little. Then again, he held out his hands: "I have nothing," he said, "all I have is with Abeyd."

"Send us camels when you come to your dira," said the young relative. "Abeyd will open your saddlebags, and he will look out and see the thirty-five camels brought in by the camel-boys at sunset. His sorrow over Haafa's flight will be shallow, but his happiness will be deep when Allah sees that you have not been killed, Oh Hamulum, and Abeyd can look into men's eyes. The circle about his coffee fires will be great. 'Look,' he will say, 'the saddlebags of the heathen filled with the magic for a wife, and look, her thirty-five camels are still with me.'"

As they rocked along together side by side, John looked over at Haafa.

"What thinkest thou now?"

"I think of our son, Oh Hamulum. He will be tall, and the sky will be in his eyes, as in the eyes of my husband. He will be neither dark nor pale. When he is a man, he will not color his beard with saffron like the merchants of Hayil. Allah will make it yellow like thine. And because of him, my son, thee will not put me away when I am an old woman." She thought a moment. "The Nasarenes do not put their women away, eigh?"

Yellow Hair

The Hotel Valles gleamed white against the dark green jungle, and the red-tiled roof was not now startling in the soft light of after sunset. It was a beacon light on the island of Sanitation in the savage sea of the jungle, and there the touring schoolteachers would find cokes, ice-water and English.

Helga drove into the valley where the Indian village had slept so long, but which had been transformed into a comfortable stopping place for travelers driving to Mexico City, with nervous care. As she let the car roll into the jungle village with its gleaming white tourist hotels, she feared the least infraction of the traffic laws, since she believed that they were interpreted whimsically. Stopped before the romantic front of the Hotel Valles, she felt relief in the thought that the first stage of the journey had been reached without incident.

Sally and Beth had a big room together, and Helga and Irma had singles. When shown to their darkened rooms with the cool tiles, they each in her own way felt that she was a part of a cinema wherein there were pith helmets, slinky half-castes, whiskey, white planters and sin. The banana leaves scraped pettishly outside their windows, when the barefooted Indian boy threw them open. The sterile odor of insecticide filled Helga with confidence, and she didn't hesitate to walk barefooted over the tiles to the tiled shower. They even gave her a sensuous feeling like sun-bathing, or lying in a tub of hot water.

The girls were highly pleased that they had guessed right about their dresses, when they saw the girl who had come with her parents in a long, shiny car, chauffeur-driven, enter the dining room. She was undoubtedly wearing jersey—a sort of lime-colored jersey. Helga and

Beth were wearing jersey; Helga's was blue to harmonize with her hair and make more noticeable her blue eyes. Beth's was Burgundy, suitable to her dark hair. The other brunettes wore cotton, and just as Helga had warned before they left, their frocks had wrinkled despite the care they had taken in packing them.

They thought it exciting to be sitting in the large oval dining room, built in imitation of an Indian jacal, opened and screened all around and thatched with palm.[1] It was an adjunct to the white, red-roofed hotel. You came into it suddenly when you might have supposed you were leaving the hotel by the back door; you opened a double door at the end of a long passage way, and debouched into this spacious oval with jungle all around it.

The usual Swiss was at the cash register, looking with approval at its American efficiency over his glasses, in a manner that suggested that he and it were alone in their efficiency in this enervating jungle. He watched the mestizo waiters with mistrust when they came up with the paid bills, his thick fingers counting the change piece by piece.

"What about a bottle of wine?" asked Beth.

The smoke from their cigarets made strings that expanded at the top, then became erratic as they floated into invisibility. They looked over the wine card, straining a little their assumed savoir faire. The waiter suggested Sauterne, since Americans, he knew, quite often called for it.

"Guess that'll be alright—what d'yu say girls?" said Helga glad to be free of the obligation of choosing.

They watched the unaccustomed waiter intently as he poured it. His courtesy and willingness to please them made them overflow with kindliness, and they smiled their sweetest smiles at him.

"Isn't he nice," said Irma.

The girl who had come in the long shiny car driven by an efficient American chauffeur sat with her parents at a table near them. The man, the woman and the girl had little to say to each other, as though they might have been quarreling. They had the manner of being the only people in the dining room. There was an atmosphere about the girl which made Helga think of *Town & Country*, and this gave her warm pleasure, since it made her feel that she was part of the world that traveled and played and was bored, sitting here in the blue jersey which had not wrinkled in the suitcase.[2]

Outside the jungle night was like a black leopard, waiting, crouched, but more nonchalant than intent. The prey was not important, since it had swallowed the Mayan civilization in its own good time, and this gash called Valles on the International Highway was nothing.

The moon was inlaid with palm and ebony as it rose out of the blackness, and added to the mysterious savagery, but exposed no tangible evil, and inspired no precipitate movement; no bird or beast of the teeming blackness spoke to it, and the diners in the room that had been made to look like an Indian jacal were unaware of it.

After her second glass, Irma said: "so this is May-hee-co." Helga was afraid that the girl out of *Town & Country* might hear her so she began to talk of Mexican art. "They say," she said earnestly, leaning her elbows on the table, "that Orozco is ever bit as good as Rivera, but you know—you hear more about Rivera in the United States."[3]

As Helga talked, Beth was facing the little bar where the stubby-fingered Swiss counted the money and looked over his glasses at the cash register. She watched the histrionics of two young men.

One was very handsome with black, shiny hair which had been oiled with care. He wore a white coat with black trousers and a black, bow tie. Beth remembered having seen such a combination in a Scotch whiskey advertisement, depicting a scene in India. The young man had got his idea from the American films. Beth was fascinated by him, although she knew that he was conscious of each of his movements, of each word spoken by himself; of the stage laugh, and of the manner in which he sipped his brandy. All this as he pretended to be insuppressibly gay and deeply amused by his companion's conversation. He kept flashing his black eyes at the girl who had driven up in the long, shiny car with the efficient chauffeur.

When the girl and her parents were leaving the dining room, the young man watched her straight back avidly. When she had disappeared behind the door, he turned his burning eyes toward the table occupied by the schoolteachers. Beth lowered her eyes just in time. He was momentarily attracted by Helga's yellow hair, with the interest all Italians and Mexicans manifest in blondness. Her back was to him, and his interest was fleeting; not urging him to speculate about her face.

He became colorless and blank now, as one who might immediately take off his shoes and unbutton his collar, after an important visitor has left. His companion attempted to maintain the conversation at the former level, but he was absent-minded and disinterested.

He started away from the bar listlessly, then turned grandly to his companion and said, "you pay for it." His companion looked at him with contempt, then turned to the Swiss who expectantly awaited the money: "Big man, eh—look, he calls loudly for brandy in a grand voice, now he says in a little voice, 'you pay for it,' eh? No, he pays for his grand manners, verdad?"

The handsome young man threw fifty centavos onto the bar, sneering a little, then left the room. His companion gulped the rest of his beer quickly and followed him.

They were standing at the desk when the four girls walked by on their way to the front court, and Beth noticed that they both stared at Helga's yellow hair, and scarcely noticed the others.

The moon had just begun to give on the court, and the troubadours in white camisas, trousers and cracked sandals were already gathered and were sitting on the edge of the silent fountain. There were only two other guests besides the four girls and the girl from *Town & Country* and her parents. The father's cigar glowed from the darkness of the colonnade, and the odor of it was like incense in the hot night.

The girls strolled out past the fountain and then to some benches where the light of the moon was let through by some tall palms and splashed on them. They sat and waited for they knew not what. As an expression of their freedom from the eyes of their community, they lit cigarets from the glowing butts of their after-dinner ones.

The handsome man came onto the porch and looked in the direction of the glowing cigar for some time, then his movements indicated a decision. Followed by his companion, he came to where the girls were sitting.

"Pardon me," he said in English, "can I make a request for you," and he pointed to the three men sitting with guitar and violin on the edge of the dry fountain.

"What about Rancho Grande," said Beth.[4]

The three Indians came forward and stood in front of the girls. They smiled deferentially. They put feeling into the song; the song the Americans always called for. The tenor held on after the others had stopped, clinging on in a high, wild falsetto; a quavering lament. The girls said "ah" almost in unison, when the lament trailed off and then died.

By the end of an hour of banter and playful conversation, Beth and Irma saw that they were in the way. Miguel, the handsome one, was sitting bent over with his face close to Helga's, and Alfredo, the other one, was apparently overwhelmed by Sally's luscious roundness. Beth had known that this would come. Men always looked hungrily at Sally. She had an animal ripeness that attracted men; an invitation that was accompanied by a carelessness that would seem to neglect all defences. Her eyes provoked interest when she didn't realize that she was challenging, and she laughed at everything, missing all fine points and subtle suggestion. She seemed to laugh as a deaf man assumes understanding by nodding his misunderstanding, but this same laughter nullified her smoldering carelessness, since it washed away all possible understanding, and ardent men became thwarted and mystified.

Beth didn't want to leave the jungle moon, and she felt a bitterness against Sally laughing brainlessly into the night, while Alfredo looked at her moon-softened shoulders, laughing absently. She felt that she would like to tell someone, anyone, how Sally kicked off her things and left them on the floor, and how she wore her underclothing too long. She had roomed with Sally three years in the little town where they taught, and she knew.

Soon the colonnade was deserted, and Sally's laughter from the bench grew less frequent and more difficult to inspire. After everyone had left, Alfredo had sung to her in a very bad voice, but the moon was too powerful and emotion under its influence was too insistent to be properly expressed by soft talk alone.

She had allowed him to kiss her, but when she laughed in the middle of a long embrace, Alfredo was defeated, and thereafter spent much time staring at the incipient swell at the square-cut neck of her cotton frock, in the splashes of moonlight.

Her feet began to hurt in the unaccustomed temperature, and she put her hand to her mouth when she felt it convulsively opening. There was a period of complete silence and her mind became a blank, and her emotions remained at ebb. She said, "guess I'll say goodnight—what do you say; buenas noches?"

Later Helga and Miguel came in from the shadows to the deserted colonnade. They stopped at the top of the steps that led from the fountain court.

"Number ten," he whispered passionately, "I know, I saw it on the books at the desk."

"No," she said, "no."

"Why should we be ashamed of laav," he said softly, "eet is laav."

He spoke English very well but used "laav" and "eet," because he believed he sounded like the French cinema hero, Boyer.[5] He had had much experience since the International Highway had been opened.[6] He knew when to be a poor, struggling Indian genius, a gay, lovable mestizo, yearning for higher education, or a drifting Don of good family destroyed by the revolution. The first role was for the rich American widows and romantic matrons; the second for American business men and archaeologists whom he sometimes guided.

Several times as they walked in the moon shadows, before he had hypnotized himself into the role of tropical lover, he had spoken of "my people," implying a proud family clinging to a decaying mansion in Mexico City. Actually he had been born in the shadow of one of Doheny's old oil derricks in Los Angeles in a shack faced with tin from grease containers and cast-off automobile licences.[7] On Saturday evenings, his youth had been spent in searching for his stone-cutter father among the cantinas in the Mexican quarter. When the International Highway opened, he found himself qualified as a driver in the White Cap organization.[8]

Helga would not allow him to come as far as her door. Something terrific had come to her, and she wanted time in which to think clearly about it. She impulsively tightened her arms about his neck when she was sure of her decision, as though instead of saying goodnight, she would hold him forever, and after her decision she relaxed her body and let it press close against his. The songs he had sung in the overpowering falsetto in the creative moonlight, ran on in the rhythm of her heart beats.

She whispered, "I MUST go." She gave him a last, long look as though she would devour him with her blue eyes that glistened. She mistook the natural mobility of his face now, and earlier, when he had been singing, for suffering.

When he realized that her decision was definite, he began to plead again: "Later, the window—from the court; it is easy. Number ten, I know—please."

"No," she said softly.

"Then I will come anyway; I'll find a way." His voice was dramatic and dramatically he turned away and was lost in the shadows. She stood and looked at the inky moon shadows where he had disappeared, for some time, then entered the hotel.

She went to her room and lay on the bed. It was cooler now since the jungle was breathing into the night. She didn't turn on the inadequate little fan, but lay there where she had flopped and tried to think, but there was only a falsetto throbbing in her brain, and two beautiful black eyes with the savagery of the jungle crouching behind them.

Finally she got up and took a shower mechanically, then stepped out from the powder mist of the shower room and put on her prettiest night gown with lace on the neck and with puffed, short sleeves laced with a blue ribbon. She put "One Night in Paris" behind her ears, and then touched her scented fingers to the hollow in her throat.[9] She stood in the shaft of light from the window and let down her glorious yellow hair. He had said that he wanted to drown—he had actually said "drownd"—himself in it when it was flooded with moonlight. A lump came into her throat, and she moved quickly to her bed believing that she might thus escape it.

She lay on the bed. The silence was heavy. A mosquito buzzed, and it seemed to her that it was more like a petulant whine than the familiar buzz of those at home. Far off she heard a strange howl which was very much like a growl that came out of the otherwise silent jungle. She wondered why she was so passive, and had a tendency to allow her thoughts to be completely absorbed by the buzz of a mosquito and the faraway jungle sound, when she had such important things to think about.

She sat up hazily thinking that in this position she could think more clearly, but she noted the moonlight on her hair. She looked at it intently, then lay back on the pillow so that the full width of the shaft could play on it, as she arranged it to flow over the other pillow, and she began to play with its silkiness. She became suffused with glory and with a sense of intoxicating power. Her full-blooded and generous body whose proportions she had to artificially restrain, and her thickish ankles had made bitter all her secret dreams and had been the primary reasons for her refuge in sublimation; the reasons for her affectation of low-heeled shoes and her assumption of bright efficiency—the stand-aside-and-give-him-air efficiency of a field nurse. But tonight the glory was undimmed for the first time since puberty, even though it was strangely confused with fear that thrilled her.

She put her face into her hair and the tears came. They had been on the edge of emergence for the last hour, but she had managed them. Now they came and fell into her hair and wet the pillow. For some time she lay thus, then she got up without knowing what she was doing, and walked to the window that gave on the court. The leaves were unstirring in the moonlight that made them metallic.

The window was open but the mosquito screen panels were fastened by elbow gadgets which allowed them to be swung out. She read carefully from them the word "Pittsburgh." She unfastened them and the two sections of the screen swung outward. She could hear her heart beat as she did this, then she began to shake a little, and went back to the bed. She shook ridiculously for a short time, and she could hear the springs shake with her shaking.

She stopped trying to think and allowed her mind to remain blank, except for its concentration on the whine of the lone mosquito. In the absence of thought, a transition to unconsciousness was easy.

Much later she awakened suddenly, and before her mind could become clear, she began to shake again. She heard a scratching on the screen, and she suddenly realized that previous scratchings had awakened her. She lay back from a sitting position to listen. She continued to shake slightly, and the springs responded. The scratch came again, and it seemed to be secretive and full of purpose like the hunting of a jungle prowler. She waited; perhaps three minutes passed, then it came again, secretive and purposeful.

After another long wait, she became suddenly calm, and walked to the window like one going to meet the inevitable, but without thinking. The screens were as she left them when she unhooked them, and she looked out on the first grey of dawn. The air was still the panting breath of a jaguar, but there was a whimsical pre-dawn breeze. In it, a banana leaf, like the sound-sifting ear of a wild elephant, moved gently, and scratched ever so gently, the half opened screen as she watched.

Only a Blonde

The twilight dropped over the Mexican village of Coyotl, as if falling from an impatient hand.[1] Better to shut out quickly the day of life-subduing sun and bring on the sharpness of the semi-desert night of the mountain valley. The dogs that had slept all day were beginning to bark desultorily and their mouthings floated up the foothill to Shelly Peters as she stood on the parapet of the little church that clung to the side of the mountain. She could hear a bell too; a mellow-toned voice that was like a habit; more like a tradition than a reverent call of the present. The bell had lost its reason for being but stayed to ring long after the spirit which had conceived it had faded with the centuries. It had fallen from the old belltower with the stones and rubble that fell during the earthquake of 1907, and since that time had been ringing from a weathered scaffold serving for a tower.[2]

That afternoon when she had visited the church in the valley below her, she had seen the Indian women with their rebozos over their heads kneeling in the dim light of the partially restored church. There she saw flowers, a papaya, and two glowing oranges at the feet of a rather sad-faced Virgin, and this unquestioning faith had brought hardness into her own face, so intense was her vindictiveness.

But now as she stood on the parapet of another church high above the valley, she was under the spell of the fading day, so wild and tran-quil and burdened with something sinister, she felt, but there was nothing romantic about it for her. The women kneeling in the half-ruined church in the valley in what she would call their abasement was the thing that generated the sinister atmosphere, she was coldly certain, and her feeling of vindictiveness left no room for the warmth of romance. She had left the church in the valley that afternoon suddenly, when she saw a woman fall on her knees on the cold, stone floor, and stretch out her arms in the form of the cross as she faced the statue of the Virgin and mumbled her prayers. She had left the dim-lighted coolness of the church to blink in the strong sunlight. A feeling of disgust arose in her even now as she stood above the village, and she scarcely heard the soft-toned pleading of the bell and the barking of the dogs that floated up to her.

The sacristan of the little church clinging to the side of the mountain had seen something hard in her face and had left her to muse alone. He had noted the hardness when he had shown her the retablos; the crude pictures which the beneficiaries of prayers and masses had caused to be painted in order to express to the various saints their gratitude for cures and protection. Furthermore she had not given him even a centavo for his trouble.

Yellow kerosene lights began to show here and there in the village below and she began her descent. The hotel seemed much farther away than she had thought, and she was glad to see the dark form of the valley church with its weathered scaffolding for reparations begun in 1913. The silent forms of women with their rebozo-covered heads padding along toward the church on their bare feet inspired her bitter vindictiveness to express itself with some quotation which would fit perfectly her feeling at the moment. But there were no neat quotations to be recalled from Marx or Weblen, or from the cynical truths of Professor Gottchalk's lectures at Harvard.[3] She was always remembering "the inevitability of gradualness" of the Fabians.[4] This phrase seemed to cling to one like Milton or Brooke or Shakespeare, but it annoyed her when it always presented itself as she was searching for the thoughts of others to express her intense religious hatred of Capitalism.[5] The Fabians were milk-toasty, she felt.

Just as she saw the dim outline of the little plaza, she became aware of a tingling in the back of her neck, as if something might be following her. The tingling fear went all over her body, and she increased her stride; her composition-soled, low-heeled shoes making no sound and her grey flannel skirt was ample for her efficient movements.

Suddenly she felt ashamed of herself, stopped and swung about, searching the darker shadows of twilight. She saw no movement. She felt like a hunter boring into the jungle undergrowth for the outlines of a wounded leopard, and like the hunter her instincts were sure.

She turned and strode on. No matter how annoyed she might be with herself she concentrated all thoughts and her eyes as well on the little plaza, and felt a relief when she saw the yellow light above the door of the Martínez Hotel.

She had just changed into a frock with a low circular neck which had a black ribbon threaded through it, and had touched up her lips when the patron called to her to say that the police wished to speak with the señorita americana. Instinctively she opened her compact again, and with her little finger erased specks of lipstick from the corners of her mouth.

There were two young men standing under the feeble light outside the hotel entrance. One wore the uniform of the police, and the other was dressed in a business suit. She smiled and bid them good evening as one comrade might greet another, but neither answered. As she came up to them, one pointed to the station wagon and said in Spanish, "señorita, is that your car?" He called it "camioneta"—little truck.

She said, "yes sirs, the little truck is mine." There was a smirk on the face of the one not in uniform as he demanded: "We must have your papers, please."

"Why?"

"You are standing your little truck contrary to regulations."

Since arriving that morning, she had not seen another motorcar. There had been only strings of burros laden and unladen, coming into and leaving the market in the plaza. One had been driven in from the mountains with a sick Indian strapped to his back. She had remembered this incident especially, and had at that time realized that there were no cars in the village. There had been no traffic except the burros and the Indians with burdens on their backs. She smiled sweetly, "Oh surely, you make a joke, sirs——," but before she could finish, the dim light showed her a hard cynicism on the face of the young man in the business suit which was close to contempt: "The señorita will give us her papers" and he smiled contemptuously.

Radcliffe girls, even the self-sufficient, emancipated ones, never deem it out of character to smile at big Cambridge traffic officers, when they run traffic lights, so she smiled again and arched her left eyebrow. This looked like trouble. She knew what it could mean to leave her papers in the hands of the police of a little village far out in the wild mountains of the Mexican State of Guerrero.

The young man in the business suit looked at her sternly now, the cynical smile gone but the contempt remaining: "This gentleman, the traffic officer," and he nodded to the man in uniform, "holds little patience, señorita—we will have your papers, please."

She was frightened now, and her thoughts darted, attempting to find an exit, but found none. She had the papers in her purse, but she said, "why surely, they are in my room—with your permission." She turned and entered the hotel. She went to the office of the patron but he was not there. She saw the crooked old porter who had moved her so unpleasantly by his obsequiousness earlier in the day.

"Where is the patron?" she asked hurriedly.

"He is departed, señorita."

"Where?"

"He is at his house, señorita."

"Where is his house?"

"Perhaps he is not at his house, señorita—who knows?"

She looked about the little inner court that was pink-tinted like so many things in Mexico. She thanked the old man and he bowed. She went to the dining room which was a roofed end of the little court. There was no one there. She even peeped over the partition into the kitchen, but heard only the bubbling in a great earthen jar on the charcoal stove. She went to the front of the hotel and looked into the little office again, then climbed the short flight of steps to the balcony and her room. She sat on her bed and tried to think. She walked to the little window that gave on the plaza. There were a half dozen women and boys staring up at her window, and a flash of anger burnt her face, then helplessness came over her. The white-clad figures and the women in their purple rebozos vaguely lighted by the dim light over the hotel door were so silent and menacing now and she was no longer interested in them as underdogs.

She thought of trickery; perhaps the young men couldn't read or write English. She fumbled about in her purse for something that looked official; perhaps a last year's certificate of vehicle ownership, but she found nothing. Finally, like an animal that becomes helpless through intense fear, she walked down the stairs and out to the young men. She would do anything that they might direct her to do now, and think of a way out later. She handed over her papers.

The young man in the business suit moved over to get under the light, and she started to explain the papers to him, reaching for them. He jerked them away and said with the utmost contempt in English, "I read your language very well." This gave her hope and as he read the papers, she said, "Oh, do you speak English?"

"Yes, certainly, why not?"

"I thought—"

He seemed not to hear her. He folded the papers and stuffed them into his purse. "'Not very official,'" she thought.

The young men paid no more attention to her. They started across the street to the dark village hall. She unconsciously put into her voice a sort of beautiful girl helplessness, "but where can I park the little truck tonight? I'll be gone tomorrow, and I won't trouble you anymore." The young men turned as one. The one in the business suit turned to the other and said "perhaps, eh?" and she could see their white teeth in the dim light as they smiled. They shrugged their shoulders simultaneously, and the one in the business suit said, "who cares; park where you like." They turned and walked on. By this time she wanted to be pleasant and wanted very much to please them, so she shouted, "but what time and where do I appear?" They held a low conversation, then from the darkness, the spokesman said, "eight o'clock." Again she called to him, "in the morning?" and the answer came from the darkness, "when else?"

The patron was in the hallway when she entered, and she, as she remembered later, handed him the notice of her arrest dramatically as if she were accusing him of crime. She also remembered later that he had scarcely looked at it as he handed it back to her and as he exploded in Spanish: "This will not go—no, this will not go at all. I shall not have my noted foreign guests in my poor little hotel insulted by the stupid police. You must know, señorita, that I shall do things about this stupid matter; I shall go with you to the office of the mayor at eight o'clock in the morning and tell him that I have something to say in this matter. I shall make them understand that the guests of my poor little hotel are under my protection. You shall go under my protection to the mayor, be assured, señorita————"

As he raved, she became nauseated. His bluff and insincerity was like a blow in the face. She thanked him feebly and walked along the little court to the dining room. There were voices in the kitchen now, and a waiter came out with a greasy menu. He said pleasantly that the evening was beautiful, and she nodded her head and attempted to smile sweetly.

As she sat waiting, it seemed to her that her thoughts must be smothered in piles of wool. A mestizo, a mixedblood, approached her with his hat in his hand.[6] As he spoke he apologized for his very existence it seemed, and at the same time handed her a note as though he would do it before she could throw up a defence against him. She took the note and while she was absorbed by it, he sat down at the table without permission. As she read, he watched her, and when she looked up from her reading, she caught his eyes fixed on the low neckline of her frock. Instead of instinctively pulling it up, she shifted her position a little. His face glistened in the light of the kerosene lamps, and his smile was fixed. She instinctively tugged at her skirts which were already in place, and thanked him very graciously, then turned to her food as if she would dismiss him.

He sat smiling his greasy smile, and again when she looked, he was looking at the low neckline of her frock. A chill came over her, and she had the strange feeling that she must seek out some woman in this strange land of black-eyed men. She found herself visualizing a motherly woman with black, soft eyes like the eyes of a Madonna. She had heard a woman's voice in the kitchen and looked in that direction.

The gate-door in the partition was slightly ajar, and peering out from the crack were the black Indian eyes of the cook. They were like the eyes of a lizard, fixed and soulless, and as disinterested as black beads. She turned from them with a slight shudder, then her anger became almost uncontrollable when she realized that she was acting like the kind of female she hated. She said to the bringer of the message with histrionic sweetness, "look sir, I give a thousand thanks to you for the bringing of this fortunate message, and you will leave now. You must know that I am very tired and that I am weary from the things that have passed. As you see, I do not touch my delicious food."

The messenger became syrupy: "My poor life is yours, señorita. I will stay outside your door and make guard during this night." He looked about as if afraid of being heard, "it is very dangerous here in this place, señorita."

She wanted to scream, but she said calmly, "no, if you wish to make me happy, you will go now; perhaps you can see me tomorrow; I mean you can help me tomorrow—perhaps." Her own stupidity added to her anger. He saw the anger in her face and deep in his heart, he was hurt. "Good," he said, but he continued seated and continued to smile his fixed smile.

Suddenly she realized that he was the one who had followed her from the church on the side of the mountain above the village, and spasmodically closed her fingers under the table into a fist. He stood up, and as he did so, he bowed and said goodnight, keeping his eyes on the neckline of her frock. At the door, he turned and said, "it is the belief of myself, señorita, that you cannot go tomorrow; for several days, I believe, you cannot go." She thought that he made a movement as though he would return to the table, but instead he said goodnight again and left the hotel.

As she mounted the stairs to her room on the balcony, she noticed a piece of paper on the table just outside her door. It was torn across diagonally, and she had noted how bare the table was when she had come up to her room before dinner. She took the note from her bag and found that it fitted the other half on the table perfectly. She looked about her like some animal, then entered her room.

She moved the only chair against the door, and placed her bag there also, then read the note again by the light of the lamp. It was written in English with long graceful flourishes:

Reputable and Beautiful Stranger:

You must not fall a victim to the Traffic Officer. He no doubt wants to unpleasant you. Tomorrow it will be convenient for you to call upon the Mayor of the City, and your cause will be in good hands.

Signed: A Professor in the High School,
Vincente Andreas Gomez y Salazar.

On the second reading, she felt courage, but she could not sleep. She sat or lay fully dressed on her bed and listened all night. She heard the boards of the little balcony outside her room creak, but there was nothing more just then. Once she went to the little window and looked out upon the dark, silent, little plaza, and she thought she could see a man; at least the conformation of a man in the shadows. She came back to her position on the bed quickly and sat staring at the door.

She thought of the day before yesterday which now seemed to have been weeks ago. Then she had left Frannie with the three Princeton boys they had picked up at Spratling's in Taxco, where they insisted on staying another day in the tourist-, artist-infested place. She had driven off to Chilpancingo in disgust with the lot of them, saying that she would meet them there when they should come along noisily and conspicuously in Charlie Fairland's Jeep.[7] She thought now of Charlie's strong forearms, and his great chest and shoulders, and the honest sweat of his ruddy face. He acted at all times like a clumsy little boy at a party.

She had wanted to come to Mexico alone to study social conditions, but for her mother's sake, she had consented to travel with Frannie. Frannie was tiresome with her simulated glee over everything when they were with young men and her fear of Mexican food and bandits when they were alone. Now, she didn't want to think of these companions who had been forced upon her by Frannie's studied insouciance, her well-studied naturalness and her stressed curves, no more than she wanted to think of Charlie's puerile attitude as an arrogant protector of American womanhood when they had entered native bars. Such bourgeois artificiality and hypocrisy sickened her, but in the menacing silence of the savage night, she had to think of something in order to drown the thoughts of the shadow that was darker than the other shadows in the plaza and took on the outlines of a man the longer she looked; the memory of the indifferent Indian eyes of Guadalupe the cook fixed upon her from the crack of the kitchen-gate door. When her thoughts were afield she wasn't so conscious of the creaks in the balcony floor just outside her door, which she imagined she heard all during the night.

She ran out of cigarets just before dawn. She could hear the cocks crowing and the shrill whistle of the nightwatchman she supposed. She heard the porter draw the bar and swing open the front door, and she experienced relief when she realized that the front door to the hotel had been barred.

When the light became strong enough, she washed her face, making certain that she didn't get any of the questionable water in her mouth, a thing she had chided Frannie for doing. She spent some time in applying lipstick and in combing her shiny hair. She seemed to be a long time in attaining the perfection she desired. Although she had been known as a "brain" at prep school, and was known as a very serious student of social conditions at college, it didn't occur to her as she studied herself in her mirror that by thus enhancing her rather striking blonde beauty, she was really aggravating the conditions which were the cause of her unhappiness.

She felt much better when she came down to breakfast and the patron bowed from his office door. She would see him after breakfast about going over to the mayor's office with her. She had finally come to the conclusion that her fine would be stiff, and that after paying off graciously—and helplessly—she might get her car papers back and be allowed to leave over the long dusty trail to Chilpancingo.

As she sat over coffee and her atrocious pink cakes, a tall man came in and went to his table without noticing her. He sat and opened a well-known North American magazine. He did this rather ostentatiously, she thought. Just as she had made up her mind that he was the professor of the note, the patron came in and bowing graciously asked permission to introduce her well-wisher to her; the estimable professor of the high school.

Gratitude flooded her and she felt great waves of confidence. The tall man looked like a pure Spaniard with no copper tint that would indicate Indian blood. He bowed and she rushed over to him, holding out her hand and flooding him with expressions of gratitude in English. She saw his face turn crimson, and his eyes become the eyes of a worshipful dog, then he stammered and said in Spanish: "I am of the note; my heart is with you, señorita, and I am sure all will go well——"

"But I thought——"

"You will forgive me," he said, "I do not speak your beautiful language, but you will make myself and my disciples happy if you come to us after your visit with the mayor. You will come to our poor little high school?"

Her heart sank. He saw the disappointment in her face, and with quickness and grace he stood at the back of one of the chairs at the table and waved his hand over it saying, "honor a poor teacher of the high school in this backward village, señorita. I shall introduce you to a delicious Mexican dish which no tourist has ever tasted." His eyes pled with her like the eyes of a dog plead for food.

"Oh, no, a thousand thanks," she said awkwardly and she went back to her table, not being able to think of an excuse, and very unhappy again and annoyed with herself because of her clumsiness.

Soon her watch indicated that it was time to go. She knew now that the patron would be gone, and she had given him up as a broken reed anyway. She walked across the plaza to the mayor's office. There was no sign of life. She waited for half an hour and no one came. She walked back to the hotel determined then to make the patron do something when he did appear. He was gone. Again she asked the porter, but again he didn't know: "Who knows, señorita," and the shrug of shoulders seemed to be an attempt to convince her that such as he knew little of the convenient disappearance of patrons, or of their fancy plans in general.

A brisk mestizo came into the hotel and pretended to be so busy that he didn't see her. He shouted to the porter, "the patron—where is he?" but as the servant started to explain something, he waved him aside saying, "never mind." He himself must have thought that he was giving the impression of Yankee enterprise and efficiency, but in the all-conquering sun of the mountain valley, his activity struck one boldly as being histrionic.

He flashed his black eyes to Shelly, and in that flash he covered her whole body. He took off his hat and said deprecatingly: "I have come to apologize for my backward village, señorita. I know of this matter. Give me your little paper, and I shall go to the mayor immediately. No, no, you do not go with me." He waved her to a chair, "the mayor's office is ugly; I shall see that you suffer no more from this backward village." He took the ticket and left.

When he came back, he waved toward the dining room and said, "come, you will honor a poor engineer of sanitation from the Department of Mexico." She sat with him out of gratitude. When she asked him the amount of the fine, he assured her it was nothing.

As they talked, the young man with the cynical smile came in and handed her papers to the engineer and he handed them over to her. She called to the young man's back a faint "thousand thanks" as he left the hotel but he made no answer.

She moved as if to go. Now, she wanted only to get started over the primitive trail to Chilpancingo. He noted the movement: "You would like first to hear about this backward place, señorita?" She knew she ought to hear that which she had come to ascertain; the condition of the Indians under the revived agrarian policy.[8] She had come for the purpose of approving of the new spirit in Mexico and of rejoicing with the uplifted people whom the overlords both Spanish and Mexican had cowed and enslaved for centuries. She believed too that this young engineer must be of the new generation of sparkling hope, and at any other time she would have been deeply interested in recapitulating the victory with him, using the bold term "revolution" in mutual understanding, but all desire had left her except the urge to get away as soon as possible. She said, however, very feebly, "yes, it would be interesting."

He was visibly happy, and said, "good," but his black eyes flashed over her in a manner which caused her to believe that he was not really interested in telling her that which he wanted her to believe was so close to his heart.

"It is this way, right?" and his eyes flashed over her again. "Right, there is the church," and he held up one finger. "There are the Federal schools," and he held up another finger, "then there is the local government," for which he held up the third finger. "There are the Federal schools under the Department in Mexico, and there is Federal sanitation, right? Good, now your poor servant before you is the Sanitary Engineer in this backward place. You may weep for me. Good, now the church contends against the Federal schools, and the local government sometimes contends on the side of the church, and sometimes not. Good, then sometimes the Federal schools contends on the same side with the Sanitary and sometimes not—both Federal, you understand? Sometimes all four fight against each other." He spread his arms, then let them fall helplessly, and allowed his lower lip to protrude. "What can one do? Good, my friend the professor was afraid to go before the mayor in your behalf, since things go well between them now. The patron was afraid because he wants things friendly at all times so that his pesos will not be disturbed, right? But the Sanitary Engineer is afraid of no one in this backward place, right? So you have your important little papers because the Sanitary Engineer is afraid of no one in this place."

His eyes sparkled and he looked at her as if he were wondering about his timing. She could see in his eyes a reserved excitement protected by his volubility over her distress and her palpable interest in such strange conditions. She had seen the same excitement behind the solicitude of both the message bearer of last night and the professor this morning.

Fear came over her again, and its strength gave her power to make a resolute move. She arose and mumbled her thanks as she strode to her room. He followed behind her saying that she must see the making of the famed Coyotl rebozos; the way they dried the freshly dyed threads by stretching them in the sun along a certain street, and how they shone in the sun as they dried, but she hurried up the steps to her room thanking him over her shoulder at every long stride.

When she came down to pay her bill the patron was there, and she failed to hear what he was saying about the thwarting of the police. The engineer was standing by the rear wheel of her station wagon directing work of pumping up her tire. The sweating pumper was the message bearer of the night before. The engineer smiled up at her, "it is nothing, señorita, this burro," and he pointed to the squatting figure, "let the air from your tires last night."

She hated the white pantaloons and jackets of the silent Indians and their bare-footed women standing about the car. Their silence and dignity and their inhuman detachment seemed to be the hereditary glazing developed through generations of human sacrifice to their ancient Aztec gods.

She started the motor and was quiveringly ready to drive off, but the engineer stood with the door open. He placed his foot on the running board and was saying, "I should never forgive myself, señorita, if something happened to you; I shall go along and protect you through this very dangerous country." When she had got into the car, the Indians had crowded closer, and many were now standing in front of it, and the thought of the horrible results if she maimed or killed one of them brought sweat to her body. She could not project her thought beyond herself; the mere fact of a wounded Indian would mean little as far as she was concerned.

As the engineer hesitated with his foot on the running board as though waiting for the slightest approval from her, which was nothing more than courtesy as his mind, she knew, was made up, she was ready to weep. He kept talking, but she didn't hear what he was saying more. She looked around attempting to find some sympathetic face.

The message bearer was smiling his fixed smile and watching her, and a little way removed from the crowded Indians and the others of the hotel, was the cynical young man standing in the doorway of the village hall, and she was startled to find something behind his cynical smile too—or perhaps in her distraction she was depending upon the distortions of fear.

The engineer was now waving the Indians away from the front of the car before climbing in with her, and her thoughts had stopped completely like the ticking of a shocked clock, when an Indian boy came running by the car with fear in his face crying, "carro, carro," and pointing to a dust cloud.

The patron came out of his doorway where he had been standing, and the Indians crowded into an investigative group like deer, and all eyes were upon Charlie Fairland's Jeep. One leg hung carelessly over the side, and Frannie and the boys were waving and shouting. Now, Indians who had been sitting placidly under the trees of the plaza feigning disinterest came up to see. The patron and the others of the hotel stared in disbelief. Charlie swung his long legs out of the Jeep, saluted and said, "hi-yu, Mother Brown, here's the Lone Ranger."

Shelly found herself hysterically introducing the crazy North Americans to the patron, the engineer and to shy Guadalupe the cook, who had come out to witness the miracle with her own eyes. "These people have been WONDERFUL to me," she was saying in English, then she turned to the smiling and dignified engineer and the others and translated, "I have said to them—your—I have told them of your great kindness———I." She broke off and turning back to Charlie, said excitedly, "let's go."

"W-a-i-t a MIN-ute," he said, "t'ell with that, les—havn't they got Carta Blanca in this dump?"

"Oh, no," she said hurriedly and loudly, to drown out what the patron would say, since she noted that he had understood Charlie's wants. "Sí," the patron was saying, "beer, beer, yais, beer—cerveza, sí, yais," but Charlie had only time to get in beside Shelly as she drove off. He leaned out of the window and shouted to Barrett Comstock, "herd the wreck in, Bink."

As the station wagon climbed up the winding, dusty trail out of the sun-subdued valley, the thorns and the straggling pines were passed, and finally as they entered the groves of big-leafed oaks, Shelly looked back at the little village far below them, but it blended so well with the sterile grey-brown earth that it was scarcely visible. A thought flashed through her mind that it was like a protectively colored animal waiting for its prey. The thought was objective now like the thoughts one might have when passing a drunken bum asleep on the subway steps.

She looked at Charlie's profile that gave the impression of irresponsibility, and she knew that he was seeing nothing of the trees, the savage cactus and the thorns, or the almost invisible Indian settlements protectively colored against the sides of the mountains. She knew he would be thinking of a cold bottle of beer, and once he had had several, he would worry considerably about how he might manage to stay with or near her most of the care-free summer; wandering half-consciously from place to place just behind her, and bumbling like a kindly, protective, happy giant.

An all-absorbing happiness came over her and when the trail became straight and level for a moment on the flat top of a water shed, she looked into the rear vision mirror to see how her carefully designed mouth was getting along.

Stories from
Indian Country

Readers who wish to avoid plot spoilers will
prefer to skip to the stories and then return.

"The Apache Woman"

It appears that the first story in this section, "The Apache Woman,"
was the first short story Mathews wrote during his flush of short story
writing in the late 1940s. He notes its composition in his diary for
August 2, 1946, reading it that very day to his wife and stepdaughter.
The next day he rewrote the ending. Within two days he had it in
the post along with three stories of theirs and began writing "Yellow
Hair," a story in the preceding section. We do not know where he
sent these four stories, nor does it appear that they were published
in his lifetime.

The landmark of Fort Osage dates the setting to 1808 or later.
Though it may seem to the uninformed reader "timeless" or a display of the myth of eternal tribal warfare, the fort, the horses, the
epidemic, and other markers all remind us that it takes place well
into the latest colonial (that is, U.S.-impacted) era of Osage history.
Mathews apparently does not write of this incident in *The Osages*,
so it is difficult to know certainly that the story is nonfiction. In
that work he indicates that the Osages named Apache *A-Pa-Tsi*, or
[Lodge] Makes-Us-Stoop People, for their short stature relative to
the renownedly tall Osages. Possibly the scene is as late as 1855 when,
Mathews writes, "the *we-lu-schkas* came again, this time the *ge-ta-zhe*,
things-on-your-face, smallpox." (*We-lu-schkas* means "little mystery
people" in Osage, a general name for disease.) If so, the Black Robe
may be Father Schoenmakers, a Jesuit of the Osage mission on the
Neosho River in southeastern Kansas, who had arrived in 1847. Wa-

Cabe Shinkah, Little Bear of the Bear Clan, is mentioned in *The Osages* as one of several men turned over to U.S. authorities in 1824, to be tried for the death of a party of whites led by Major Curtis Welborn; he may have lived until at least 1863.

While it deserves comparing to the other stories written about Native Americans in the direct postwar era, "The Apache Woman" also bears an eerie resemblance to an incident in James Welch's *Fools Crow*. In that story, however, a young, arrogant warrior stumbles into a room filled with sick and dying enemy women and does not return in sickness to his people. The two testify to the ubiquity of the experience on the nineteenth-century Plains. The story also bears the marks of a mind actively connecting his own experiences to his tribal history. Mathews adorns the old Apache woman with a ceremonial headdress of quetzal feathers and silver bracelets. The detail likely emerges from his stay in Mexico in the early years of World War II, though Mathews had also hunted in the U.S. Southwest where Apaches live. Significantly, he also features not only an Apache pictograph but the Osages' ability to read the writing of their enemy. Though the consciousness of indigenous writing systems is not pervasive in his work, the inclusion of this indigenous literacy and its theme—the defeat of the Spanish cavalry by a large Apache force (symbolically or actually)—flag his attempts to educate his reading public. Mathews moves beyond the tribal consciousness of the nineteenth century that denigrated the Apaches, promoting an appreciation for pan-Indian accomplishments, while retaining that Osage consciousness as the primary means toward historical recovery of an intricate history increasingly erased.

"The Talk of the Face"

When Mathews penned "The Talk of the Face" over two years later, in November 1948, it was probably already one hundred, perhaps as much as two hundred, years old. Though associated with no certain year, its features place it prior to 1865. The relative sparseness and accommodation of white traders and trappers suggest that it is not yet 1849, and the camp at Marais-des-Cygnes suggests that it might even be earlier than the treaty in 1825 that excluded the Osages from the Missouri territory, though that river flows through Kansas as well. It is another story he associates with the Bear Clan of the Osages: Bear People in "The Apache Woman." Given that his grandmother was a Big Hill girl of the Buffalo gens, this genealogy implies that he heard it from one of the men who also informed his books *Wah'Kon-Tah* and *The Osages*. It can be contrasted nicely to his narration of the despairing separation of a young Osage man and a young Arapaho woman in *Wah'Kon-Tah*. The two meet at Carlisle, the Indian boarding school in Pennsylvania, but the man's pursuit of marriage to this woman about whom he cannot stop thinking is met by both their families with intransigent though somewhat well-reasoned refusal, clearly rooted in their antagonistic tribal history. It is intriguing, too, that Second Son initially sees the Cheyenne as tall, pale warriors, pale as a sick Osage. Some scholars have argued that Indians east of the Rockies may have had comparatively pale or white skin. The detail may suggest some interest on Mathews's part in ideas of multiple migrations within North America, or to North America from continents beyond Asia. It certainly suggests his lifelong interest in various Osages' ideas of their own superiority, even in the face of the humiliation of unguarded capture, and consciousness of their imposing stature.

"The Flower on Cadron Creek"

The next story in this section, "The Flower on Cadron Creek," sees Mathews ranging away from Osage-centered plots. He would return to the Cadron Creek incidents in his masterwork on Osage history. That eight-hundred-page tome devotes chapter upon chapter to the conflicts that arose between the Osages and the "chain-pressured" Cherokees. As early as the last quarter of the eighteenth century, many Cherokees saw little alternative but to remove west, often into Osage territory in Arkansas and Oklahoma, once decades of mutual accommodation and racial mixing were thrown aside by the new citizens of the new United States. There as well as here, Mathews narrates the Cherokee side of the story with empathy, despite the outrages committed on both sides of the Cherokee-Osage divide. "The Flower on Cadron Creek" captures the tension between the survivance of the ending, in which accommodation and cross-national marriages are given new hope, and the powerful irony of an attraction between seemingly inimical forces. Lieutenant Thomas Fuller, whose actual name was Joseph W. Harris, is humbled and transformed by his witnessing. Yet the reader must wonder, has he become at the last any less an agent of coercion than when he first saw Anne MacDonald or yearned for dire situations from which he might rescue her? Like Laban J. Miles in the *Wah'Kon-Tah* of seventeen years earlier, Fuller begins the journey full of the romance of Indian tribulation, but entirely an alien to its meaning. He outpaces Miles in understanding through action. Whereas "sullen fullbloods" critique that reservation agent's lack of awareness of events under his watch, the lieutenant in charge of removal in "The Flower on Cadron Creek" feels finally like the fullbloods look as they sit among the cedars, waiting. He also acts, in ways that Miles fails to act, and refrains from imposing modes of behavior on his charges. Whereas Miles seems unable to control his compulsion to control.

Mathews apparently had access to the journal that Lieutenant Harris kept, as he quotes from it in *The Osages*. He also writes of the real events that formed the basis for some final scenes of the fiction:

> The settlers were afraid to come to the camp to give him aid in caring for the stricken, and he struggled along aiding the local doctor, Roberts, until the doctor died; then he himself was stricken, but recovered.
>
> They had only opium and calomel to treat the disease, one-half of a grain of opium and from fifteen to forty grains of calomel. These two men, Lieutenant Harris from Portsmouth, New Hampshire, only a few years out of West Point, and the country doctor, Roberts, originally from Alabama, personified the nobility in man that seems sometimes to be only his own poetic assumption or just a chimera until it rises from and above greed, salacity, panic,

fear, and ghoulish theft, as it did that April and May on Cadron Creek in 1834.

When the survivors of these people and others of the immigrants reached the rivers of the Little Ones, they separated to find their new homes, and soon soldiers at Fort Gibson, the missionaries and their families, and the Little Ones were dying like flies.

The missionaries lost Rev. Montgomery, and the Redfields lost all of their children, and many others died of the cholera. As if the cholera and the measles and the smallpox were not enough, this summer of 1834 was the summer of the great drought following the year of the greatest floods. The thermometer registered 100, 110, and 116 degrees at the fort.

The dragoons off on their expedition to the plains must have died from cholera as well as from heat and malaria.

The wife of Mr. Vaill of Union Mission became insane.[1]

One wants to imagine that Mathews heard the story first not from Lieutenant Harris's journal but from an Anglo-Cherokee-Osage granddaughter or great-granddaughter of the pair. It seems unlikely. Harris did quit the army following the incident, but he returned to Portsmouth and died three years later at the age of thirty-two. Mathews was, however, one of the earliest writers to insist upon telling the stories of Cherokee removal not as a single punctuation upon a theme of Jacksonian treachery but as the phenomenon of a half-century of complex, multifaceted decisions by Cherokees of various Cherokee nations and towns, made necessary by Federalist, Jeffersonian, and Monrovian policies and their confluences with French and Spanish imperial interests. That this story conflates the 1838–39 Cherokee Trail of Tears with one of the last of the earlier "voluntary" migrations displays how much more sophisticated grew Mathews's understanding of continental history between 1949 and 1961.

"Moccasin Prints"

If only one of this collection of newly published stories lives on, it should be "Moccasin Prints." It is an extraordinary account of Bull

Head's ancestor Standing Bull and the Battle of the Monongahela of 1755. Mathews appreciated greatly the significance of this story, as he wrote of Braddock's defeat at least four times—here, in his *Sooner Magazine* story "Man Not Afraid," in *Talking to the Moon*, and in *The Osages*—and in the last used it as a ripe occasion to meditate on the woof and warp and weave of gentile (clan) and tribal memory and their often-occluded relation to European memory. But nowhere is the narrative more stirring, more stunning than in the version appearing here. Rather than standing as a mediator between the keepers of the memory and his audience, Mathews not only stands aside but embeds the speaker and listener—direct lineage descendants—in the present. It is a present where the stakes are high. Immortality is no guarantee. Indeed, it seems that everything is against it: not merely the weakening of the Dorset line, and the falling away of the sons responsible for keeping the story, but all of historiography.

Rarely are the French-allied Indian forces of the North American side of the Seven Years' War named, either tribally or individually, in English-language accounts. When they are, there seems rarely to be any acknowledgment that the French allies against Braddock ranged beyond the tribes of the Ohio valley and the Great Lakes. Such forethought, organization, solidarity, and geographic range are unthinkable. One account narrated to Zebulon Pike in 1806 saw a brief revival, but the local societies of the late nineteenth and early twentieth century concerned in its preservation frame Chtoka's account of the battle to Pike in skeptical, provisional rhetoric. French sources are absent from our historiography of the event. Even some of the more recent English-language accounts seem intent on slandering the French and multinational Indian alliance, minimizing or discounting the cleverness of their strategy, and repeating ungrounded and exaggerated claims of drunken debauchery following the victory, even while admitting that Braddock defeated himself, that British and Americans sometimes lose and lose big. Apparently the French and Indian allies did not win the battle: Braddock lost it. Bull Head finds amid this rot and cant the perfect rhetorical situation. No British ambassador could deny Great Britain's later defeat by Washington, nor could any British ambassador deny their pride in his showing during this embarrassing British defeat years earlier. Will his fame carry along the footprints of Maria's grandfather into immortality? We cannot know, but Bull Head and Mathews have given it a fighting chance.

"Bad Medicine"

Both *Talking to the Moon* and *The Osages,* not to mention *Wah'Kon-Tah* and *Sundown,* contain passages on the centrality of peyote religion within Osage society in the early twentieth century. In *The Osages,* the chapter on Moonhead follows one entitled "Disintegration and Confusion." However, his sentiments toward the phenomenon were complex. In *Talking to the Moon,* he wrote:

> I have been intrigued over the last ten years with this cleaning-up activity of militant, devouring Christianity; the cleaning-out of the machine-gun nests of the native religion, and the gradual roundup of the guerrillas left in odd corners as the advance sweeps on. As I watch with my sympathies fired and my sense of the dramatic inspired, a new force makes its appearance and seems intent on conquering the conqueror, Christianity. The natural, slow-moving local drama, wherein the original paganism of the blackjacks had to adjust itself through Peyotism to Europeanized Christianity, now becomes a tragedy in the wild confusion of adjustment to the new force of natural science, mechanically conceived.[2]

Christ was able to capture the imagination and hearts of some Osages because, as Mathews observed in *The Osages,*

> As a man they could understand Him, because He had come from the stars as they themselves had, and He had come down to earth by the command of his father, as any young man among them must have done, showing obedience to and respect for age. He was both *Tzi-Sho,* of the Sky Lodge, and *Hunkah,* of the Earth, and now in their own unsureness and anxiety, they became more interested

in what the Heavy Eyebrows said about Him, and suddenly they were identifying themselves with Him.[3]

The mysteries of "Bad Medicine" are overshadowed to a large degree by Mathews's more caricaturing than insightful treatment of the Christian African American woman whose participation in the Otoe man's ritual in this story is indispensable to its effectiveness. Yet it seems that the story is a triumph for "paganism." Eagle Feather is a Road Man in the Peyote Church, yet he is unable to discover through western medicine or his syncretic faith the cure for his son's occult ailment. Me-Ompah-We-Lee seems to turn his ears away; even his clan and social songs at Red Horse's grave are of no effect. He must look beyond his own knowledge and rely on McMann's powers. And he must rely on a method that is simultaneously nativist and accommodating of non-Indian—but not so much of Amer-European—presence on the continent and within the community.

The Apache Woman

The drums on the Cimarron were like the pulse beats of the earth. They took up and sonified the earth rhythm which all life feels. They inspired emotion to the point of bursting in the hearts of the men who danced against the illimitable space; pounding their moccasined feet against the red earth of the upper waters of the river.[1]

During the day when the sun attempted to silence all sound, the throbbing was deadened as though moving away in the distance, but when the red August sun slid into the red tableland behind the cottonwoods of the river, and the wind-twisted junipers stood against it like bent, old women searching for buffalo chips, the drum's TUM-tum, TUM-tum, TUM-tum carried the earth's rhythm far into the night. The buffalo wolves sat with tongues lolling, listening before taking up the mesa trails, and the coyotes howled to express some mysterious emotion of their own.

Against the flame-dance of the fires, the black-, yellow- and vermillion-daubed bodies of young men danced in religious fervor. Each carried a coup-stick with a downy eagle feather on the end of it. The body of each glistened with sweat, when he danced out of the shadows into the whimsical flame-dance. In the scalp-lock of each, the tail feather of the eagle spun, or inclined forward as the young dancer bent low to the ground, tracing the trail of his imaginary enemy with his coup-stick.

The young men had been dancing for four days and nights, and for four days and nights they had fasted; given only water from the spring, that welled under the roots of a lone sycamore, and spread its fingers over the sand before disappearing into it.

Hunger makes men ferocious, but it also gives to men thoughts of metal brightness with the sharpness of flint, and capable of sparking like flint when struck. And when men are hungry they also see visions that are like the dreams of the night; the true experiences of man's other self, released from the body for a short time; visiting for a few moments the future land of the spirit.

Thus when man is hungry after four days of dancing, he is better prepared to enter into the land of the spirit and understand better, and carry out more effectively the laws of Wah Kon Tah, the Great Spirit. His body becomes numbed by the great fatigue and the first pangs of hunger have passed to leave the body in a state of passivity, giving the feeling that it is temporarily absent; allowing the spirit to take complete control.

On the fourth night, the pulse of the earth on the upper reaches of the Cimarron stopped and the silence was complete. The flame-dance brought out the bent figure of a woman sitting at the edge of the dance ground, which had now been worn bare of even the sparse vegetation which characterized it. Only the bent figure of the old woman, whose sitting form, with the head on its breast, was the very symbol of futility that death brings. The dancers had disappeared into the shadows of the lodges where the flame-dance could not follow.

The old woman moved. She pulled her robe about her, and lifted her face to the stars, then broke the silence like the sudden yelping of a close-by dog coyote. For some minutes, she sobbed the Song of Death, with her face turned to the spirit world above. The chant rolled over the tableland on the heavy air of night in crescendo. When it seemed to be about to express the height of emotion, the voice snapped into a sob, like the snapping of the A-string when the violinist has burdened it with his attempt to express an emotion which it cannot carry.

After the sob, there was action. The three ponies stared, and one snorted and circled the man holding the rope; with his head high and his tail up like a banner. Three of the dancers ran toward the ponies, and when they reached them, they bounded onto their backs, and broke into a run completely circling the camp four times, then the hoof beats were lost in the night far to the southwest, where the war song of the three young men also faded.

The old woman got up slowly and went to the river to wash the ashes from her hair. The talk became light again and the old woman laughed with her attendants, as she washed away the badge of her grief in the red-tinted water. She was happy again because Wah Kon Tah had thus willed; that after four days of lamentation, the spirit was on its way to heaven if all the ceremonies of death had been carried out. With the happiness of spiritual relief came the odors of the feast that was being prepared.

After they had left the camp and they could no longer see the light of the fire, the young men pulled up their ponies and rode abreast in a walk. They said nothing as they rode along, but they knew where they were going. A scout had seen twenty lodges of Apache, and had seen them go into camp. The Osage scout was angered by the fact that the Apache had put out no scout to warn the people of the proximity of the Osage. Though they did not say so to each other, the Osage felt that this was an insult. They liked to sit in their camps, returned from their hunting expeditions to the plains, and laugh with pride about the numbers of Pawnee, Cheyenne, Apache or Caddo scouts sent out to watch the movements of the Great Osage when they came to hunt on the flanks of the seasonal buffalo migrations, but no scout was seen to serve as eyes for the Apache band.

This fact had much influence on the instructions given the young men setting out to take a scalp after the mourning dance, just ended. Little Bear was an important man who had died on the horns of a mangy, solitary old bull he had wounded, and the old men had thought that only the scalp of the fighting Pawnee would propitiate an angry Wah Kon Tah. But the Apache were also great enemies of the Osage, and this insult would not be overlooked. And perhaps this would be one of the few chances the Osage would have to take Apache hair, since they hunted farther west by tacit agreement. The two tribes had had only one clash in recent years, and the Apache had lost a chieftain, and the Osage warriors had counted coup on the big fellow who looked important. Surely the Apache would not soon forget this victory and the strong medicine of the Osage.

Thus, the more the old men of the camp thought about the story of the scout, the more annoyed they became, so they instructed the young men who were to take a scalp from the enemy to assuage the bad will of Wah Kon Tah, to go to the Apache camp for the trophy.

So filled with religious fervor were the young men that they glowed with self-righteousness as they rode along in the night. Each had his dreams, but suffusing all of them was a great emotion. One of them kept reaching up to his scalp-lock and feeling of the fluffy eagle feather stuck alongside the spinning tail feather, to be sure that it was still there, and Wah Kon Tah could see it as they rode along, and would make no mistake about the young men's affiliation with the Bear People, to which Little Bear had belonged.[2] And this same young man taking part in his first mourning dance, or war dance as the white man called it, nervously looked at his coup-stick periodically to see that the undertail feather of the eagle was still floating on the end of it.

As they neared the little stream where the scout had seen the Apache go into camp, they became cautious, even though their glow of religious fervor urged precipitate action. They rode so that a scout could never see them against the night skyline, and they rode apart so that the group would not make a noticeable concentration of blackness against the blackness of the night.

Soon they could smell the camp of the Apache, so they left their horses in a dry wash, and crept on their bellies onto a ridge that over-looked the little stream where the camp was situated. They couldn't see much in the darkness, so they waited. They were downwind and the odor of camp fire was strong, and their forgotten hunger came back momentarily.

Beyond the camp, the coyotes talked excitedly for a few minutes, then silence again. Far off in the foothills a wolf sang, but there was no answer to the song from the camp dogs; however, this absence of bluff-barking was not noticed by the watchers. The silence was deeper than before, except for the dry rattle of a weed caught in another one, and the sound seemed loud in the almost windless night. One of the party crawled over and released the prisoner weed. It could drown the footsteps of an Apache scout, slight though the sound was.

The nervous young man felt his belly tingle as the darkness gave way, and he felt of the feather in his scalp-lock again and carefully examined the end of his coup-stick. There must be no mistake; Wah Kon Tah must identify them so that full credit would come to them. The leader felt of his arrows slung over his back.

Then the light gradually revealed the twenty lodges, just as the scout had said, and the three young men waited for movement. The water hole was just below them and someone would come out soon to water his horses. They had no plan but each would act instinctively and perfect cooperation would result. Someone would come down to water his horses, and they could put an arrow through him, each hit him with his coup-stick, then take his hair and be away before the camp was aware.

The sun came up, and stabbed the mesa with its lances of light. The shadows of the yucca and sage grew shorter, and still there was no movement. They could see far across the red land on the other side of the little stream, and they saw no horses dotting it. As one they crawled back to the arroyo where they had left their horses, and there they remounted, and rode together down its dry bed, then, hidden by a ridge, began a wide circle about the camp. They saw no life. Finally at the opposite point on the circle from which they had been hiding, they came across the hoof prints of the Apache horses, and the parallel traces of the travois. Among the prints were the traces of the camp dogs, but there were no moccasin tracks, so the young men knew that there was no use following them. However, they did follow for a mile, then from a high ridge, lying on their bellies, they could see the dark marks of the travois wriggling across a blinding salt flat far in the distance.

Satisfied, they rode back along the trail until they came up to the camp, then the leader gave the horses to the nervous young man to hold, while he and the other crawled up to the very edge of it. They returned after a half hour and the leader pursed his lips toward the place. All three rode up to the lodges. A cur with ribs like a washboard circled around the camp; the tip of his tail touching his belly.

There was one large lodge with a pictograph completely encircling it. They could read it; it was the story of the meeting with Spanish cavalry, and all the Spaniards were falling from their horses like leaves from the cottonwood, pierced by the arrows of an abnormally large Apache.

It was a handsome lodge. They walked toward it cautiously, then the leader gently opened the flap. He turned and motioned to the others but the nervous young man stayed outside to again hold the horses and watch for evidence of a trick. The leader went to the other end immediately and raised the edge of the lodge so that they would not be trapped, then both stood and looked at a figure seated in the center of the lodge on a rich buffalo robe. The head of the figure was on its chest, and seemed unaware of the presence of the mourning party. The figure was draped in a gorgeous blanket, and wore a ceremonial headdress made of quetzal feathers from the jungle of Mexico. Silver bands hung from its emaciated wrists, and hanging down its back was an otter skin tailpiece taken from the Sioux. The nervous young man opened the flap and also stared.

"Oh—ho," said the leader and hit the figure with his coup-stick. It moved, then the other man snatched the headdress and buried his war ax in the figure's skull. It rolled over and lay still.

The young man looked at the quetzal feather headdress and his eyes shone, then both of them began to rip the finery from the figure. When the fancy shirt came off, they stopped and the leader said, "ha, ha, ha, hey." The naked body was withered and diseased, and the breasts hung flabby like empty pemmican sacks. It was an old woman.

The supreme insult did not strike them immediately; only when they had ridden off some distance, and the leader was arranging the gorgeous blanket across the withers of his horse did it occur to him, then he became embarrassed over his own actions. He said; "if they do not hear you say it, they will not know that I struck an old woman with my coup-stick; if you do not say it, the people will not know about this old woman."

They cached the blanket, the headdress, the shirt, the bracelets and the arm bands, then continued their quest for a scalp to appease Wah Kon Tah so that Little Bear could enter into Spiritland.[3] The hair of a woman would be an insult, especially a useless old woman who had been left behind to die.

At noon they came across the hoof prints of a scout's horse, and later they saw the scout against the skyline. He was sitting his pony watching them. He was on a hill and he could see in all directions. They could see by his dress and by the decorations on his pony that he was a Pawnee. They couldn't surround him, so being three, they rode toward him. They became filled with religious excitement again, and gave little thought to the possibility that there might be a Pawnee band on the other side of the hill.

Soon they were in a dead run toward him. This action was so strange that the Pawnee waited to see what the trick might be, then looked wildly about for others. His band was far away and he became excited, and turned to flee too late. The young men overtook him and took his scalp, then after the three had made coup on his body, they tied the scalp to the leader's coup-stick and raced into their own camp singing: "we have met the enemy—now our brother can enter paradise."

Attendants took over their lathered ponies, and they were treated as heroes.

The Beaver Band had come out to the plains in late summer to hunt a few old bulls and cows that had not gone north with the spring migration, or had drifted south before the autumn migration. There were always a few stragglers on the upper waters of the Cimarron to be hunted in years of scarcity or epidemics among the whitetail deer in the woodlands.

They packed up and set out for their permanent camp on the Osage river. They left two days after the mourning dance since the scouts had seen several Pawnee scouts, and they desired to avoid a clash with their ancient enemies. They rode across to the Salt Fork of the Arkansas, then to the old ford on the main stream.[4] They traveled leisurely after they left the plains since in the woodlands between the

Arkansas and the Missouri rivers they were supreme. They imagined their very name shriveling hearts with fear.

Within two weeks after leaving the Cimarron camp grounds, they were camped among the laughing streams of the Ozarks. They idled there in the cool shade of the great trees, where they could lie in the clear streams and sing songs they had made in honor of their own deeds of bravery, as the cold water gurgled over them.

But soon the evil spirit crept into the camp. It sat on its haunches in the lodge of the leader of the mourning party who had taken the hair of the Pawnee. It touched him on the forehead then crept back in the dark corner to wait. Fire came into the veins of the leader and sweat poured from his body. His frightened wife scolded him in her deep fear, and the medicine man came with an eagle wing fan and fanned away the invisible tools of the evil spirit, and sang to the accompaniment of a water drum, but the leader became worse. For two days he lay looking at the ceiling of his lodge where he saw little black men with hairy tails grinning at him, and the fear in his heart was so great that it pushed the water from his body out through his skin and his wife held the gourd dipper to his lips constantly. On the third day the fire died down, but little red pimples came on his face and on his belly, and soon they spread all over his body. Then they grew and the evil spirit crept stealthily from his dark corner and crawled into his body, and a terrible odor filled the lodge.

Thus encouraged the evil spirit crept into other lodges and soon many people lay on their robes looking at the ceiling of their lodges, and saw there visions of evil which they were afraid to mention. Then the leader of the mourning party died, and the nervous young man died, and the third member of the party died, and one morning there were twenty-five people ready to be taken to the hills and placed in cairns. These people had become someone else; their faces were covered with red pustules, like the sores that covered the body of the Apache woman.

The Song of Death would not come from the throats of the people now because of the fear that came up from their hearts to lodge there. Many of the stricken ones crawled away into the woods to die alone, and many of the healthy ones furtively packed their belongings and stole away from the camp where the evil spirit had visited. And soon, only the dead ones remained and the camp was silent, except for the howling of the dogs that wandered about hungry and afraid.

Then one day a Black Robe from Fort Osage came down the trail on some business of the white man's God.[5] His careful mule stepped mincingly down the mountain trail, then stopped, and with his great ears like wings turned toward the silent camp, gazed in wonderment. The Black Robe dismounted, and understanding came to him as he put his fingertips to the pits on his sun-tanned face, left there by smallpox.

There were many things which told him that there was no one in this awful silence in need of either physical or spiritual succor. The sun flashed on his crucifix as he held it up toward the deserted camp, and as he said a few words in Latin. Then he remounted and turned the willing mule's head back up the trail whence he had come.

Three nights later when he wrote his report to his superiors in St. Louis, he informed them only that the Beaver Band of the Great Osage had been wiped out by smallpox. He did not know of the Apache woman and that men of the Plains had advanced to virus warfare.[6]

The Talk of the Face

The Osage can associate no certain year with the time when Flower-That-Sways-In-The-Wind followed Second Son back to his people. They are not certain about the year, but they remember their thoughts when they saw her. When the Cheyenne named her, the Osage say, there must have been plenty of meat in their lodges and their hearts must have been singing. They in their heart-singing had called her right; she was the tall flower of the prairie. She was the tall flower that bows to you when you come upwind to hunt the whitetail buck, and her beauty made you forget that you must take meat back to camp; made you want to lie on your back on the prairie and make a song about her.

But the Osage remember that Second Son was captured by the Cheyenne in August after the Bear Clan of the Osage had gone to the headwaters of the Cimarron to establish a hunting camp for the autumn migration of the buffalo, and they will tell you that within a space of twelve moons, Second Son came back to his people. He came back on his own horse and this beautiful girl of the Cheyenne rode behind him with much talk of the heart in her face.

They said that Second Son's body talked too in its straightness; that it spoke of great pride and courage, while his face challenged the world to say that he was not a man; to hint that he was not a warrior to whom the people could point, even when he rode among many warriors.

The story of Second Son and the Cheyenne maiden will have no ending as long as grandmothers like to remember the days when they themselves were straight and young and talked with their eyes, and lay tingling in their lodges waiting for the first notes of the love flute coming from the inky moon shadows. But the story had a beginning.

Second Son stood on the banks of the Arkansas River and watched the Bear Clan of the Great Osage cross to the red earth on the other side. He watched until the breezes of the plains wiped out the pale dust cloud that marked the progress of the many horses of the hunting party. The friendly breeze of the plains did this quickly so that the Pawnee could not judge their number from far across the red earth that was like the flat chest of a mourning warrior.

He was eighteen and he wanted to show his prowess as a hunter of buffalo, but the chieftain had said that he must stay with his old father and mother. If the Commanche or the Pawnee struck suddenly while the band was on the plains, the party must be mobile, and the old people would only make them slow and weak and indecisive.[1]

Second Son and his family had come with the band to the edge of the Osage range at the Arkansas River and had stopped there among the ash, the walnuts, the cottonwoods, white oaks and the blackjacks that covered the hills. Here were plenty of deer, and here no Pawnee or Commanche dared come. But across the river on the red plains, many hunting parties of other tribes roamed, and here the Osage, the Pawnee, the Caddo, the Cheyenne, the Commanche and other tribes had their balance of power skirmishes. Thus on the edge of the woodlands, Second Son must stay and hunt for his old parents, so that they would be comfortable until the band returned from the hunt. They could do little for themselves. Their movements were like the movements of the bullsnake when the leaves turned and the cold winds of autumn played with them, and their minds were like the mornings when the fog made mystery on the prairie.

When he entered the lodge of his father, the heaviness of his heart seemed to pull his head down so that he could only look at the ground in his unhappiness. His old father looked up at him but the challenge of youth was gone from his eyes. His father sitting in the lodge running his fingers up and down the edges of the trader's blanket, looked only questions now. When he looked up at his tall son, his filmy eyes asked only questions. Second Son answered his father's question of the eyes: "I am going across the river. There is broken earth on the other side of the river that may be the trail of a stray bull that was thirsty. I shall ride the yellow horse which we got from the Kiowa; the grass that hugs the earth on the other side of the river is yellow now."[2]

The old mother who was like the brown leaf of the winter oak stopped her puttering and listened to the man's talk, then went on with her work. Second Son looked at her and then said: "If I do not come back before the sun goes to sleep, do not worry; I can take care of myself."

He kicked his yellow horse hard in the belly with his heels, and put him across the river, causing the water to splash above his head. He came out on the other side onto the plains where there are few secrets. When drought has visited the land, there is the tall dust cloud that tells your enemy much about your strength in numbers; there are inquisitive pronghorn cutting the skyline with a dozen heads turned toward you, and there is the wolf which your horse's hooves have disturbed, taking one last look at you over his shoulder before he melts from sight over the long swells of the plains. But the Kiowa horse was yellow and the short grass of the plains was yellow in this time of drought.

Soon he saw a black dot far out on the plains. It was a tiny black dot on the crest of a swell, but there were no drainage fingers leading to it. He looked about him, then jumped from his horse and picked up a handful of fine dirt and threw it into the air. The plains breeze carried it away from his hand and carried it toward the black dot far away. He knew that he must approach from the other side, and this meant that he must ride for several miles; he must ride in a large circle and come up from the other side.

From the other side, he saw that the black dot took on the definite conformation of a lone buffalo bull. As he approached low over his horse's head, taking advantage of a ravine that headed near the bull, he could see him swing his great curly head abruptly alongside of his body to brush away the great black horseflies that sting like the trader's iron things when heated in the fire.[3]

When the ravine grew shallow and there were no longer the bushy-headed tumbleweeds to hide him, he kicked his horse with his heels and rode straight at the startled bull. He stared stupidly at the oncoming horseman, then turned and lumbered off across the plains.

Second Son was surprised at his speed, but he soon saw that the bull was poor and would therefore have more wind than a fat one. He could hear the heavy breathing of his horse and he could see the tongue of the bull hanging out from his open mouth. Suddenly the bull stopped and faced him. When he circled him, the bull turned only his lowered head.

One shot from the white man's rifle brought him to his knees, then like the bank of the Arkansas loosened by many rains slides slowly down the slope, the bull rolled over and died.

The sun was low now and Second Son's long shadow fell across the buffalo as he skinned him. He was busy with the skinning. His horse wandered off and he could not watch his ears for signs of danger. There was a tumbleweed loosened from the earth and caught in others still standing, and the breeze played with it like the Pawnee play with their captives tied to a tree, and like the white captives of the Pawnee, it sang in the wind a little song of despair.

Thus with his horse out of sight and with no pricked-up ears to give him warning, and with the song of the imprisoned tumbleweed; and in his eagerness to get back to his father's lodge with the tongue, the humpribs, the heart and liver, before darkness, he heard no sound of the Cheyenne warriors behind him. It was only that his shadow thrown across the carcass became thicker.

He froze like a rabbit, but it was too late. His arms were caught and tied behind his back, then he was turned around to face the Cheyenne warriors who had come out of the sun.

They put him astride the yellow horse. Two of them examined his white man's gun diffidently. Another walked about the carcass spitting on the ground as a message for the wolves; a warning to them and the coyotes that this carcass belonged to man. They took the tongue, the heart, the liver and the humpribs, and rode with their captive back into the sun.

They rode through the night, and all night these tall, pale warriors talked in a strange tongue. It was not like the tongue of the Sioux, the Omaha or the Missouria which was the captive's own tongue, but like the chatter of coyotes, he believed.[4] They were as pale as a sick Osage, these tall warriors who had come out of the sun.

When they rode into camp, the women came to look at him, and he looked into the distance not seeing them. When one of his captors hit him across the face with a coup stick, he kept his eyes wide open and would not lose control of the muscles of his face. When they tied him to a gnarled cedar, the dogs sniffed at his legs and some of them growled. When one lifted his leg against him, the men jeered and the women laughed, and the round-faced children pointed to him and chattered like titmice.

He kept his eyes on the tall red butte in the distance, which was a sentinel of the Rocky Mountains; an outpost on the foothills. The men jeered him in the sign language of the plains. They pointed to him, and with the cupping of their hands on their chests indicated that underneath his shirt he was a woman.

All day he stayed there tied to the gnarled cedar, and many times that day, an old woman, who was like the dried peaches in the trader's store, would pass on her way to the spring, and each time she would spit at him. The men pointed to a fat dog and asked him if he was hungry, but he pretended that he did not hear the insult and kept his eyes on the red butte.

Then the sun went away and cold air slid down the slopes of the Rockies. Soon a great roaring could be heard which was repeated many times in the canyons of the mountains. The wind struck the lodges of the Cheyenne and the disturbed dust of the camp blinded him.

Soon he was alone and the rain came down like the mane of a stallion flowing in the wind. He opened his mouth and drank. As he looked up, he saw a magpie sitting in the top of the cedar, using the branches for shelter. The magpie was talking as magpies always talk, but this one was trying to tell him something. He listened. The magpie shook his wet feathers and drew them close to his body, then said, "you will see your father and mother again," and with this, he flew across to some friends in a tall aspen.

As the storm roared, Second Son strained at the lashings, and soon the wet and slippery elk thong came over his small hands, and he was free. He bent close to the ground and slipped into a ravine, then down it until he could walk upright. But soon he had to climb out as the reddish, swirling water rushed above his knees. He sat under a bushy cedar, with his head between his knees, and with his hands over his head and waited for the storm to abate.

Darkness came before the storm grew tired of its boasting. He walked out from his tree but could see nothing, so he went back to the spot where his body had kept the ground dry and attempted to sleep, but his thoughts and the fear that was like some animal in his heart kept him awake.

He thought of the glistening land between him and the camp far down the Arkansas; the land that was as hard and as barren as a buffalo-hide shield. There would be nothing but dry washes to hide in or the long sand dunes of the river with their sand-blasted willows and stunted cottonwoods crawling over them like hunger people. In this hard, shining land, the Cheyenne and the Arapahoe saw every thing that moved. Even if he could travel through the Cheyenne range at night, the Commanche were always proud to have an Osage scalp-lock to boast about. A lone warrior on foot in a strange land was a heaven-sent gift to the enemy of his people who first saw him.

By the time the light was barely coming into the horizon of the east, he had made up his mind. He was stiff with cold, but he stole silently back to the Cheyenne camp. There were no sentinels, since the Cheyenne were at home, and few enemies were bold enough to attack a home camp of the fighting Cheyenne. There were no sentinels but the horses were under guard. He crept up close to make sure; he was so close that a horse snorted. He lay still, then inch by inch crawled away. With no chance to get his yellow horse, or stampede the herd, he had only one chance to live left to him.

In the customs of the Osage, the Peace Chief's lodge is sanctuary for anyone who takes refuge there, no matter whether he be enemy or tribal transgressor, and Second Son believed that since the Great Osage had such a custom, the Cheyenne might have a like custom. He chose the largest of the lodges and crept toward it on his belly.

The camp dogs were suddenly aroused. He froze with his face in the damp earth. When his heartbeats became less insistent, he felt better, because then he could hear the far-off howl of a wolf. When he thought the dogs were back in their places, he crawled on. The morning was cold and damp and the light of the day came slowly as though reluctant to reign over such damp dreariness left by the storm of the night.

Again, just as he came close to the lodge of the chief which loomed in the darkness as a solid mass more extensive than the other masses, the dogs exploded from their windbreaks and their shelters and yelped excitedly. Some of them howled long and dolorously like wolves. Again his heart seemed to thump against the damp ground with the rhythm of the dance drums, and from the way it sounded in his ears, he felt that the damp earth must be carrying it to every ear in the camp.

He lowered his face into the heavy scents of the earth and waited. He waited for the excited, intensified, eager baying that would indicate his discovery by the camp mongrels, but it didn't come. One by one, they went back to their shelters, and only one remained to howl into the greying darkness for some time. Suddenly he broke his mournful mouthing and yelped with injured innocence, and Second Son knew that some woman had thrown a stone at him.

He crawled swiftly then and came to the opening of the chief's lodge, and there he sat just within the opening.

The light came slowly, and soon the people were astir. They stood and pointed at him and talked like coyotes. Children came to stare at him as he sat there, looking at nothing. He felt a movement behind him but he did not stir.

After some time the flap of the lodge was pushed aside, and he heard the plop of a doeskin robe, as a girl passed out of the lodge, brushing against him. She turned and looked at him, then quickly looked at her feet. His heart came into his throat, he felt, and he tried to look away but couldn't. When she looked at him again, the muscles about his mouth tingled, and the little people with tiny, fluttering wings began to work in his stomach. He thought of making the sign-language sign for Osage by brushing his hand along his roach, but the movement was clumsy and he felt deeply ashamed, and his face was burning.

She looked into his eyes a moment, then looked modestly at her feet again, hesitated, then with a quick movement touched him with her swinging robe as she re-entered the lodge.

With the touch of her robe and the scent of its clean smokiness, he forgot that he was cold and miserable and afraid. His heart found its normal position again, and he could feel it swell and send a warmth through his body which he thought must be his old courage coming back. When a young man stopped to leer at him, he looked back with defiance.

Second Son was asked to come into the lodge and food was placed before him. The chief called a council of the chieftains and they talked long in their coyote tongue. Second Son sat in the darkness of the lodge away from the light that streamed in at the flap and was like a beam pouring into the smoke hole. He sat motionless as the chieftains talked. One of them pointed to him with a long, crooked finger and talked with anger.

They departed. The chief sat and looked into the fire for a long time, and when a white man came into the lodge, he didn't look up from his gazing. The white man was grizzled and his eyes were almost hidden by his eyebrows like ferns hanging over the hole of a bank beaver. He and the chief talked, then the white man came over to Second Son and sat down beside him after taking his limp hand into his own horny one. The young man was surprised to hear his own language come from the mouth of the grizzled white man. "The chief says you will be his son," said the white man. "He says he wants this thing. He says his daughter wants him to buy you. He has no son, he says, and he says he wants a son in his lodge. He says his daughter wants a brother. It will be good, he says, if he has a son to hunt for him when he is old. He says it will be good for his daughter to have a brother."

The white man rose and walked out of the lodge without another word. Having lived with the tribes of the plains, he had lost his white man's volubility.

Thus Second Son, the Osage warrior debased by captivity and discouraged by the thoughts of the people about his seeking sanctuary in the lodge of the chief, was absolved of disgrace by his adoption. But he could see that the respect which the people now showed him came only from the teeth. He could see this but he didn't feel it because of the singing of his heart which shut out all other things. No thoughts could drown this singing. Being close to his new sister Flower-That-Sways-In-The-Wind made his heart sing all through the hours of the day, and during the night in his dreams. He watched her pack his horses for the long hunts, which was a sister's duty. He watched her pull the fringed sleeves of her robe above her elbows, as she fastened the packs and tied the thongs with her long copper fingers working like the delicate legs of the tarantula.

He built fires with cedar when hunting in the foothill country, because the smoke of the cedar was like the scent of her robe. He hunted for the right kind of willow and made an Osage flute. When the long nights of the hunting moon covered the foothills with silence, he dreamed by the fire. He dreamed in the light of his fire without fear in the region claimed by the Cheyenne as their range. As he dreamed he made songs, but there was never a song of hunting or of war; they were songs of sadness; songs about the beauty of Flower-That-Sways-In-The-Wind.

Sometimes when his deep emotion brought tears to his eyes, he would take out his flute and let its clear, monotonous plaintiveness express that which was in his heart. When he finally wrapped himself in his robes, he would dream that she was there beside him, and when he reached out to touch her, there was emptiness; emptiness and the eternal questioning of the coyotes somewhere in the darkness.

He learned to speak the Cheyenne tongue, but it was unnecessary when he was with her. There was then only the language of the heart that came into their faces, into their eyes and into their movements. The plop of her robe and the feel of it as it touched him, and the smoky, doeskin scent of her person made the little people crawl through his body and dance in his stomach.

She was his sister. She could pack his horses for the hunt, and serve him food, and they could talk together about his hunting and about the moccasins she made for him, but they never talked of the tall warrior with the scar that reached from his ear to his mouth. They never talked about the things this warrior did; about the red hair he had taken from a white trapper, or the unauthorized foray which he and his young men made against the Utes. When the town crier chanted the deeds of this young man, and especially when he stopped his horse in front of the chief's lodge to be sure that she had heard, they could not express the fear that was in their hearts.

They knew that this young hero had offered ten horses to her father for her and that the chief had declined only because his daughter had asked him to do so, and because he loved this beautiful daughter. They knew that someday the chief would say that it was time for a grandson and he would accept fifteen or twenty horses from the tall young warrior.

The tall young hero could also read the language of the heart that came into the faces of the brother and sister, and he hated the young Osage when he read these things. When their eyes met, there was hatred. Also, the tall young warrior, being a hero, was a leader and his young men began to look with contempt at Second Son, and there were whisperings that underneath his shirt he was a coward who had sought sanctuary.

These rumors arose above the singing in his heart when they grew under the subtle guidance of the tall young hero. One day, unable to stop his ears against the rumors that were like the buzzing of hornets, Second Son climbed to a high foothill, and there under the shade of a cedar, he took out a fragment of a trader's mirror, and with his paints, painted his face in the Osage manner. He then whetted his knife and walked into camp singing an Osage song; a song of war.

When the people came to look, he began to insult the tall young warrior in Cheyenne. In the middle of the camp circle, he stood and chanted insults, and the people came and stood about expectant.

Soon they began to whisper. "He knows Greybull is gone," they said. "He has come to challenge the air, this Osage. Greybull is hunting."

When he heard these whispers, he left the center of the camp as if he had not heard them, but his heart was filled with bitterness. For two days, he sat in the lodge with his head low. He would not look up. He knew that he must kill Greybull now, and the poison in his heart stopped his ears to the words of Flower-That-Sways-In-The-Wind. But they were like the cardinal that flashes in front of your horse, and drives away all thought of sadness; they were like the notes of the woodthrush, these words, and soon he listened.

He remembered only that she had said that she would "wait for six moons for his return." The arrangements were hers. It was soon learned that Second Son, the adopted son of the chief, would visit his people. He was given a horse and an escort of young warriors by the chief, and the leader of this escort was Greybull.

They rode through the sun-splashed plains to the east. As young Cheyenne, they rode boldly. They sang and laughed but said nothing to the chief's adopted son. Sometimes Greybull looked at the back of his shaven head or at the area between his shoulder blades when because of the sun, he had let his blanket slip down to his waist. Greybull's face was hard when he looked thus because his thoughts were urging him to draw his bow. The laws of the tribe kept it at his side, however.

When the party reached the woodlands Greybull, the Plains hunter, became nervous. He was worried that he couldn't see through the boles of the trees, and every shadow became an enemy. He kept looking back over his shoulder to the west; to the plains where one could see what was happening.

One night he couldn't sleep. He heard footsteps in the darkness of the trees, and it was very easy for him to convince himself that his young men were being led into an Osage ambush. He stealthily awakened his men one at a time, and they rode off through the trees back along their trail, leaving Second Son in his robes. They knew, however, that he had seen them go.

The next day Second Son rode on toward the permanent camp of the Osage on the river called Marshes of the Swans in the drainage region of the Missouri.[5] This was now Osage range and he rode singing a song of his people. Suddenly he fell silent. He left his horse and crept slowly among the trees. He saw his brother First Son bent over an elk he had just shot. When he saw him, First Son was frightened. He backed away saying, "you are dead." Second Son soon convinced him that he was not a spirit, and they went on to the camp together.

His father's eyes questioned, then his old hands trembled more than ever, and his mother came up to him and laid her head on his arm, mumbling.

Every day he spent talking with the young men of his band, and every night he saw the image of Flower-That-Sways-In-The-Wind, and some nights he cried in his robes because his heart was full of sadness.

For several moons he talked with his young men. He sent out bands to take horses from the Pawnee, and he sent parties to far-off Red River to take horses from the Caddo, and from the white trespassers and hunters. When they came back with horses and everything was ready, he went to his older brother and asked for the medicine bundle and for the war songs that went with it. But First Son was jealous of his stories about his adventures and wouldn't let him have them.

There was no use. All was ready but he couldn't go on the war path without the medicine bundle and the war songs. He went into the woods and sat for a long time, and as he sat, the crows taunted him, saying that he had lost his courage. He got up and shouted at them, and waved his bow at them.

That night in his dream Flower-That-Sways-In-The-Wind came to him, and the next morning he was filled with determination and courage. He called his young men together and they rode away to the west, without the sacred bundle. As they rode, he made up his own songs, and each one had in it the defiance that stirs the heart of the singer.

Bands of Pawnee watched them from a distance but were afraid to attack such a large party of painted warriors. When they neared the

Cheyenne range, they scattered and traveled in pairs and traveled only at night, ever alert for signals from each other.

They reached the place of meeting at sunset and watched the activity of the Cheyenne camp. The intensity of Second Son and his songs, which came from the depths of his heart, inspired them as though they had danced the war dance for four days and nights.

All night they lay and just before dawn they struck; they struck when they heard the hooves of the stampeded horses. Members of their party had crawled up in the darkness and killed the guards, then stampeded the herd. This was the signal for the attack.

The Cheyenne, taken off guard, were overwhelmed by the shouting, diabolically painted Osage. During the terrific fighting, Second Son had a guard placed about the lodge of the chief.

When the fight was over and the horses were herded ready for the trip back to the Osage camp, Second Son ordered the chief's horses to be left with him. As he told the chief of this, the haughty old man looked coldly at him, and said nothing.

Then Flower-That-Sways-In-The-Wind stood before him. They looked at each other and there was no thought of anything outside themselves. There was no thought of the smoke that hung over the camp in long ribbons. They did not hear the first dismal keening of a woman from the foothills, or notice the tired, bedaubed followers of Second Son, standing in groups waiting.

They stood for a moment only, then the relaxed, soft muscles of Second Son's face became taut again. He looked about him like the golden eagle on his hunting station, then walked toward his horse, and Flower-That-Sways-In-The-Wind followed.

The Flower on Cadron Creek

The Cherokee were gathering at the designated spot on the Hiwassee River in eastern Tennessee under orders of the military, to await removal to their new homes west of the Mississippi River.[1] The flatboats were tied up waiting on the opposite bank of the river; waiting for the people to come reluctantly, bitterly, vindictively, hopelessly to the rendezvous with what property was left to them after the opportunistic whites had swarmed over their land and had with the aid of the military driven them from their great and small houses. Some of their faithful slaves had come with them, but many had been appropriated by the whites along with the other property, and some had fled to become lost in the mountains and the forests.

In Andrew Jackson's first message to the Congress, he had asked for the removal of the Cherokee along with other tribes, and later a treaty had been signed by a minority gathering of the Cherokee Nation and they had signed away their lands in eastern Tennessee, in North Carolina and in Georgia, and the United States Government was in the process of forcing the conditions of the treaty upon the Nation as a whole.[2] They were forced from their manorial homes, from their huts hidden in the forests of the Great Smokies; from their cotton plantations and their tobacco plantations and from their little corn fields. Now they were being gathered to be sent to the new lands west of the Mississippi on the fringe of the domain claimed by the plains warriors.

They came to the rendezvous on the Hiwassee through the dripping forest and across the yellow, frothy stream in ox carts, horseback and afoot and in six-horse wagons sent by the military to gather them. The

"Mountain Towns," the fullbloods from the mountain sides, came quietly afoot or in the six-horse government wagons. The mixedbloods came burdened with their property, their children, their weeping slaves and their hurt dignity.

At the shelters which the government had constructed for their convenience, they unloaded their things and waited. The fullbloods sat as though detached from the world; from both the good and the ill of the world, and the mixedbloods gathered into knots and talked and berated the President, Andrew Jackson.

Lieutenant Thomas Fuller in charge of the detachment, strutted now, after the shock that had brought dejection when he learned that he would be in charge of sullen Indians migrating halfway across the continent. He had been deeply disappointed when he realized that there would be no balls in stately white columned mansions; that there would be no strains of the minuet and beautiful southern belles with whom he might flirt.

But after the first pangs of disappointment, he had begun to feel that there was some compensation. He had been out of West Point only eight years and here he was in the responsible command over a large party of emigrants. And he was pleased to note that not all were sullen fullbloods, but many were people of education, of culture, and this made his command all the more important, even though the cultured ones might also ignore him. And there was glory here in this command. There had not been much excitement in New Hampshire where he grew up, and when he left the Point, the wars of glory were over, and the Indian wars of the Plains were still in the future.

He put his dress uniform away carefully, and he would leave it at Chattanooga when they floated by on their flatboats. He had now reconciled himself to the prospect of barbaric adventure, and there would be soldierly responsibility instead of sparkling eyes, soft lights, dreamy music and romantic moonlights.

As the members of the Nation gathered, the shifty-eyed white men of the lowest order followed to squeeze the last benefit from their tragedy. Trade boats floated down from the Clinch and the Holston rivers, and from the headwaters of the Tennessee to the mouth of the Hiwassee, thence up to the encampment.[3] They sold cakes and pies and fruits; cider applejack and whiskey, and some carried hard-eyed women.

Lieutenant Fuller could do little about this; he sneeringly called the trade boats "floating doggeries."[4] There was no plan by the military to obviate this menace, and soon there was shrill feminine laughter cracking the silence of the darkness, loud swearing and weeping violins disturbing the peace of the little encampment. Being a West Point man, he wanted authority to deal with this barbaric orgy, but having none, he had to stay close to his quarters in fear of insults that no gentleman could brook without himself causing bloodshed.

The rains continued and the dejected tribesmen crawled into camp in government wagons or in their own conveyances; or they came on horseback and afoot, and Lieutenant Fuller stood and watched them from his shelter. He felt impatience now, and he was filled with excitement in anticipating the great adventure. It would mean that he, a young man, would be in full command of a horde of people until they should arrive at the lands across the Mississippi. His word would be the law; he would be the judge and the jury. He was only a young man and there is no wonder that he appreciated his own importance.

He had appointed his assistants and delegated authority to them, and they stood about pointing out the camping places to the arrivals as they came up. As the days wore on, all the government shelters were taken, and the remaining families must be shown to camping places in the open. He felt a responsibility toward these people who being obviously people of culture, must be treated in such a manner with their slaves and their valuable equipment. He wanted to do something for them, but there was nothing to be done. He knew that they in their hauteur would accept no special favors from the symbol of their persecution. Many of them spoke English with strange accuracy and purity, and he would respect their opinion of himself. He would sometimes express his unhappiness that they had only the weeping sky for a roof, but there would be no smiles from these people and no interchange of the amenities. They thanked him with dignity.

But he believed it was better that way. He had authority to exercise, and even the mutual understanding and respect of the cultured and the lettered was not conducive to efficiency, and this emigration certainly had a military nature and flavor.

Then, the day before the flatboats were brought over from the opposite banks of the Hiwassee to be loaded for the departure, a wagon stopped just opposite to where he was standing. The Negro driver sat upright and straight with great dignity as though instead of driving a creaking, hub-knocking wagon, he were seated on the driver's seat of a landau.[5] Sitting beside him was a tall man with greying black hair resting on the shoulders of his broadcloth coat. He was dark; perhaps like a Spaniard, but he was a Cherokee mixed-blood gentleman. Lieutenant Fuller was quick at such appraisals of social status.

The bed of the wagon was piled high with personal effects, and when the tall man climbed out over the wheel, Lieutenant Fuller instinctively folded his arms across his chest, suddenly feeling his authority and his dignity in the presence of this gentleman who would certainly make a point of ignoring him.

When the dignified driver had climbed down, the tall man began to give him instructions about the unloading, and the former waved to the wagon that had stopped behind the first one, and several slaves came running forward to get their instruction from the driver of the first wagon. When several more came up to help with the unloading, Lieutenant Fuller looked back to see several more wagons coming up, piled with goods and slaves. All the wagons were pulled by horses of high breeding, and they were splashed with yellow mud and sweat foam flaked off from under their collars and their breeching. He saw that the tall gentleman intended to camp right there without anyone's leave. He would take no offense at the tall gentleman's attitude in ignoring him, but about his obvious contempt of the authority which he represented, he was not quite sure. There was something about the tall man's presumptions that caused him to hesitate, especially when it occurred to him that the tall gentleman would negotiate with him through his black man. He thought he might call one of his assistants but the tall gentleman would certainly pay no attention to a civilian of his own Nation. He decided to bow courteously and speak to the tall man himself.

But as he started to the wagon framing his courteous salute and his perfectly formal military attitude in his mind, he noted that a girl had descended from one of the wagons in the rear and was coming toward the first wagon where the tall man stood. She lifted her skirts from the mud and there was a smile on her face which seemed to express her contempt for the situation. Immediately behind her waddled an old mammy, black and fat and grumbling. She carried the girl's shawl, sprawled across which was a great angry Chinese dragon in red.

The Lieutenant stopped his motion and stared. He could do this since he was absolutely unnoticed, even in uniform. Most of the gathering people looked at him, he had noted; some with open hatred, some with casual interest and some with a look of fear, as if they were thinking "what now." But to these recent comers, he might have been a hitching post.

And now his urges were colored by the girl. Suddenly he had no thought of directing the tall man to camp in a certain place; he only wanted to walk up to the gentleman, make a proper bow and place the United States Army at his service, then walk away as though he had very important business elsewhere; at the other end of the encampment, hoping that the girl's eyes might rest with deep interest on his very broad shoulders as he hurried away. He could trust his shoulders to serve his vanity well.

He did just this, but as he walked away he was not sure that he had made the gallant picture he had visualized. He felt with some degree of discomfort that he had almost said too much and stayed too long after his correct bow to the tall gentleman. His hard military efficiency had been effected by clumsiness and the evidence of a terrible weakness which urged him to stay in the presence of the girl he had pretended to ignore, as he bowed to the tall gentleman.

When he had arrived at the other end of the encampment to which he had so efficiently hurried, he had nothing to do and he thought only of keeping out of the sight of the latest arrivals. However, he soon regained his feeling of importance. A circle of men had formed quickly about the two white hangers-on, slashing at each other with knives. This gave him the occupation he needed. He had his assistants take the knives and he banished the two from the encampment, and he fondled the hilt of his sword as he gave the command.

This diversion compensated him for the recent lack of confidence when his whole being was disturbed by the grace and the beauty of the girl stepping daintily across the mud holes. He noted the expressions of respect on the faces of the men who had formed the circle about the slashers. The "I allus try to do what's right" look had come into the eyes of the shifty men of the circle as he gave his commands, and this aided his self-esteem tremendously.

The next morning the boats were loaded and there was the muddle of leave-taking. Men and women, having said goodbye affectionately to relatives and friends on the banks of the river, would with brimming emotion jump up from their places where they had piled their personal effects and rush back up the slippery banks to fall into waiting arms again. Tears would stream and grimaces of fear and black unhappiness would distort their faces. Some in blind despair jumped from the boats after they had been pushed out into the current of the river, attempting to say one more goodbye to those left weeping on the bank. These had to be rescued and the Lieutenant would have been very hard with them if he had not been conscious of the fact that the screen on the stern that gave some privacy to the tall man and the girl was near. He realized that she might not be interested in what was going on, but the very fact of her presence caused him to stoop over himself to help haul in a wet, weeping Cherokee woman, mourning her fate in some strange tongue.

From the deck of a flat boat, he had watched the fat mammy show the whites of her eyes as she lifted her streaming face to the sky to say something to God, then lay her head upon the shoulder of the girl and weep with the abandonment of a child. He had watched the other slaves standing with their hats in their hands listening to the last instructions of the tall master, then the tall gentleman and the girl had torn themselves away from the now weeping and shouting Negroes and came aboard without looking back. He had seen the set face of the tall gentleman and the flash of the dark eyes of the girl looking at nothing as they went to their allotted space in the stern.

The Negroes then had drawn his full attention. One man chanted as he looked at the sky, and he turned completely at intervals as he chanted. Several dropped to their knees and rolled their eyes to heaven as they prayed and wept. The fat mammy now wept silently and shook like a great doll made of jelly. Then as the flatboat floated in the current of the Hiwassee, the group disappeared, suddenly screened by the new leaves of the trees as the boat curved with the current. Even the black man who had detached himself from the group to run along the bank weeping and praying in some rhythmical chant was lost to view.

The boats floated silently on the current of the Hiwassee to its mouth, then came onto the swifter current of the broad Tennessee River and the days passed like the hours of eternity. All seemed calm and purposeful, and there was no danger or other emergency to occupy the people's time so they could wonder about what lay ahead of them far away up the Arkansas River in the savage lands that lay on the fringe of the forests where it melted into the plains. There the painted Osage would be waiting for them with war axe and arrow but before they reached the lands west of the Mississippi, there might be malaria and cholera. They knew malaria. Many a yellow-faced white man carried it about with him, and as they glided along the current of the Tennessee, they saw hollow-eyed children clinging in fear to their staring mother's wide skirts, gazing at them, and they knew that malaria had touched them.[6]

But cholera drove fear into their hearts past the sentries of reason. They knew it as an evil spirit that hovered over the waters of the lower Tennessee, or hid in the forests in the mists of the early morning and wandered in wisps of poison vapor at night creeping into their bodies as they slept among their things on the flatboats.

For Lieutenant Fuller, the rumors of cholera along their route had crystallized into hard, glittering fact and he had spent several days worrying, but he was young and he was starting on the adventure of his short life, and he was filled with the thrill of it as one might be filled who expects battle. Then added to the expectations of adventure and danger there was romance on the stern of the boat in the form of a girl. He would welcome danger for the sake of becoming her protector; perhaps so that he might even sacrifice his own life for her, so greatly had he been affected by her eyes, her manner of complete indifference to his existence, and by her daily presence on the same flatboat.

The measles broke out on the flatboats and there would be times when they would tie up to bury some child who had died of them. They would solemnly dig a grave in the alluvium and a fullblood minister of the gospel would dedicate the soul to God, and the boat would glide on with some tragic woman standing with her eyes fixed on the disturbed earth made into a mound, chanting to some dimly remembered god.

The days passed and several times during a week, they would tie up to the bank for an hour or more, leaving a fresh mound of earth as they pushed out to the current; a mound which the wolves would sniff at and wonder about.

They struggled over Muscle Shoals, and at the little settlement of Waterloo, they left their flatboats and boarded the steamboat Western Sun and took keelboats in tow so that the whole party could be transported.[7] At Waterloo, they had to wait until the boatman paying homage to a river tradition got blind drunk and recovered, before they could proceed.

Now they floated and were aided by the great paddlewheels of the side wheeler Western Sun, as they traveled north down the Tennessee and finally onto the current of the very broad, chocolate-colored Ohio.[8] Day by day on the overwhelming Ohio, the forest slid by with occasional clearings like distance markers. In some of the clearings, there were settlements and in some, only solitary log cabins, with women and children standing on the bluffs or the steep banks as silent and as motionless as wax figures. In some of the clearings, men would leave their oxen and their plows to stand and stare at the dark-skinned people on the decks of the Western Sun and on the keelboats towed behind.

They were only a short time on the Ohio, then they came out of the mouth of it onto the Mississippi before they were aware. When the people heard that they were on the Mississippi they began to take fresh interest and to gaze across the broad waters to the forested banks far away. It seemed to them now that they had escaped the evil spirit, the deadly cholera that they had expected to come out of the mists of the Tennessee. Here in the middle of the great Mississippi, the mysterious forests and the sinister mists where the cholera might lie hidden seemed to be safe distances from the boats.

There was more activity with people coming on deck to cook their food over one of the designated fireplaces. Lieutenant Fuller even caught glimpses of the girl as she came up to busy herself about a fire. At all other times, she stayed below in her cabin.

Then he had to order that the fires must be put out as darkness came, after Red Fox's wife, starting below from one of the fires, was blinded by the glare momentarily, and had slipped, falling overboard. The great river's current was carrying them swiftly, and they were unable to rescue her. There was only a shriek in the darkness, then calm again after the excitement, and then Red Fox standing looking out over the blackness refusing to go below. He stood there until the sun made blood splashes on the water the next morning, then he went below to mourn.

There was a ripple of excitement like a wind that comes up suddenly after a suffocating day, when they reached the mouth of the Arkansas.[9] Somewhere up this river lay the land which the government had traded to them for their ancestral homes back in Tennessee, Georgia and North Carolina. They had floated down the Tennessee, the Ohio and the Mississippi, now the paddle wheels of the steamboat labored and thrashed like some great beast up the Arkansas, and its groans and its thrashings echoed along the forest walls seeming to hem them in now after the broad Mississippi. Soon Lieutenant Fuller had to order some of the keelboats in tow cut loose and their occupants to make camp on shore until other arrangements could be made. He had difficulty in making them understand that they were not being abandoned and when some members of the same family had to be separated, their fear and unhappiness touched him.

He wasn't the hard military man anymore. He had begun to develop a helpless sympathy for these tragic people who were not in the least tragic in their calm acceptance of fate's decrees. There was a nobility in them he noted that shone out brightly in contrast with the whites and some of the mixedbloods who whimpered quite often. When he had picked up a doctor to attend his measles patients, he could only persuade him to stay with the boat for sixty or a hundred miles, and he would then be compelled to find another for the same distance of travel. At first he could plan the stops for the burials with cold efficiency, telling off certain men to dig the graves and attend to details, but the silent fullbloods standing at the graveside like trees with their limbs broken began to affect him. Now he dreaded the moment when he had to give the order to tie up and tell off his men for the duty that was becoming more and more tragic to him.

As the disease grew in intensity, so did the mechanical troubles seem to grow in the shallow current filled with sandbars and "sawyers," and death and trouble came together as the Western Sun labored and thrashed the waters of the Arkansas into white, crystalline sparks and foam. There were frequent stops to repair paddles or for getting wood for the boilers, and sometimes they buried a child, repaired paddles and got wood all at the same stop.

The young Lieutenant often walked the deck in the darkness alone, and he felt no more the glory of his position and had forgotten West Point. As he walked, he often found himself thinking of the girl somewhere below. But sometimes during his thoughts of grave responsibility that grew like some malignant pressure, he found himself building up conditions wherein she was in great need of his aid. He saw in fancy a hairy-faced boatman who had got a jug of whiskey during one of the stops, and red-eyed and wandering had insulted her. He could see himself running the beast through with his sword or perhaps putting him in chains, then bowing to her and walking off coldly and efficiently while her beautiful, and now adoring eyes rested on his broad shoulders. He, on discovering himself enjoying such fancies would become very much ashamed of himself, especially did he become chagrined one star-dominated night when he realized that his sword arm was actually extended in imaginary thrust.

Disaster followed disaster. The stops became more frequent, as children continued to die and the paddles were constantly being broken on buried tree trunks and on rocks. They traveled only during the daylight hours now; the Arkansas was too dangerous at night. During the long waits of the nights, the boatmen would become restless through idleness and there were fist fights and fights with hunting knives and some drunkenness, but now when Lieutenant Fuller needed his military hardness most, it had been weakened by the human despair about him, and instead of military justness toward these men, he hated their shifty eyes, their hairy faces and their braying laughter that disturbed the silences of the nights. His orders were harsh to them and sometimes unreasonable as his sympathy for the emigrants grew.

It was the day they passed the mouth of Cadron Creek some miles above the settlement of Little Rock when he believed that the climax had been reached. Across the river stretched an impassable sand bar, and he had to order the boat back to the mouth of the little creek, so that they might go into camp and await the spring floods from the Rocky Mountains. Here at the confluence of Cadron Creek and the Arkansas River, they went into camp among the cedars and the oaks that stood like staring people.

During the activity, he saw the tall man and the girl carrying their equipment up from the boat to a chosen place for their camp. They worked easily, denying themselves the aid of a slave offered by a mixedblood family. The tall man was genial and spoke to the others about him with a smile, and once the laughter of the girl rang out when the tent suddenly collapsed on the tall man. There was a child to be carried away from camp for burial and there was a fight between two boatmen which shouted for his attention but still he wanted very much to approach the tall man with the offer of manual aid. But of course this was not even a thought, but an instinctive urge, and he knew that his presence near them would only bring contempt into their faces.

For several days, he rode over the countryside visiting the lonesome little cabins and the little settlements in search of teams and wagons to take his party overland if the Arkansas' rise was delayed. It was the planting season and the settlers needed their horses, but he found a cheerful settler who was also a doctor, who agreed to relieve the doctor who had come this far with the boat, and attend the sick. He believed that the water would soon come from the melting snows of the Rockies, or that he could eventually find horses and wagons to transport the migrating people.

But in the forests of Arkansas, the evil spirit that waited there saw the weakness of the people on the little creek called Cadron, and struck suddenly. Dr. Wills tired from his attendance on the sick sat on a log and stared at the ground between his feet. Lieutenant Fuller walked over to him and sat beside him. He had to tell someone about his horse being stolen; the only one in camp and one which he had procured for his use in riding out to search for transportation and food. It had been stolen by white renegades. Dr. Wills didn't even comment but looked at the young man sadly, then he said with false strength in his voice:

"Lieutenant, two members of the Bruce family died this morning—of—of—cholera."

The young man sat for some time, then he said quietly:

"Can you stay with me, doctor?"

The doctor had returned his gaze to the spot between his feet and answered; "I can't leave, Lieutenant, they'll need me more than my own patients."

Several boatmen were caught sneaking off when they heard about the deaths in the Bruce family, and they had to be overtaken and brought back to aid the stricken ones. The fullbloods began to move their camp fires away from the center of the encampment, and smoke curled from among the cedars in widely scattered spots. And when members of their families were stricken, Dr. Wills and Lieutenant Fuller had to cover an increasingly greater area to attend them.

They stepped among the people lying among the cedars and to the living they gave from one half grain to a full grain of opium, and from fifteen to forty grains of calomel. The dead they buried immediately.

Blond hair came upon the face of the young man and black hair sprinkled with white came upon the face of the doctor, and their eyes were deep in their sockets. They had little aid. They had to keep guard on the white men to keep them from sneaking off into the forests, and the fullbloods silently aided them in burying the dead, but otherwise sat and waited.

They could get no aid from the settlers. They ran into their homes and shut their doors when they saw one of these haggard men approaching them. The whites and the mixedbloods became afraid of each other, and their imaginations became acute. They picked up every rumor and wept and prayed and became savagely protective of their own persons. The young officer saw a white man standing over the body of his mixedblood child, shaking his fist at the sky, while his fullblood wife stood with her hands folded in front of her looking down at the small body. This picture became a symbol to him for the rest of his life.

Smoke filled the air. The fullbloods burnt the dead grass of the last season and the cedars crackled in flame. Thus did they attempt to kill the evil spirit or send it back into the forests, or keep it at bay, but still they died three and four and even ten on some days, and the burial parties got no sleep.

Just as the young officer's military efficiency become absorbed by his sympathy for the dignified suffering of the fullbloods in their silence and their dry-eyed submission here and on the river, so did his romantic fancies woven about the girl become absorbed by his constant thought and his endless activity in behalf of his charges. He became stupefied with fatigue.

He scarcely realized that she and the tall man were also busy caring for their people and that he now saw her quite often. He had now forgotten that she hated him as a symbol of the power that had forced the removal of her people from their homes, and by indifference had made this tragedy possible. He did, however, know that now he might approach her and feel some comfort in being close to her, but his sympathy and his duty overwhelmed all.

She and the tall man had attended Red Fox, and when he came with a party for the body, he caught her looking at him as he gave directions in his tired voice. The tall man nodded; he knew now that the tall man was her father. She had looked at him with approval, but the look that would have made his heart sing a month earlier, now was not even dignified by his consciousness as an incident of any importance at all in this drama of death, and tragic tears that never welled from the heart.

When he spoke to her finally, he was no more the proud officer from West Point with his histrionic courtesy, but a very brave young man who having reached the end of his strength and will was almost ready to accept the fullblood philosophy and wait. As he rode by the settlers' cabins this time, he was not interested in the children fleeing toward their cabins to fear-crazed mothers waiting for them in the open doors; he had no contempt for them. He was aware only of the hands of the little Wills boy clutching his shirt as he rode behind him on the lame plow horse he had finally managed to capture. That clutching hand gave sharpness to his feeling of futility because the very clutch of the dirty little hands was expressing hope and confidence that must be deceived. The little boy's face had changed from expressing fear to the expression of peace like in one who has found shelter, when he had arrived at camp breathlessly to tell him that his father Dr. Wills was ill. The young man knew from that moment that he was alone now, and now as he approached the cabin of Dr. Wills in the woods, he felt like the fullbloods looked as they sat among the cedars, waiting.

He saw her as he entered the room. She stood looking at him and he could say nothing. It must have been that seeking expression on his face; that seeking for refuge in the maternal spirit which brought the mother beauty into her face, but he scarcely noticed it. It was only for a moment that they looked at each other, then he glanced at the sheet-covered body of Dr. Wills. There were only the children and Mrs. Wills in the room besides themselves. The children watched him expectantly but Mrs. Wills lay on a pallet in the corner of the room with her face to the wall.

"Where—can I get some neighbors?" He knew the question was stupid after he had asked it.

"They are afraid," said the girl calmly.

They looked at each other again over the mound of fresh earth back of the cow lot, then he rode to Little Rock to get a conveyance for Mrs. Wills and children, so that they could go into the settlement.

As he rode back stirrup to stirrup with Dr. Baird, he couldn't even begin to tell him the story, and the doctor did not press him.

After three days more, the disease left as quickly as it had come, and a day came when there was no funeral, then three days passed and a week went by and there was no calling off of names for the burial parties. Those who were in good health began to talk about the hellish tragedy with the comfort people have when they have escaped the fate of others about them.

Then one day, Lieutenant Fuller slept all day with his clothes off, and when he came out from his shelter, the sun was lancing the cedars both charred and green with its late afternoon shafts. All was quiet. He smelled the now almost sickening odor of salt pork frying. The salt pork and the flour, both cornmeal and wheat, were the only foods to be found in camp. The sick had been sustained by salt pork and the well had eaten it three times a day. Now the odor seemed to be carried along on the coalescing smokes of the cooking fires and seemed intent on following him.

He walked up among the cedars beyond the fullblood fires and sat on a log trying to make himself think. Most of the boatmen had succeeded in getting into the woods despite his constant watch, and the water in the river remained clear and unstained by flood sediments. Tomorrow, he must find horses and wagons. He noted that there were several horses in camp now procured by the mixedbloods. He felt too weak to ride out. He had taken opium but he knew he must show himself every day or the morale of the camp would be shattered, and anyway he felt like fighting again now since the disease had gone and he had slept.

Then he saw the girl coming toward him. She must have some business with some of the fullblood families, he thought, but with all his heart he wanted her to come to him and sit by him on the log. She wouldn't need to say anything. As she approached her dark eyes were on him and they had that look he had seen at the Wills cabin. She was coming to him. He rose and bowed, and she smiled.

She put out her hand: "Father approves of my coming to you," she said. "When he is stronger, he wants to thank you for what you have done for our people, and in the meantime allow me to offer my thanks."

He looked into her eyes and they were filled with something he needed terribly, but he couldn't have expressed what he felt about his need. It was as deep as hunger or thirst. He became as canny as a dope addict to influence her to stay for a moment, for an hour, forever by him.

"Please sit down," he said. He tried to be facetious, "on this Chippendale piece."[10]

She sat by him on the log. He could smell sandalwood strangely mixed with wood smoke. Her shining dark eyes seemed to bore into him and he felt ashamed of his ragged beard and moustache.

Then she laughed: "I might introduce myself—I'm Anne MacDonald and my father is Coosa MacDonald, an assistant chief of the Cherokee Nation, although he's only an eighth Cherokee.[11] He insisted on traveling with the people; to share the worst of their ill fortune. He seems to think that he is someway responsible for their tragedy by his not having more influence with Mr. Jackson."

"I am Lieutenant Thomas Fuller, trying to carry out the orders of my superiors," he said. He felt his lips crack as he attempted to smile.

She looked at him, and the expression which he had seen in the Wills cabin; that maternal expression came to her face again, even though behind it, she seemed to be in deep thought.

"Father and I are going on ahead tomorrow. We've got wagons for ourselves and some of the fullbloods who are still weak and ill."

There was a long silence. The sun had taken its lances with it as it sank, and its blood-colored reflection on the river was fading.

Lieutenant Fuller had no dope-addict cunning now. He felt weary and lost. Human goodness and the high glory of self-sacrifice had passed with the passing of Dr. Wills, to leave him alone in his end-of-the-world unhappiness, and now beauty would pass from this awful place leaving him staring after it, forsaken. He didn't want to speak but his weariness and sense of being lost forced the words:

"Anne—Anne MacDonald, beauty will go with you. Forgive me; I'm weak from all this," and he waved his hand toward the smoke from the many fires that in the heaviness of the late afternoon air hung like a silken scarf just above the tree tops, "or I guess I wouldn't say it like this—but—but I love you." In his weakness, he felt like crying. He continued; "I loved you from the first day I saw you at the gathering grounds on the Hiwassee." There was long silence. "That's all," he said as he sighed almost inaudibly, "that's all there is to it." He wanted to explain to her that he realized he shouldn't be placing himself in a position to be rejected but there seemed to be a species of sweetness in defeat now, and he might as well kill everything; every hope and begin all over again.

She looked at his sunken cheeks and his eyes that retreated into their sockets. She had stolen many a glance at him when he strutted in the encampment on the Hiwassee and on the rivers, and she had seen his handsome, arrogant face clean-shaven, and his glances that darted with assurance. Now she saw his soul in the sunken eyes and heroism in the hollow cheeks covered with a wild growth of blond hair, and tears came to her eyes. She put her hand on his for an answer, but he would not feel the completeness and the deep significance of that response to his confession until he could think clearly and feel sharply again.

And they sat thus looking at the burnt-over ground in front of them, and their eyes were fixed on a little flower that had sprung up after the fire had destroyed the grass of last season and the green cedars. It nodded bravely and boldly and was filled with hope in this acrid blackness of destruction.

Moccasin Prints

The old chief sat, running his thumb and forefinger along the edge of his red and blue blanket. He was impatiently waiting for the big day; tomorrow. A frown came to his face when he heard the slamming of a car door. He dreaded that sound when he sat alone at the little ranch house among the hills, with only his old body servant to protect him.

His frown deepened as he waited. Then he heard the sharp tapping of high heels on the porch and the frown faded. His granddaughter Maria came into the room quietly and with a quick smile for him that revealed her well-cared-for teeth. They were very white against her copper skin.

"How," she said as she raised her hand and smiled. She went to the little mirror on the wall which was always awry, straightened it, then gave her hair as black as a crow's wing several strokes with her pocket comb.

She looked back over her shoulder: "Tomorrow, hein?"

The old chief answered simply, "how."

"We must have a good speech," she said in English. "This man is a Lord—from England. He is an Ambassador. He has come out here to see the Indians. We must have a good speech."

"How," said the old man in English, "good one."

"The committee is decorating the Crystal Room with flags; American and British flags." She saw the lack of comprehension in his old face, then she said in Wah-Sa-She,[1] "white men are doing many things. He is a great man, this man from England. They want to make him happy. They do many things; they eat their cigars now and talk

160

with their hands. There will be many people there at that feast; many white people. But you will sit by this great man at that feast. You will make the good-friend talk."

"How."

"This talk must be good-friend talk. This great man knows about the Wah-Sa-She. This man knows that they are great people. But you will make friend-talk; you will not talk about greatness of your ancestors. You will not talk about fights with Pawnee and Commanche lo-o-o-ong time ago" (where Wah-Sa-She always won, she thought). She continued: "This man wants to know if you are glad he came here. He wants to know what is in your heart because he has come many sleeps to see you."

"How."

Maria was quick. She fumbled her bag and got out a notebook and a pencil. Her grandfather watched her. She was like a dark flower, he believed, but she was like the white nurse at the hospital, when his horse fell. She would make him do something; he knew the sign. She was acting like that white nurse at the hospital.

But he was happy that she was here. That slammed car door might have been his son, her father, with white man's whiskey on his breath, asking for money. It might have been one of his many grandchildren coming to visit with him, but always in the end asking him for money. It might have been the fat man from the Chamber of Commerce in a great hurry, eating his cigar that had no fire, talking pidgin English and waving his arms; telling the chief of the Wah-Sa-She what to say to the great man from England; how to say the welcome.

He was glad Maria was here. She would protect him from all the others. There was a pile of papers by his chair with her picture in them, and he had studied them over and over during the long hours. They were pictures of her in a short skirt, balanced on her toes, as though she would fly away.[2] He knew that Maria was important, although he couldn't understand why. If she were not important, white man would not put her picture in the papers and in the magazines. His heart sang when he thought of this, and that which she told him had weight because of those pictures.

He heard her pencil on the notebook and he looked at her for some time. She would make paper talk for him to say to the great man. She was like the white nurse at the hospital when his horse fell. He became irascible. He waved his hand which held his eagle-tail fan. He waved it toward her and over the notebook as though he would wipe out the paper talk.

She looked up at him indulgently, then continued writing. He scolded her, holding up his cane this time, menacingly.

"Pee-she, bad," he said. "Throw that thing away. I shall tell this man about Washon'ton," he said in Wah-Sa-She.

Again the indulgent smile from Maria. "He knows about Washington. He lives there. He has a great home there. He is great messenger from England."

She wondered if he could get the significance of Lord Dorset's position. There was no word for Ambassador in Wah-Sa-She.

She saw that her grandfather was angry, and when he motioned for her to come near him, she humored him. He shut his eyes as he did when he visited his ancient memories. He did this to shut out the modern world of which he was not a part.

"I shall tell this man about Standing Bull who was many times my grandfather."[3]

(Here it goes, she thought.) But she knew she must humor him. He laced his long, bony old fingers and seemed to shut his eyes tighter against the world of the present.

"He was young man, my grandfather many times back, lo-o-o-o-ong time ago. He was Standing Bull. When he was old, he told this thing to his son Buffalo Hide. This Buffalo Hide told this thing to his son White Bull, and White Bull told this thing to Bull Pawing Earth. He was my father, Bull Pawing Earth, and the others were my fathers too, and I, Bull Head, will tell this thing which Standing Bull said lo-o-o-ong time ago. I will say to this great man that one day when Standing Bull was young man, Ee-Sta-Heh, Heavy Eyebrows, came to camp of my people. My people said, 'there are the Ee-Sta-Heh, Heavy Eyebrows—they have come to bring our little girls back.'

"But these Ee-Sta-Heh were soldiers. They knew nothing about the little girls other Ee-Sta-Heh, Heavy Eyebrows, had carried away to make women of them. My people had heard them crying like crows carried away by the owl who comes before the moon goes to sleep. Like crows the owl has taken, my people heard the voices of their little girls die far away in the night. These Ee-Sta-Heh with hairy faces had killed our bull-boats, and there was no trail on the water of the river to follow.[4] My people could not follow the bateaux of the Heavy Eyebrows. Now when they saw the soldiers of Heavy Eyebrows, they said: 'tompa, Heavy Eyebrows have come to tell us about our little girls, which their people with hairy faces have carried away like the owl carries away the crow in the night.'

"But these Ee-Sta-Heh, Heavy Eyebrows, soldiers said nothing about their people with faces like the coon, who carried away our little girls. There were many gifts. There were the rifles of the white man, and tobacco and many beads with all the colors when you look at Grandfather the sun with your eyes closed. There were these beads for moccasins and there was shrouding for the women, and there was much powder and lead, and there was pet-sa-ne, fire water.

"They gave our young men a little pet-sa-ne. Then they said that the Long Knives were coming to kill us and carry our women away. They said they knew where the Long Knives were. If we came with our friends, the Heavy Eyebrows, many sleeps, we could kill the Long Knives, and then we would not have to think about this thing. We could sleep on our ears, and only a small boy could guard the horses. Many words came from the tongues of the Heavy Eyebrows, and our young men turned their ears to them, and followed the Heavy Eyebrows toward the place where Grandfather the sun rises from his robes.

"There were many of us. A hundred of our young men followed the Heavy Eyebrows. For many days, we walked. Soon the tall trees cut off the sky and we were afraid. Little Bear, leader of the Bear Clan, said there was no sun now, and during the night, there were few stars, and there was evil spirits in the darkness of the tall trees.[5] They gave Little Bear much pet-sa-ne these Heavy Eyebrows, and soon he was singing a song of war. He stood by the fire when his head was sick with pet-sa-ne, and he dreamed that he had killed many Pawnee. He had a hard time to get up from his knee when he showed them how he had killed Pawnee but he had only spirit bow in his hands. Little Bear, with the evil of white man's pet-sa-ne singing in his head, forgot the evil spirits in the darkness of the tall trees. The Heavy Eyebrows laughed at Little Bear.

"There was a great river and another great river, like the legs of a man coming together, and there at that place were the houses of the Heavy Eyebrows.

"There was a great wall made of trees, so their enemies could not take them in the dawn. There were many Heavy Eyebrows with the white man's gun in their hands looking down upon us from the great wall made of trees.

"The Heavy Eyebrows brought many things to us to eat, and we killed deer and turkey and the skunks were very fat in that place.

"There were other people there. Some of these people had the scalp-lock like our people, but we could not understand their tongue. They came to us with their hand raised and touched those things which we wore, and sang their strange talk at us. There were other people there with hair long like the hair of a woman, and they made their houses of the bark of trees. But many of the Heavy Eyebrows talked in many tongues, and we gave our words to them and they made them into the talk of other people there at that place.

"We went toward that place where Grandfather the sun comes from his robes; for many sleeps, we had gone toward that place. Then one day, Heavy Eyebrows left the wall of dead trees, and we went with them, and the other people who had come to that place went with them. The other people with the scalp-locks like ours and with the long hair of a woman went with them. Again we went toward Grandfather the sun, but in the tall trees we could only see his fingers. His fingers touched the guns of the Heavy Eyebrows and they were like live things.

"One day Standing Bull went with Reevers—he was Heavy Eyebrow scout.[6] They went through the tall trees like buck with antlers on his back stepping like the cougar. They climbed a ridge. When they got there, Reevers told Standing Bull to take the eagle feather out of his scalp-lock, then they pulled weeds and lay on their bellies and crawled for a long time like the terrapin. They put these before their faces and looked down into a little valley. There in that place they saw the Long Knives. They were coming through the trees like buffalo going to water. But where there is only one buffalo in each place like beads on a string, there were two Long Knives in each place like a double string of white man's beads. There was no end. Their chiefs were on horses. Their coats were like the maples in the Deer Breeding Moon. The long line of Long Knives was like blood from the heart of a bull flowing back through the trees.

"They knew the Heavy Eyebrows were close. They wanted to scare them, these Long Knives; they would scare the Heavy Eyebrows. One soldier beat a drum and some of them played the white man's flutes.

"Standing Bull and Reevers came back to the Heavy Eyebrows. There was much talk. The Heavy Eyebrows said we would go to that place where Standing Bull and Reevers had seen the Long Knives. Soon my people heard chopping with the white man's ax. They heard the same noise the Heavy Eyebrows make in the trees when they build their high walls from trees. It was the same noise the Heavy Eyebrows make when they build their bateaux.

"Soon there was much talk again, and my people moved with the Heavy Eyebrows and the other people. My people ran from tree to tree or crawled on their bellies, and there was no talk among the Heavy Eyebrows now. When they looked, they saw only a few of the Heavy Eyebrows, and only one or two of the other people. This was the Indian way. It was like horse taking.

"My people came to a ridge and looked into a little valley. The Long Knives were there, but they could not get through the trees now. The people with the Heavy Eyebrows knew of this place; they knew the Long Knives could not get through this place without the white man's ax. Now they were chopping the trees so they could get through. Standing Bull saw a chief get off his horse and hit a Long Knife soldier over the back with the flat of his long knife. Our people do not hit their soldiers. Our people saw the chiefs of the Long Knives look into the trees but they could not see our people and they could not see the other people and they could not see the Heavy Eyebrows lying like our people when they attack the enemy before dawn; like my people when they take horses.

"There was a cry of war. It was like the hunting cry of the buffalo wolf. My people began to shoot and the other people began to shoot and the Heavy Eyebrows began to shoot. My people could hear the song of the long bow and the scream of the bullets and the smoke from the guns made them cry.

"The soldiers of the Long Knives were like horses when the prairie burns. They shot into the trees with their guns, and not seeing their enemy, they ran like horses when the prairie burns. Standing Bull had a gun; the Heavy Eyebrows had given him a gun. He said he shot at a tall Long Knife on a good horse. The fear was in this horse's eyes, and the foam came from his mouth, but the tall man was not afraid. The arrow of Striker killed this horse, and Standing Bull's bullet went over this tall man's head. This tall man got on another horse. He was brave, this tall man, and he rode with his long knife over his head, yelling to the Long Knife soldiers who were afraid because they could not see their enemy.

"Standing Bull aimed again at the heart of this tall man, and a bullet from Reevers' gun killed this other horse. He was not a good horse; the one with the foam was a good horse. Standing Bull's bullet again sang over the tall man's head when his horse went down. He was a chief, this tall man, and four bullets went into the coat of this tall man. Standing Bull saw the dust come from the coat of this tall man when the bullets hit, but this man who was a chief did not fall when the bullets went into his coat that was like the maple leaves.

"This tall man got another horse and this time he rode close to the trees where Standing Bull was hiding. He aimed at this tall chief's heart but there was no thunder from his gun. It was cold in his hand, and his heart was cold too, and had much fear in it when this tall chief would not go down.

"Striker was close to Standing Bull and he looked at Striker. He had his bow drawn but he did not shoot at the tall man. He looked at Standing Bull and there was fear in his heart too because the tall man would not die. Then Striker pulled his bow and the string broke. The tall man would not die of bullets. Striker's arrows seemed to bend around him, and then his bowstring broke.

"Striker had fear in his eyes now. He said to Standing Bull: 'it is Wah'kon; Mystery,' and Standing Bull said; 'it is Wah'kon; Mystery.' They shot no more at the tall chief. Striker put his hand over his mouth with surprise and fear, and looked at his broken bowstring. Standing Bull aimed at a Long Knife soldier who was running away, and the thunder came again to his gun, and the soldier fell.

"The tall man came close to them with his long knife flashing over his head, but they would not shoot at him, because of Wah'kon; Mystery.

"Soon they could not see this tall man for the thickness of the smoke. Soon the smoke went away and there were no more Long Knives there in that place. They carried their big chief away and the tall man who was a little chief went with them. Their big chief was dying. On the ground were many Long Knives. The ground in that place was like the ground when the sumac has lost its leaves.[7]

"The hair of the Long Knives came away in my people's hands without cutting. My people threw this hair on the ground. It was evil spirit. My people took their coats which were like the maple when the buck deer runs. We, our people were like the cardinal, the fire bird now, in the coats of the Long Knives, but we had no wings."

The old chief opened his eyes and looked on the floor in front of him, as though the transition from the past must come slowly. Maria was still looking out the window, lost in the story. With a quick movement, she threw her notebook onto the table.

"Braddock's Defeat," she said aloud to herself. She saw the question in her grandfather's face as he looked up at her, then he smiled at her and said the one word "Washon'ton."

"How," she answered, "Washington." Then she said to herself, "the tall man who lived because he was brave." Another question came to the old man's face, and she answered it in Wah-Sa-She, "Washington; Wah'kon."

"How," he said, pleased.

Again, she said aloud to herself, forgetting his presence, "yes, Washington; Wah'kon—Mystery—Fate." To the old man's questioning eyes this time, she said simply, "good."

The old chief looked at the floor in front of him again and said as if to himself, "I'll tell this great man this thing. I will tell this great man from England that my people met his people lo-o-o-o-ong time ago."

Maria rose and walked over to the bed where the gorgeous warbonnet lay, and fingered its eagle feathers.

"Good?" asked the old man in English.

"Sure," she said, "good."

As she fingered the eagle feathers, she tried to imagine the country house of Lord Dorset somewhere in a very green English countryside. He would hang this warbonnet in the hall? In the gun room? Where? In the hall, she guessed.

"This man will tell his sons this thing?" asked the old chief suddenly.

"How, we will tell his sons this thing which you will tell him," she assured him. It is his own moccasin prints he is thinking of, she thought. She thought: What a boast; what a grand boast. He knows my father will never remember or tell the story, nor his sons. He knows that there is only the white man's road. It is the end. But Lord Dorset will tell his sons; the story will live at Dorset House for—ever—. She walked to the window without finishing the thought. As she looked out at the chickens scratching in the yard, she thought, but it's the end there too. There may be no more Dorset House and tradition at this moment. Will some future custodian know the story to tell to the crowds who have paid their shillings to see the seat of the Dorsets, while the current Dorset is raising apples in British Columbia?

She went back to her grandfather. "It will be good," she said "to tell this great man this thing. He will hold your hand a long time in his and laugh. When you give this warbonnet, his face will be like the face of a chief in council and it will be full of memories of the story of his people. He will put this warbonnet in his house. He will remember."

The old man's face was happy.

"He will remember," she continued in Wah-Sa-She, then in English said as if to herself, "but his moccasin prints; the moccasin prints of his tribe are dim too."

But there was no question in the old man's face this time. He was contented and happy.

"How," said the old chief as he rose. He picked up his cane and left the room, in a manner that suggested that all was well.

Maria looked at the closed door behind him, then picked up her bag and fished for her cigarets. She lit one, and sat for a long time looking at the warbonnet. "I guess," she said to herself, "the tall man who was too brave to die, has left some pretty plain moccasin prints." Then with a catch in her voice, "I hope."

Bad Medicine

Spirit Iron lay with his long copper-colored hands flat on the white sheet of the hospital bed. The window was open a little at the bottom and the breeze from the south-east played with the tail feather of an eagle which hung from the head of the bed by a buck-skin string. The bead work on the base of the feather scraped a little, and that was the only sound from within the room. There were sounds of the cars along the highway which passed in front of the hospital, and the occasional buzzing of the bell down the hall.

He wanted nothing. He just lay there looking at nothing; looking through the roof into space. Sometimes he closed his eyes, but the nurse couldn't be sure when he slept—if ever.

Big, ripe, red-headed Helga just couldn't believe that there was nothing wrong with him, even though the doctor had said that there was nothing wrong. He hadn't found that which he had expected to find in the spinal fluid, and there was nothing else. He always said that an Indian had no will power; that an Indian just gave up. Only thing wrong here was the need of a little will power, and the right kind of food; just get him to eating—not the heavy greasy stuff, but good sensible food.

Every chance she had, she would slip into the room in her white uniform, which seemed about to burst and let her heavy breasts come tumbling out. When she came tip-toeing in her white shoes on which her feet made bumps, she had a side-sway which seemed dangerous for her patient. She would look down solicitously on the face that looked like copper with a patina, and ask: "How you feelin', chief—huh?" Then look closer and tuck the covers under the mattress, and smooth out the top covering, still looking intently at his face: "Don't wanta drenk, do you?"

But there was never an answer, and she would stand there longer, then go over to the window, pull the shade down a little, and push the curtains over. At the door she would sometimes look back at the quiet form on the bed and say: "well, if you want anything, just push the buzzer—see?"

This silent man had been brought to the hospital by his father two weeks before. In the two weeks, Helga had become maternally protective toward him. His silence appealed to her as weakness and she responded with her strength. His copper color was symbolical to her of souls outside the grace of God, and her faith responded. For the last week she had been saying five Hail Marys every night for his recovery.

Every afternoon, Eagle Feather and his wife came to see their son.[1] They would come down the long corridor in their moccasins, looking neither to right nor left; intrigued neither by patients nor flowers glimpsed through open doors.

His mother would set the jug of water down by the bed—water which she had brought from the spring at home—then waddle over to the only chair in the room.

Eagle Feather would go up to the bed and gaze at his son. He would stand there for a while, then begin to fan the pale face gently with an eagle-wing fan. Sometimes he would chant prayers as he fanned, but most of the time he stood in silence, praying only with his thoughts.

After an hour or more, they would leave as silently as they had come, and Helga would slip back to the room with fluttery interest, expecting to find some change; some evidence of mysticism.

When Eagle Feather and his wife came in at three o'clock, the doctor was there. He stood by the bed, but they said nothing. The mother set the jug of water down and went to her chair in the corner, and Eagle Feather walked up to the bed.

The doctor picked up the patient's wrist as though he would feel the pulse, then dropped it and looked up at Eagle Feather, with an expression which assumed that only men understood. "Better take him home. He'll be alright. Nothing the matter with him; no use running up a bill here."

Eagle Feather smiled and said to Spirit Iron in Osage: "Doctor says you can go home. Tomorrow you will go home."

The doctor bustled out followed by Helga attempting to tip-toe. The smile left Eagle Feather's face and was replaced by a thousand crinkles. He fanned the face of his son for a few minutes, then turned to the door. His wife got up, pulled her blanket about her shoulders and followed him out. They walked out of the hospital and to their large car in single file.

The negro chauffeur climbed behind the wheel indolently.

Eagle Feather and his wife talked much about Spirit Iron. In fact, they had talked much about him for several years and it seemed that he was growing worse. This was the third time he had been in the white man's hospital, and since he had come home again, they said to each other, that they should do something about him. The fact that they were very unhappy; the fact that Eagle Feather himself had had to go to the white man's doctor about his stomach because of this evil thing, seemed less important than the fact that Spirit Iron was the head of the clan in his father's absence. They said that at this time they must do something about this evil thing—this evil thing which had come to make its home in First Son.

Eagle Feather was Road Man in the Peyote Church, and he had prayed for the relief of his son, but he knew that only one thing could take this evil from him. It was the Evil Spirit himself who had made this evil and he must take it away. He had gone to the hill above his ranch and had sung all the songs he knew, but Me-Ompah-We-Lee seemed to turn his ears away, and his son still had the evil, and was pale and dull.[2] Now his son was back from the white man's hospital.

He decided to do a very dangerous thing. He went to the open structure where his son was lying on a raised platform under a roof of blackjack boughs. He sat there for some time, then he said: "My son, I have heard the story of this evil which Red Horse gave you. I said you were young and that you did not know that you must not take this thing from Red Horse. You had only sixteen summers, now you have twenty-five summers. You have gone to the white man's hospital and you have taken white man's medicine. I have prayed to Me-Ompah-We-Lee to ask Wah-Kon-Tah to make this evil go away. I have talked to Father Fire, but this evil which is in you will not go away. I am an old man. Soon I shall go away, but I say to myself, I cannot go away with evil spirit in First Son."

A pet crow flew up onto the platform, cocked his head and croaked; food absorbing every hour of his converted life. Wah Pokah, the owl, boomed from the creek bottom. Wah Pokah's voice made Eagle Feather feel hot; coming out of the bottom in midafternoon. It seemed to sneer at the words that had just come out of his heart. He made a mechanical movement in tying his blanket tighter around his waist. He looked at his hands and continued:

"I said, I shall take this thing and give it to the sister of Red Horse. I shall say: your brother gave this thing to my First Son. I shall say to this sister of Red Horse, that many times, I warned my First Son about these things of evil, but that he was young and turned his ears away. I shall say, Red Horse, your brother gave this thing to my son, and told him he would have power over white women. My son had sixteen summers and juices in his body were strong. He was Tah Tunkah in rut running after doe.[3] I shall say that now this evil is in heart of my son and he will die."

He did not look at Spirit Iron. He squinted his eyes and looked out over the prairie. He arose suddenly as through determination and said: "How, give me this thing and I shall take it to sister of Red Horse."

Spirit Iron lazily reached into his trouser pocket, took out an old-fashioned coin purse and handed it to his father without saying anything. The old man tucked it into his blanket and went into the house. He told his wife where he was going. She looked worried but said nothing.

The house of Red Horse's sister was at Grayhorse Village.[4] She was seated on the platform of a bough-covered open structure. She was very fat and she flowed out over the blanket which she had spread.

Her legs were ridiculously short in buck-skin leggins, and her moccasins were very small.

After Eagle Feather had sat with her for some time, he said: "Sister, I have come about a thing which makes my heart heavy. I have come to give you that thing which Red Horse gave to my First Son." The fat old woman became frightened.

"Huhn," she said, and her voice became shrill, "this thing is not mine. I do not want this thing. You must go." She slid forward as if she would leave, but stopped, overcome with the effort.

"It is bad," said Eagle Feather, "this thing does not belong to my son. This thing belonged to your brother. I am troubled about this thing. I have come to ask you what I should do."

Then he told her how Red Horse had given his son this thing. This thing of evil which he knew how to use, but he had not told Spirit Iron how to use it. He had said simply: "Take this—white women will come to you when you have them in your head; their hearts will sing when you pass."

The old woman was worried. She made no more attempts to move, and she said "huhn" several times, then, "I don't know how to tell you." She played with her blanket edge nervously as she looked far away: "I am a woman and I do not know about these things. My father was a medicine man and he knew about these things. I have heard my father say that the giver of these things of evil must take them back. Evil Spirit is only one to whom these things belong, he said. I am a woman. Only medicine men know about these things."

There was a long silence. The wind rattled the leaves of the bough-roof. A lean cur got up and scratched himself vigorously and whined softly. Red Horse's sister looked down on her fingers moving over the edge of her blanket: "You ought to take this thing to my brother's grave, I believe."

Eagle Feather went to Fire Walker's house. He sat there until sundown, talking. He went out to his car and told his chauffeur to drive out on a road that was in reality only two parallel ruts. He got out of the car and told him that he would be back soon; he said he wanted to gather some lily-roots. He walked as though he were going to the bend of the creek. Out of sight, he waited until darkness fell. He pulled his blanket up over his head and climbed to the cemetery on the prairie.

A new flag had been placed on Red Horse's grave. He looked closely at the picture of Red Horse inlaid in the granite tombstone. He lit a match to make sure.

He squatted by the long mound of earth, and began digging with his knife. As he dug, he sang softly a war song of the eagle clan. The song that would indicate to the Evil Spirit that he was Eagle Feather of the eagle clan and that he was not afraid.

When the hole was completed, he reached in his blanket-folds and took out the old-fashioned coin purse. He opened it with trembling fingers. He reached in and took out a piece of the skin of a black squirrel. He quickly placed it in the hole and covered it with care.

On the way home, he sat straight in the back of the car and sang one of the social songs of the tribe; softly, barely audible. His heart felt light again, and he was sure that he would be able to sleep better now, and that the evil which had come into his stomach would not come back. He wondered what kind of present he should give the sister of Red Horse.

Every day he looked for some change in his son, but none came. Several weeks passed and the same old worry came to Eagle Feather and his wife. He lay awake at nights and listened to the booming of Wah Pokah from the creek bottoms, and the evil came back to his stomach. His wife scolded more and did not laugh as much over the doings of her grandchildren. Every day they saw the pale face of their son and the eyes which were dull and seemed to be looking into space. He spent many hours alone standing and looking at the horizon, or lying on his back on the platform under the blackjack bough-roof.

Eagle Feather got his son into the sweat lodge again, but there was no response. Spirit Iron took his place in the horseshoe-shaped group of naked men. When the water was poured on the hot limestones and the others, with heads bowed, began to sweat, he seemed cool. His father looked at his gray face from his position at the head of the group and wondered why the evil in the form of sweat did not come from his son's body; why there was no heavy-hearted sadness showing in his face.

He attempted to pray for his people, but the thoughts of his First Son swarmed. He attempted to turn his ears to those who had heavy hearts; to talk to Father Fire in behalf of his people, but the heaviness in his own heart buzzed in his ears so that he could not hear, and Father Fire turned his ears away and added to the heaviness which had built a home in his heart.

His thoughts were disturbed by a movement. A glistening man came up to him, and slowly rolled a cigarette of sumac leaves and handed it to him. He lit it at the fire and the prayer smoke ascended. The man told of his troubles and Eagle Feather the Road Man listened.

This man was an Otoe. When Eagle Feather had given his advice, he lowered his voice and told the Otoe of his own troubles. The Otoe said that nothing could be done. He thought that only one man could do something. This man was a medicine man of the Otoes—his name was McMann.

Just before sunrise, when the men in the sweat lodge had unburdened their hearts, and were ready to go out and pray to Grandfather, the Sun, as he crept up over the blackjacks, Eagle Feather called Second Son to him and said: "Go tell that Otoe to come to me."

The Otoe arose and walked around to Eagle Feather. The flame of the fire glowed on his naked body. Eagle Feather said to him: "Go get this Otoe. This Otoe they call McMann."

After sunrise the Otoe was on his way to this reservation in the luxurious car of Eagle Feather.

The Otoe man known as McMann was very serious. He asked Spirit Iron many questions, but Spirit Iron answered him in monosyllables. He assumed an air of mystery. Almost the same air he assumed when white people came out to see the Otoes dance. He raised Spirit Iron's sleeve and cut his arm with a razor, but he ignored the medicine man. He stood for some time singing a song in a low voice, and looking at the sun. A flock of crows flew over the valley cursing, and McMann stopped his song and seemed to curse back at them until they were lost to sight.

He left Spirit Iron sitting on the platform detached from the world, and went into the house. He went up to Eagle Feather and pompously asked for a drum. He examined it carefully. His face crinkled as he examined the taut buck-skin wetted by the water within. He tried the marbles around the edge of the jar over which the buck-skin was stretched. Then frowning to indicate the importance of the occasion, he sat on the floor cross-legged and began to sing and beat the time with his fingers on the drum head. For an hour, he sat there and chanted in the Otoe language.

He put the drum aside and motioned for Second Son to come to him: "Go tell it your father to come here," he said in English. He arose and walked to the window with great importance, smoothing the braids of his hair which hung down in front.

When Eagle Feather came, he spoke Osage: "My father, you said that this evil thing had been buried on the grave of Red Horse. You said that you did this thing. Tonight we must get this evil thing. I have talked with Evil Spirit. Only I know how to do this thing. He says that we must get this evil thing from the grave of Red Horse. He said it will be good—every thing will be alright if we burn this evil thing. He says we must give this thing back to Father Fire. He says that Father Fire made every thing—that this thing is to be given back to him who made it. Your son will be alright again. Your son will smile and his heart will be light again if this evil thing has not rotted on the grave of Red Horse. If this evil thing is not rotten, it will be alright. Tonight we shall get this evil thing."

Eagle Feather's old face sagged with pain. He looked down at the floor, then looked up at McMann with the look of a dog that has been punished; hope and fear were in the old man's face.

They did not take the Negro chauffeur to the Grayhorse cemetery. Second Son drove McMann and Eagle Feather. There was no conversation. Eagle Feather sat straight with his blanket wrapped about his head, and McMann sat on the edge of the seat as though ready to jump. He was an Otoe and was unaccustomed to such luxury. He held to the strap by the window and watched the lights float by.

As they walked up to the grave of Red Horse, Eagle Feather chanted a song, the song of his ancestors; chanted under his breath. His blanket felt very heavy, and he was uncomfortable with sweat. When they reached the grave, he stood like one of the dark tombstones. There was no wind; the flags drooped on their poles. He handed his knife to McMann, then returned his hand to the folds of his blanket. Second Son stood off a little way attempting to hide his intense interest.

At the first stab in the dirt, McMann said, "if this thing has not rotted, it will be good." Eagle Feather felt that the knife had pricked his heart. He was sweating more now and he began to sing audibly.

He realized that McMann was saying something, and he saw Second Son bending over his shoulder. McMann placed the thing they had been examining in his pocket, and turned down the hill: "The evil thing has not rotted," he said.

Back at the ranch, McMann took command: "Go get this Black Woman who cooks for you," he said to Second Son. Then he turned to Eagle Feather: "You must go in the house. No one with Indian blood must see this thing. We must make a big fire. We must give this evil thing back to Father Fire. The Black Woman must do this thing. No Indian must do this thing."

The Black Woman appeared at the door and looked at Second Son through cheap glasses. The fire was burning and she looked at it; the light shining on her face. The flames agitated the leaves of the oaks and traced the branches on the side of the conical Peyote church. She came forward and over her shoulder watched Second Son disappear in the house. Then there was no one in sight except the medicine man. The whites of her eyes shown as she looked at McMann. This inspection took note of the shabby coat and the hat with a greasy band. She saw he was a poor Indian, and her fright subsided. She didn't see how this shabby man could be very important, so she became almost bold.

"Ah aint go'in do no finigglin' with the sper't and de bounty of de Lawd——Ah's a chu'ch woman—Ah—."

McMann motioned her closer. He was very serious and she came as under a spell. He watched the fire and she stood watching his face lit up by the flame. He looked like the devil hisself, sho 'nough. She was too frightened to protest further. He left the fire and she watched him into the darkness. Her eyes glistened.

When he came back, he was carrying the drum. He sat down in the light of the fire, fixed his gaze on the flames and began to beat the drum with his fingers. The rhythm rose above the crackling of the flame and he began to chant; high, almost falsetto, like the beginning of the coyote song.

Fright seized the Black Woman. She lost all her boldness born of the contempt for this shabby Otoe and inspired by the security of being a chu'ch woman. And this fear held her there like the fear that causes a jackrabbit to forget his legs when an eagle comes out of the sky whistling like a bomb. Sweat made her face shine. Her white apron shown like a truce flag to the evils of the unknown darkness.

Even the flames danced to the rhythm of the drum and the night was stilled by the spell of the chant. Soon excitement welled in the Black Woman. She found herself shaking her fat in time with the drum. She felt that she wanted to dance; that the sper't of de Lawd was sho 'nough flagelatin' over that dark valley. She had an impulse to declare her joy, and retch up and tech Heav'n—the sper't was a-comin' to be that strong.

The chanting stopped and with it, the rhythm of the drum beats. With the drum stilled her excitement left. McMann came toward her, holding out his hand. She watched his face in the light attempting to see something there which she might understand.

"Put it this thing in far," he said, and handed her the piece of squirrel skin. It was pliable and warm like a live thing, and she almost dropped it. She wanted to cry out, "oh Lawd," but her throat was dry and she could make no sound. She felt McMann's hand pushing her toward the fire, and all thought left her. She threw the little piece of skin and it was immediately lost in the flame. There was no more pressure on her back and she stepped back. She had been sweating and now she was shivering with cold.

As she stared, the drum beats began again, and above them the chanting. But this time she felt no emotion. The flames charmed her as they danced with the drum beats—as though the drum beats were the pulse of the night.

"Lawd, Lawd," she said the next Sunday, when she arose to tell of this 'sperience, "them flames was red and blue and purple—and vi'let, and they wuza hissin' like nobody evah heard. Hit seemed lak de earth was go'in to dissinsect, and swalla evah livin' thing—man and beast and burds of de ai'ah. And a-roarin' lak de secon comin'. That Otoe man wuz a-setting' there lak a stature, and Ah means he wuz sho 'nough a-beatin' that little drum ana singin.'"

The White Boy hired by Eagle Feather stopped the truck by McMann's shack on the plains. The skeleton of a T-Model Ford made mournful songs in the wind. The wind kept getting behind the tail feathers of nondescript hens, causing them to go places they had no desire to go. A hound looked at the truck sadly, then with the utmost indifference, crawled back under the house. The White Boy turned the button of the radio and slouched down under the wheel.

McMann and Eagle Feather came out of the shack, and the White Boy crawled slowly out of the driver's seat, picked up the halter, and started to let the end-gate down and place the ramp. McMann stopped him, then turned to Eagle Feather:

"Father, I cannot take this horse. You must not give me this present. That which you have told me is good. It is good that evil has left the heart of your son, and he is well again. That which you have told me is good. You have told me that he talks only to children now; that he does not talk to men and women. After this great evil has left his heart, there is no room in his heart for the evil of men and women. He has in his heart only room for the talk of children. That is good. You must say that Father Fire has done this thing."

The crinkles radiated from Eagle Feather's eyes as he shook hands with the Otoe Medicine man, and the latter continued to smile as the great car was lost in its own dust. The White Boy followed, driving the truck. As the dust settled on the buck brush at the side of the road, the medicine man watched the mane of the white horse flow with the wind—but he knew that he would never be hungry again.

Stories of World War II and the Cold War

> Readers who wish to avoid plot spoilers will
> prefer to skip to the stories and then return.

I like to think of these final pieces as stories for a nuclear age. Like his travel stories, this section of stories displays for readers a side of Mathews with which few readers are familiar: his introspections about the Second World War and its new military technologies, about the rise of communism and socialism, and about the advent of the Cold War. That these contemplations remain relatively unknown is partly due to the fact that, as a writer of mixed heritage, writing between the 1930s and the 1970s, Mathews found that publishers often marketed him to audiences on the basis of only one aspect of that heritage—his Osage identity. The points of view shaped by that aspect certainly do not absent themselves from these five narratives, but nor do they take center stage. They are subtle; they are interwoven with his European heritage; they may even to some readers today seem incongruous with the apparent thrust of his attempted interventions here. It is not to be forgotten that Mathews thought of himself in many ways as a military man. The stories cannot be assessed without taking into account the complexity of that identification and its valences within the overlapping communities of Native and Middle America.

"No Time"

The first story in the section stands out amid the other four. On June 2, 1943, Josephine M. Caudill, Mathews's eldest sister, received a telegram informing her that her son Henry Benjamin did not survive an airplane crash during practice training in service to the war effort. The news broke the hearts of the entire family. Mathews particularly noticed the pain of his younger sister Marie. Other than his father, who had died before the first war, his entire family was there to receive the young man's body four days later. Much was going on in Mathews's life. Earlier that year he had taken the manuscript for *Talking to the Moon* to Chicago. The country was in a paper shortage due to the war, so his prospects for swift publication were unsure. He was struggling with debt and financial worry as well as with the Osage Tribal Council, with whom and on which he had worked for a decade. "I should like to forget the silly affairs of a jealous, ignorant treacherous lot of mixed bloods and misguided fullbloods. I have already given too much of my time to them." His fiancée Elizabeth Palmour Hunt was in a state of high stress over unspecified financial and management struggles with Philips Petroleum, which was involved in her deceased first husband's gasoline bulk plant. "Dibbs will crack up if she doesn't come out from under the burden of worry and high tension." He had seen her son, his niece, and another family member off to private colleges and boarding schools that winter, having worked to secure his future stepson a better education than what he felt Pawhuska could offer. He also notes in his diary for later that year that he was funding his daughter's first-year tuition at Goucher College and his son's at St. George's School in Rhode Island. He was trying to build and sustain a new, more independent relationship with eighteen-year-old Virginia, from whom he had been distanced by estrangement from her mother. Meanwhile he wrangled with his ex-wife over Virginia's education, alimony, and what he perceived as a lack of understanding regarding his financial situation—matched or exceeded, apparently, by his lack of understanding over his ex-wife's. Six weeks before learning about Henry Ben, he had attended the funeral of his friend Les Claypoole, who appears in both *Talking to the Moon* and his autobiography.

It is hard not to read "No Time" in the context of his response to Henry's death. Two weeks after learning of it, he was second-guessing his nephew. Should Henry have bailed out? He considered the "mistake" for only a moment before writing that he understood in context why he had not. "God, what parents Henry Ben had." Mathews had not been close to Josephine in his childhood: she was six years his senior; the family dynamics were calm, but complicated, for the two eldest siblings; three children born between them had died in childhood. Perhaps what Mathews meant by this private comment is reflected in the loose rein the mother in this story gives Jimmy, yet Mathews himself as a child did "exactly what" he wanted. He often rode out onto the prairie-plains and camped overnight away from home during his second decade. But Jimmy's mother is not Mathews's mother: she tries to exert control over her son's activities, but does not do so authoritatively, firmly. (That does not sound at all like the Josephine of his youth!) At the same time, there may have been a sense of guilt on Mathews's part: the role model, the WWI night-bombing instructor, the uncle Henry must have looked up to as a pilot even when too preoccupied to fish or hunt with him. And then, why *Huckleberry Finn*? What does Jimmy's mix of love for the book and freedom from it imply? Certainly, in the end, Jimmy Johnson's story is a different story from Henry Benjamin Caudill's.

By the end of the year Mathews and Elizabeth were seeing her son John off, after his enlistment as a private in the Marines. Their tension would not end for another eighteen months. On Christmas 1944, he remarks John Hunt's and Henry Ben's absence. It was their good fortune that by June, John at least was home safe, a second lieutenant in the Marines, and about to embark on a long career and a long, fulfilling life.

"The Liberal View"

"The Liberal View," a story with quite a different tone from "No Time," seems shaped by Mathews's developing relationship with his stepson, and perhaps the young man's attractions—mystifying to Mathews—to the privileged pretentiousness of the Eastern literati. Despite the trail of breadcrumbs left by the mentions of well-known writers of the early twentieth century, a magazine in which they published, Grace Monroe's husband's trip to Russia, and the title of the story, any specific targets remain enigmatic. Theodore Dreiser had traveled to the Soviet Union and was good friends with H. L. Mencken, the founder of the magazine the *American Mercury*. He had also died before this story was written for Mathews's planned June 1949 show-ing in his story-a-month line. Yet Dreiser's marriages hardly follow the Monroes' pattern. Of the four writers mentioned plus Mencken, both Dreiser and Sinclair were open socialists; the latter was accused of communism from the right and capitalistic affinities from the left. Anderson also affiliated with socialism. The other two, while critics of American life, do not fit this profile so neatly. In fact, by 1964 Mathews would be using Sinclair Lewis's 1935 antifascist novel *It Can't Happen Here* as a touchstone for his own political treatise against Goldwater fascism. (Incidentally, Lewis's first wife was named Grace, and his second was an anti-Nazi journalist who had been expelled from Ger-many in 1934.) The *American Mercury* itself would become associated in the 1950s with right-wing ideals and ideologues: it was a platform for the writings of William F. Buckley Jr., Billy Graham, and J. Edgar Hoover. These dates and the passage of time in general best help us to assemble the puzzle. The battles in the United States against fascism, socialism, and communism and their enmeshment with populism were and are shifting sands. Mathews sketches a composite of no particular writer but has as his target the widespread hypocrisy of all four of these social movements as played out in the American political and literary theatres. Irony—in Grace's ignorance of political philosophy, her toothless ultimatum, her refusal to approve her son's freedom of thought and pursuit of true knowledge, her engulfment in her own special privilege, and perhaps even her denial of a son's latent homosexuality—is the word of the day.

"What Thing Is Fairest"

"What Thing Is Fairest" preceded "The Liberal View" in chronology of invention. By New Year's Eve 1949 Mathews was on a tear. Driven by financial worry, he had in September of the previous year embarked on a scheme to fund his research for his book on oil magnate E. W. Marland by writing enough short stories to publish one per month, if all went well. All did not go well, and this story slated for January 1949 was one of the thirteen he had sent to his agent Brandt & Brandt in New York City that were never published. The title comes from Algernon Charles Swinburne's "The Song of the Standard," an ode to Italy and its tricolored flag, to the Roman Empire, and to the besieged promise of freedom.

Green thing to green in the summer makes
  answer, and rose-tree to rose;
Lily by lily the year becomes perfect; and none
  of us knows
What thing is fairest of all things on earth as it
  brightens and blows.

This thing is fairest in all time of all things, in all
  time is best—
Freedom, that made thee, our mother, and
  suckled her sons at thy breast;
Take to thy bosom the nations, and there shall
  the world come to rest.

This poem's end is fitting given Charles A. Wiggins's nostalgic reminiscence and its ties to Mathews's own history as well as the stories of the many oil magnates with whom Mathews was both acquainted and intrigued, including Marland, William Skelly, and others. In his 1921 diary Mathews recounts a similar relationship to his own Diana Tennant, one B.G., at Oxford, whose full name is lost to history. It ends much differently, with the post-WWI Mathews telling her that he does not love her, knowing he does not want to marry, recognizing that primal urges and being full of spring are not love, and loving his freedom too much to part with it. The details down to the presence of a motorbike with side-car and a prospect to explore oil with a large company in Portuguese Africa are the same. Yet Wiggins's path remains only Mathews's alter ego, his what-could-have-been, just as Diana Tennant remains Wiggins's. In Wiggins, and in Wiggins's relationship both to east Africa as represented by his half-caste lover and to Diana, Mathews also seems to recognize the ambitious, acquisitive colonialist that he the author could never have become.

Floating ominously over Wiggins's memories are cottony clouds in the form of mushrooms of atomic reaction. This thrust into a nihilistic future negates all Wiggins's complacent ponderings regarding biological succession, the illusions of youth versus age, and his hopeful teleology. Yet again, these ponderings are Mathews's. Colonialist or anticolonialist, this is a Mathews who understood himself ironically as shaped and privileged by oil discoveries in the Osage, unwilling to deny his implication in the formation of the mushroom cloud that might destroy it like the oil madly gushing down Antelope Creek.

"Natural Science"

Mathews had to have had a great deal of fun writing "Natural Science." Despite its ominous subject, despite its long-salient international oppositions, he was clearly also playing, finding his futuristic feet. Even the allies have a nightmarish title for their unlikely leader: Supreme Commander. Where has democracy fled? Like a later Arlo Guthrie, he also invents a peace-preserving advance on the original nuclear technology, but unlike Guthrie's "un-neutron bomb," he leaves it to the readers' imaginations to decide what the Sun-bomb actually did. What he suggests is much less flowery than the folksinger of the next generation would wish for. It better fit his profile as a veteran of the war of 1914–18, a man who had hoped to serve in the war of 1939–45, and someone who like many of his generation had applauded Hiroshima and Nagasaki when they occurred. Possibly his selection of an Asian enemy recalled Japan, but "Tamberlania" has the feel of a much larger nation. It seems likely that the story was written in response to the Communist victory in China and that country's efforts to acquire nuclear weapons. The names Khan and Gheng narrow the field from a generalized Sino-Soviet identity for the futuristic empire to a definitively Chinese or South-Central Asian superpower oppositional to a Russian-dominated USSR. Perhaps the creation is as late as 1964, when China detonated its first nuclear weapon. Mathews was definitely writing short stories in the early sixties. Given that he never mentions this one in his extant diaries, however, an immediate postwar or early Cold War advent seems more likely. Mathews's treatment of Asians here hardly deserves the dignity even of the name Orientalism, for it is unstudied, unresearched, a creation of the news media rather than careful attention to historical detail. For a World War Three antithriller, his is marginally more respectful than he might have been and participates slightly less in perpetuating Yellow Peril scares than many did: Dr. Gheng is able; Tamur is worth preserving until the day when things change.

Totally weird, totally Mathews: a likely story for a nuclear age.

"The Meek Shall Inherit?"

"The Meek Shall Inherit?" is the ugly alter ego of "Natural Science." The delight of the first 80 percent of the story in which we follow David's beleaguered life and belabored thought processes with amusement stops dead once we arrive at the paragraph about "fanatical little brown men." A paragraph hinted at when David, belabored in his thinking, recalls talking to Carol about how Stuffy talks "just like a 'Nigger.'" We can fight the impulse to conflate the character David—perhaps one of Mathews's "unfit, who will eventually destroy us"—with the author: the anticommunist author has given us quite enough ammunition to do so, and indeed so has the last half-century of literary criticism. "The author is not his character!"[1]

Yet it is very hard to deny, despite Mathews's ironic tone born of his outsidedness from David, that many of the thoughts following that split at the news of Hiroshima seem to be Mathews's. Granted, from a distance of over sixty years, we can be smug. We can judge the optimism about atomic weaponry in the decade preceding and following the blast misguided, sick, racially aggressive. We have the wisdom of hindsight; those of us who were teenagers in the Reagan era have the experience of mass anxiety over the predicted nuclear winter and the apparent headlong rush of two superpowers toward mutually assured destruction. Mathews's experience, on the other hand, had been one of piloting nuclear scientists and their nonnuclear research experiments through the clouds during World War I.

But it is hard to forgive him. As late as 1970, as long as twenty-five years after this story was penned, he continued to believe that

Hiroshima had been the most heroically "effective 'bluff' of Homo sapiens, and the postponement of World War Three," rather than one of humankind's greatest atrocities. So, yes, David's thoughts after Hiroshima continue to carry the author's double-voiced irony, his doubt, his skepticism, his mockery of his character's overblown idealism, his hatred of his character's political affinities. And yet that irony, doubt, skepticism, mockery, and hatred fail to convince us that he did not share even as he mocked them David's hopefulness, his idealism, his grandiosity, his prejudices, his foolishness, his self-destructive will-to-power.

Unfortunately Mathews was also all too prescient about the international monitoring of delinquent countries, which has come to reveal both the arrogance of the nuclear nations and the sinister psychopathy of the rogue states and their dictatorial leaders.

No Time

The age of tyrants had come again to the old world, but in the modern times these faraway tyrants could reach with their knotted clubs across the Atlantic Ocean to America. One of these mad men had risen in Germany. An unlettered barbarian without culture had risen in a cultured world and had demanded that the world kneel to him and his whims. He was demanding that there should be no more tranquil twilights on the farmsteads after the work was done, and no more summer evenings of peace in the villages and towns of America. This paranoiac came into every home in wide, humanitarian America and shattered the peace and tranquility. The Godless barbarian shouted from every radio and his name aroused fear and frustration and bitterness in every heart.

In order to bring peace and pleasant living again to the land, so that its people could dream again, Jimmy Johnson with millions of other young men said good bye to their parents, their sweethearts, their brothers and sisters. In order that the people of the land need not bow to this crazy tyrant, these young men drilled in the hot sun of camps from Ocean to Ocean and circled monotonously day after day over the new airfields.

The people set their jaws and hid their tears and veiled their thoughts with hope, and said "we've got to do it to remain free and live our own lives as we wish to live them, and we shall see that another will not be allowed to rise and take from us our dreams and our hope and our peace."

A telegram came to inform Jimmy's family that he had "failed to survive a crash" in his fighter plane. It was one of many received over the land. The day he was twenty-one he had fallen off from close formation at 6,000 feet and had crashed to earth like a winged wild goose; out of the white puff-clouds over Florida which that day had been spaced with the deep blue of the sky.

His crazy college jackets and his dinner jacket and shoes were put away along with his collection of model planes in a pitifully small box and taken to the dark attic. His picture in his new uniform was placed on the table and its eyes looked out over the room with the cocky assurance of youth which made his family feel that he might actually come back.

As they put the little planes away they remembered the day nine years before when Jimmy was twelve. The family had gone on his birthday to a grove of hickory far out into the country, where no house could be seen, for a picnic. Jimmy had insisted that his fighters and his bombers and the materials for his hangars be brought along.

Under the shade of a tall wide-armed hickory, he had built his airfields, carefully and accurately. While the others built the fire and prepared lunch, Jimmy walked about holding a fighter and then a bomber, and sometimes one in each hand high over his head, making the sound of the motors with his lips. Oblivious to everything, he had walked out and back from his little airfields, circling and buzzing with his lips as he held the planes high in his hands. He would sometimes walk far out into the field buzzing with his lips, then circle back and make a new sound as the plane glided in to a landing.

Sometimes he had a battle between two fighters as high as his hands could reach, and one would always fall softly to earth with his dirty hands guiding it.

The family remembered the mockingbird sitting on the very top of the tall tree that shaded him, singing ecstatically; jumping into the air and looping without losing a note in its mad happiness. They remembered the quail whistling from every quarter with that tranquil assurance that the cock quail has in the mating season. They also remembered the leaf shadow playing lazily on the picnic basket, and the blue spiderwort with their flowers waving gently in the breath of a breeze. But as they remembered, these things were only a back-of-the-scenes chorus to Jimmy's buzzing lips and in his complete absorption. They were the muted orchestra during dinner hour drowned by the buzz of conversation, or like the careful splendour of the room to a gourmand.

When the sandwiches and chicken were ready, Jimmy's mother had called to him, but he was slow in coming. When he finally came, he brought the favorite fighter with him; he flew it to the spread cloth holding it high in the air.

He drank from his soda water and bit into his sandwich, then holding them in one hand so that his right could be free to fly the fighter, he buzzed back to his flying field under the hickory.

The members of the family were absorbed in conversation and didn't miss him until his mother started to put the things away.

"Jimmy," she called, "have you had all you want? One sandwich is not enough; come get another."

It was then that they noticed the half-eaten sandwich placed carefully on a tuft of grass with the ants swarming on it, and the flies settling on the bottle's mouth. Jimmy's mother shrugged and smiled indulgently. "THAT boy," she said.

Uncle Mack had put a flyrod together, then he put a line on a cane pole, and shouted to Jimmy, "look," as he held up the tackle.

"Ina minit," said Jimmy, but went on with his fighter battle as high as his arms could reach, vibrating his lips and frowning, as he circled in the field.

Finally after several calls to Jimmy, uncle Mack laid the cane pole against a tree, and set off across the fields alone.

"If that boy comes to," he had turned to say, "tell 'im I'll be at the sycamore hole."

Much later, uncle had come back with his catch of perch, and the family admired them, and uncle Mack was visibly proud. He called to Jimmy and held up his string, but Jimmy only stopped momentarily and asked, "how many?" then without waiting for an answer circled again buzzing. This time a fighter in the right hand was attacking a bomber in the left.

The shadows lengthened and the cicadas began their rasping chorus. Jimmy's mother called again:

"Come on; we're ready to read *Huckleberry Finn*. You said to bring it. We'll take turns reading, or you can read to us for the whole time if you want to."

"Ina minit," he said.

Fifteen minutes passed. Twilight was coming lazily on this summer's day, and Jimmy's mother shouted to him again.

"Jimmy Johnson, do you want to read *Huckleberry Finn* aloud or don't you, after we brought it purpose'ly for you? Come on now put those things away, or we won't have time before dark. JIMMY, please answer me; I'm serious."

Jimmy stopped and let the plane in each hand dangle nose down. His dirty face showed the pain of frustration and the lack of under-standing by comfortable grown-ups.

"Mother," he said, "I hav'nt got time. Don't you understand, mother? I hav'nt got time."

The Liberal View

Grace Monroe stood straight and calm at the speaker's stand. Her beauty had always owed much to her bright intellect, and to her ever-bubbling intensity. Even now as she stood with her handkerchief clutched tightly in her hand, speaking to the room full of people, her beauty of middle age was like a carefully changed oil portrait of her twenty-five-year-old self. It was as if a portrait painter under the customs of a much earlier age, had come back every five years to make changes in the portrait to harmonize with the aging of the subject. The lines of middle age and the very slight looseness of her jowls, were the delicate lines and shadows painted in by the re-visiting artist, who had been careful to make the lines carry out the original flattery.

She was not militant, despite the nature of her subject, and the people who made up her audience were with her in full sympathy so that she could make extravagant statements with tranquil assurance. She sneered very attractively and the sea of sympathy represented by the faces before her, made her customary sharp and damaging witticisms unnecessary. The seas' rollers were the periodic waves of her audience's intense and almost neurotic vindictiveness. When she stressed some gospel, some of the people in the room would squirm in their seats, as though they were urged to stand and re-affirm the truth spoken by her.

She had the power of tranquil certainty. Most of the fervent speakers against the restraints put upon civil liberties and freedom of conscience adopted the certain, very adequate, and highly satisfying phraseology of the learned disciples of Marx and Veblen, which would very often pass as original to the great majority who had never read the 19th century thinkers, and knew them only as oft repeated names.[1] Grace Monroe, however, could give original expression through clever phraseology to rather unoriginal maxims on freedom of thought.

She knew when to pause and when to become angry with righteousness and this confirmed the listeners in their soul's dedication to the new religion of the mechanized civilization of the 20th century.

They believed in her as a fervent disciple of her late husband, Marc Monroe, who had become famous with his novels of reaction against the narrow, stodgy smugness of America when questing readers made scripture of the Mercury magazine and devoured Lewis, Dreiser, Sinclair and Anderson.[2] He had ridden the trend of national self-analysis, and had died a millionaire.

"All we ask," she assured her listeners, as she moved her hands forward above the stand in the manner of a mendicant, "is the liberty the Constitution allows us. We only want the teachers in our schools and colleges to be allowed to teach and think as they choose, and teach that which they know to be the glaring truths of man's history. We want the masters of this nation of ours to let our nation—their nation—be a democracy in fact as well as in name. We don't want Neanderthal ignorance holding the club over our intellectuals; over our teachers, telling them what and how to think, thus barring our children from the fields of true knowledge." Here she smiled her dimpled little smile which scarcely broke the line of the left corner of her mouth. This little smile covered the slight feeling of rising hatred that might impose undignified speech or gesture upon her. "These Neanderthal men seem to think that our children might find the goblins of historical truths if they allow them into the fields of true knowledge. Oh no, they don't want that, so they cow their teachers with the primitive club of ignorance and special privilege."

She paused, then continued: "We know the task before us. We know the size of the job we have taken on. We know the nature of the fight we must carry on every minute to give back to the people of this country freedom of thought and speech and assembly. We will not allow the intellectuals of our schools and colleges to be cowed by the slant brows of special privilege. Open up the gates to the fields of knowledge and give our teacher and children freedom to search there for truth; give them freedom from fear and suppression."

At this point, several members of the audience started instinctively to raise their hands as though they were in a schoolroom and were asking permission to speak. But the movement was only instinctive, and with their faces frozen with intensity, they lowered them from the half-raised position. It was in the very nature of their intensity, that even though they approved heartily of what she was saying, they felt almost overwhelming urges to testify against their imagined oppressors like camp-meeting witnesses against the devil.

When the meeting was over, Grace walked sedately among the people of the room, and a small company formed about her, suggesting points that she might have made, and turning her role into that of a listener; a role incidentally which she played with impatience and boredom prettily concealed. Knots of people formed in the middle of the room, in the doorway, and in one corner, seemingly talking each at the same time with jerky gestures, and every face wore a white intensity, and there was not a smile in the room.

Grace, in passing the newsstand at the station, bought a copy of *Vox Populi*, and turned immediately to her column, passing up the bold headlines of the story from the White House.[3] She glanced over it hurriedly and finding it had not been cut, looked it over more carefully to ascertain if her meaning was intact and had not been destroyed or enfeebled through typographical errors or by plain carelessness on the part of the proofreader.

The next afternoon, as she climbed the steps to her son's room in Petrie Hall, she had forgotten about her column, had given herself up to worry about him.[4] He had refused to accompany her to Stalingrad where she was to write a series of articles on the postwar spirit of the heroic citadel.

She found him packing for the summer vacation. She kissed him fondly on both cheeks, then sat on the lounge and watched him.

"Will there be any tennis where you're going?"

"Mother, really; I thought I told you we'd be camping in Maine, then to Quebec for as long as we can stand each other—that's what Hank says."

"How old is this Dr. Mason; this Hank as you call him?"

"I don't know—what's the difference?"

"What on earth will you do all that time?"

"I don't know; go boating perhaps, hike, read. We're reading *The Republic*—you know, Plato."

"Is he head of the department or just——?"

"No, just a professor."

"Good gracious, I thought they'd stopped teaching Greek and Latin long ago."

She watched her son pack with a look of adoration. How much he looked like his father. She was extremely nervous. She looked at her watch: "Look, honey, I'll be back in half an hour to say goodbye. I won't have too much time for the boat."

Even after twenty minutes with Dr. Mason of the department of Greek and Latin, she was still upset. She had studied his face and had tried to draw him out, treading lightly in the fear of exposing her ignorance in his field. He had not committed himself, and seemed intent on drawing her away from a field wherein she might stumble and hurt her self-esteem. He was very kindly and extremely courteous.

As she talked, Dr. Mason recalled the much honored novelist, her husband, who the year before his death had visited Russia and had returned bubbling with enthusiasm. He had proclaimed to the avid reporters who had come to meet his ship in tug boats to hear his latest oracles, that Russia had the most significant government ever devised by man. Then he had died leaving instructions to Grace to keep his son in the political faith to which he had dedicated him; leaving him a million dollars.

She realized as she talked with the kindly scholar that she couldn't talk young Marc out of vacationing with his beloved Hank, and as she stood ready to leave, at the door which the professor held open for her, he could see her face grow suddenly cold and very hard, as she said without the usual embarrassment of one deciding suddenly in his extremity to be ruthless: "I understand you will be reading Plato this summer. I want to know this; is there anything in these classics, in Plato, that would influence Marc's thinking—that would affect his belief in the Marxist theory of government." She paused; she didn't like the word "theory"—"in his political beliefs. His father would turn over in his grave, and I—well, I might as well be frank with you, doctor, I simply won't have it."

What Thing Is Fairest

Spring had come to the Red Bed plains. It had come on the spring breezes from the faraway Gulf of Mexico. It had brought green to make artistic contrasts with the red erosion gashes of the ravines which with their bushes and stunted trees were like veins of the red earth feeding the arterial river that wandered lazily now, once out of the canyons of the Rockies. Its bright light and its balmy air spread over the land, created dreams and hope again. It inspired cottony clouds to form a woman's head with flowing hair, an elephant, grazing white buffalo; which soon re-formed into piles of cotton, fantastic castles or mushrooms of atomic reaction.

As spring came over the land, it seemed to concentrate upon Charles A. Wiggins' gardens and his great expanses of lawn. It sent the flowers into competitive blooming, but it touched with its magic the dandelions and the weeds into new life as well, and this to Charles A. Wiggins, sitting in his chair at the big window of the mansion, seemed to be a personal insult. He watched his gardeners busy cutting the grass back from the walks and picking up sticks and twigs, and raking the wind-blown petals from the lawn.

The bronze Pan that stood among the lilacs had meaning now, and you could make out the lascivious smile back of his pipes. At one time Chas. A. had set his heart on an Aphrodite as well, to be placed on the other side of the lawn from Pan. He had ordered her done in white marble, with her arms in conventional guard position, which would indicate sincere modesty so satisfactorily that it would excuse her pagan nudity. He had had Borghessi make her so that her head was turned back over her shoulder; looking back with an expression of sincere fear at anyone who might be coming along the walk.[1] The position of her arms and her expression would have made her acceptable, despite her lusty, female curves. Borghessi had suggested that goddesses were never uncomfortable in the presence of mere humans, but Chas. A. was not convinced when he thought of Caroline.

When he had said tentatively to her some years ago, "I think I'll have a statue set up on the other side by the trellis, of Daphne or Aphrodite or something," Caroline had answered, "yes dear, why not—you'd love that." The way that she said it made him feel that she was surely holding Diana Tennant in reserve to bring her forth at the proper time as evidence of his general unworthiness as husband and father. Diana Tennant had been his secret; his precious secret enshrined in a secret chapel, and Caroline's silent allusion to her had annoyed him. He had had Borghessi sell the statue for whatever he could get for it.

But these incidents of a few years ago didn't disturb his comfort as he sat by the window watching the gardeners modify nature's enthusiasm. It was after breakfast and the doctor said that he might have one of his three daily cigars after breakfast, and he was waiting for a time before indulging in that great pleasure. The morning had been regular, and now, in his comfort, his business was the important one of watching the gardeners.

He wondered if Jules would ever see that dead limb slanting down from the catalpa. He couldn't understand why he had not been able to see it before this, but that was the way the thing went; no pride anymore. But he'd better get to work on that limb before the mockingbird started her nest. The male was singing from the flagpole right now.

He liked the up-side-down catalpa, or umbrella catalpa, he guessed they might be called. It was decorative and cast a very dense shade on hot days, and the mockingbirds liked to build their nest in the dark foliage where it could be completely hidden. People were always saying that it looked artificial there on the lawn, but what about the willows along the Cherwell he had loved so much, and which he remembered so well. They were even spaced as though they had been planted.

He began to think of days long ago when he had floated in a punt on the Cherwell near Oxford. Much had happened to him since then. From a poor undergraduate he had become a man of great importance, and people had the highest respect for him. When he was on the Chamber of Commerce program, the dining room was filled and overflowed. His millions made what he had to say very important to people. He was the perennial chairman of the Red Cross drives because his name was associated with wholesome things, and wherever it was seen it inspired confidence. He took all this for granted. Certainly he believed that he had done much that would inspire people to look up to him.

Even so, there were people who minimized his importance; they said that the Minnie Eagle Feather Well No. 1 had been blind luck; that he was just another lucky wildcatter in discovering the most important oil field in the state with his well on the Minnie Eagle Feather allotment.[2] That was years ago, but he could remember the well coming in as if it had been yesterday. He and the driller had washed their hands in the oil and had washed each other's faces with it, and had run around the derrick shouting as if they were mad, while thousands of barrels of oil ran down into Antelope creek.[3] The town of Eagle Feather grew up and became a boom town, but now it was the cleanest little town in the state. The name had been changed from Eagle Feather to Wiggins long ago.

He supposed he had been set up over the notice he had received since that day, and he had actually thought of himself as being one of America's most important people. Attesting to his importance were symbolical keys to cities, testimonials on parchment, group pictures of the American Petroleum Institute members with himself in the center and caricatures done by noted artists and cartoonists. There were the life-size painting of him in the People's National Bank, looking down upon customers with dignity and goodwill, and the Wiggins collection of historical documents at the State University. The symbolical keys to the cities, the caricatures, the testimonials and the clipping books were in the large den where no one ever went now. Only the maids went there to dust like the caretakers of a cemetery.

But the disappointing thing about it all was that Caroline was even less interested in these things than she ever was. Since the Minnie Eagle Feather No. 1 came in, she had been busy, it seemed to him with a lot of fol-de-rol, which had ever as its background a smug confidence in her importance as the social leader of the city. He thought this background; this backdrop to her stage was a bit too obvious, since the play and the players alike seemed to be for the purpose of bringing it out, instead of the play itself being the thing. She had ever been absorbed with that intangible "the thing to do" social business.

He had hoped that Tom or Charles Jr. might be interested in the things in the den. They were doing well, he guessed, but they had grown up into just ordinary men, after the assurance which the mere fact of their birth had given him, and after all his dreams for their becoming outstanding men. They were just like anyone's sons. They weren't even as physically handsome as he had been. You might take Charlie for a bank clerk instead of the son of Chas. A. Wiggins, the oil millionaire and civic leader. And Tom; well, Tom was smothered in a conventional domesticity, and followed the pattern Mabel had set for their lives among other nonentities of their two-car set.

He lit his cigar and changed his already comfortable position as though he would attain a climax of comfort to harmonize with his complete enjoyment of the cigar. The mockingbird volplaned and put the stray cat crossing the lawn into a crouch and a snarl of defense, then zoomed and circled for the second attack. He wondered why the gardener Jules couldn't keep the stray cats off the place. There you are again—that's what the world was coming to; no responsibility anymore.

The cat took refuge in the bushes just under the window where he sat, and he wondered why Jules had not seen him. He ought to be run out of those bushes; there wouldn't be a bird on the place. He tapped the glass with his stick, but Jules couldn't hear. He tapped and frowned, but neither conveyed anything to Jules's humped back as he stood looking at something on the ground with his gnarled hands hanging loosely at his sides. From his right one, the shears dangled hopelessly.

A cloud threw a momentary shadow over the grass, and the mockingbird began to sing again, believing that the cat had been discouraged. Chas A. forgot the cat too, as he came back to his thoughts about his family which gave him a secret feeling of failure. They, all four of them had taken things for granted, and grown up to be commonplace people. He remembered their curls and their beautiful faces, and what had seemed to be their brilliant observations. The promises which their brightness and beauty symbolized had made his dreams for them fantastic. He had no doubt that they were superior to himself and Caroline, and had less of human frailties.

His little girls had made him feel like a hero and he had been made happy by the idea that perhaps he could project his protection over them to the end of his days, and they would ever come to him as a refuge. Having been born in the west and during the latter part of the 19th century, his ideas had been colored by the hint that women had a certain divinity absent in men. But when he had a family of his own, he realized that women were not closer to heaven than men, but he still expected Jane and Emily to be like some of the staunch heroines in the novels he used to read. They would be just, virtuous, reasonable, magnanimous and have womanly tenderness and kindliness that were poetic. When they had climbed upon his knees and put their moist, warm arms about his neck, he had felt his strength, confidence and promises that were sure of fulfillment, send their warmth over him to bring restless happiness. He knew he could be protective unto death, and he knew at that moment that nothing should ever bring ugliness into their lives, or disturb their humane and poetic thoughts. The world of men in general and sons-in-law in particular might take warning.

That had been his dream. Now as he sat at the window worrying about his lawn and his up-side-down catalpa, he saw his daughters as matrons whose concerns and pleasures were definitely earthy. They would rush into the room flushed with silly excitement and peck at his cheeks without really being conscious of him, then find Caroline as usual. From the time they were leggy school kids, they and Caroline patronized him, and they came to him not as one goes to court for an interpretation or decision, but as one might go to some agitating stockholder to get a confirmation which the strong board of directors do not need, but for the purpose of following the letter of the law. There were mystical understandings, which gave them mystical power to show him indulgence where respect was actually a shadow.

When they came to the house, they got with Caroline immediately, and from what he could overhear of it, their conversation was about on the level of that which one might expect from fishwives over a fence. Ed says this and Jim says that, and "I just tole him—now look, I said, two can play that game." They talked about their children; the way they ate their cereal, or the manner in which they refused to eat their cereal, and how one of them, Jane, had a "perfect jewel of a nurse" and the other, Emily, had to put up with a second rater.

As far as he knew, Charles A. 3rd had never been taken into the den since he had been old enough to understand things, to be shown the keys, the testimonials and the books of clippings. The boy was one of those bright, disinterested, irresponsible, fact-bearing, argumentative products of book training. His big feet in some mysterious manner seemed to, at one time or another, touch and displace everything in the room. His manner was superior and tolerant, with bad grace showing through courtesy, when he came to "speak" to his grandfather. Someday, he would rush into the room—possibly just after his freshman year at college, and say, "heck gramps, didn't know you were in WHO'S WHO—musta been quite a boy."

That's the way it was, he thought. It was all like the coming of spring; a bright promise which inspired dreams and action, then the romantic, vivid life filled with beauty and song and hope, grew yellow and monotonous and silent, and dreams died. Dreams needed the sap of spring; that's what they were made of, after all; the urges of spring, the disturbances of the spring of a man's life, when there were babies' bright faces, roses, bird song and faces flushed with love and eyes filled with earth's unlimited promise. It must be a thing which

God holds out to man so that he will not become discouraged in each succeeding generation. The old ones can't possibly convey their disillusionment to the younger ones, nor can the dead grass leaves and the brown leaves of the trees and the shriveled empty seed pods, color the new grass with their yellow, the new leaves with their brown and the flower buds with their ugly dryness. Then if it's God's design, each spring is a little better than the last one, and man's dreams about his superior babies must be planted in him; instinctive and natural. It would be like climbing a stairway, where each step gives under your weight, but never falls quite to the level of the one under it. In this way the promise will finally come true, is that it? Man will reach a stage where he will finally have some intelligent understanding of God, and he will no longer create hatreds and fumble and spill blood in the insistence upon his ignorant interpretations.

That may be it, he thought. Old men like himself were dull and useless tools, which once had been sharp and bright. Or they were relay runners with batons ready to hand on. We can only run once, and we can have only one springtime promise. I suppose if we had known that, he thought, we might have known how to appreciate it, or we might have stopped running. Our one spring was the most wonderful thing that ever happened to us, and we weren't even aware of it, just as we can't appreciate the flowers, the freshness, the scents, the bird song, and the cloud shadows across the lawn until they have passed; until the July and August suns beat down without pity and the flowers die, the birds are silent, the moonlights un-scented, the grass turns pale and the earth cracks.

He had been proud of the estate he had fenced in, and of the large house at the end of the winding, graveled road. The spotless lawns and gardens and the big house with its striped awnings, gave the impression of coolness on the hottest days, and gave him the feeling as he approached through the years, that somehow he had overcome the temperamental attacks of nature on the plains; that he, the important man, might even have the respect of nature as a creator in his own right. But the estate that had been pictured in a national magazine, along with his skyscraper business building with its tall spire topped by a beacon inspired by Lindbergh's transatlantic flight, were not so important now. Only in those days of his spring when the girls were so fat and moist and sincerely affectionate and adoring, and the boys were so exceptionally bright and promising, did he believe that his spring would not pass. It was amusing now; you might as well believe other impossible things; that roses would bloom and nod all summer and winter, and there would be eternal singing of the mockingbird, and scents of the earth would not be killed by the mid-summer sun's heat.

The ash of his expensive cigar finally dropped onto his vest, and he looked at the short butt with discomfort. He couldn't have another one until after lunch. Chas. A. Wiggins couldn't have another cigar when he wanted it, and he couldn't have bacon and eggs or fried chicken or beer anymore, ever.

What did man get out of life; was everything an illusion? What good was memory of bacon and eggs and the first bottle of cold beer. Was life really just a garden of roses in the short spring, which foolish young men believed would remain full-blown forever? Foolish young men believed this; not old men like himself. They could detect dreams from realities because they had seen the spring pass; they knew about the yellowing grass and shriveled seed pods of flowering promise. Those nodding roses out there in the garden couldn't fool him—now.

Jules was looking up out there in the garden; surely he couldn't help seeing that dead limb slanting from the catalpa, yet he went on about his methodical clipping of the grass from the edges of the flagstone walk. The tree with its bright new leaves was casting quite a shade. It didn't look too artificial there on the lawn. He didn't know that he had been striving for a natural effect anyway. People were crazy. What he wanted was man-made beauty; the picture-book kind of beauty you saw in England, and that catalpa reminded him of the willows along the Cherwell near Oxford. They must have been planted long ago. The memory of them thrilled him.

He could see again the cows grazing on the perfect emerald of the meadows bordering the "Cher"; sprinkled with a sort of buttercup and daisies, he guessed them to be. He could see again a tall girl with a dripping punting pole as he sat on cushions in the prow. He had difficulty in accustoming himself to her sincere desire to do part of the punting. She had insisted upon doing her share from the first day they went out on the river, and she had actually enjoyed it. He would never forget her standing there in a frock like a sheath tied at the waist, with her wheat-colored hair cut in the manner of a Shakespearean page boy's bob. Her teeth had gleamed in the sunlight when the punt floated out of the shade, and her eyes sparkled as they talked. He could hear her beautiful English voice now. It had reminded him of three sounds at different times, and he could never make up his mind which sound it most resembled in general. It was like a mountain brook hidden by moss, and it was like a strong breeze passing through the crystal pendants of a chandelier, but when they were on the river, it was exactly like the tinkling of the water at the prow of the lazy punt.

He moved his body in the chair so as to be more comfortable when thinking of Diana Tennant. After a few trips on the river, he noticed the manner in which she had begun to look at him, and he could remember her curt little English ways, as though she might be embarrassed by the knowledge that there was a soft look in her face and a revelatory sparkle in her eyes.

And soon they were not even noticing other people on the river as their punt slid along. They almost forgot to say "sorry" when they barely avoided bumping another punt coming around one of the many bends of the Cher. She thought everything he said was very amusing, and he thought her laughter was the most beautiful sound he had ever heard, and the Roman Diana couldn't possibly have been as beautiful as she.

He remembered that she had carried no mirror or powder puff and her face was flushed and sometimes the inner threads of her bobbed hair were moist, when she bent forward at the end of a pole thrust.

While he had liked this freshness and frankness, he had been bothered a little by them. She was always striding along with the grace of a deer, and he was always too slow in taking her arm to assist her. She was discouragingly self-sufficient, and he had been accustomed to frail helplessness among the girls of Updike College out on the plains of the United States. Their simulated frailty had been the standards against which he measured girls, and he found Diana falling uncomfortably short. And another thing: he was not sure that he approved of her smoking cigarets. Back at Updike he had known one or two daring girls who lit up cigarets back of bushes, or as they traveled along some country road in a car. But Diana had a craving for them, and lighted them and smoked them as an accustomed man might do, to let them dangle from her beautiful lips. All these things brought the slightest shadow of doubt concerning her virtue, and this shadow of doubt tinged slightly with indefinite expectation, tempered his growing infatuation. But this feeling had had a very difficult time against the English spring; against Diana's eyes, her whimsical thoughts and her animal grace; her laughter and her words that were like the tinkling pendants of the breeze-disturbed chandelier, and against the growing softness of her eyes, this feeling came only after intervals.

But still he had missed the simulated helplessness which to him had been natural to girls, when Diana helped him moor the punt, or took the pole as he sat in the prow. All this which he had then thought was feminine frailty in the girls of Updike, he knew about now. He actually frowned as he had this thought of the present. Now, he knew it to be what it was: window dressing. The girls were the sellers and the young men the buyers, and more than once the young men he believed had been oversold. He thought of Caroline, Jane and Emily.

Why, they were always selling him something with that histrionic benevolence and deep concern found in the voices coming over the radio. It had been like that from the beginning. Caroline had been one of those frail things who carried her powder puff and her mirror, and took them out frequently along with her comb with which she would give her hair a few strokes, then fluff it with her fingers right at the table after a coke or after a dinner. After marriage and during his springtime when he was busy amassing millions, it never occurred to him that window dressing had been too optimistic, even when he realized that her attitude had indicated that he was a sort of obstacle to her ambitions. She had frequently mentioned the stage and had intimated that his existence as her husband and her sacrifices in bearing his children had made the flowering of her histrionic ability an impossibility. He had caused her to remain mute and inglorious. He supposed that Jane and Emily's husbands were obstacles as well.

The shadow passed and he was back in England surrounded by an English spring with Diana and himself in its center. He could still hear the cuckoos calling from every garden, and he could still see the skylarks hanging against the sky, spilling their song to float earthward as a rocket spills its sparks.

The warmth of extreme happiness that tingled a little came over him, and there was no distinct incident; just a blur of re-captured happiness. Having no sharp, thrilling incident to keep his memory focused, he returned to the present, and he had suddenly fallen from the crest of happiness to the trough of reality. He actually said aloud, "what a damned fool." It had been his personal rose of his personal springtime, and he had failed to appreciate it in the garden of roses. He could remember that he had thought at the time, he was appreciating this part of his spring. They expressed their own glory of tragic youth by reciting poetry to each other. She liked Rupert Brooke and he liked Swinburne.[4] He realized now that he had spoken Swinburne's lines in an attempt to express his own deliciously sad yearnings, not understanding the truth in them. Now he could understand "what thing is the fairest of all things on earth as it brightens and blows."

The image of Diana in her wide hat and heavy string of large beads that hung as she bent over St. Paul's barge to smile down at him, was clear in his memory now. It was Eights Week on the Thames. He was not much concerned whether his own college crew held its place on the river, and he paid little attention to the ruddy-faced mothers with their ruddy-faced eager daughters and nieces in tow, flowing in an organdie stream toward the river. He had no time to wonder at the boyish boastfulness of the ancient oarsmen wearing their Leander ties and their old blazers, who came back each May for years to strut with amour propre.

The figure of Diana in white sitting at the tea table on his college barge, looking at him with devouring eyes, was all he could see or think about. Amid the chatter and the clinking of tea cups, he heard only her voice. The rooks in the elms that grew along the river banks were hopeless in their chatter against the conversational buzz over the barges. But still he could remember the colored pennants floating over the barges, and the trees dancing in reflection on the Thames, reaching beyond the gay reflections of the barges dancing closer to shore. Beyond the tree reflection was the reflection of the English sky.

They had walked to Meadow Road where she lived after dinner at the St. George, and hidden by the bushes by the gate, they had said good night. He could remember her body coming to press against his as if it had been drawn by a magnet, and he could remember the moist kiss that had made their words afterward, hesitant, meaningless and broken.

He could remember how he felt as he walked back toward his college and he could remember that he had never felt that way before or since. There had been some high moments in his life; when the Minnie Eagle Feather No. 1 came in for instance, but that was the emotion of high excitement, not the calm feeling of glory and power that could conquer all things. He could remember how his glory had imposed action and how after reaching his college, he had walked through its centuries-old garden and climbed to a crumbling piece of the thirteenth-century wall of the city of Oxford. From there he had looked over the meadows and the winding Thames. The Roman Eagles had marched here, and Charles's queen Henriette had walked in the garden with her flirtatious ladies-in-waiting. Immortal scholars and warriors and statesmen had walked here, but none of them was as important as he at that moment.

His memories flowed smoothly now. He remembered the road to Chipping Norton, and Diana's hair streaming back from the sidecar of the motorbike he had borrowed, and he could remember the echo of the exhaust along the walls that bordered the little out-of-the-way roads.[5] They stopped by a field of poppies flaming in the sun. The languor was complete. The bees buzzed soporifically, and even the song of the skylark as it came pouring down from the sky was lazy that day. The rooks flapped indolently across the poppy field, from wood patch to wood patch, and even their voices seemed to be softened. The wheat beyond the poppies waved ever so slightly.

He remembered the flood of emotion that came over him even more powerful than the happiness that seemed to race constantly through his body, as he looked down at Diana from the driver's saddle. Her hair matched the slightly waving wheat, and the black and white of her frock, and the flush of her face blended with the emerald of the meadows and the flaming poppies. A languor had crept over her. There was no whimsical action or other expression. When she finally spoke, her voice was like the moss-hidden brook.

They made no move to leave the motorbike. He had no desire to do so; he only wanted to sit and look at her without thought; in complete subjection to the humming glorification. He knew now though, after the passing of years of experience, that she was under the spell of the song, the brightness and the color, and the rhythm of the earth, at that long ago moment, and that her love had been in full tide.

He must have sensed something instinctively, he could now suppose, and his kicking of the starter must have been an expression from the prudery of the campus of Updike.

They spent the afternoon at the inn in Chipping Norton, sitting across from each other over empty tea cups, talking, laughing, and carrying on silly conversation. They didn't even notice the landlady who served them as she watched them from a far corner of the room with her face a picture of bitter-sweet softness. He remembered that Diana had suggested that it would be "frightfully odd, if I suddenly became you, Charles dear, and you should become me," and they spent most of the afternoon imagining the manifestations of this silly confusion of identities.

Then there had been The Clary. The lounge had several parties but again they were alone. He had grown used to the cigaret hanging from her lips with its end against her very white, even teeth. He remembered that there were two distinct lights in her eyes; one a sort of hunger expressing an inscrutable yearning and the other a soft light that poured over him, and made him feel that he could attain any objective he might wish to attain. That day in the Clary lounge, the hunger light and the soft light came and went alternately, and both made him feel that he had somehow failed in some mystical promise.

She had made one of her characteristic movements to rise, the quick kind when you might expect to see bag, handkerchief and gloves fall at her feet, but nothing of this sort ever happened. She said she must be going, then she sat again and looked at him with poignant sadness: "Charles darling, I daresay the war has taken something from me—done things to my femininity, y'know. I'm perfectly stupid." She hesitated a moment, then said, "I'm quite sure American girls are wonderful—it's hot and bothering to know it," then she laughed. She paused: "Y'know, I was on the land during the war—I think of myself as being a piece of ordnance or something. Y'know, standing ready to be used; to be shot off or something at a certain moment for old England, sort of business, then left alone incapable of self-action—impossible unless ordered by military thing—necessity; the war was frightfully long here, darling. I've lost the art of finesse—I love you. I can do nothing about it, I simply love you."

What about this against Updike standards? He looked into her eyes and saw there a primitive kind of submission; not a sudden yielding under the power of emotion, but there was the submissiveness of an animal.

He remembered a brief feeling of embarrassment; not over the situation, but a vicarious embarrassment for her. She seemed to be looking for something in his eyes. Her eyes were searching his face and his eyes he could remember, then she said, as though she had not found what she sought, "I must know if you love me at all—if you care a farthing."

He didn't even see his gardener Jules now as he came up under the window to scare the cat away from the bushes, and he became uncomfortable from the effect of his memories, when he suddenly realized that long ago in the Clary lounge, he had actually enjoyed the dramatics of the situation. He recalled too clearly for comfort why he had not told her that he loved her. He did love her but he didn't want to lose her. He remembered the obstacle of his poverty, and this made him feel better, but soon the sweat came to his forehead, when he remembered what had been behind his feelings long ago; it was the standards of Updike and the criteria set up by the co-eds—the window dressing as he would call it now. Also her cigaret hanging from her lips suddenly became a barrier again.

He remembered how her eyes shone with love that hurt him, when he had assured her that words were not necessary, and that she must judge by his actions. Then a cheap cockiness came over him as they had sat looking at each other, and the passing cloud representing the criteria of Updike, put her in a new light and she became fair game. He had trembled with the thought that he could pick her up and carry her upstairs, and the world would have been forgotten by her, but he would have been sweaty with embarrassment.

Her eyes were twinkling and dancing as she arose from her seat. She hurriedly snatched one of the pink tea cakes from the table and made for the door exactly as the Roman Diana might have done, and he felt slow and clumsy as he followed the lithe huntress.

Jules was having trouble with the cat in the bushes and he looked up at the window as if expecting irascible directions, but Chas. A. was not aware of him. He had suddenly become very unhappy, since he had to reminisce in sequence, even though he didn't want to do so. He wanted to stay in memory with Diana and the skylarks and the poppies under an English sun. He had to remember how he had resigned his scholarship to go with a geological reconnaissance party to east Africa. He had been given a Rhodes Scholarship because there were no ex-Rhodes scholars on the examining board at that early date, and because he had been president of the YMCA, president of the Student Council and had run the hundred in ten seconds.[6] He had even played the lead in the college play, to make sure of his qualifications in campus activities. He managed to become president of the senior class as well. His grades even at Updike had been a matter of good business and business-like maneuvering, rather than an indication of academic worthiness.

In Portuguese East Africa, he worked hard because he saw his opportunity in proving himself with the big oil company who had sent his party down, and he had felt like a Kipling character, and the Portuguese half-caste girl with whom he lived secretly gave him the proper coloration for a fiction hero in the bush.

His letters to Diana must have become pale, and their cheapness must have reflected upon his promises to her when he left Oxford. Back in the United States he began laying the foundation for the Chas. A. Wiggins fortune, and he was so absorbed in this that he scarcely noted the arrival of his letter which had come back from England, scrawled over with station markings, after two months in search of Diana Tennant. He was in a high fever of ambition now; he was on the geological staff of the great oil company.

After these compulsory sequential memories, he wanted to get back quickly to the pink and white girl, the Cher, the buttercups and daisies on the emerald meadow dotted with picture-book cows; back to the call of the cuckoos from the Oxford gardens, the suspended skylarks singing in ecstasy, the romance of the Thames during Eights Week; the little inn at Chipping Norton and the poppy fields across which the rooks flapped so indolently. He wanted to remember the pink and white girl across the table from him at the Old Oak associated with the sweetest hours ever stolen from lectures; the hours between ten in the morning until noon, after she had finished with her singing lessons.

But it was difficult to get that long ago English spring back with its beauty, its singing, its tranquility, that were the especial backdrop for his glory with the Dianesque girl with her voice like a moss-hidden brook's merry tinkle. He tried to hear her laughter and see her eyes so softly lighted with love and hunger. There was a translucent slide now that came between him and his images of memory, so that they lost their sharpness, and it seemed to be the quite logical sequence of Africa. He didn't want to come back to the rich room in which he sat and be conscious of Jules' puttering about the perfect lawns and gardens.

He shifted his body again, as one might shift during a dream, unconsciously acting as if the shift might facilitate the bringing back of that faraway spring with its images; allow him to escape from the wilted roses and the yellow grass leaves of disillusionment.

Natural Science

General Joe Higgins sat at his desk at General Headquarters. The light from the window, what light there was since General Headquarters of the Westarmies were in London, shone on Joe's bald head. The feeble light also picked out the flakes of dandruff on his new uniform; gathering in the wrinkles like drifted snow, since the tunic fitted him like a flower-girl's coat.

His hands were blue-veined and spidery as his long fingers seemed to crawl over the papers on his desk. His pince-nez were far down on his nose, and he had even clung to the black ribbon; the civilian ribbon to which they were attached. He even mumbled to himself as he had done for the last thirty years over his laboratory experiments.

Outside his quiet office, the General Headquarters Building was filled with excited and exigent people like the hibernating activity among red wasps. Tamberlania had dropped the first atomic bomb since the war of 1940–45.[1] As a matter of fact, Tamberlania had mis-dropped the first atomic bomb. One of her planes had got through the radar screen and, being harassed by the Westarmies' fighters, had dropped the bomb off the coast of Britain, missing its objective, the city of Latium, by three miles.[2] The other bomb-bearing planes had failed to get through the Westarmies' radar and jet fighters, and had sped back to their base without firing a shot at their jet attackers.

The American press was still free and had been taking the line only recently that Westarmies' defences were unbreachable. Hence Tamberlania suspected the opposite and attempted a sneak attack.

The surprise attack aimed at the most important ports of Britain had a deep effect on Joe Higgins, and the miss gave him little comfort.

There was the evacuation of Latium, especially of those people within five and two-tenths miles of the center of the explosion, which was of course about three miles out to sea. But soon Joe Higgins pushed the accomplished fact of the bomb back into a dark corner of his mind, since it didn't prove anything he didn't already know, and devoted himself completely to the study of more effective defense.[3]

He reproached himself audibly as he spread his spidery fingers over the papers on his desk, but his mumbled reproaches were inarticulate. He felt like a noted scientist standing before a conference of scientists from all nations, who had made an error in his calculations.

He had been sure that the radar warning system had been as perfect as man could make it, yet the plane had got through, and had just missed with its bomb the most important port in all Britain. Latium was the port through which all supplies and men from America were funneled. There were also essential factories there.

But there sat General Joe Higgins. Not like the Supreme Commander of the Westarmies, calling for conferences on strategy for retaliation but mumbling his chagrin over his error, and searching for a remedy with intensity of concentration.

Joseph A. Higgins, Ph.D., the most advanced scholar of atomic energy in all the world, and now Supreme Commander of the Westarmies had closed his doors to the world. His subordinates had seen fit to place a guard at the door, which was changed periodically. He had ordered that no one should be allowed to enter while he vindicated himself; while he searched for his error.

Outside his office, the world was in nervous excitement, and newsboys ran down the streets of London, Paris, Rome, Berlin and New York waving papers with black headlines. His staff waited in another part of the great building which covered forty acres.

His staff consisted of bluff generals and higher officers of lesser grade. They sat in their neat uniforms and waited with small grace. They talked with each other in American and English, and in their voices, bitterness was evident. Why, they asked each other by intimation, did the Westboard of Military Affairs select Joe Higgins as Supreme Commander? He who wore his uniform like a pair of overalls. He had never been inside Westpoint or Sandhurst or Annapolis.[4] Why, they wondered by inflection and indulgent smiles, did their Westboard select a detached idealist who had become fascinated by the miracle of atomic power?

From what they knew of his strategy, it was based upon his exact knowledge of geography, animal behaviour and the number of people in certain areas of the earth and what they did, and what they believed about God. He knew the number of people in any given spot on the globe, the earth's terrain and fruitfulness, the works of man both peaceful and military. He knew the economy of every unit of society, and how a bomb dropped in any given spot would affect that economy. He knew the destructive effect of the waves of the atomic explosion, which he said often, were like the concentric wavelets set up by a pebble dropped into a placid pond. He knew the diminishing deadliness to the number of people in the area where the bomb would be dropped.

But all this seemed as crackpot-ism to the generals, and they were continually embarrassed by his lack of military manners and social graces. When the King of England gave him an audience, he immediately forgot everything the American ambassador had told him, and had failed to remember even one item in the instructions given him concerning palace etiquette. He became the object of sneers wherever people gathered. Only the well-trained guard at the West-building ever saluted him.

Once when he had rushed out of his office with his hands full of papers, he as usual had forgotten his tunic, and a new American guard had shouted, "Hey, buster, where yu think you're goin'?"

The hours dragged on. The staff officers left by twos for lunch and then for dinner, then returned to wait and chafe over the delay of definite action. It meant war, they knew, and in war you must take very definite action. Their pride was hurt and their disgust profound. They brought papers back with them and the headlines were asking in a blatant, this-has-gone-too-far manner, what the Westcommander was doing. When would there be retaliation? Was Westeurope prepared to defend and attack as the people of Westeurope had been assured? In the text under the screaming headlines, the question was asked, why had not some message—an ultimatum—been sent to the dictator of Tamberlania, or why, better, had not the Tamberlanian capital, Tamur, been bombed? Everything was intensity. Human interest stories came from frightened Latium.[5]

But the door of the Supreme Commander of Westarmies remained closed, and the guards were changed many times in the military manner. Another night came on, and there was not a pin point of light in all of London, and people waited in their shelters with no confidence in their protection.

The newspapermen got their information from the staff officers who wanted desperately to give their views, even though cautiously and in the military form. But behind their talk was the deep disgust; the seething contempt for the little man who had been selected as Supreme Commander because of his almost heavenly knowledge of atomic power and strategy. The Chief of the Westboard was flooded with telegrams and with telephone questions, and ex-statesmen over the world berated the little scientist with dandruff on his new uniform.

Crowds formed and flowed about Times Square, in Piccadilly, around the Madeleine, at the Brandenburg Gate, along the Corso.[6] The crowd around Times Square shouted, "Joe Must Go," and carried the same on banners. Other banners shouted, "Joe's Too Slow—Let's Go." This in New York even as the darkness fell, but in Europe and England, people went underground scampering and barking like prairie dogs.

But General Joe Higgins was unaware of this. He hummed his worry and searched for truth and vindication before his imaginary conference of international scientists. His pride as a scholar would not let him even for a few minutes lie on his luxurious couch. He must find the error that let the Tamberlanian plane through the radar screen, which he was sure had been airtight.

Down in the staff room, the officers had their tunics unbuttoned, put their feet on the tables and some of them studied maps. Wrath pervaded the room.

"Hell," said General Carter, "give me the 58th Bomber outfit with plenty of fighter protection, and I'll guarantee to get every bomb concentration they've got, and even get old Khan himself with all his yes-boys."

"Daresay we are sure about bomb concentrations and plants?" said Sir Gerald Tapps.

"Yeah, we got them spotted alright," said Intelligence Colonel Crawford.

General Carter rose and let his hands fall helplessly before him as though they were unable to bear the weight of his contempt. Then he walked over to the window to look out upon the darkness, and there to fume.

"I must say I don't quite understand," said Sir Gerald. "What IS he doing up there? Does anyone know?"

There was no answer; only the shaking of a few heads, as if they were weary of wondering what he was doing up there in his office alone.

Sir Gerald continued: "You know, I was aware of him at Oxford. Just that—aware. He was a Rhodes Scholar; from, from, from some state with a most beautiful name. That doesn't matter. He wasn't KNOWN, you understand. He walked about the Meadows alone on Sunday afternoons. A friendly dog really. He looked into every face he passed as if he wanted to speak, and I daresay no one ever spoke to him. He wore glasses even then. There was a bit of egg on them one morning as he flew across the Quad, with his set face. He was always early for tutorials and lectures. I mean, you got the idea that he might actually commit suicide if he missed one.

"Naturally, he played no games. But one time my college, of which he was also a member incidentally by grace of myopia on the part of our Provost, divided up into two Rugger teams—intra-mural business. Here this bloke showed up in shorts and stood about during the game. Of course, he wasn't chosen on either side." Sir Gerald looked about the room and seemed to see something in the faces of the others which made him quite uncomfortable. He smiled apologetically, and said: "Of course, he wasn't our Supreme Commander then, was he?"

He felt the interest of the officers. Even General Carter at the window was listening. He continued: "I daresay, I shouldn't have remembered him from that incident, if I hadn't also seen him running with pained determination along the Tow Path during Eights Week, shouting between labored breaths, 'well rowed, well rowed' to our crew. His face was red; a very curious red. I remembered him and he fascinated me. I waited to see him each May during the races, and each year he stumbled along on his thin legs shouting with the others, 'well rowed, well rowed.'

"No one ever chose him to dance in hilarity, after our crew bumped Merton or The House.[7] He just stood aside and wiped the perspiration from his glasses, with that, you know, unhealthy red over his face. It wasn't a full-blooded red, but a sort of rash. Then as the others shouting and clutching at each other for dancing, crowded onto the barge to cross the river, he was always the last one on, and had to hold on for dear life to keep from being crowded into the river. He walked back to his college quite alone.

"Daresay, I shouldn't have remembered quite so clearly the incident of the Tow Path if he hadn't got a First in Natural Science, or something. People who get Firsts are pointed out, you know. He suddenly became worthy of notice, since he was an all-time high as you Americans say, in something or other having to do with science. Mind, that was of much importance when one considers the age of Oxford, and thinks of the mighty men who have worn the gown there during the centuries."

Victor Vitupi pointed at the ceiling above which were the General Headquarters offices, smiling, and said: "Well, this is one time when the playing fields of England had a dry haul. With apologies," he continued, "to all you gentlemen here." Vitupi, Brigadier-General, wore the Congressional Medal.

"Yeah," said General Carter turning from the black window, "Sir Gerald there was stroke on the Varsity boat, and the rest of these gentlemen were outstanding as oarsmen or on the Rugby field. Like me: I was All-America at the Point, and Vitupi here was one of the greatest ends the Point ever produced."

Just at that moment Lieutenant Ray appeared and walked up to General Carter, placed his heels together and said: "The Supreme Commander conveys his compliments to General Carter, and commands the presence of all members of the staff in his offices immediately."

There was the business of buttoning tunics, and grabbing briefcases. On the way, General Carter whispered to General Vitupi.

"Bet the Commander didn't say anything of the sort. Bet he said: 'Lieutenant, would you mind telling the gentlemen of the staff that I would like to see them if it is convenient?'" They both smiled sardonically.

When they appeared, General Higgins seemed to remember something suddenly. He stood and saluted his inferiors, before they could even have time to present themselves with the usual formality. Then he smiled pleasantly and said, "have seats, gentlemen."

He laced his long spidery fingers and looked at them with a wide smile.

"I have found the hole in our radar, gentlemen. I can assure you that we shall be more effective next time—in the future."

After he smiled at them for a moment with his Cheshire cat smile, he picked up some papers from his desk and began to study them.

The officers looked at each other and in the face of each one was the question: "What's this? No retaliation?"

The Commander laid the papers aside. He was highly pleased since he found that the error was not really his error, but the natural error that is ever associated with human frailty in execution. The Tamberlanian plane had got through the radar screen by accident. He laced and unlaced his long fingers and his Cheshire cat smile remained for some time as he studied the faces of his inferiors. Then he picked up a dispatch. He held it up.

"Here," he said, "is the report on the effects of our Sun-Bomb dropped tonight within the Arctic Circle, and here—," he held up another paper, "is the Tamberlanian apology and peace proposal." His smile was almost a gay one now.

"Sir," spoke up General Carter, "does this mean that we are taking no retaliatory action, sir? That we shall not take immediate action?"

"Oh, but we have General," and the Cheshire cat smile came again. "This dispatch."—Here he handled the paper again. "We've dropped the Sun-Bomb within the Arctic Circle close enough to the scientific Tamberlanian station there, so that they could get the full significance of its devastating power. Dr. Gheng is stationed there, and he'll be able to interpret the thing accurately. He'll know what the Sun-Bomb means, be assured." He picked up the other paper, "hence this peace proposal."

"Hee, hee, hee," he laughed diabolically, "they had no idea we had the Sun-Bomb, or I assure you, they never would have been brash enough to attempt a surprise attack. Hee, hee, hee, they know now—yes, they know now. With all of Gheng's puttering, hee, hee, hee, it'll take them ten years—yes, maybe twenty. By that time, things change; things change."

"But sir," spoke General Carter again, "why drop the Sun-Bomb on the Arctic waste. Pardon me sir, but I'm afraid I don't understand." He looked about at the others. "I'm sure these gentlemen———"

Commander Higgins looked genuinely surprised. He said: "General, perhaps you didn't understand me." He picked up the second paper again and continued. "I have here a peace proposal from Tamberlania. Able Dr. Gheng got in touch with Tamur immediately after our Sun-Bomb shook the top of the world, you see. I knew he would, hee, hee—I knew he would."

"But, but———," stammered General Carter. His tie seemed to be choking him.

The Supreme Commander paid no attention to him. He fumbled with the papers on his desk. As he fumbled, he said, "Mm-m-m-m-m, let me see. Yes. Quite right. If we had dropped the A-Bomb on Tamur, we would have destroyed—let me see. Yes, exactly—no, not exactly, but approximately, three hundred thousand men, women and children, and if we had dropped the Sun-Bomb on Tamur———." Here he looked at the faces about him, saying, "assuming that we got through, we could have wiped out the city completely. As one might rub out a dot on the map which symbolizes it."

He laid the papers down and looked around at the faces of his staff with obvious pride.

After some moments of his Cheshire cat grinning, he asked: "Any questions, gentlemen? Any suggestions? You understand, gentlemen, that the dictator would not have been in Tamur, don't you? Only the people; the fear-dominated and obedient people."

Then there was a very long silence.

The Meek Shall Inherit?

David stood before the mirror, parting his hair. He wasn't thinking of the parting, which was after several minutes of stroking, perfect. But combing so that the parting was straight and neat was a habit, and tonight he was doing it mechanically, as though some very familiar action were necessary to offset his unpleasant thoughts.

Finally, he laid the comb down and picked up his Phi Beta Kappa key which dangled from a chain which in its turn connected a watch with a fingernail clip. He put the watch into the watch pocket of his pants, then shoved the clip into the side pocket, fingering the key to make sure that it would hang on the outside, and be visible. It was too hot for a coat.

He waited for the heavy footsteps of his landlady to indicate that she had made another trip into the kitchen with things from the supper table, before he descended. Her sweaty face and her back hairs waving like antennae were too much for him tonight.

Ordinarily she seemed to be just one of the homely, good-hearted people of the world, who enjoyed doing nice things for others; the ordinary people of the world who did things for the people of more importance than themselves. She was in the front room every night when he left to have a date with Carol, and she made him happy on such nights, as a sort of symbol of the peasant rabble giving godspeed to the prince. On such occasions he was a prince, you know, in a way. He loved Carol, and the fact that he was sure Carol loved him, made him a little, just a little arrogant, though he realized that scholars should be above such things.

Thus was he the prince when he descended the stairs, and Mrs. Shelly, beaming as she dried her hands on her apron, was the loyal people on ordinary nights when he descended, scented and combed. She always said, "got your key, I guess," and he would answer with a smile. Then a little later, he would feel of his Phi Beta Kappa key alongside of his pants pocket, to make sure that it was hanging outside and had not slipped into his pocket.

But this night, he didn't want to see Mrs. Shelly, so he waited until the heavy footfalls could be heard in the kitchen and the swinging door had puffed shut, before he left quietly. Out in the darkness he didn't feel of his key.

As he walked down the street, he could feel the presence of the people sitting out on their front porches; a hint of white, a murmur of lazy voices. It was so hot and dry this summer that the insects were silent. The little southern town was sleepier than ever, and even the pines that seemed to guard it from the hurry of the world, were somnolent. People, it seemed to him, were waiting for something which they really didn't expect to happen.

Carol's house set back among the magnolias was dark and quiet, but he knew that Dr. and Mrs. Shirley would be sitting out on the porch talking desultorily. He believed he could smell the doctor's cigar.

Before he came to the house, he crossed the street into the darkness of the trees on the other side, then when past the house he re-crossed, and continued along the street until he came to the edge of town. He came to the wagon bridge which spanned Haynes Creek, and he could smell the mule droppings on the splintery flooring. He stopped and looked over the railing and attempted to see down into the darkness of the dry bed. He looked at his watch by the light of a match. He would wait until just after the second show ended. They would stop at George Monk's drug store after the show, he knew.[1]

He was a highly intelligent young man so he conscientiously attempted to analyse the reason for his deep hatred of Stuffy Wilson. Carol was too fine a girl to ever have anything in common with old

Stuffy. When you thought of it, it was really ridiculous; to put it into Stuffy's own words, "what a laff."

That bird, he believed, could sweat when the glass was at zero, and he could remember, when they went on picnics, how Stuffy got his mouth greasy with food. It was disgusting the way he lifted the lids of the picnic baskets long before it was time to eat, and he thought of the way his summer sport shirt, with low V neck was lower than the hairline on his chest. He couldn't talk about anything except Mr. P.J.'s money. He talked about his father in that clumsy, consciously offhand way that showed anybody that he thought he was being kind to the boys who didn't have money.

David winced as he remembered the splash old Stuffy made at the University last autumn in football. What it was though, he thought, was what he, David, called the magic of repetition. Granted, old Stuffy was good, but after that ninety-five-yard touchdown against MSU, the sportswriters' eulogies grew like a snowball rolling down hill, and every time the State University was mentioned, they had to bring Stuffy's name into the story, whether he had done anything or not. One smart aleck started calling him "Willie the Weaver," but that didn't last long since Stuffy usually ran like a playful horse.

He concluded finally, as he turned and leant with his back to the railing, that he didn't really hate Stuffy; he was just disgusted with his big hairy arms, and the assurance with which he slouched about town in his tight duck pants; the white ducks that failed to meet the tops of his big, soiled tennis shoes; failed to meet the bright yellow socks, above which black, glistening hairs showed, and were so tight across his hammy buttocks. He guessed it was disgust with the way he towered over and overwhelmed you, and put his big earnest face close to yours, when he was emotionally interested in the thing he happened to be telling you; always ending with "am I right?", in a manner which suggested that the world must know that he was right; that the rightness of that which he was telling had been known by men from the beginning of time, and only fools would believe otherwise.

It was just that he was disgusted with the beastliness and the sanguine, sweaty, ham-handed earnestness of Stuffy, and hated the thought that Carol was having to put up with him tonight. He was sure that whenever she went out with him, she was doing it in order to be nice to him; like patting a bear on the head, when he attempted to lick your hand. He liked that simile and he resolved to use it sometime when he talked with Carol with cynical indulgence about old Stuffy. They had talked before about Stuffy's childishness and his thick head, and the way he used big words that were often miles from their actual meanings, just like a "Nigger." He had made Carol laugh one time when he was talking of the thickness of Stuffy, when he had said that the word "inconceivable" with him was like deuces wild in poker. He never played poker, but he could explain it to Carol, since scholars usually knew a little about everything.

An insect ticked down in the dry bed of the creek, and since he had "thought his unhappiness out," he began thinking of the insect. He had a desire to know more about insects, and he would get a good book on them some day. There was some reason why this little fellow was down there ticking away; he sounded sad, as though he missed the water, or maybe he was a drought lover and was glad the water wasn't there.

He looked at his watch and he could almost read it without a match, since the light of the waning moon, dulled by the heat haze, was almost strong enough. He decided to go home. He didn't know what he had really intended to do; how he had intended to express the jealousy that had come to him like a chill that afternoon, when Carol had told him that she had a date with Stuffy.

After being soft-voiced and expressing sorrow over the telephone, she seemed to have grown impatient, when he kept insisting that he had thought that it was understood he would call. He couldn't call any sooner, he stubbornly repeated. Then she had said, "don't be an oaf," and had hung up.

He guessed he had shown his deep disappointment, and now he realized that he had actually been upset because he knew she was going out with Stuffy. He wouldn't have minded if she had dated Harold Acton or somebody else. Harold was a brazen, clever fellow who could say rude things and get away with it, and was always depreciating himself and his wealthy father with such clever words and gestures of mock hopelessness. He considered his own existence a joke, and since nothing was sacred with him, he was fascinating to both sexes.

Thinking thus, everything seemed to be alright again as he started home. He walked in the shade of the trees that arched the walk, and was invisible in the inky moon shade as he approached Carol's house. Then he saw them coming along the walk, and he stopped and watched. They turned into the yard, and he wouldn't have noticed that Stuffy had been walking with his arm around Carol, if he hadn't had to shut the picket fence gate; then calmly returning it as they walked toward the house. In the milky moonlight, there was no mistake about it. The chill of the afternoon came again, and something hard came into his stomach.

By the time they had reached the porch steps, David had crawled through a hole in the picket fence, and then moving bent over, concealed himself behind a lilac bush. He had a good view of them and he waited. He didn't know why he was there, or why he had moved so quickly and so definitely. He had no definite thoughts and no definite feelings, except a high emotion that seemed to flood his thought plant. This emotion was warm and tingly and not too unpleasant, and the hand that held a branchlet of leaves to clear his view was shaking.

He heard Carol's laugh and it was gay and ringing, and he could see beyond them the empty chairs of Dr. and Mrs. Shirley.

Then he saw Carol put her hand on Stuffy's shoulder and smile into his face, then she laughed again, just as though she were laughing at the wit of Harold Acton. There was a silence, then the murmur of conversation again, and since he couldn't hear anything and his senses were strained, he fixed his gaze on the back of Stuffy's bull neck. He was excited, and he felt that he would be vaguely disappointed if the something fundamental which seemed to be promised him, didn't happen. There was the anticipation of something primordial.

He saw Stuffy place his great, hairy powerful hands on each side of Carol's soft waist, and he thought Carol was straining against him with both hands on his shoulders. Then with the purposefulness of a plunging fullback, he stepped up to her level on the porch, drew her body to his and lowered his mouth to hers.

There they stood; her body almost absorbed by his. They stood thus for some time, and David began to shake all over with vicarious bitter-happiness and excitement. He saw Carol's hand creep up from under Stuffy's arm and find its way to his broad back, then to his bull neck, and there it rested. He watched it carefully, as though in it; in its slow seeking movement, he would find the proof which he sought. He watched the hand so intently that he saw pressure in the fingers.

Under the influence of palpitating excitement, he followed Stuffy home. He kept back in the shadows with the alertness and caution of a hunting cat. He watched the broad shoulders appear in the glare of the street light, then become almost extinct under the moon shade of the trees, to appear again in full forcefulness and arrogance under the next light. When Stuffy turned into the spacious yard and walked with springing assurance toward the white pillars, he watched him. He watched him jump the flight of five steps leading to the porch, swing open the screen door, and almost simultaneously switch off the light in the hall.

When he reached his room, the queer, incomprehensible anticipation of primordial happenings had left him, and in its place came frustration and the most helpless kind of hatred. He wanted to kill Stuffy, and he felt that if Stuffy were in the room with him, he could do it. But the realization of the fact that he wouldn't do it, and further that he couldn't do it, plunged him into bitter frustration and self-pity. "Oh God," he groaned, as he fell on his bed. For two hours, he sobbed like a broken-hearted child, and the springs creaked rhythmically with his convulsions.

Thereafter, everything connected with Stuffy Wilson gave him a sensation of fear. An enervating wave ran over him when the noon whistle blew at Wilson's Textiles, and the sight of the family car, with Bigfoot Simpson, shiny and black, at the wheel, made him quiver. To see Stuffy's maroon convertible parked in front of Monk's made his blood turn to water.

He grew bitterly vindictive, and set out to translate the Iliad with a martyr's selflessness. He took the book with him when he drove out to collect from the red clay farmers and Negroes when their notes became due at the First National Bank.

He had been working at the bank since he was in high school in the little town that was protected from the world by its pines. He had come from his home of two rooms and a box kitchen, perched on the side of the foothills, where the original red topsoil had been eroded and had found its way down the Tennessee River perhaps a hundred years ago. A country school teacher ever hopeful and ever eager to give to others the pleasures of education which he so smugly enjoyed, believed he had found a genius, and brought him into the little town and got him a job at the bank, doing little odd jobs that Negroes couldn't do.

He had saved his money and had worked hard, and during his freshman year at the University had risen to be collector; the last of the onerous jobs. The next one would be of some importance.

The summer wore on. Translating the Iliad was like sucking an orange that was all fiber and no juice, but he kept at it like the martyr he knew himself to be, and he could think contemptuously of the people of the town and their blank looks if he told them what he was doing.

Then the tragic summer ended with tragedy. Jim Searcy, a fast-talking extrovert, who impressed you as being ever ready to jump through a fiery hoop on the command of old J.D., was promoted over his head to a cage in the bank.[2] Jim was brassy and as aggressive as a stallion, yet as adjustable as a hunting dog. You could see the "yes sir" forming on his lips before old J.D. had finished giving him orders.

He couldn't believe it. After his making Phi Beta Kappa in his junior year, the Saxons had written congratulations in a letter loaded with such phrases as "the town is proud of you," and full of praise for his enterprise and his manifestation of "the American spirit," ending with, "your job will be waiting for you for as long as you want it." He also saved the letter from Congressman Jerry Saxon, and the left-hand half-column of the local paper.

But with that same key glinting at the side of his pants, old J.D. called him in on September 1st and told him how sorry he was that—er—well, he didn't have the temperament for a banker—perhaps. He was cut out for bigger things, etc., etc.

With the money he had earned at the bank that summer, and with the last of the loan from Uncle Ben, he was able to finish his senior year at the University. The disturbance of his private life seemed to have extended to the universe, when he read of the Japanese attack on Pearl Harbor, and Christmas at the cold empty boarding house at the University would have been entirely tragic if Dr. Betz had not decided to stay in town.

Dr. Betz was in Economics, and he was very clever. His students loved his satirical remarks about capitalism. He could quote Marx and Veblen and any of the worthwhile writers on economics and sociology you could name, and his brilliance was a sort of rallying monument of granite covered with silver leaf.[3] He confirmed every suspicion about capitalism among his students, and finding himself somewhat restricted, inspired them with others, which he immediately found pleasure in expanding and confirming.

He was young, and a shock of hair would flop down over his right eye when he talked, giving just the right impression of intensity, since he never manifested intense feeling or drooled hatred. He was as cold and purposeful, and as efficient as the big spider that runs to the web-entangled grasshopper, and winds him into complete helplessness. The grasshopper of capitalism had no chance to fly through the perfect web of his logic, and once entangled, the procedure was cold and deadly and sure, from the first sting that brought paralysis to the last binding of a kicking leg.

Not only was Dr. Betz young with a shock of hair that fell over his right eye when he talked, but he had a mannerism in which he raised his thick eyebrows and allowed his lips to pout. The shock of hair of intensity, the satirical questioning of the eyebrow, and the judicial weighing of the pouted lips, were stronger criticisms than words, of the beliefs of capitalism. He would state an obvious truth, then push his lower lip out and cock his eyebrow as if interrogating some invisible umpire, and the statement would suddenly become ridiculous; even be transformed into an unusually stupid capitalist belief.

The students loved him; especially the bright ones, who were intelligent enough to understand him. There were only a few of these, however; to others, he was just another "prof" to be got around somehow. Naturally there was an inner circle of the few, who sat with him at a large table at the Varsity Tea Kettle and felt liberated and smugly detached from the ignorance of the world.

David, unhappy, vindictive and filled with injured innocence, found refuge with Dr. Betz and his inner circle, called the Wooly Worm Club. They were dedicated to the purpose of not only enlightening the world, but of bringing the social scales back to balance, and in their bright youth, they not only saw the mistakes of man down through the career of history but were disgusted by the fact that they were and had always been so obvious. They were resolved to swallow no more of the slick worms of desert theology, stuffy middle class maxims and capitalistic credo.

As they sat between classes at the Varsity Tea Kettle or in Dr. Betz's rooms, they told with cynical pleasure of little personal experiences with social arrogance and heartless greed. One young man told them of holding the door open for a Negro woman, and he pictured so graphically the gratitude in the old woman's eyes as she said, "God bless you," that a very pretty brunette, who sometimes disturbed Dr. Betz through the careless manner in which she sat on the floor eagerly listening to him, wiped her eyes without shame.

Then David, who had now regained his intellectual smugness in the collective expression, told the Wooly Worm Club of the very difficult time he had since Jim Searcy had been promoted to a cage at the First National Bank at home, and he had been let out. He didn't mind washing dishes at the Delta House, but to be displaced by Jim because he was more successful in collecting from the poor whites and the Negroes was really amusing. That's what he was saying now from his new attitude—amusing. David told them how he used to sit for an hour on the tongue of a wagon talking to a bent and gnarled old Negro, not having the heart to take his mules as the bank had instructed him to do. He would say with a cynical smile, which in itself seemed to say, "there you are; what are you going to do about it? The same old story."

This dismissal from his job; the job which he had considered to be the third rung in the ladder of life's success, had hurt him deeply and his frustration was so profound that he had spent a day in bed, saying over and over in his impotent rage, "the ignoramuses; the beastly skinflints." But now his vindictiveness was strengthened by collective glory, and with this feeling of herd security, and from behind the blinding shield of Dr. Betz's wit and satire, he could treat the incident of capitalistic persecution with amused contempt. He could assume this new attitude toward his old collecting job, but he couldn't forget so easily his vindictiveness which was born from bitter impotence on the summer night of milky moonlight.

In June, when the graduating class were going through their three days of ceremony, he sneered at the traditions with other members of the Wooly Worm Club; at the decadent mummery and ikon worship. They sat in the back row and exchanged significant glances, when a speaker mentioned "the Christian spirit," and "the American way of life." When the degrees were conferred on sections of candidates, instead of individually, to save time, they sneered at the omission of the tradition, surprisingly. He sat next to Iggy Stavinsky on the back row, and when the young men and women in their gowns stood up to have the privileges and benefits of educated people conferred upon them, he and Iggy slumped down on their sacrums in languid, cynical protest.

He sat at his window and watched the golf sticks, tennis rackets, stadium rugs, radios and expensive luggage being carried out from the big fraternity house across the street. He hated the black, sweaty chauffeurs who took orders from the pot-bellied fathers and fat, thick-ankled mothers, who in turn deferred to their sluggish, nonchalant sons, answering their solicitude in monosyllables.

He waited until the last shiny car had left the curbing of the house across the street, then came out of the drab boarding house, carrying his scarred, imitation leather suitcase in one hand, and holding the neck of a laundry bag thrown over his shoulder, with the other. The laundry bag was filled with pamphlets on the economic and social condition in the South, and soiled clothing.

In the desolate, heat-shimmering, sterile foothills, he thought of Carol and of the shade and the pines that guarded the little town's tranquility, and of the First National Bank, where he had many times visualized his name in gold lettering on a door. The cynical aloofness which he felt with Dr. Betz and the Wooly Worm Club at the University began to fade, and herd security to give way to his old feeling of frustration. As he sat on the sagging porch of his father's house, tears of impotence and self-pity came to his eyes. He made a gesture of hopelessness, when he smelled his father's sweaty body as he picked up the washpan and held it under the handpump at the edge of the decayed porch flooring. As his father sniffed and snorted, a dolorous old hound with the perfect expression of injured innocence got up and moved out of range of the splashing water.

He looked out over the rows of scraggly cotton which came right up to the yard gate that hung only from the top hinge, then at the barn that listed almost to the point of unbalance. The siding curled at the bottom and the paint had long since peeled off, and at the west end the jimson weeds were attempting to hide its scars.

The screen door opened and his mother with that apologetic manner which mountain women have when they trespass on Man's domain, said as she handed him a letter; "looks like a letter fur yew; Cason Bently fetched hit this mornin'."

It was a command from the War Department to appear before the local board.

He waited with others in the hot ante-room. The Wooly Worm Club had agreed to have nothing to do with the capitalistic war. There was not really an agreement, but a tacit understanding, that if called, they would stand on their constitutional rights and conscientiously object to the carrying of arms. He had said over and over to himself, the speech he would make to the members of the board. He even put the stereotyped statements characteristic of capitalist hypocrisy into their mouths, and answered them with the cant and the clever cynicism of the Wooly Worm Club.

Then the door opened and the board members came out for the lunch hour. Old Mr. J.D. Saxon, millionaire president of the First National Bank looked down at him severely, then spoke with studied kindness. At that moment, the whistle at the Wilson Textiles blew, and the vision of those women and girls coming out of the works like a herd of ewes and lambs, at the will of bluff, implacable old man Wilson, made him feel weak and unsure. Under emotion, he stood up and answered "yes, mam" to one of old J.D.'s kindly questions.

As he left the building, he made a sound that was supposed to drown completely his profound humiliation.

After lunch, he made no mention of his conscience, but he was turned down, and put in "4F" classification.[4] Skinny Platt passed, as did most of the others, it seemed to him. He walked over to the court house and sat on a bench, hating the world.

The court house people were coming back from lunch. Ben Simmons who had had a job there as long as he could remember was telling old Joel Pennington about something; a bright moment when he could savor the importance of being the informer instead of the subordinate under orders. His chalky hands made pictures in the air as he talked, and David could see the stained collar of the sombre alpaca coat and the dandruff flakes on the shoulders. Greying women came up the walk singly or in pairs; tools voting for the machine every election in order to hold their jobs. "Lick-spitals and prostitutes to the big-bellied gods of capitalism," thought David.

May Toll came along with three pasty young clerks, swinging her hips and tossing her "permanent." She saw him; she never missed a man. She raised her hand and wriggled her fingers at him. His eyes followed her to the entrance, and he lost interest in those who came later.

The careering flow of his hatred slowed up and spread out like the agitated waters of a mountain stream when coming suddenly to a reedy, marshy flat; fingering as they seek their way among the weeds and flowers. He thought about May, and the liberties she was allowed all over the court house. He smiled at his own cleverness; "and the liberties she allowed outside the court house," he thought.

He used to go there to record mortgages and sign releases for the bank, and he could remember how she brightened up the place with her creative hip swinging, and her empty little challenges, which forced indulgent smiles on the faces of the fusty old office holders.

Then being an intelligent young man, he began to wonder why he was thinking about her; why she had stopped the mad dashing of his stream of hating. Was it because she was the only embodiment of the creative spirit among all the sallow, dull, burnt-out embers that he had watched coming back from lunch? She had power; she was force, no matter what the ministers of the town might think about her. She was neither the vain, hopeless little words of Ben Simmons or the mild, sugary exchanges of greying women, and all the words that floated through the court house—from the janitor's cubicle to the County Court Room—couldn't prevail against the fact of her being.

In this mood, being extremely intelligent, he even dared to question the words of Dr. Betz; that is, the words that express the ideas of lightning brilliance but ignite nothing. Better the poster displaying the clenched fist behind "Mike" Mikailovitch when he spoke at the meeting in Lordstown last winter. He could remember his wild hair that shook as a punctuation to his fervent sentences, and the little flecks of foam that formed at the corners of his mouth, when he pointed to the clenched fist, and shouted that you "hadda meet force with greater force; meet hypocrisy with greater hypocrisy, and chicanery with more subtle chicanery, then when you finally have the superior power; when you are SURE you have the greater force, then strike without mercy."

He got up and pulled his pants from his sticky body. He felt better; he was protected by the herd again, if only in thought. He felt comfortable and important once more, and could feel this way since youthful cynicism—the rose of idealism nourished by the Wooly Worm Club, which was born on a dewy June morning and had not yet felt the ominous patter of dead, falling leaves; this rose and the clenched fist rising over the sprawling, bloody body of capitalism—could be fused into one symmetrical embodiment, to be covered by his cloak of sympathy.

When the government moved into the sleepy little town with bulldozers, shovels hissing steam, tractors, and every mechanical destroying device known to man, he speculated with the rest of the surprised citizens. The pines toppled like weeds before a mower, and great, naked red patches appeared in the earth. A woven-wire fence was erected to enclose an area of several hundred acres, and cavalrymen were brought in to ride around inside on eternal guard duty. Sentry boxes were set up, and armed guards appeared at the gate with fixed bayonets. The very tops of shiny buildings could be seen peeping over the pine tops, from the center of the mysterious area.

When David applied for a job, he was examined very carefully, and he had a long talk with a soft-spoken, gentle man wearing thick-lensed glasses about his qualifications. He had majored in Physics at the University and he was careful that the Phi Beta Kappa key hung on the outside of his pocket.

His advancement astonished him, and soon he was in charge of a department dedicated to the development of a gadget which would be a part of a bigger gadget, being developed elsewhere. No one knew what the gadget was to be used for, and the community in general not even knowing about the gadget, wondered constantly. The mystery that lay behind that woven-wire fence with its armed, stern-faced guards and its cavalry riders; with its signs that warned the curious away from it by indicating that it was charged, became complete. The people of the community could only squint across at the tops of the buildings showing above the trees and speculate.

David's salary overwhelmed him. He stayed at Mrs. Shelly's but he often had dinner at the hotel, and he started smoking cigarets at the time they became scarce. He couldn't figure out why this should give him such satisfaction. He perfected a smile that had in it both mystery and indulgence for those who asked what they were "doing out there," and he was made happy in watching old J.D.'s face expressing its worried eagerness, when he came close to him to whisper the question.

Stuffy was in England and Carol was waiting for the end of the war in an army wife colony in Virginia. He was a major now, it was said. Harold Acton was a private first class, and Jim Searcy had been deferred for obscure reasons which were never questioned.

The "Blue" army from the Lebanon maneuver terrain came through town, rumbling for hours down Main Street, with its interminable jeeps, trucks, guns and motorcycles. For some reason a band struck up. As the music sounded hidden wires in his body, he felt himself grow gloriously important as he stood watching. There was something in this collective expression of power and glory that brought an obstruction into his throat, and the kind of joy that brings tears came over him. He was at that moment part of the greatest man force in all the history of man.

As he came from the plant one day, he saw Dr. Shirley and Judge Henry Briggs talking. Judge Briggs adjusted his glasses and traced with his crooked finger the lines under the banner headlines on the afternoon paper from Lordstown. World attention was centered on Hiroshima in faraway Japan.

David bought a paper and went to his room to read the story. It took him some time to get his thoughts past the stone wall of factual statement, then he thought of the gadget they were making at the plant, and being an intelligent major in Physics, he knew.[5]

He bathed mechanically and went down to dinner. He didn't hear a word Mrs. Shelly said, and he didn't know what they were having for dinner. He went back up to his room with his thoughts not on the people of Hiroshima as one might expect of a member of the inner circle of Dr. Betz's students, but he was thinking of himself and his relationship with the world, now. He sat at the window and as the day died, his thoughts piled up so fast that he had to tear them down repeatedly to get at the smothered key thoughts.

He knew enough about chain reaction, now perfected apparently, to know that the war with Japan was over. He thought of the millions of men under arms on the islands of the Pacific, and on the home islands, and the great battleships with the little brown men crowding over them like monkeys; of fanatical little brown men waiting in caves all over the Pacific, waiting, ready, even happy to die for their god and their Emperor, suddenly frozen into inactivity. These millions of fighting men trained for the last twenty years for one purpose, now made useless by a single incident. Made useless by—by—by the hand of God in a way; at least as men had always imagined the hand of God might be held up with palm outward to stop force.

Force, he thought, that's what it was; the stopping of brute force for the first time in the whole history of the world, and making it impotent; useless. What would happen now to force that had its being in size, and strength, and courage and aggressiveness. What would happen now to the age-old balance among the species in the forests of the upper Nile, in the savage Rockies, and on the deserts, as well as among the grassroots in the vacant lot which his window overlooked. Perhaps the bull elephants would trumpet their bluff and give tacit recognition to respective ranges when the contenders were of equal strength, and the grizzlies would recognize power in each other which must be respected, and the balance would continue to be kept in the grassroots, or man even, might not be able to adjust himself quickly enough to the resulting chaos. But what would man do now?

If force is useless now, what of the clenched fist on the poster back of "Mike" Mikailovitch; what of the swarming brown men spread like an invasion of monkeys over the Pacific, and what of the endless line of trucks and guns and the thousands of men representing the millions of men who had glorified the modesty and flooded the fear in his loneliness through the dramatic expression of collective might?

The image of the animal earnestness of Stuffy Wilson, as he sprang up the steps to take Carol in his arms, came to him; old J.D.'s cold, sleepless calculations, and his grim caution, and then an image of the relentless, fanatical Mikailovitch with the foam specs in the corners of his mouth. He thought of May Toll and the rounded, soft creative force of her body. These forces all, would adjust to, compromise with, and recognize only equal or superior force in others, to create the balance, to create the pattern for all harmony on earth.

"That thing in Hiroshima," he thought, "it won't know how to play the game; it won't know the rules." He enjoyed for a moment his own cleverness, then he became serious again: "What if it is God? What if he is answering the prayers of the meek that have been wafted to Him from the beginning of man's thought. Then, again, it is really like the Greek Deus ex machina—Deus grown weary of man's little comedy." He liked this thought also. Then back to natural science again: "There's no germ of life in this disintegration at Hiroshima—always in disintegration, there is the germ that swells, and bursts and grows and reproduces the image that has gone. In this stopping of force as if God had suddenly held up his hand; finally deciding to take action in the affairs of man, and making force impotent, what will happen to the chain of life?"

He wondered if man finally had his own destiny in his hands. His thoughts came to the shy scholar from Washington, who blushed a little when you spoke to him. You knew now that he had played a very important part in the perfection of the atomic bomb. He remembered that he seemed to be always on the verge of exposing a deep mystery, especially after he recognized the scholar in David, and he remembered how he had often stopped in the middle of a sentence, as though he must review the first part of the sentence before going on.

He began to think of this highly civilized scholar, who was mild and shy and modest, coming out of his laboratory where he had been in harmonious balance with the great pattern, stepping daintily over the torn earth where the bulldozers had passed. He remembered him as he stood with his delicate hands behind his back, watching through his thick-lensed glasses the hairy, sweating, swearing work-men, as though he were afraid to attract their wrath to his person. Now he thought he was like a quiet, graceful animal of the deep forest perfectly adjusted to the lions and the ticks and the raging storms; confident in its protective coloration, its fleetness, its knife-edged senses, suddenly forced out onto the gashed and riven man-made clearing to become completely bewildered.

Insect stridulations came up from the grassroots of the vacant lot as he sat in the darkness. The night silence was broken by the coarse laughter of the men at Cotton Sellers' garage as they baited the half-witted Negro handyman Sam. He got up emotionalized by a thought.

He walked back and forth across the room, and he felt that he could scarcely wait for the morrow. He was thinking: "We could organize the scientists of the world; we the inventors could control our invention, use the power we had created for good. We could have world brotherhood and a society of nations that would work. A board of scientists could control the world, and there would be no more war, and no more race inequality, or poverty or suppression, or slums or crime. The board would punish the first nation that even thought of starting a war with the threat of the atomic power which we controlled exclusively; we the chosen of the thinkers of the universe."

As he paced, he glowed with bubbling glory. He could picture the members of the World Board of Scholars seated about a great table, considering the case of the large nation that had concealed from them the exact figures on the production of jet planes for the fiscal year. The man at the head of the table rose from his high-backed chair to speak, and the others sat back to listen. The scholarly speaker said that his patience was at an end; that if the nation under consideration did not make available the figures requested by the Board by May 1st, or give to the Board a more satisfactory account of the new movement which he understood was making difficult the Board's government in the southern provinces of the nation, that the Board trusting in God, and with reluctance, and a deep feeling of distress, must resort to punitive measures.

The great scholar sat down amid cheers, and the other members nodded their approval at each other. The great scholar at the head of the table was himself.

Source Acknowledgments

John Joseph Mathews's short stories are reproduced here by permission of his granddaughters Sara Dydak, Laura Edwards, and Chris Mathews and courtesy of the University of Oklahoma Libraries, Western History Collections, John Joseph Mathews Collection:

"The Thinkin' Man" (box 4, folder 24)
"Too Small for a Horse" (box 4, folder 25)
"Old Bob" (two versions) (box 4, folder 17)
"Lady of the Inn" (box 4, folder 9)
"Allah's Guest" (box 4, folder 2)
"Yellow Hair" (box 4, folder 29)
"Only a Blonde" (box 4, folder 19)
"The Apache Woman" (box 4, folder 3)
"The Talk of the Face" (box 4, folder 23)
"The Flower on Cadron Creek" (box 4, folder 7)
"Moccasin Prints" (box 4, folder 14)
"Bad Medicine" (box 4, folder 5)
"No Time" (box 4, folder 16)
"The Liberal View" (box 4, folder 12)
"What Thing Is Fairest" (box 4, folder 26)
"Natural Science" (box 4, folder 15)
"The Meek Shall Inherit?" (box 4, folder 13)

Notes

Introduction

Among sources for this introduction was private correspondence with the University of Oklahoma Press, spring 2012 and May 2015–December 2016, and with the University of Nebraska Press, January 2020.

1. The three longer Mathews works following *Wah'Kon-Tah* and *Sundown* were *Talking to the Moon* (1945), *Life and Death of an Oilman: The Career of E. W. Marland* (1951), and *The Osages* (1961). Source texts referred to in writing this paragraph were, in order: Henry Seidel Canby, "*Wah'Kon-Tah* by John Joseph Mathews," *Book-of-the-Month Club News*, October 1932, ed. Harry Scherman, p. 2, Oklahoma University Press Collection, Western History Collections, box 4, folder 5, University of Oklahoma Libraries; Mathews, *Wah'Kon-Tah*, 43–57, 359, 13, 330; Special Collections page for *Wah'Kon-Tah*, University of Missouri, https://exhibits.lib.missouri.edu /items/show/354; Mathews, *Wah'Kon-Tah*, 343–59; Mathews, *Sundown*, iv, 52–53; Warrior, *Tribal Secrets*; Mourning Dove, *Cogewea*, 15; McNickle, *The Surrounded*, 3–5.
2. John Joseph Mathews Collection, Western History Collections, University of Oklahoma Libraries, Norman, Oklahoma. Published and referenced with the permission of the Mathews family, works in this collection are hereafter referred to by initials, box number, and folder number, as in JJM 1.1. See also Mathews, *Old Three Toes* (hereafter cited as *OTT*); Susan Kalter, preface and introduction to John Joseph Mathews, *Twenty Thousand Mornings: An Autobiography* (hereafter cited as *TTM*), xiii–lii.
3. *TTM*, 105, xxxi, 78–79, 83, 85, xxxviii.
4. *TTM*, 295–96; Owens, "'Disturbed by Something Deeper,'" 163; Kalter, "John Joseph Mathews' Reverse Ethnography," 26, 45n2; "President's Uncle Dies: Kinsman Who Reared Mr. Hoover Succumbs at Age of 87, *Cincinnati Enquirer*, 13 April 1931; "The Herald's Daily Book Review:

Wah'Kon-Tah," *Dayton Herald*, 23 February 1933; "Old Diaries Published,"
Tahlequah Citizen, 7 July 1932; "Plan Series on Civilization of Indian
Nations," *Seminole Morning News*, 6 July 1932; "Free Public Library Latest
Books," *Central New Jersey Home News* (New Brunswick), 15 January 1933;
Osages, ix–x; Kalter, "John Joseph Mathews' Reverse Ethnography," 29, 24,
44 passim; *Osages*, ix–x, 789–90; *TTM*, xvii, 257n2; Snyder, "'He Certainly
Didn't Want Anyone to Know,'" 28–29; *TTM*, xliii, 257n2; Mathews, *Talking
to the Moon*, 1–17; *TTM*, 91 passim; *TTM*, xxxi, 261n29; JJM 3.5 (29, 31 January
1967 passim); JJM 1.1–4.45, 8 (framed sketches and sound recordings); JJM
4.1–29; *TTM*, xxiii, xxxii, xliv; JJM 4.31–35.

5. JJM 1.48, 1.50, 2.1 ("Wrote 11 short stories and sent 13 off to my agent, [2 of
them written in 1948] to carry out a-story-a-month plan."), 4.2–3, 4.5, 4.7,
4.9, 4.12–17, 4.19, 4.23–26, 4.29; JJM 4.1, 4.11; *TTM*, 265n61. Unfortunately,
there are no indications of which magazines may have rejected his short stories of this 1940s and 1950s era, if his agents at 101 Park Avenue did indeed
send them on. Recent pandemic conditions have slowed ongoing efforts to
track down archival records of his agents' holdings and the publishers they
may have contacted regarding successful and unsuccessful placements for
authors they represented. Experts in the history of the book and in publishing studies located in the New York City area may have better luck.

6. *OTT*, 137–49; JJM 1.48 (August, September); JJM 1.49 (the 1947 diary com-
prises 1 October through 30 November only); JJM 1.48 (31 December
1946); *TTM*, xx; Mathews, *Sundown* 235–37, 240–44.

7. *TTM*, 7, 267n75; JJM 1.50. A genealogical researcher might be able to
answer whether Carl and Carol Brandt of the literary agency Brandt &
Brandt were related to Joseph Brandt, Mathews's editor at the University
of Oklahoma Press. This editor's efforts have been unsuccessful.

8. JJM 1.50; JJM 2.1–2. "The White Sack" is a story Mathews revised for publication in his children's book and so is not included here in our present
volume, although its themes certainly appeal to adults, and it too is a
story for a nuclear age if ever there were one. See *OTT*, 43–54.

9. JJM 2.1–2 (1949 diaries) versus JJM 2.3–4 (1952 diaries); JJM 3.2–3 (1963
diaries); JJM 4.2, 4.5, 4.13–16, 4.24–25; MSS in JJM 4.1, 4.3–4, 4.6–12, 4.17–
23, and 4.26–29 compared for type and formatting indicators; JJM 2.3;
TTM, xli.

10. Kalter, "John Joseph Mathews' Reverse Ethnography," 26–27; *TTM*, xix.

11. *TTM*, xlv–l, 234–52; JJM 1.1–25, 1.27–28, 1.36–47, 3.14.

12. See *TTM*.

13. Before them, there were also Native writers like Simon Pokagon, Sarah
Winnemucca Hopkins, John Rollin Ridge, William Apess, and Samson

Occum going back to the beginning of contact and before (in indigenous, nonalphabetic writing forms). See Simon Pokagon, *Ogimawkwe Mitigwaki (Queen of the Woods)* (1899; East Lansing: Michigan State University Press, 2011); Sarah Winnemucca Hopkins, *Life among the Piutes* (1883), ed. Mrs. Horace Mann (Reno: University of Nevada Press, 1994); John Rollin Ridge (publishing as Yellow Bird), *The Life and Adventures of Joaquin Murieta, the Celebrated California Bandit* (1854; Norman: University of Oklahoma Press, 1955); William Apess, *On Our Own Ground: The Complete Writings of William Apess, a Pequot* (first published between 1831 and 1836), ed. Colin G. Calloway and Barry O'Connell (Amherst: University of Massachusetts Press, 1992); Samson Occum, *The Collected Writings of Samson Occum, Mohegan: Leadership and Literature in Eighteenth Century Native America* (New York: Oxford University Press, 2006). See also Mathews, *Wah'Kon-Tah* and *Sundown*; Mourning Dove, *Cogewea*; McNickle, *Surrounded*; Zitkala-Ša, "American Indian Stories" (1900–1902; 1921), in her *American Indian Stories, Legends, and Other Writings*, ed. Cathy N. Davidson and Ada Norris, 68–160 (New York: Penguin Classics, 2003); John Milton Oskison, *Black Jack Davy* (New York: D. Appleton and Company, 1926); Ella Cara Deloria, *Waterlily* (written between 1945 and 1954; Lincoln: University of Nebraska Press, 1988) and *Waterlily*, 237 (Raymond J. DeMallie, afterword to Deloria); Luther Standing Bear, *My People the Sioux* (1918?; 1928), ed. E. A. Brininstool (Lincoln: University of Nebraska Press, 1975); Francis La Flesche, *The Middle Five: Indian Schoolboys of the Omaha Tribe* (1900; Lincoln: University of Nebraska Press, 1978); E. Pauline Johnson, *The White Wampum* (Toronto: Copp Clark Company, 1895) and *Flint and Feather, Collected Verse* (Toronto: Musson Book Company, 1916); Charles Alexander Eastman, *Indian Boyhood* (New York: McClure, Phillips and Company, 1902), *Old Indian Days* (New York: McClure Company, 1907), *The Soul of an Indian* (1911; Mineola NY: Dover Publications, 2003), and *From the Deep Woods to Civilization: [Chapters in the Autobiography of an Indian]* (1916; Mineola NY: Dover Publications, 2003); Alexander Posey, *The Fus Fixico Letters: A Creek Humorist in Early Oklahoma* (1902–8), ed. Daniel F. Littlefield and Carol A. Petty Hunter (Norman: University of Oklahoma Press, 1993); Arthur Caswell Parker, *Seneca Myths and Folk Tales* (Buffalo NY: Buffalo Historical Society, 1923).

14. *TTM*, xxxix–xl; JJM 1.47–50, 2.1–14, 3.1–13.

15. La Vere, *Caddo Chiefdoms*, 1–39; Francis Jennings, *The Ambiguous Iroquois Empire: The Covenant Chain Confederation of Indian Tribes with English Colonies from Its Beginnings to the Lancaster Treaty of 1744* (New York: W. W. Norton, 1984); various historical and literary works regarding Cherokee

history from the pre-Columbian era to the present; *TTM*, xix, 258n6; Rollings, *The Osages: An Ethnohistorical Study.* See also Reilly, "People of Earth, People of Sky," 124–37; Hall, "The Cahokia Site and Its People," 100–103, particularly 102; and Brown, "The Cahokian Expression," 104–23 (all in *Hero, Hawk, and Open Hand,* ed. Richard F. Townsend).

16. *Osages,* 789–90, 3–19, 7; Hall, "The Cahokia Site and Its People," 102; *Osages* 28–29.

17. JJM 2.3–14.

18. *Wah'Kon-Tah,* 63, 91, 138, 142, 144, 149, 151, 253, 257, 259, 288; *OTT*, 174n12; *TTM*, xxxviii; JJM 1.1–4, 1.6, 1.20–22, 1.24, 1.46, 1.48, 1.50; "Michael Aloysius Feighan, 1905–1992," Biographical Directory of the United States Congress, https://bioguide.congress.gov/search/bio/F000060.

19. JJM 1.48–50, 2.1–2; Saunders, *Cultural Cold War,* 1–6, 21–22, 241–43 passim; *TTM*, 266n73; Pevar, "1953–68: Termination," 7; Fortunate Eagle, *Heart of the Rock,* 15–27; Tebbel, *History of Book Publishing,* ix–xi, 1–102. In my reading of Mathews's diaries, I have not taken specific, nonmarginalia notes about his entries related to termination and relocation. However, I do recall mention of these concerns in the diaries between 1950 and 1970 (folders accessed: JJM 1.26, 1.29–32, 1.34–35, 2.3–14, 3.1–9 4.38, 4.42).

20. Private correspondence, January 2020; *TTM*, 263n52; Schedler, "Formulating a Native American Modernism." In 1950 only 36 percent of Americans still lived in rural areas; by 1990 that number had reduced to less than 25 percent. During Mathews's childhood, the figure was between about 50 and 60 percent. United States Census Bureau, table 4, "Population: 1790 to 1990. United States Urban and Rural." See also Mathews, "Author Joseph Mathews Discusses . . . Dollar-Importance," 10.

21. Tebbel, *History of Book Publishing,* 1–102; Saunders, *Cultural Cold War,* 1–6, 21–22; Mathews, *Talking to the Moon*; *TTM*, xxxix–xl.

22. Private correspondence, January 2020.

23. Mathews, "Author Joseph Mathews Discusses . . . Dollar-Importance," 10–11; *TTM*, xxiv–xxv; *OTT*, 140; *TTM*, 263n52.

24. Mathews, "Author Joseph Mathews Discusses . . . Dollar-Importance," 10.

25. Private correspondence, May 2015–December 2016, January 2020.

26. H. W. Wilson's Readers' Guide Abstracts; H. W. Wilson's Readers' Guide Retrospective: 1890–1982, https://www.ebsco.com/products/research-databases/h-w-wilson-databases. Other prevalent short story writers, perhaps in some cases less well known today, included John O'Hara, Frank O'Rourke, Georges Carousso, Arthur Joyce Cary, Margaret Cousins, James Thurber, Frank O'Connor, Wallace Stegner, Booth Tarkington, Sean O'Faolain, Conrad Richter, and Roald Dahl as well as James Baldwin.

27. *TTM*, xliii; Mathews, *Life and Death of . . . E. W. Marland*, 65–105 passim.

28. *TTM*, 158–230, xx, xxvi, 295–96.

The Thinkin' Man

1. Mathews may be referring or giving tribute to Packsaddle Ridge in the Bridger National Forest, south of Jackson Hole, Wyoming. Bill Maze may be a tribute to Bill Barron, described in the headnote to this section and also mentioned in *Twenty Thousand Mornings* and *Old Three Toes and Other Tales of Survival and Extinction.*

2. In his autobiography Mathews writes: "We crossed Two Ocean Pass and came into the drainage of the Snake River, and finally camped on Pilgrim Creek, a feeder of the Buffalo Fork of the Snake." The Buffalo Fork runs along the northern part of the far eastern edge of the Grand Teton National Forest. Mathews was somewhat mistaken that Pilgrim Creek feeds the Buffalo Fork. The Buffalo Fork joins the Snake just south (downstream) of Moran, Wyoming, while Pilgrim Creek runs into Jackson Lake and the Snake River west (upstream) of Moran.

3. Aside from the aptness of the name Fortune for a big boss from New York City, Mathews may have chosen this name as a tribute to his relative Tony Fortune. Tony Fortune, with whom Mathews hunted coyotes during high school, was the husband of his mother's niece Mamie; his cousin's husband.

4. Two Ocean Pass is a pass that crosses the Continental Divide in the Teton National Forest about fifty miles northeast of Jackson Hole, Wyoming. North Two Ocean Creek divides in two here to flow toward both the Atlantic and the Pacific Oceans. A National Natural Landmark designates this point on the Divide.

5. The Hole is Jackson Hole. Stinking Fork trail could be a reference to the Shoshone River, within and east of Yellowstone, and near Cody. A Stinking Fork is referenced in diaries of emigrants on the Jim Bridger Trail and appears to be an indication that one has reached the Shoshone (also referred to as the Stinking Water or Stinking River because of the volcanic fumaroles and hot springs near Cody) in a journey north from the Greybull River. That area seems far out of range for this location, but there are of course many geysers, fumaroles, and hot springs within Yellowstone Park.

6. Rocinante is Don Quixote's horse. The implication when the nickname is first introduced as a joke between Grace and Jack is that Fortune is an idealist with his head in the clouds. Don Quixote believes himself to be living in the chivalric Middle Ages rather than in his own more mundane time. Perhaps also, Grace and Jack believe him to be easily deluded and deceived. The title

comes into play as well, as Don Quixote reads too much, perhaps is seen as thinking too much, whereas the story exhibits Fortune as thinking just enough, just right, accurately and effectively. Though still perhaps with regret or remorse, as sitting by the fire with his head in his hands might indicate.

Too Small for a Horse

1. In the typescript at this spot, "care" is crossed out and "cake" written in, leaving "car" alone. The "old Model T" is mentioned; possibly Buff is saying he ordered a new car. Cake in the final paragraph of the story refers to animal feed; Buff may have ordered a carload of this.

Lady of the Inn

1. The Picts lived in eastern and northeastern Scotland when the Romans occupied the British Isles. Unknown is whether they were Celts or another ethnic group, but Argyllshire where this story takes place was not their domain at that time. They first appear in written sources by outsiders at the end of the third century, when they attack Hadrian's Wall along with the Irish (Scots having their origin in Ireland). By the 600s the Picts had united their domains and encountered Christianity. In the ninth century they unified with the Scots into the kingdom of Alba. They were known for body painting and carved stonework.

2. Girard was the maiden name of Mathews's mother, thus the last name of his maternal uncle and grandmother.

3. Plus fours are sporting trousers that end at the upper shin, their name indicating that they are four inches longer than knickerbockers. In the 1920s they were associated with the Prince of Wales.

4. In his 1963 story "The Royal of Glen Orchy," which he wrote for his book for boys aged eight to twelve, Mathews noted that a gillie (ghillie) was a "guide to deer stalkers for shooting in general." McCarriker appears as a ghillie in that story as well (as McCarricker). The later story takes place about twenty miles southeast of Glencoe, where a vignette from "Gallery," another published story found in his archive, is located.

5. Vauxhall is a British car company founded in 1903 in London. Its 1920s models include both closed and open carriages.

6. Whin or whinbush is also known as gorse or furze. It is a variety of evergreen shrubs with an abundance of yellow flowers. These shrubs thrive through fires, which usually accelerate their germination from seed and can allow their ability to sprout from the stem to give them dominance for a time afterward. Bracken is a variety of fern, large and coarse, often found on the moors. A brogan is a heavy, laced, ankle-high work boot.

7. Dottle is the unburned tobacco at the bottom of a pipe, often wet from the smoker's saliva and the moisture in the tobacco. Mathews was a life-long pipe-smoker from at least the 1930s on. Blackcocks are the males of the *Lyrurus tetrix* species known as black grouse. The females are referred to as greyhens.

8. Compare to the jaguars and other large cats in Mathews's Mexico stories and elsewhere.

Allah's Guest

1. Bedouin is a name for several tribes and tribal confederations of Arabic-speaking herders tied together "in networks of real and fictive kinship" whose people generally lived a nomadic lifestyle until the changes in the region wrought by Western imperialism, including the advent of global oil production. The Aneza or Aniza is a confederation of Bedouin tribes that live in northern Saudi Arabia, western Iraq, Syria, and neighboring states. I have let Mathews's spellings for these groups stand.

2. A Nazarene is a follower of Jesus (of Nazareth). There was also a fourth-century sect of Jews in Syria who accepted the divinity of Christ. Here too I have left Mathews's spelling alone.

3. *Sheikh* means "elder" in Arabic, and is used to designate a tribal leader among Bedouins. A *sheikha* or *shaykhah*, however, does not necessarily mean elder, but wife or daughter of a sheikh (in this case, both). Women may become sheikhs, as opposed to shaykhahs, though it is rare. A contemporary writer might capitalize sheikh (or Mathews's spelling "sheykh") before a proper name, as one capitalizes the chief in Chief Joseph, but he might have been onto something by refraining from doing so.

4. The Anglo-American Oil Company was founded in 1888 by Standard Oil of New Jersey to market oil in the British Isles. It is a predecessor to Exxon.

5. The Shammar, a confederation of three smaller groups, is one of the largest tribes in the area recently known as Iraq, Saudi Arabia, Kuwait, Palestine, Syria, and Jordan. They held hegemony in the region in the mid-1800s. Historically, they have been rivals to the Aneza.

6. A beyt is a tent, or household.

7. Rabia is a variety of wheat.

8. *Wellah* appears to be Mathews's way of writing Wallah, or "by Allah." *Billah* means "with Allah," or "in Allah," as in *Audhu billah* (I seek refuge in Allah) or *la hawla wa la quwwata illa billah* (there is no power or strength or transformation or progress except with and through Allah).

9. El Wejh, or Wejh, is a city in northwestern Saudi Arabia on the Red Sea. It lies several hundred miles due south of Damascus. Today one would travel through other nations to reach Damascus.

10. Hayil, or Ḥāʼil, is a city in the central northwestern part of Saudi Arabia. It served as an oasis along a route frequented by caravans making the pilgrimage to Mecca. Between 1834 and 1921 it was the center of the dynasty of the Rashīdī emirs, one of the clans of the Shammars.

11. A league is the distance a person can walk in an hour, or about three miles. However, the actual distance of a league has varied over time and culture.

Yellow Hair

1. A jacal is a style of house found in Mexico and the U.S. Southwest, made of adobe and supported by poles. Its architectural heritage reaches back into the eras prior to European intrusion.

2. *Town & Country*, a magazine founded in 1846, describes itself as a site of elegance shaping "readers' discerning tastes in fashion, travel, design, beauty, health, and the arts and antiques," and chronicling the achievements of the most famous figures in the United States.

3. José Clemente Orozco (1883–1949) was most famous as a muralist in the social realist vein. Like Rivera, he left his mark not only in Mexico but in famous and regional locales in the United States. One well recognized section of his mural "The Epic of American Civilization" at Dartmouth College is known as "Gods of the Modern World." He was critical of the impact of the Mexican Revolution (roughly 1910–20), though an apparent champion of the working classes. Just after this story was composed, his illustrations for John Steinbeck's *The Pearl* were published. Diego Rivera (1886–1957) was another founder of the renaissance in Mexican mural art of the early twentieth century. Married in 1929 to the artist Frida Kahlo, Rivera painted not only in Mexico, Europe, and elsewhere but in major cities in the United States, such as San Francisco, New York, and Detroit, and influenced the murals of San Francisco's Coit Tower. His active communism and brief stay in the Soviet Union—though complicated by equivocal and changing relationships to Stalin and the Soviet state—is likely an important contrast here to Orozco given Mathews's antagonism toward communism. Both muralists were influenced by the indigenous heritage of Mexico.

4. "Rancho Grande" is a corrido, later covered as a country and western song—sometimes with lyrics vastly changed from the Spanish original—by Elvis Presley, Dean Martin, Freddie Fender, and Roger Creager. Its first lines are: Allá en el rancho grande / Allá donde vivía / Había

una rancherita / Que alegre me decía / Que alegre me decía // Te voy a hacer tus calzones / Como los que usa el ranchero / Te los comienzo de lana / Te los acabo de cuero (There on the large ranch / There where I lived / Was a little rancher girl / Who happily told me / Who happily told me // I'm going to make your breeches / Like those that the ranchers wear / I start them with wool / I finish them with leather).

5. Four-time Academy Award nominee Charles Boyer (1899–1978) was famous for his roles in *The Garden of Allah* (1936), *History Is Made at Night* (1937), *Conquest* (1937), *Algiers* (1938), *Love Affair* (1939), *All This, and Heaven Too* (1940), *Back Street* (1941), *Hold Back the Dawn* (1941), and *Gaslight* (1944).

6. Mathews appears to refer here to the Pan-American Highway, initiated at the fifth Pan-American Conference in 1923. By 1950 Mexico became the first country in the Americas to complete its portion, though at this writing that achievement was yet a few years away. The highway runs from Nuevo Laredo, Tamaulipas/Laredo, Texas, through Monterrey, Mexico, to Mexico City before continuing south. North of Laredo there is no official Pan-American Highway, but one branch goes through San Antonio to Dallas while another heads west toward Albuquerque. The connection to Los Angeles made here is unclear but consistent with Miguel's transnational mobility and border identity.

7. Edward Laurence Doheny and Charles A. Canfield discovered and drilled the first successful oil well in the Los Angeles oil field in 1892–93. The oil boom created there may have been one of the attractions drawing Mathews, newly married and in his midthirties, to Los Angeles in 1925. Doheny also drilled in Tamaulipas, a province of Mexico where Mathews stayed in 1940, and was involved in the Teapot Dome scandal that temporarily took down the founder of Sinclair Oil, a company with which Mathews had a prospect as an exploratory geologist in the early 1920s. Doheny and others like him were made famous by 1927 through the characters in Upton Sinclair's *Oil!* During his stay in Mexico, Mathews sought out conversations with oil men and others affected by Mexico's 1938 nationalization of the oil industry. Of course, he later published his fourth book on the oil tycoon Ernest W. Marland.

8. On October 13, 1939, Mathews wrote in his diary: "I went to the 'White Cap' office and chose an Indian boy to drive for me so that I could enjoy the mountains. He has a bright face and a white toothed smile, and calls himself Ray Bayez. I made arrangements with him to drive to Mexico City. I also asked him if he could answer the many questions that I should likely ask about everything we passed. He assured me solemnly that he

could. He said that he could speak English and a little French. As we climbed, I soon exhausted his English, and tried him on French, but that was, as far as I am concerned, only a selling point in order to get the job of driving. So with bastard English-Spanish we climbed into the most interesting country in the world." A different White Cap organization was "las Gorras Blancas," described by one historian as an organization of masked, native night riders resisting Anglo land encroachers in territorial New Mexico. (Still other White Cap organizations in Indiana and Tennessee were associated with the Ku Klux Klan, a decidedly pro-Anglo movement.) Las Gorras Blancas nominally faded out by the end of the nineteenth century, yet is credited with being the root of the Alianza movement of the 1960s.

9. A reader may be able to discern that Mathews chose Helga's perfume carefully. The scent called One Night in Paris was invented in 1929 by the aptly named Bourjois cosmetic company, founded by Alexander-Napoleon Bourjois, a cosmetologist in the Paris theatres. The scent became a worldwide hit during World War II. It blends ylang, violet, cedar, Turkish rose, vanilla, peach, musk, and bergamot. Its association with the bourgeois and semianonymous atmosphere of World War II seems precisely the target at which the author aims.

Only a Blonde

1. Coyotl appears to be a fictionalized name used to disguise the identity of Chilapa, a town to the east of Chilpancingo in the Mexican state of Guerrero, south of Mexico City.

2. A magnitude 7.7 earthquake affected the state of Guerrero on April 15, 1907.

3. Thorstein Veblen is well known for his 1899 work *The Theory of the Leisure Class*. He originated the idea of conspicuous consumption. While critiquing capitalism and the unproductive business class, his views were not perfectly coincident with Marxism, not particularly supportive of organized labor movements, and "castigated 'vested interests' and the 'common man' alike." The appearance of "Weblen" here may imply that Shelly Peters does not realize how much she is a part of the leisure class Veblen attacked, nor is she a strong enough student to understand the incompatibilities of his thought and Marx's. It also deserves some notice that Gottschalk's is the name of a department store catering to the small town market.

4. The Fabian Society was a precursor to the Labour Party in Great Britain. It was a socialist movement that advocated gradual change over revolution and promoted democratic socialism.

5. Although Mathews mentions Rupert Brooke in another story, "What Thing Is Fairest," as well as in his January 1940 diary from which "Only a Blonde" derives, he might mean Arthur Brooke, the sixteenth-century English poet, here. Milton and Shakespeare are the other two writers mentioned, and Arthur Brooke was the main source for Shakespeare's *Romeo and Juliet*.

6. Mathews wrote extensively in both *Wah'Kon-Tah* and *Sundown* about the relationships in the Osage nation among persons fully of Osage ancestry and persons whose ancestry was both Osage and European. In using the common terminology and ideology of the day (full blood, mixed blood), he changed his spellings through the years, perhaps due to different editors at his presses, who perhaps themselves were not always internally consistent within one text. In *Wah'Kon-Tah*, we see full-blood (or simply Indian) and mixed-blood; in *Sundown*, fullblood and mixedblood; in *The Osages*, mixed-blood but fullblood. For this text, we have followed Mathews's typescripts.

7. Taxco is a town southwest of Cuernavaca (south-southwest of Mexico City), also in the state of Guerrero. Chilpancingo is directly south of Taxco, on the road between Cuernavaca and the coastal city of Acapulco.

8. Mathews is probably referring here to the Constitution of 1917, which included land-reform and agrarian programs. The revolutionary Emiliano Zapata had championed these reforms. Shortly following its adoption, the president was unseated in a coup because he was not implementing the constitution's policies. Following the coup, Presidents Obregón and Calles began land redistribution and the restoration of *ejidos* or communal lands belonging to villages. Though slowed by Obregón's assassination and the Depression, these efforts resumed by 1934 and continued until 1940 under Cárdenas. After the election of Manuel Camacho that year, Mexico entered a period of slowed reforms and increased industrialization and urbanization, so the setting here may be prewar, though agrarian claims from U.S. interests were settled during the later era.

In July 1940 Mathews wrote in his diary: "Pépé [his host] has told me without the least bitterness of the partition of some of his best land into community plots of about two hectares each (about 7 acres), and he has given me a picture of the effects of this agrarian policy of the Government—naturally from the Hacendado angle. However, he is fair and gives both sides, and valuates the whole system objectively. However I should like very much to attend one of these meetings of the members of the board of the Ejido, sometime when a representative of the Agrarian Bank comes to talk with the members. Or, I should like to visit sometime when they discuss the affairs of the community."

Stories from Indian Country

1. Mathews, *The Osages*, 568.
2. Mathews, *Talking to the Moon*, 84.
3. Mathews, *The Osages*, 740–41.

The Apache Woman

1. The Cimarron River flows from the northeast corner of present-day New Mexico through western Kansas and the panhandle of Oklahoma to the Arkansas River at present-day Tulsa. At its height, the Osage hegemony stretched across most of the four current states of Missouri, Arkansas, Oklahoma, and Kansas. By locating the action at the headwaters of the river, Mathews indicates that the Osages are far to the west within their territory or westward of it in common hunting grounds or another tribe's territory. He does not indicate which Apache group is encountered, perhaps because his sources did not record it or, if wholly fictional, he did not think it important or did not know the different divisions.

2. This sentence is of interest for two reasons. It is the only place where Mathews originally typed "Beaver Band," but crossed those words out in favor of "Bear People." Whether he forgot this correction while proofing the subsequent pages or intended to indicate a smaller division of the former group is unclear. Also, in his autobiography, Mathews writes long passages about the fetish objects that World War I pilots brought aloft with them, which tie the anxiety of this nineteenth-century character to Mathews's generation:

> They were often tied to the struts of the planes, almost ceremoniously before the pilot of the bomber climbed into his cockpit, but more often they only fondled them in their pockets, or wore them on the person. But for some reason or unreason some of them—a small percentage perhaps—had to be seen to be effective. . . .
>
> One can't help wondering about the reversion of modern civilized man (by his own estimate) to the primitive stage in his development, when face to face with man-contrived mechanical dangers, and who seems to have an urge to propitiate this man-made power manifestation, just as his primordial ancestors tried to propitiate the natural manifestations after attributing to them super-natural power and designs. . . .
>
> Man had got himself into the air—toward heaven—by mechanical means and this was a new experience, and there was nothing in his earth-dwelling, racial experience (since his concepts and creations were based on earthy things like floods and fires and lightning,) out

of which he could create the omnipotence and mysticism which had given him security on earth, but not above the earth in flying mechanisms. . . .

But why visible; why not secret amulets? Perhaps the idea here is also primordial, since primitive man took no chances, and wanted them to be seen, but by whom? Not his brother flyers, not the command staff; in the latter case the result might have been new regulations or revived old ones.

Logically, the primordial urge was to have some non-entity, some not-yet-conceived Mystery to notice them.

3. Mathews crossed out "the great mysteries" in favor of "Spiritland" here.

4. The Osage River is far to the east of the headwaters of the Cimarron, in what are now central Missouri and eastern Kansas. Since the Salt Fork of the Arkansas River runs west of Ponca City, Oklahoma, the band is likely still a week away from their permanent camp in the Ozarks when they cross it.

5. Mathews wavered here between writing "white man's god" and "white man's God," apparently opting for the latter.

6. In the draft Mathews changed this last line to: "He did not know of the Apache woman but even if he had no one in those [illegible—looks like "lakns of"] virus warfare." In an apparently earlier draft, the lines read: "Three nights later when he wrote his report to his superiors in St. Louis, he wrote that the Beaver Band of the Great Osage had been wiped out by smallpox. He had never heard of virus warfare."

The Talk of the Face

1. Though often normed in his published works, Comanche is frequently spelled with two *m*'s by Mathews.

2. In *The Osages*, Mathews writes: "These chain-pressure disturbed and displaced ones . . . flowed north of the domain of the Little Ones to become enemies. These enemies, the Kiowas and Cheyennes and Arapahoes rather mild ones as far as the Little Ones were concerned, were added to the traditional" enemies (Pawnees, Wichitas, other Caddoans). The Little Ones are the Osages and the time is the second decade of the eighteenth century.

3. The manuscript leaves us guessing whether Mathews meant "trader's" or "traders'." Though multiple white traders worked in the region and were familiar to the Osages, I have tentatively chosen the former, because Second Son is likely thinking about a specific man.

4. The Sioux, Omahas, Missourias, and Osages all speak languages derived from a common tongue of the Siouan language family, with Omaha and

Osage related more closely than the others as Dhegiha Siouan languages. Cheyenne, on the other hand, is an Algonquian language, related to many more easterly tongues, such as Ojibwa, Abenaki, Delaware, Wampanoag, Cree, Kickapoo, and Shawnee (as well as two Californian tribal languages). It is most closely related to the Blackfoot and Arapaho languages.

5. Also known as the Place-of-the-Many-Swans and Marais-des-Cygnes, this is a river that flows from eastern Kansas, joining the Osage River to flow into the Lake of the Ozarks in Missouri and then into the Missouri. In *The Osages* Mathews ceases reference to it just before discussing the 1825 treaty, indicating that despite its origin in Kansas, the Osages removed from their permanent camp there at the time of that treaty.

The Flower on Cadron Creek

1. The Hiwassee River runs westward through far southwestern North Carolina, northeastern Georgia, and far southeastern Tennessee. It joins the Tennessee River north-northeast of Chattanooga.

2. Although Mathews appears to refer here to the Treaty of New Echota, signed by The Ridge, John Ridge, Elias Boudinot, and others on December 29, 1835, these historical events on Cadron Creek took place in April 1834. Possibly he refers instead to the Treaty of 1828 with the Western Cherokees, which offered incentives to Cherokees still living in the Appalachian Mountains to remove west. Given the 1949 date of composition, Mathews may simply have mixed up the dates. He had not yet begun work in earnest on *The Osages*, and even there it is unclear that he researched Cherokee chronology as closely as that of the Osage.

3. The headwaters of the Clinch River are in western Virginia. It flows southwest across the Tennessee border, emptying into the Tennessee River west-southwest of Knoxville. The Holston River runs a parallel course to the east of the Clinch, flowing through Knoxville on its way to meet the Clinch. Knoxville, where the Holston meets the French Broad River, is considered to be the headwaters of the Tennessee.

4. A doggery is a cheap saloon or a dive.

5. A landau is a carriage with four wheels. Its passengers face one another and can be covered with a top that divides into two sections for maximum versatility. Its driver sits on a raised seat outside the main carriage.

6. Mathews's mention here of malaria as a disease of the 1830s United States and adjacent regions of North America (Indian Country, the Arkansas River country) may surprise some readers who think of it as an African or South American illness. The disease was not eliminated here until the middle of the twentieth century, through the efforts of programs to

control it and other vector-borne diseases, programs that called for the draining of areas where mosquitoes breed, the implementation of sanitation measures such as killing adult mosquitoes trapped in houses, and the screening of residences and other buildings, as well as the use of DDT in the South during the time in which this story was composed. Mathews's grandmother treated patients of another mosquito-borne illness, yellow fever, in mid-nineteenth-century New Orleans. The related West Nile virus has been on the upsurge in North America as well, since 2001, though the efforts to control the transmission may be having some impact.

Cholera is a water- and food-borne bacterial disease characterized by severe abdominal pain and causing excessive diarrhea and vomiting. Death usually results from the dehydration associated with these symptoms. In the United States the disease has been largely eliminated through the preventative use of proper sanitation, such as hand-washing, purifying treatment of water, and adequate sewage systems that segregate untreated waste from food and water.

7. Muscle Shoals is a thirty-seven-mile stretch of rapids on the Tennessee River in northwestern Alabama noted in history for its role in the wars between the Chickamauga Cherokees and other southeastern tribes and the nascent United States. In early 1780 a large party of invading Anglo and Scotch-Irish colonizers led by the Wataugan leader John Donelson (later the father-in-law of Andrew Jackson) traveled through Muscle Shoals. They were attacked while going through Chickamaugan towns near present-day Chattanooga, Tennessee, and again six days later, a few days after running the rapids. This "flotilla" consisted of thirty boats that held about two hundred people bound for the French Salt Licks on the Cumberland River (now Nashville).

It appears that the first Cherokees had settled in the Muscle Shoals area, formerly the territory of neighboring tribes, by the middle of the 1780s. Due to extensive intermarriage, strategic alliances, and migrations caused by encroaching Amer-European settlers, the area was multiethnic in character at this time, consisting mainly of Creeks, Chickasaws, Shawnees, and Cherokees. It was part of the lands reserved to Cherokees, Creeks, and Chickasaws in the 1785 and 1786 treaties of Hopewell. Nevertheless, in 1786, speculators from the State of Franklin led by Valentine Sevier tried unsuccessfully to take the region. They sent an expedition of three to four hundred men to the region, briefly opening a land office there. Their attempts were frustrated by Chickamaugan leader Dragging Canoe, whose forces were allied with Creek forces. John Sevier continued to try to obtain the region for Franklin, and made overtures to individuals in the Spanish government toward that objective. Meanwhile, in 1787, two Chickasaws informed the settlement at Nashville that a new settlement, the town of Coldwater, had appeared near the shoals. When James Robertson went there to try to destroy it, believing that the Indians there had been harassing Cumberland settlers, he found a deserted town on the south side of the river and followed a trail eighteen miles west to Coldwater Creek, where Coldwater town had been established. In the ambush that followed, twenty Indians and six French, including one French woman, were killed. Among those killed were six Creeks who had been trading with the eight or more French traders there.

In March 1790 a group attempting to establish a settlement at Muscle Shoals was turned back by a joint force of Cherokees, Creeks, and Shawnees. The leader Doublehead (brother of a respected chief, Old Tassel, murdered by James Hubbard's men under a flag of truce two and a half years earlier) may already have been living there by that time. Reports say he settled there with a multiethnic group of forty Cherokees, Creeks, and other Natives in 1790, apparently with the permission of his mixed-blood Chickasaw son-in-law George Colbert. In early 1791, when the Tennessee Company under Hubbard attempted to establish an illegal settlement and blockhouse at Muscle Shoals, Chief Glass of Nickajack town and a party of sixty warriors evicted them. Then, in the autumn of 1791 and winter of 1792, Doublehead came into conflict with various settlers and the extended Sevier family during a hunting expedition along the Cumberland River, reportedly on the offensive and in violation of the Treaty of Holston. In October 1792 the Cherokee leader Bloody Fellow may have advised the Spanish, who were trying to back Cherokee resistance against the United States, to build forts in the Muscle Shoals area, though such reports by western powers of invited fortresses are notoriously unreliable due to their self-serving potential. In June 1794 Anglo-American invaders were again repulsed when a boat containing five white men, three white women, four white children, and twenty slaves was captured by a Cherokee war party after the men—and possibly more of the party—were all killed. This event was one of those used by Robertson to justify attacks three months later against the Cherokee Lower Towns of Nickajack and Running Water at the Georgia-Alabama-Tennessee border, approximately 150 miles away. By 1800 Doublehead was encouraging the establishment of a Moravian missionary school in the Muscle Shoals area, inviting trade with the regions west of the area, and helping to open a wagon road into Tennessee. Accusations of unauthorized land selling in the area in 1806 led to his assassination.

Waterloo is a town in northwestern Alabama downriver from Muscle Shoals. It is on the border with Mississippi and quite close to the Tennessee border.

8. The Tennessee River loops northwestward from Waterloo to Savannah, Tennessee, then jogs back northeastward and runs almost due north through Tennessee to Paducah, Kentucky, where it meets the Ohio River. The Cherokees are traveling hundreds of miles more than the distance between their homes and Indian Territory in order to take advantage of the less physically demanding waterways, yet they do not escape the intense physical punishments of removal.

9. The Arkansas River meets the Mississippi below Rosedale, Mississippi, on the border between present-day Arkansas and Mississippi, about equidistant between Memphis and Vicksburg.

10. Chippendale was a kind of furniture originating in England and named for the cabinetmaker Thomas Chippendale. It had been fashionable particularly between the 1750s and 1770s. It blended Gothic, Rococo, and Chinese styles. The backs of Chippendale chairs were often delicate in the sense that they were not solid but consisted of decorative carved traces of wood supporting a mostly open framework.

11. Given that Mathews chooses a pseudonym for the historical Lieutenant Joseph W. Harris, it appears that Coosa MacDonald and Anne MacDonald are also pseudonyms. John Ross, who was the principal chief of the Nation in 1834 and who was one-eighth Cherokee if measured only by "blood," had descended from a family named McDonald on his mother's side. His grandmother was Anna Shorey. One of his homes was located at the headwaters of the Coosa River (now Rome, Georgia). After fighting the Treaty of New Echota in every way possible short of war, Ross organized his people's removal by dividing the tribe into thirteen parties of about a thousand refugees each and then journeyed to Indian Territory by water with a smaller group of invalids. His first wife Quatie died en route in 1839 in Little Rock.

Moccasin Prints

1. Mathews first wrote Osage, then crossed it out in favor of Wah-Sa-She. As he explains in *The Osages*, Wah-Sha-She is a subdivision of the Grand Hunkah division of the Ni-U-Ko'n-Ska (Children of the Middle Waters) tribe. The subdivision Wah-Sha-She were the Water People and Name Givers, and their Deer gens was known to the Illini, who told that name to the French as though it named the entire tribe. It became Ouazhaghi, then Osage.

2. This detail allows us to recognize that this Maria is not a fictional name, but a reference to Maria Tallchief, the famous Osage prima ballerina of George Balanchine's New York City Ballet and mother of living Osage poet Elise Paschen. The recognition is poignant, as we see better the gulf in the story between Maria's westernized education and the grandfather's traditional education through the telling of father-to-son stories of historical import. It is poignant due to both the progress for Osage women in education and the loss of Osage-controlled education and history brought about by the reservation era of U.S. policy as well as by the oil riches shared by the Osages. It is also important that while the father-to-son chain may be broken, a man-to-daughter or man-to-granddaughter survival of the history is forged. Maria Tallchief's grandfather does not appear to have been named Bull Head, as Maria's grandfather in this story is named, so Mathews has worked both to fictionalize (or perhaps double-attribute) the story and to drop too large a hint of its possible origins for us to pass over.

3. Neither Standing Bull nor any of his descendants named here—Buffalo Hide, White Bull, Bull Pawing Earth, Bull Head—appear in *The Osages*. In that book Mathews says the story about to be told by Bull Head is one of many about the same events told by members of multiple gentes (patrilineal clans) of the Osages. His source for this particular one may have been the Tallchief family, or his own family, as his great-grandmother was Buffalo gens, or possibly Hi'n-Ci-Mo'I'n or Se-Se-Mo'I'n or Tse-Zhi'n-Ga-Wa-Da-I'n-Ga through Mathews's father and a trader he knew, or even Mo'n-Ci-Tse-Xi, Mrs. Fred Lookout, of the Bear gens. Hiu-Ah-Wah-Kon-Tah (Alex Tallchief) and Tse-To-Hah (Eaves Tallchief), both Buffalo Face gens, of the Big Hills, are also listed in the bibliography to Mathews's *The Osages*.

Another possibility is Chief Lookout himself. On Monday, 19 March 1945, Mathews talked to Chief Lookout regarding a speech he was to give at Woolaroc welcoming Lord Halifax, almost certainly a model for his "Moccasin Prints" story. The previous day he had written: "Supposed to go out to Chief Lookouts to talk with him about his speech at Woolaroc Wednesday, to welcome Lord Halifax, but the rain came in the afternoon, and I satyed [*sic*] at Dibbs house" (JJM 1.47). The next day he was able to visit the chief and subsequently wrote the speech for him. "Out to Chief Lookouts this morning to talk with him about his speech. This afternoon I arote [*sic*] it for him:" The colon appears to lead to a blank space on the bottom of the typescript page where he likely intended to insert the speech. Woolaroc is both a location near Clyde Lake in Osage County and the nearby museum and wildlife preserve founded in 1925 by Frank

Phillips, the oil magnate, as a ranch and retreat for himself. Mathews was also writing about the theme of that story, Braddock's 1755 defeat at the hands of the French and the part Osages played in it, in diary notes of 3 March 1952.

In "Man Not Afraid" Mathews puts the story in the mouth of Ee Sa Rah N'eah. "My father told me this thing. . . . His father told this to him too, and it is true. . . . My grandfather was Wy Zte Kee Tompa (Eagle That Dreams). When he was this high (holding his hand about three feet off the ground) his father went toward the morning sun. . . . This father of my grandfather was Wy Nah She Zhee (Eagle That Swoops)." Later the narrator tells his father of hearing the story, and the father responds: "Yes I have heard that story and many more that have been handed down from generation to generation. Like all stories they lose something as they are handed down, but they are all based on facts; that is those that are not based on dreams. What do they teach you in school about Braddock's Defeat? Sounds like George Washington on the white horse."

4. A bull boat is a small, round boat made of a wooden frame with buffalo hides as the waterproof shell. Bull boats were light enough for a single person (often a woman) to build and portage, but could carry weighty goods, and were usually used to carry provisions, such as buffalo meat from a hunt, or to ferry rivers. When Maria's grandfather says that French men killed their bull boats, he may mean they killed off many buffalo in the area whose hides would have been used to make the boats.

5. See the comments in the section note about "The Apache Woman." It is clear that these would not all be the same Little Bear of the Bear Clan, however, given the three dates: 1755, 1824, 1863. Mathews also mentions another man named Little Bear of the Bear Clan of the Little Osages: Mi-Tsu-Shee. Mi-Tsu-Shee was alive in 1793 and may or may not have met Zebulon Pike.

6. It may seem strange that a man named Reevers appears here as a military leader for the French. In the Pike account the Osages were recruited by a man named McCarty stationed at Fort Chartres. Nationality and national loyalties were not necessarily as fixed in the eighteenth century as we often imagine. There are many Irish surnames, for example, that make up portions of Spanish Louisiana's history. Perhaps Mathews created Reevers as a fictional name. Perhaps it is Rivière or a similar French name Anglicized. Or perhaps a British man became a trader or soldier or captive of the French prior to this action.

7. Mathews's original title for this piece was "Like Leaves of Sumac." Sumac leaves turn bright crimson in the autumn, so this line is saying that the

ground was covered with blood and/or redcoats. Once again, Mathews uses the color red symbolically in this story, as he had in *Sundown*, to indicate multifarious interconnected associations of great significance. Sumac itself reinforces the eastern woodlands setting of the battle. Some sources place the Osages along the Ohio River valley prior to their seventeenth-century presence west of the Mississippi. This would put their origin not far from present-day Pittsburgh, where the action takes place, and would shed some interesting light on their responses to forest warfare. Other sources associate them with Cahokia, the urban center of the seventh through fifteenth centuries near present-day St. Louis. The two ideas are not mutually exclusive.

Bad Medicine

1. There is also an Eagle Feather in *Wah'Kon-Tah*, though he seems to be of a different generation from this man. After his death, his will informs the agent Laban J. Miles that he has been entrusted to raise his two daughters. Miles was agent from 1878 to 1885 and from 1889 to 1893. Mrs. Edna Maze is also listed as Eagle Feather in Mathews's bibliography for *The Osages*.

2. Mi-Ompah-We-Li was Moonhead, a French-Delaware-Caddo medicine man also known as John Wilson. He was a founder of the peyote religion and built two fireplaces or moon altars for the Osages. The moons symbolized the grave of Christ. In *Wah'Kon-Tah*, Mathews has a character Eagle That Dreams talk about Moon Head as Kiowa, but he corrects this designation in *The Osages*.

3. Ta means buck deer in Osage, while Tonkah means Big or Great, so in context Tah Tunkah seems to be "great big buck deer."

4. Grayhorse Village was the place where the Big Hills People settled when the Osages made their last removal to the area now known as Osage County, Oklahoma, in 1872. Mathews's great-grandmother (father's mother's mother) was a Big Hills Osage, a member of the Buffalo gens.

Stories of World War II and the Cold War

1. The first two quoted items are from the story "The Meek Shall Inherit?"; the third ("unfit") is from Mathews, Diary, 1 January 1970, Oklahoma University Press Collection, Western History Collections, box 3, folder 9, University of Oklahoma Libraries; and the final one is a well-known dictum in the teaching of literature.

The Liberal View

1. See note 3 to the earlier story "Only a Blonde."
2. The *American Mercury* was a magazine established in 1924 by author
   H. L. Mencken and drama critic George Jean Nathan. Under Menck-
   en's direction through 1933, it published and promoted a large number
   of now well-known writers, activists, and scholars, including scholars of
   Native America, many of whom were associated with left-wing political
   views. Those published included Sherwood Anderson, Theodore Dreiser,
   Edward Sapir, F. Scott Fitzgerald, Vachel Lindsay, Carl Sandburg, Marga-
   ret Sanger, Franz Boas, Countee Cullen, W. E. B. DuBois, Max Eastman,
   Mary Austin, Sinclair Lewis, Frances Densmore, Upton Sinclair, Robinson
   Jeffers, James Weldon Johnson, Alfred Kroeber, Lewis Mumford, Margaret
   Mead, Bernard DeVoto, William Faulkner, Edgar Lee Masters, Edward
   Robinson, Chief Standing Bear, Langston Hughes, John Dos Passos, and
   Robert Frost. Even Leon Trotsky received "airtime" from the relatively
   conservative Mencken. Some of Mathews's own friends and professional
   associates published with Mencken: Walter S. Campbell (as Stanley Ves-
   tal), B. A. Botkin, Henry Seidel Canby, Frank Dobie, and George Milburn.

   After Mencken departed, the magazine continued to publish in
   much the same vein, mostly under the direction of publisher, and then
   publisher-editor, Lawrence Spivak. During this period Spivak helped
   found the radio show that became television's *Meet the Press* in 1947.
   In 1949 "Gerhart Eisler Meets the Press" appeared in the magazine as
   apparently the first joint endeavor between it and the television program
   (which Mathews watched). Authors included Anton Chekhov, William
   Saroyan, Arthur Schlesinger, Pearl Buck, Aaron Copland, Ford Madox
   Ford, Havelock Ellis, G. K. Chesterton, George Santayana, Bertrand
   Russell, Paul Sears, Alfred Kazin, Claude McKay, Abraham Cahan, Her-
   bert Hoover, Walter de la Mare, Zora Neale Hurston, Gypsy Rose Lee,
   Theodore Roethke, Dorothy Thompson, Shirley Jackson, Ray Bradbury,
   W. A. S. Douglas, Grace Milburn, and Hodding Carter. Mathews knew
   Sears and Milburn, would eventually use Santayana's and Russell's autobi-
   ographies as models for his own, and would have been attracted to titles
   by lesser knowns about horses and dogs "I have known."

   By the early 1950s a turn toward the right was taking place, with a
   mixed list of contributors that included William F. Buckley, Marshall
   McLuhan, James Baldwin, Bernard Malamud, J. Edgar Hoover, Billy Graham, and William Saroyan. Whether Mathews would have been stirred or
   disgusted by some of the new titles—"Communists in the White House,"

"Reds and our Churches," "Red Infiltration of Theological Seminaries," "America Is Losing the War against Communism," "Communist Christianity," "International Bankers and the Communist Conspiracy," "The KGB Murder Apparatus," and "Red China and the Moral Conscience of America"—is anyone's guess, as is whether he received the publication regularly at all.

Sinclair Lewis was the author of *Main Street* (1920), *Babbitt* (1922), *Arrowsmith* (1924), *Elmer Gantry* (1927), and *It Can't Happen Here* (1935), a novel in which a fascist candidate wins the presidency of the United States. Theodore Dreiser is best known for his novels *Sister Carrie* (1900), *Jennie Gerhardt* (1911), and *An American Tragedy* (1925). He is one of the key figures in the movement toward literary naturalism. The novels of Upton Sinclair often attacked the cynical foundations of American industry. In *The Jungle* (1906), he uncovered the unsanitary conditions within the meat-packing industry; in *Oil!* (1927), he goes after the big oil industry in the Southern California, where Mathews had moved with his family a year or two earlier to pursue a prospect with Standard Oil. Sinclair was a very prolific writer, publishing more than ninety books and nearly thirty pamphlets between 1898 and 1968. Sherwood Anderson is perhaps best known for his widely anthologized short story "Death in the Woods" (1933) and his novelistic exposé of small town America, *Winesburg, Ohio* (1919).

3. Vox Populi means "voice of the people." The Library of Congress lists many Vox Populi newspapers, though none from the period of this story that seem to fit. It may be used here as a general allusion to publications catering to populist and/or socialist sentiment. Anderson published in a journal called *The Masses*, edited by Max Eastman, who, like Dreiser, had visited the Soviet Union.

4. There is a Petrie Hall at Auburn University in Alabama, though its features seem to fit neither the vaguely northeast location of the action, nor the use of it here fictionally as a residence hall, nor the sentiments of the story. The setting and observations seem to emerge from Mathews's visit to Harvard for his stepson's graduation in June 1948.

What Thing Is Fairest

1. Mathews may mean to allude here to the Villa Borghese Gardens and the Borghese collection of "Roman" sculptures. Their heir, Scipione Borghese (1871–1927), an adventurer and detached business owner who dabbled in socialism, would have been about a generation or less older than Wiggins.

2. Much of the oil discovered in Oklahoma, both in and beyond Osage County, was discovered on allotments owned by Native Americans and leased—usually through the federal government's reservation agency—to oil prospectors. Mathews may be playing here with the name of the Nellie Johnstone No. 1 well; drilled near Bartlesville in 1896, it was the first commercial well that paid, starting the rush into Osage County. The atomic references and Diana's allusion to World War I, however, make Wiggins a tycoon of a later generation.

3. There is a Big Antelope Creek outside the well-named Blackwell, Oklahoma, which is about ten miles northwest of Ponca City, one of the major oil towns of northern Oklahoma. This reference may be a direct linking of Wiggins to Marland (who, however, never attended Oxford University), as Marland leased his land from the Ponca tribe and worked out of Ponca City. Mathews possibly also knew of the Antelope Creek Phase in archaeological terminology. Sites in the panhandles of Texas and Oklahoma are associated with this phase, which named the period from 1200 to 1500 AD in that area. Mathews went on one archaeological dig in northeastern Oklahoma while at the University of Oklahoma.

4. Rupert Brooke (1887–1915) was an English poet, a graduate of Cambridge, and an acquaintance of Virginia Woolf and E. M. Forster; Brooke died of blood poisoning from an otherwise minor incident while serving in World War I. Diana's fondness for him may derive in part from this romantic loss, as well as his intriguing love life. He first published in 1905 and is remembered for his war sonnets. A phrase in his poem "Tiare Tahiti" became the title for Fitzgerald's *This Side of Paradise*. Algernon Charles Swinburne (1837–1909) was a graduate of Oxford and friend to the poets Dante Gabriel Rossetti and Christina Rossetti. His poetry explored scandalously alternative sexualities, medievalism, and patriotism, among other things. This choice of Wiggins may reflect a contradictorily conservative character who is nevertheless attracted to taboo-breaking but not as up-to-date, daring, or frankly modern as Diana.

5. Chipping Norton is a town about twenty miles northwest of Oxford, so Wiggins and Diana are "in danger" there because they are relatively anonymous.

6. By 1877 individuals were recorded running the hundred-yard dash in ten seconds. Post-WWI intercollegiate records were about 9.4 seconds, so Wiggins would have been quite the athlete, though perhaps no Olympian.

Natural Science

1. *Tamburlaine the Great* is a play written by Christopher Marlowe in 1587. Its subject is Timur the Lame, an emperor of Scythia in Central Asia of the late fourteenth and early fifteenth centuries. Around 1370 he had proclaimed himself "sovereign of the Chagatai line of khans and restorer of the Mongol empire," and began fighting against other khans. Chagatai was the son of Genghis Khan. At one point, Timur's troops nearly occupied Moscow. Like Mathews's WWI hero, Allenby, Timur conquered Aleppo and Damascus, among a large number of other cities and areas. His empire included all of present-day Iran, Uzbekistan, Afghanistan, Azerbaijan, Nakhchivan, Kyrgyzstan, Tajikistan, Georgia, Armenia, and Turkmenistan as well as parts of Iraq, Kazakhstan, Pakistan, India, China, Turkey, Syria, and Russia. Mathews may also have known the name Tamburlaine through Edgar Allan Poe's poem "Tamerlane." This reference, with the others to Khan and Gheng, solidifies our sense that Tamberlania is not associated with the Soviet Union in Mathews's mind. However, it also raises the question of whether Mathews was alluding to a Central Asian or a Chinese superpower.

2. Historically, Latium was the region in Italy where Rome is located.

3. Note that Mathews spelled this word in both American style (*defense*) and British style (*defence*).

4. Sandhurst is the location of the Royal Military Academy (formerly Royal Military College) of Great Britain, an officer training center.

5. There is a Tamur River in eastern Nepal.

6. By the Madeleine, Mathews appears to be referring to L'Eglise Sainte-Marie-Madeleine, a church in Paris that is designed in the form of a Roman temple with columns. Napoleon commissioned the design of the structure in 1806 as a monument to celebrate his army. The Bourbons turned it into a church in 1816. Brandenburg is the Brandenburg gate in Berlin, built at the end of the eighteenth century, restored in the late 1950s, and isolated from use by both East and West Germans between 1961 and 1989 by the Berlin Wall, which enclosed it on both sides. Corso is the Via Del Corso in Rome, which Mathews visited on his honeymoon in 1924. The Corso is the main street in central Rome and has been used since the Classical era. At one end is a monument to the first king of united Italy and the tomb of the unknown soldier from World War I, the war of 1914–18.

7. It is humorous that Mathews specifically chose Merton, his alma mater, to be one of the colleges that the Supreme Commander's college bumped,

marking the Supreme Commander as definitively NOT one of Mathews's fellow Mertonians!

The Meek Shall Inherit?

1. Mathews apparently fictionalized his setting, as Haynes Creek, the Tennessee River, Lordstown, and other geographical markers do not seem to coincide. There is a Haynes Creek near Atlanta, Georgia, where the Tennessee River is not, and a Lordstown, Ohio, where David is not. Both Atlanta and Nashville have state universities, but neither is near that river nor in the same town with David's apparent future employer. George Monk's drug store here may have been a tribute to P. J. Monk's drug store in Pawhuska. A Mr. P. J. appears two paragraphs later.

2. In his autobiography, Mathews mentions a college sweetheart whom he names Circe, admitting that her last name was probably Searcy. His summer enrollment at Sewanee, Tennessee's University of the South, may have been one of the reasons he chose the Tennessee River Valley as his setting, and he may have drawn upon it for some of the small town and rural details here.

3. See "Only a Blonde" and "The Liberal View" and their notes for other mentions of Marx and Veblen.

4. The 4F classification means that the board believes David unqualified for military service physically, mentally, or morally. Mathews leaves nicely ambiguous the question of which of these has been the cause, and whether David's intent to avoid the draft launched him into the last category or whether they would have rejected him regardless.

5. The Manhattan Project's location in Los Alamos, New Mexico, is only its best known. It spanned over thirty sites, including several universities, a facility to separate and enrich uranium in Oak Ridge, Tennessee, and an ordnance works in Sylacauga, Alabama. The editor's maternal grandfather worked for the project through General Electric in Chicago, Illinois, and Ames, Iowa, as an electrical engineer.

Selected Bibliography

"About 'Meet the Press.'" MSNBC.com. National Broadcasting Corporation, 2010. www.msnbc.msn.com/id/3403008/ns/meet_the_press-about_us/?ns=meet_the_press.

"About Vauxhall." Vauxhall. General Motors UK Limited, 2010. www.vauxhall.co.uk/about-vauxhall/index.html.

"About Vauxhall: History and Heritage." Vauxhall. General Motors UK Limited, 2010. www.vauxhall.co.uk/about-vauxhall/vauxhall-history-heritage.html.

Abrams, M. H., et al., eds. *The Norton Anthology of English Literature, Volume 2*. 5th ed. New York: W. W. Norton, 1986.

Ahouse, John. *Upton Sinclair: A Descriptive Annotated Bibliography*. Los Angeles: Mercer and Aitchison, 1994.

American Automobile Association North American Road Atlas (#2800). Quebec: Quebecor Aurora, 1999.

The American Mercury. Vols. 1–34, 36–61, 63–71. New York: Knopf, 1924–50.

———. Vols. 74–83, 109. Torrance CA: American Mercury, 1952–56, 1973.

"American Mercury Magazine." Namebase.org. Public Information Research, 2010. www.namebase.org/main1/American-Mercury-Magazine.html.

"Antelope Creek Ruins: Chronology of Exploration at Antelope Creek in the Texas Panhandle." Panhandlenation.com. Plain Media Studios, 2008. www.panhandlenation.com/exploration/antelope_2.html.

Atlas of the River Basins of the United States. 2nd ed. Soil Conservation Service, U.S. Department of Agriculture, June 1970.

Baas, Jacquelynn. "José Clemente Orozco, Orozco: Man of Fire." *American Masters*, 19 September 2007, PBS.org. WNET THIRTEEN, 2016. www.pbs.org/wnet/americanmasters/episodes/jose-clemente-orozco/orozco-man-of-fire/82/.

Barzini, Luigi. *Peking to Paris: A Journey across Two Continents in 1907*. New York: Library Press, 1972.

Berkman, Leslie. "Department Store Chain Gottschalks to Relaunch in California." *Press-Enterprise*, 26 April 2010. Enterprise Media, 2010. www.pe.com/business/local/stories/PE_Biz_W_gottschalk27.3af117f.html.

Bevington, David, ed. "Romeo and Juliet Headnote." In *The Complete Works of Shakespeare*, 991. Glenview IL: Scott, Foresman and Company, 1980.

Bierhorst, John, ed. and trans. *Cantares Mexicanos: Songs of the Aztecs*. Stanford: Stanford University Press, 1985.

"Borghese Gallery and Museum, the Villa Borghese." Galleria Borghese.it. N.d. www.galleriaborghese.it/default-en.htm.

"Bourjois Paris: History and Background of Bourjois." FragranceX.com. 2016. www.fragrancex.com/products/_bid_Bourjois-am-cid_perfume-am-lid_B__brand_history.html.

Boyd, Dan T. "Oklahoma Oil: Past, Present, and Future." *Oklahoma Geology Notes* 62, no. 3 (Fall 2002): 97–106. Oklahoma Geological Survey website. Board of Regents of the University of Oklahoma, 2000–2009. www.ogs.ou.edu/fossilfuels/pdf/OKOilNotesPDF.pdf.

Brown, James A. "The Cahokian Expression: Creating Court and Cult." In *Hero, Hawk, and Open Hand: American Indian Art of the Ancient Midwest and South,* edited by Richard F. Townsend, 104–23. New Haven: Yale University Press, 2004.

Brown, John P. *Old Frontiers: The Story of the Cherokee Indians from Earliest Times to the Date of Their Removal to the West, 1838*. Kingsport TN: Southern Publishers, 1938.

Butler, Adam, Claire Van Cleave, and Susan Stirling. *The Art Book*. London: Phaidon Press, 1994, 345.

"Cadron Creek Settlement, Conway, Faulkner County, Arkansas: Memorial Plaque Erected by the Conway Chamber of Commerce, Faulkner County Historical Society and the U.S. Army Corps of Engineers, October 1989." Arkansas Ties. N. d. www.arkansasties.com/Faulkner/Structures/CadronCreek/cadron.htm.

Case, Theodore S., ed. *The Kansas City Review of Science and Industry, Volume 5*. Kansas City MO: Press of Ramsey, Millett and Hudson, 1882, p. 56. Google Books, 6 July 2007. https://books.google.com/books?id=EW4EAAAAYAAJ&source=gbs_navlinks_s.

Centers for Disease Control and Prevention (CDC). Cholera, "General Information." CDC.gov, 2010. www.cdc.gov/cholera/.

———. Malaria, "Elimination of Malaria in the United States (1947–1951)." CDC.gov, 2010. www.cdc.gov/malaria/about/history/elimination_us.html.

———. Malaria, "History of Malaria, an Ancient Disease." CDC.gov, 2010. www.cdc.gov/malaria/about/history/.

———. Malaria, "The Panama Canal." CDC.gov, 2010. www.cdc.gov/malaria
/about/history/panama_canal.html.

———. West Nile Virus, "Statistics, Surveillance, and Control Archive." CDC.
gov, 2010. www.cdc.gov/ncidod/dvbid/westnile/surv&control_archive.htm.

———. West Nile Virus, "Virology: Classification of West Nile Virus." CDC.gov,
2010. www.cdc.gov/ncidod/dvbid/westnile/virus.htm.

———. Yellow Fever, "Yellow Fever." CDC.gov, 2010. www.cdc.gov/ncidod
/dvbid/yellowfever/index.html.

"Charles Boyer (I) (1899–1978)." The Internet Movie Database. IMDb.com,
1990–2016. www.imdb.com/name/nm0000964/.

Chatty, Dawn. "The Bedouin in Contemporary Syria: The Persistence of
Tribal Authority and Control." *Middle East Journal* 64, no.1 (Winter 2010):
29–49.

Churchill, Suzanne, et al. "Synopsis: The Masses." *Little Magazines & Modernism: A Select Bibliography*. Department of English, Davidson College, 2004.
www.davidson.edu/academic/english/little_magazines/masses/synopsis
.html.

Conley, Robert J. *Cherokee Dragon: A Novel of the Real People*. Norman: University of Oklahoma Press, 2000, pp. 282–83.

Costello, Bartley, Jorge Del Moral Ugarte, Emilio Uranga Donato, and
Miguel Urban Ramos. "Elvis Presley: Alla en el 'Rancho Grande' Lyrics."
MetroLyrics.com. MetroLeap Media, 2004–16. www.metrolyrics.com/alla
-en-el-rancho-grande-lyrics-elvis-presley.html.

Curry, Martha. "Sherwood Anderson 1876–1941." *The Heath Anthology of American Literature, Volume D*. 5th ed. New York: Houghton Mifflin, 2006.

Dargusch, Carlton S., and John D. Alden. *Selective Service and Military Policies
on Classification, Deferment, and Delay*. 3rd ed. New York: Engineering
Manpower Commission of Engineers Joint Council (Office of Education,
U.S. Department of Health, Education and Welfare), October 1967. ERIC,
2016. files.eric.ed.gov/fulltext/ED034678.pdf.

Davis, Margaret Leslie. *Dark Side of Fortune: Triumph and Scandal in the Life of
Oil Tycoon Edward L. Doheny*. Berkeley: University of California Press, 1998.

Denby, David. "Uppie Redux? Upton Sinclair's Losses and Triumphs." *New
Yorker* 82, no. 26 (28 August 2006): 70–77.

Deutsch, Babette. *Poetry Handbook: A Dictionary of Terms*. New York: Funk and
Wagnalls, 1962.

"Diary Descriptions of the Trail between the Greybull and Shoshone Rivers." *The Bridger Trail Route, The Bridger Trail*. Wyoming State Historical
Preservation Office, Wyoming State Parks and Cultural Resources, 2016.
wyoshpo.state.wy.us/btrail/diarydescriptions.html.

Doughty, Charles Montagu. *Travels in Arabia Deserta, Volume 1.* Elibron Classics, Adamant Media Corporation, 2006. Google Books. https://www.google.com/books/edition/Travels_in_Arabia_Deserta/kgspAAAAYAAJ?hl=en.

Edwards, Laura. Personal correspondence, 2013–18.

EHP Web Team. "Historic World Earthquakes: Mexico." Earthquake Hazards Program website. United States Geological Survey, 23 November 2009. earthquake.usgs.gov/earthquakes/world/historical_country.php#mexico.

Evans, E. Raymond. "Notable Persons in Cherokee History: Dragging Canoe." *Journal of Cherokee Studies* 2, no. 2 (1977): 176–89.

Ewart, Gavin, ed. *Rupert Brooke: The Collected Poems.* London: Sidgwick and Jackson, 1987.

"FAQ." *Town & Country Magazine.* Hearst Communications, 2010. www.townandcountrymag.com/faq.

Fiore, James J., Office of Nuclear Energy, to Carl Schafer, Office of the Deputy Assistant Secretary of Defense for Installations, 29 May 1987 (AL.02-1-DOE Letter). Office of Legacy Management, U.S. Department of Energy, 25 June 2009. www.lm.doe.gov/Considered_Sites/Alabama_Ordnance_Works_-_AL_02/AL_02-1.pdf.

Fitzgerald, F. Scott. *This Side of Paradise.* New York: Oxford University Press, 2009.

Fort, Alice B., and Herbert S. Kates. "Tamburlaine: A Synopsis of the Play by Christopher Marlowe." *Minute History of the Drama.* New York: Grosset and Dunlap, 1935, p. 35. Theatrehistory.com, 2002. www.theatrehistory.com/british/marlowe003.html.

Fortunate Eagle, Adam. *Heart of the Rock: The Indian Invasion of Alcatraz.* Norman: University of Oklahoma Press, 2008.

"Freddie Fender—Alla en el rancho grande Lyrics." STLyrics.com. 2002–16. www.stlyrics.com/songs/f/freddiefender7872/allaenelranchogrande520032.html.

"FUSRAP Considered Sites, Alabama Ordnance Works (AL.02)." Office of Legacy Management, U.S. Department of Energy, 25 June 2009. www.lm.doe.gov/Considered_Sites/Alabama_Ordnance_Works_-_AL_02/.

Googlemaps. Google map data and Europa Technologies, INEGI, Google, 2010. maps.google.com/.

Groueff, Stephane. *Manhattan Project: The Untold Story of the Making of the Atomic Bomb.* Boston: Little, Brown, 1967.

Guthrie, Arlo, and Pete Seeger. "The Neutron Bomb." *Precious Friend.* Warner Brothers/WEA, 1990.

Hall, Robert L. "The Cahokia Site and Its People." In *Hero, Hawk, and Open Hand: American Indian Art of the Ancient Midwest and South*, edited by Richard F. Townsend, 91–103. New Haven: Yale University Press, 2004.

Hamal, A., M. Benbella, S. B. Rzozi, M. Bouhache, and Y. Msatef. Abstract of "[Competitiveness of Hard Wheat (*Triticum durum* Desf.) Varieties against Ripgut Brome (*Bromus rigidus* Roth)]" (French). *Meded Rijksuniv Gent Fak Landbouwkd Toegep Biol Wet* 66, no. 2b (2001): 673–79. PubMed.gov. National Center for Biotechnology Information, U.S. National Library of Medicine, National Institutes of Health. www.ncbi.nlm.nih.gov/pubmed /12425092.

Hamer, Philip M. *Tennessee: A History, 1673–1932*. New York: American History Society, 1933.

Harkness, John. *The Academy Awards Handbook*. New York: Pinnacle Books, Windsor Publishing, 1994, pp. 50, 56, 82, 162.

Harris, Leon. *Upton Sinclair: American Rebel*. New York: Thomas Y. Crowell, 1975.

Harrison, Anthony H. *Swinburne's Medievalism: A Study in Victorian Love Poetry*. Baton Rouge: Louisiana State University Press, 1988.

Hasan, Omar. "Shammar Tribe Recalls History for a Key Role in Iraq's Future." Agence France-Presse, 2 June 2004.

"Hayil." *Saudi Aramco World* 14, no. 7 (August–September 1963): 13–17. Aramco Services Company, 2004–15. archive.aramcoworld.com/issue /196307/hayil.htm.

Henderson, Lieut. T., R.E. & R.F.C. "Route Report, Wejh to Mathar via the Wadi Hamdh, 6th May 1917 till 10th May 1917." *Roger's Study*. Roger Bragger, 2002–16. www.rogersstudy.co.uk/hejaz/hejaz_narative/route_report _2/wejh_to_mathar.html.

Hickman, Kennedy. "Glorious Revolution: Glencoe Massacre." Military History. About.com/The New York Times Company, 2009. militaryhistory .about.com/od/battleswars16011800/p/glencoe.htm.

"Hiwassee River." Geographic Names Phase I data compilation (1976–1981), 31 December 1981. *Geographic Names Information System*, United States Geological Survey, U.S. Department of the Interior, 2010. geonames.usgs.gov /pls/gnispublic/f?p=gnispq:3:328842074410688::NO::P3_FID:1328447.

Hoig, Stanley W. *The Cherokees and Their Chiefs in the Wake of Empire*. Fayetteville: University of Arkansas Press, 1998.

Hughes, Teena. "Evening in Paris Perfume." *A-Night-in-Paris.com*. 2004–16. www.a-night-in-paris.com/what-to-do-in-paris-france/evening-in-paris -perfume.html.

Hutchisson, James M., and James L. W. West, III. "Theodore Dreiser 1871–1945." *The Heath Anthology of American Literature, Volume D.* 5th ed. New York: Houghton Mifflin, 2006.

Jennings, Francis. *Empire of Fortune: Crowns, Colonies, and Tribes in the Seven Years War in America.* New York: W. W. Norton, 1988.

John Joseph Mathews Collection, Western History Collections, University of Oklahoma Libraries, boxes 1–4 and sound recordings.

"John Steinbeck, Novels 1942–1952: *The Moon Is Down, Cannery Row, The Pearl, East of Eden.*" Library of America. Literary Classics of the United States, 1995–2016. www.loa.org/books/179-novels-1942-1952.

"Jose Clemente Orozco." All-Art.org. N.d. www.all-art.org/art_20th_century /orozco1.html.

"Joseph Alexander Tall Chief." Geni.com, 2019. MyHeritage Ltd. www.geni .com/people/Joseph-Tall-Chief/6000000039974456884.

Kalter, Susan. "John Joseph Mathews' Reverse Ethnography: The Literary Dimensions of *Wah'Kon-Tah.*" *Studies in American Indian Literatures* 14, no. 1 (Spring 2002): 26–50.

Knopf, Alfred A. "H. L. Mencken, George Jean Nathan, and the American Mercury Venture." *Menckeniana: A Quarterly Review* 78 (Summer 1981): 1–10.

Kurth, Peter. *American Cassandra: The Life of Dorothy Thompson.* Boston: Little, Brown, 1990.

Lankford, George E. "World on a String: Some Cosmological Components of the Southeastern Ceremonial Complex." In *Hero, Hawk, and Open Hand: American Indian Art of the Ancient Midwest and South,* edited by Richard F. Townsend, 207–17. New Haven: Yale University Press, 2004.

Larson, Robert W. "The White Caps of New Mexico: A Study of Ethnic Militancy in the Southwest." *Pacific Historical Review* 44, no. 2 (May 1975): 171–85. www.jstor.org/pss/3638001.

La Vere, David. *The Caddo Chiefdoms: Caddo Economics and Politics, 700–1835.* Lincoln: University of Nebraska Press, 1998.

Lehmann, Gerald M. "Descendants of Samuel Riley (Page 8 of 152 of 'The Cherokee Rileys')." User Home Pages, FamilyTreeMaker.com. Ancestry .com, 2009. familytreemaker.genealogy.com/users/l/e/h/Gerald-M -Lehmann/BOOK-0001/0002–0006.html.

Lingeman, Richard. "Mencken and Dreiser: Friends, When Speaking." *New York Times Book Review,* 8 March 1992, 1, 25, 27, 29. New York Times Company, 2016. www.nytimes.com/1992/03/08/books/mencken-and-dreiser -friends-when-speaking.html.

Lintz, Chris. "Antelope Creek Phase." *Oklahoma Historical Society's Encyclopedia of Oklahoma History & Culture.* Oklahoma State University Digital Library, 2007. www.okhistory.org/publications/enc/entry.php?entry=AN006.

"LM Sites." Office of Legacy Management, U.S. Department of Energy, 25 June 2009. www.lm.doe.gov/Sites_Map.aspx.

Mabey, Richard. *Flora Britannica.* London: Chatto and Windus, 1997.

Maltin, Leonard. "Boyer, Charles" and related entries. *Leonard Maltin's 2003 Movie and Video Guide.* New York: Signet, 2002.

Mann, Barbara. "Man with a Cross: Hawkeye Was a 'Half-Breed.'" Presented at the Cooper Panel of the 1998 Conference of the American Literature Association in San Diego. James Fenimore Cooper Society Website. James Fenimore Cooper Society, August 1998. external.oneonta.edu/cooper /articles/ala/1998ala-mann.html.

Marlowe, Christopher. *Tamburlaine.* Edited by J. W. Harper. London: Ernest Benn, 1971.

———. *Tamburlaine the Great, Parts I and II.* Edited by John D. Jump. Lincoln: University of Nebraska Press, 1967.

Martin, George W., ed. *Transactions of the Kansas State Historical Society, Volume 6.* Topeka: W. Y. Morgan, State Printer, 1900, p. 330. Google Books, 25 January 2008. https://books.google.com/books?id=vbUUAAAAYAAJ&dq =braddock%27s+defeat+osage&source=gbs_navlinks_s.

Mathews, John Joseph. "Admirable Outlaw." *Sooner Magazine* 2, no. 7 (April 1930): 241, 264. University of Oklahoma Digital Collections. digital .libraries.ou.edu/sooner/articles/p241,264_1930v2n7_OCR.pdf.

———. "Author Joseph Mathews Discusses the Limited Impact, Influence and Dollar-Importance in Books of the Indian and the Southwest." *Sooner Magazine* 34, no. 10 (July–August 1962): 10–11. University of Oklahoma Digital Collections. digital.libraries.ou.edu/sooner/articles/p10-11 _1962v34n10_OCR.pdf.

———. "Beauty's Votary." *Sooner Magazine* 3, no. 5 (February 1931): 171, 181– 82. University of Oklahoma Digital Collections. digital.libraries.ou.edu /sooner/articles/p171,181-182_1931v3n5_OCR.pdf.

———. "Ee Sa Rah N'eah's Story." *Sooner Magazine* 3, no. 9 (June 1931): 328– 29. University of Oklahoma Digital Collections. digital.libraries.ou.edu /sooner/articles/p328-329_1931v3n9_OCR.pdf.

———. "From the Osage Hills." *Sooner Magazine* 3, no. 8 (May 1931): 280, 308–10. University of Oklahoma Digital Collections. digital.libraries.ou .edu/sooner/articles/p280,%20308-310_1931v3n8_OCR.pdf.

―――. "Hunting in the Rockies." *Sooner Magazine* 1, no. 8 (May 1929): 263, 278–80. University of Oklahoma Digital Collections. digital.libraries.ou .edu/sooner/articles/p263,278-280_1929vln8_OCR.pdf.

―――. "Hunting the Red Deer of Scotland." *Sooner Magazine* 1, no. 7 (April 1929): 213–14, 246. University of Oklahoma Digital Collections. digital .libraries.ou.edu/sooner/articles/p213-214,246_1929vln7_OCR.pdf.

―――. *Life and Death of an Oilman: The Career of E. W. Marland.* 1951; Norman: University of Oklahoma Press, 1992.

―――. "Man Not Afraid." *Sooner Magazine* 4, no. 5 (February 1932): 140. University of Oklahoma Digital Collections. digital.libraries.ou.edu/sooner /articles/p140,147,157_1932v4n5_OCR.pdf.

―――. *Old Three Toes and Other Tales of Survival and Extinction.* Edited by Susan Kalter. Norman: University of Oklahoma Press, 2015.

―――. "Ole Bob." *Sooner Magazine* 5, no. 7 (April 1933): 206–7. University of Oklahoma Digital Collections. digital.libraries.ou.edu/sooner/articles /p206-207_1933v5n7_OCR.pdf.

―――. *The Osages: Children of the Middle Waters.* 1961; Norman: University of Oklahoma Press, 1982.

―――. "Passing of Red Eagle." *Sooner Magazine* 2, no. 5 (February 1930): 160, 176. University of Oklahoma Digital Collections. digital.libraries.ou.edu /sooner/articles/p160,176_1930v2n5_OCR.pdf.

―――. *Sundown.* 1934; Norman: University of Oklahoma Press, 1988.

―――. *Talking to the Moon: Wildlife Adventures on the Plains and Prairies of Osage Country.* Norman: University of Oklahoma Press, 1945.

―――. "The Trapper's Dog." *Sooner Magazine* 3, no. 4 (January 1931): 133, 141. University of Oklahoma Digital Collections. digital.libraries.ou.edu /sooner/articles/p133,141_1931v3n4_OCR.pdf.

―――. *Twenty Thousand Mornings: The Autobiography of John Joseph Mathews.* Edited by Susan Kalter. Norman: University of Oklahoma Press, 2012.

―――. *Wah'Kon-Tah: The Osage and the White Man's Road.* Norman: University of Oklahoma Press, 1932.

Maxwell, Catherine. *Swinburne.* Tavistock, Devon: Northcote House Publishers, 2006.

McGill, Meredith L. "Edgar Allan Poe 1809–1849." *The Heath Anthology of American Literature, Volume B.* 5th ed. New York: Houghton Mifflin, 2006.

McNickle, D'Arcy. *The Surrounded.* 1936; Albuquerque: University of New Mexico Press, 1978.

Mestrovic, Stjepan. *Thorstein Veblen on Culture and Society.* London: Sage Publications, 2003.

Metrailer, Jamie A. "Waterloo, Alabama, the Trail of Tears National Historic Trail: A Site Report." Sequoyah Research Center. Daniel F. Littlefield, Bob Sanderson, and James Parins, University of Arkansas at Little Rock, American Native Press Archives, 2002–7. https://ualrexhibits.org/trailoftears /places/gunters-landing-alabama/.

Moore, John Trotwood, and Austin P. Foster. *Tennessee: The Volunteer State, 1769–1923.* Vol. 1. Chicago: S. J. Clarke Publishing Company, 1923.

"Motor Vehicle Use Map 2009, Bridger-Teton National Forest, Kemmerer Ranger District." U.S. Forest Service, United States Department of Agriculture, 2010. https://www.fs.usda.gov/main/btnf/maps-pubs.

Mourning Dove (Hum-Ishu-Ma). *Cogewea: The Half-Blood.* 1927; Lincoln, University of Nebraska Press, 1981.

Newlin, Keith, ed. *A Theodore Dreiser Encyclopedia.* Westport CT: Greenwood Press, 2003.

Nishenko, S. P., and S. K. Singh. "The Acapulco-Ometepec, Mexico, Earthquakes of 1907–1982: Evidence for a Variable Recurrence History." *Bulletin of the Seismological Society of America* 77, no. 4 (August 1987): 1359–67. GeoScienceWorld website. Seismological Society of America, 2014. bssa .geoscienceworld.org/content/77/4/1359.

Noe, F. P., and K. W. Elifson. "An 'Invidious Comparison,' Class and Status, 1929–60: Effects of Employment, Cost and Time on Veblen's Theory of Class." In *Thorstein Veblen: Critical Assessments,* vol. 2, edited by John Cunningham Wood, 153–66. London: Routledge, 1993.

"'Oil!' and the History of Southern California." *New York Times,* 22 February 2008.

Owens, Louis. "'Disturbed by Something Deeper': The Native Art of John Joseph Mathews." *Western American Literature* 35, no. 2 (Summer 2000): 162–73.

"Packsaddle Ridge–Wyoming." SatelliteViews.net. N.d. www.satelliteviews.net /cgi-bin/g.cgi?fid=1601986&state=WY&ftype=ridge.

Parry, Sally E. "The Changing Fictional Faces of Sinclair Lewis' Wives." *Studies in American Fiction* 17, no.1 (Spring 1989): 65–79.

———. Sinclair Lewis Society (website). Illinois State University, 2012. english .illinoisstate.edu/sinclairlewis/index.shtml.

Peterson, Roger, Guy Mountfort, and P. A. D. Hollom. *A Field Guide to the Birds of Britain and Europe.* London: Collins, 1974.

Pevar, Stephen L. "1953–68: Termination." In *The Rights of Indians and Tribes: The Basic ACLU Guide to Indian and Tribal Rights.* An American Civil Liberties Union Handbook. Carbondale: Southern Illinois University Press, 1992.

Poe, Edgar Allan. "Tamerlane." In *Tamerlane and Other Poems* (1827). Edgar Allan
  Poe Society of Baltimore. www.eapoe.org/works/poems/tamerlna.htm.
"Rancho Grande Lyrics." Roger Creager Lyrics. Lyricsmode.com. MTV
  Networks, 2016. www.lyricsmode.com/lyrics/r/roger_creager/rancho
  _grande.html.
"Record Group 75, Records of the Bureau of Indian Affairs, Chero-
  kee Removal Records, Entry 220, Emigration Rolls, 1817–1838."
  AlabamaTrailofTears.org. Trail of Tears Association–Alabama Chapter,
  n.d. alabamatrailoftears.org/photos/10.pdf.
Redish, Laura, Orrin Lewis, and Nancy Sherman. "Native American Boats."
  *Native Languages of the Americas: Preserving and Promoting American Indian
  Languages.* Native Languages of the Americas website. 2019. www.native
  -languages.org/boats.htm.
Reed, Alma. *Orozco.* New York: Oxford University Press, 1956.
Reilly, F. Kent, III. "People of Earth, People of Sky: Visualizing the Sacred
  in Native American Art of the Mississippian Period." In *Hero, Hawk, and
  Open Hand: American Indian Art of the Ancient Midwest and South,* edited by
  Richard F. Townsend, 125–38. New Haven: Yale University Press, 2004.
"Remembrance of Things Past." SI Vault, *Sports Illustrated,* 27 December
  1999. Time, 2010. sportsillustrated.cnn.com/vault/article/magazine
  /MAG1018019/2/index.htm.
Renois, Clarens. "Cholera Cases Flood Clinics in Haiti Slum." *9News, Sydney.*
  ninemsn Pty Ltd, 1997–2010, 11 November 2010. news.ninemsn.com.au
  /health/8122464/haitis-cholera-death-toll-jumps-to-643.
Richter, Sara Jane. "The Life and Literature of John Joseph Mathews: Contri-
  butions of Two Cultures." PhD diss., Oklahoma State University, 1985.
Rollings, Willard H. *The Osage: An Ethnohistorical Study of Hegemony on the
  Prairie-Plains.* Columbia: University of Missouri Press, 1992.
Ross, John. *The Papers of Chief John Ross.* Edited and with an introduction by
  Gary E. Moulton. Norman: University of Oklahoma Press, 1985.
Roys, Ralph L. *The Book of Chilam Balam of Chumayel* (1933). Norman: Univer-
  sity of Oklahoma Press, 1967.
"Rupert Brooke." Poets.org. Academy of American Poets, 1997–2016. www
  .poets.org/poetsorg/poet/rupert-brooke.
Rusch, Frederic E., and Donald Pizer, eds. *Theodore Dreiser: Interviews.* Urbana:
  University of Illinois Press, 2004. Google Books. https://books.google
  .com/books?id=tQL7UitACW4C&dq=dreiser+and+the+soviet+union&
  source=gbs_navlinks_s.
Rusche, Harry. "Rupert Brooke, 1887–1915." *Lost Poets of the Great War.* English
  Department, Emory University. english.emory.edu/LostPoets/Brooke.html.

Saunders, Frances Stonor. *The Cultural Cold War: The* CIA *and the World of Arts and Letters.* New York: New Press, 1999.

Schedler, Christopher. "Formulating a Native American Modernism in John Joseph Mathews' Sundown." *Arizona Quarterly: A Journal of American Literature, Culture, and Theory* 55, no. 1 (Spring 1999): 127–49.

Sheehan, Tim. "Era Came to End for Gottschalks: Regional Department Stores Seen as Obsolete." *Fresno Bee,* 5 April 2009. EBSCO Industries (database), 2010.

"Shoshone River Crossing." *Shoshone River, the Bridger Trail.* Wyoming State Historical Preservation Office, Wyoming State Parks and Cultural Resources, 2016. wyoshpo.state.wy.us/btrail/shoshoneriver.html.

Silverstein, Jake. "Highway Run: Touring Mexico in a Death-Race Revival." *Harper's Magazine* (July 2006): 71.

Snyder, Michael. "'He Certainly Didn't Want Anyone to Know That He Was Queer': Chal Windzer's Sexuality in John Joseph Mathews' *Sundown,*" *Studies in American Indian Literatures* 20, no. 1 (Spring 2008): 27–54.

Souter, Gerry. *Diego Rivera: His Art and His Passions.* New York: Parkstone Press International, 2007.

Stabile, D. R. "Thorstein Veblen and His Socialist Contemporaries: A Critical Comparison." In *Thorstein Veblen: Critical Assessments,* vol. 1, edited by John Cunningham Wood, 259–84. London: Routledge, 1993.

Stace, Clive. *New Flora of the British Isles.* 2nd ed. New York: Cambridge University Press, 1997.

State Farm Road Atlas. Skokie IL: Rand McNally, 2000.

Steele, Valerie, ed. "Golf Clothing." *Encyclopedia of Clothing and Fashion.* Detroit: Charles Scribner's Sons, 2005. Gale Virtual Reference Library, 2010. https://1lib.us/book/465516/582582?id=465516&secret=582582&dsource=recommend.

Stonor Saunders, Frances. *The Cultural Cold War: The* CIA *and the World of Arts and Letters.* New York: New Press, 1999.

Swinburne, Algernon Charles. *Poems and Ballads and Atalanta in Calydon.* Edited by Kenneth Haynes. New York: Penguin, 2000.

———. "The Song of the Standard." In *The Poems of Algernon Charles Swinburne, Volume II: Songs before Sunrise* and *Songs of Two Nations,* 187–90. London: Chatto and Windus, 1904. Google Books.

Tahir, Nawroz Abdul-Razzak. "Assessment of Genetic Diversity among Wheat Varieties in Sulaimanyah Using Random Amplified Polymorphic DNA (RAPD) Analysis." *Jordan Journal of Biological Sciences* 1, no. 4 (December 2008): 159–64. Hashemite University (Jordan). jjbs.hu.edu.jo/files/vln4/final%20version%20to%20be%20producedl%20modified.pdf.

Teachout, Terry. *The Skeptic: A Life of H. L. Mencken.* New York: Harper Collins, 2002.

Tebbel, John. *A History of Book Publishing in the United States, Volume IV: The Great Change, 1940–1980.* New York: R. R. Bowker Company, 1981.

Tedlock, Dennis, ed. *Popol Vuh.* Revised edition. Translated by Dennis Tedlock. New York: Simon and Schuster, 1996.

"Tennessee River." Geographic Names Phase I data compilation (1976–1981), 31 December 1981. *Geographic Names Information System,* United States Geological Survey, U.S. Department of the Interior, 2010. geonames.usgs .gov/pls/gnispublic/f?p=139:3:591087856238101::NO::P3_FID,P3_TITLE: 517033%2CTennessee%20River.

Thompson, Eric V. "A Brief History of Major Oil Companies in the Gulf Region with Corporate Contact Information." Petroleum Archives Project, Arabian Peninsula & Gulf Studies Program, University of Virginia with support from the Kuwait Foundation for the Advancement of Sciences, n.d. www.virginia.edu/igpr/APAG/apagoilhistory.html.

The Times Atlas of the World. New York: Times Books, Random House, 1995.

"Title Search Results for Vox Populi." Chronicling America. Library of Congress, 2010. chroniclingamerica.loc.gov/search/titles/results/?state=& county=&city=&year1=1690&year2=2009&terms=vox+populi&frequency= &language=&ethnicity=&labor=&lccn=&materialType.

Todd, James G., Jr. "Social Realism." *Art Terms* (From Grove Art Online, Oxford University Press, 2009). Museum of Modern Art, Metropolitan Museum of Art, 2010. www.moma.org/collection/theme.php?theme_id= 10195.

Torrez, Robert J. "The Jacal in the Tierra Amarilla." *El Palacio: Quarterly Journal of the Museum of New Mexico* 85, no. 2 (Summer 1979): 14–18.

"Treaty of Washington, May 6, 1828 7 Stat 311." GeorgiaInfo. Digital Library of Georgia, 2010. georgiainfo.galileo.usg.edu/washing6.htm.

"Treaty with the Western Cherokee, May 6, 1828." First People: Treaties and Agreements. Paul Burke, First People of American and First People of Canada: Turtle Island, n.d. www.firstpeople.us/FP-Html-Treaties /TreatyWithTheWesternCherokee1828.html.

"Ulex europaeus." Fire Effects Information System. U.S. Forest Service, n.d. www.fs.fed.us/database/feis/plants/shrub/uleeur/all.html.

United States Census Bureau. "Table 4. Population: 1790 to 1990. United States Urban and Rural."N.d. https://www.census.gov/population /censusdata/table-4.pdf.

Untermeyer, Louis. *Modern British Poetry: A Critical Anthology.* New York: Harcourt, Brace and Company, 1930.

Veblen, Thorstein. *The Theory of the Leisure Class* (1899). New York: Cosimo, 2007. Google Books. https://www.gutenberg.org/ebooks/833.

"War Eagle Girls and Plainsmen Tour Information." War Eagle Girls and Plainsmen website. Division of Student Affairs, Auburn University, 2010. http://wp.auburn.edu/wegp.

Warrior, Robert Allen. *Tribal Secrets: Recovering American Indian Intellectual Traditions.* Minneapolis: University of Minnesota Press, 1995.

Watson, John. "Geysers, Fumaroles, and Hot Springs." 31 January 1997. United States Geological Survey, U.S. Department of the Interior, 2016. pubs.usgs.gov/gip/volc/geysers.html.

Welch, James. *Fools Crow.* New York: Penguin, 1987.

"White Plymouth Rock Chickens." eFowl.com, The Web's Source for Waterfowl, Chickens, and Game Birds. aJay Holdings, 2010. www.efowl.com /White_Plymouth_Rock_Chickens_p/1054.htm.

Williams, Samuel Cole, ed. "Voyage of the Donelson Party (1779–1780)." In *Early Travels in the Tennessee Country, 1540–1800.* Johnson City TN: Watauga Press, 1928.

Wilson, James C. "Upton Sinclair 1878–1968." *The Heath Anthology of American Literature, Volume C.* 5th ed. New York: Houghton Mifflin, 2006.

Woolaroc Museum and Wildlife Preserve. "About Woolaroc." N.d. https:// www.woolaroc.org/about-woolaroc.

World Almanac and Book of Facts, 1938. New York: New York World Telegram, 1938, p. 830.

"Wyoming Snake River Map." ALL JacksonHole.com. ALL Trips Travel Guide Network, Vertical Media, 1995/2010. www.jacksonholenet.com/maps /snake_river_map.php.

Yahoo! Maps. NAVTEQ, Yahoo!, 2016. maps.yahoo.com/.

Yellowstonenationalpark.com. "Yellowstone Main Map." Yellowstone Media, 1999–2013. www.yellowstonenationalpark.com/maps.htm.

Yellowstonepark.com. "Full Regional Map" (2006).

———. "Interactive Yellowstone National Park Map & Itinerary Collection" (2006).

———. "National Park Service Official Park Map" (2006).

www.ingramcontent.com/pod-product-compliance
Lightning Source LLC
Chambersburg PA
CBHW060552030726
47498CB00005B/1357